Acclaim for George ⬛

The Way Home

"*The Way Home* is an action-packed, suspenseful mystery story that explores family loyalty and friendship. Pelecanos, as usual, writes crackling prose that propels the reader forward, turning the pages deep into the dark night."
—Chuck Leddy, *Boston Globe*

"George Pelecanos is the sharpest crime writer working today—and a lot like Richard Price, except prolific."
—Benjamin Alsup, *Esquire*

"Pelecanos, I think, is our best crime writer, a very literary writer, he's almost an anthropologist, he digs down deep in the layers and examines all angles of the crime.... It's totally inspirational to me as a writer."   —Michael Connelly, Salon.com

"With *The Way Home*, Pelecanos has once again crafted a genre-transcending novel of rage and redemption guaranteed to appeal to a broad-spectrum audience."
—Bruce Tierney, *BookPage*

"Pelecanos orchestrates the novel's climax for maximum impact, laying bare emotional truths about friendship, loyalty, and betrayal, as well as the mysterious bond between father and son. *The Way Home* finds him still blazing his unique path through the territory of the crime novel."
—Michael Berry, *San Francisco Chronicle*

"Nobody can teach George Pelecanos anything he doesn't already know about the inherent drama in the father-son dynamic." —Marilyn Stasio, *New York Times*

"A crime novel, yes, but the talented Pelecanos shoes it out of its comfort zone.... Redemption the hard way, well crafted and deeply felt." —*Kirkus Reviews* (starred review)

"*The Way Home* remains true to its titular purpose; as a result, the structure is perhaps less weighted toward a classic narrative arc and more toward the journey itself. As with his last two novels, Pelecanos demonstrates that redemption, if it comes at all, is hard-won." —Sarah Weinman, *Los Angeles Times*

"Between the wonderful dialogue, the characters who unpeel like onions before your eyes, and action that punches from the shoulder and hip—the very technique Thomas Flynn taught young Chris—Mr. Pelecanos brings things off with bravura." —John Weisman, *Washington Times*

"A well-written and touching story.... The latest novel from this master crime writer revisits familiar territory: family bonds, moral choices, and a young man's struggle to find his place in the world.... As so often happens in Pelecanos's novels, those who take the moral high road are dragged into a scenario of murder, greed, and retribution." —Carol Memmott, *USA Today*

"Notions of revenge, redemption, and justice fuel this thriller.... Pelecanos, a seasoned novelist and a writer for *The Wire*, means to provoke more than quickened heartbeats." —*The New Yorker*

"Good suspenseful writing."

—Michael Helfand, *Pittsburgh Post-Gazette*

"Labeling Pelecanos a crime novelist is as much an understatement as describing *The Wire* as a TV show set in Baltimore....Pelecanos spreads his fictional net wide, exploring the effects on his flawed characters of corruption, violence, racial conflict, and the struggle for redemption."

—Connie Ogle, *Miami Herald*

"Pelecanos writes with an unflinching eye; his descriptions of violence and those who perpetrate it are harsh as reality. He isn't sympathetic to society's underbelly, but he's quietly passionate in calling for change and suggesting some steps along that road. His language is spare, his characters tightly imagined. *The Way Home* is, at times, a painful read, but one that feels true."

—Robin Vidimos, *Denver Post*

"George Pelecanos has been moving in a new direction in his recent work, focusing less on the crimes in his novels and more on the characters. While readers might miss that previous emphasis, this change adds a richness that is a real pleasure....The power of the book is in Pelecanos's exploration of themes like the relationship between fathers and sons, and the possibility of redemption." —David J. Montgomery, *Chicago Sun-Times*

"In *The Way Home*, it's the little things that matter....Pelecanos is fascinated by the minor decisions that end up making a huge difference in the long run, and the ripples that result when good but imperfect people try to do the right thing—even when they're not exactly sure what the right thing is."

—Kevin Allman, *Washington Post*

GEORGE PELECANOS

THE
WAY HOME

A NOVEL

BACK BAY BOOKS

Little, Brown and Company

New York Boston London

Back Bay Books / Little, Brown and Company
Hachette Book Group
237 Park Avenue, New York, NY 10017
www.hachettebookgroup.com

Originally published in hardcover by Little, Brown and Company, May 2009
First Back Bay paperback edition, January 2011

Back Bay Books is an imprint of Little, Brown and Company.
The Back Bay Books name and logo are trademarks of Hachette Book Group, Inc.

Library of Congress Cataloging-in-Publication Data
Pelecanos, George P.
    The way home : a novel / George Pelecanos. — 1st ed.
    p.   cm.
    ISBN 978-0-316-15649-3 (hc) / 978-0-316-08733-9 (pb)
    1. Fathers and sons — Fiction.   2. Problem youth — Fiction.
3. Redemption — Fiction.   I. Title.
    PS3566.E354W39   2009
    813'.54 — dc22   2008054837

10 9 8 7 6 5 4 3 2 1

RRD-IN

Printed in the United States of America

For my father, Pete Pelecanos

Last night I dreamed that I was a child
   out where the pines grow wild and tall
I was trying to make it home through the forest
   before the darkness falls
                  —Bruce Springsteen, "My Father's House"

PART ONE
BAD CHRIS

ONE

No ONE could say why it was called Pine Ridge. Wasn't any pines around that Chris could see. Just a group of one-story, L-shaped, red brick buildings set on a flat dirt-and-mud clearing, surrounded by a fence topped with razor wire. Beyond the fence, woods. Oak, maple, wild dogwood, and weed trees, but no pines. Somewhere back in those woods, the jail they had for girls.

The facility was situated on eight hundred acres out in Anne Arundel County, Maryland, twenty-five miles from Northwest D.C., where Chris had grown up. At night, lying in his cell, he could hear planes coming in low. So he knew that they were near the Baltimore airport, and close to a highway, too. Some days, if the wind was right, playing basketball on the outdoor court or walking to the school building from his unit, he'd make out the hiss and rumble of vehicles speeding by, straights going off to work or heading back home, moms in their minivans, kids driving to parties or hookups. Teenagers like him, only free.

Of course, he had been told exactly where he was. The director of the district's Department of Youth Rehabilitation

Services, the superintendent, the guards, his fellow inmates, his parents, and the lawyer his father had hired to represent him had explained it to him in detail. He'd even been shown a map. But it was more interesting for him to imagine that he was in some kind of mysterious location. *They are sending me to a top secret place in the woods. A facility for boys they cannot control. A place that can't hold me. I will now plan my daring escape, ha-ha.*

"Chris?" said his mother.

"Huh?"

"Is something funny?"

"No."

"You're grinning."

"Was I?"

"Chris, you seem to be treating all of this very lightly."

"I don't mean to, Ma. I was thinkin on something, was all it was."

"You were thinking *about* something," said his father.

Chris smiled, causing the muscles along his father's jawline to tighten.

Chris Flynn was seated at a scarred wooden table in the Pine Ridge visiting room. Across the table were his parents, Thomas and Amanda Flynn. Nearby, several other boys, all wearing polo shirts and khakis, were being visited by their moms or grandmothers. A guard stood by the door. Outside the room, through a square of Plexiglas, Chris could see two other guards, talking to each other, laughing.

"How's it going, honey?" said Amanda.

"It's all right."

"How's school?"

Chris glanced around the room. "I go."

"Look at your mother when she's talking to you," said Thomas Flynn.

Instead, Chris stared into his father's watery eyes. He saw a husk of anger and hurt, and felt nothing.

"I'm asking you," said Amanda, "are they treating you all right? Are people bullying you?"

"You don't need to worry about that. I know how to jail."

"*You*," said Flynn, his voice not much louder than a contemptuous whisper.

"Do you have one of those level meetings coming up?" said Amanda.

"Not that I know."

"They're supposed to have them monthly. I'll follow up with our attorney. He's in contact with the superintendent."

"Fine."

"Let's pray," said Amanda.

She laced her fingers together, rested her hands on the table, and bowed her head. Chris and Thomas Flynn dutifully did the same. But they did not speak to God, and their thoughts were not spiritual or pure.

When Amanda was done, the three of them got up out of their seats. Amanda looked at the guard, a big man with kind eyes who surely would understand, and she embraced her son. As she held him, she slipped three folded twenty-dollar bills into the pocket of his trousers.

Amanda broke away from him, tears heavy in her eyes. "We're doing everything we can."

"I know it."

"You're in my prayers. I love you, Chris."

"Love you, too, Mom." He said this quietly, so the other boys would not hear him.

Neither Chris nor his father made a step toward each other. After a long, empty lock of their eyes, Chris gave Thomas Flynn a tough nod with his chin, turned, and left the room.

"Should we try and talk to the superintendent before we leave?" said Amanda.

"What for?" Flynn shook his head. "Let's just go."

ALONG WITH an escort guard, Thomas and Amanda Flynn walked out of the building toward the gatehouse, Thomas in front of Amanda, his heavy steps indenting the mud beneath his feet. Inmates, between classes and lunch, were moving from unit to unit, their arms behind their backs, one hand holding the wrist of the other, accompanied by a guard carrying a two-way radio. All of the boys were black. Flynn had seen one Hispanic kid, waxy eyed and wired on meds, on his last visit, so maybe there were a few Spanish here, too, but that was immaterial to him. What weighed on him was that Chris was the sole white inmate of the facility.

My son, here with all these . . .

Flynn stopped himself before ugly words spelled themselves out in his head.

He rang the bell on the door at the rear of the gatehouse, looking through bars and Plexiglas to get the attention of one of two uniformed women behind the counter. Like most of the female guard staff Flynn had seen here, these women were wide and generously weighted in the legs and hips. He and his wife were buzzed in, and they passed through the same security aisle, similar to those used in airports, they'd entered. Neither of the guards looked at the couple or spoke to them as Flynn and Amanda collected their keys and cells.

They exited the gatehouse and walked along the chain link and razor wire fence to Amanda's SUV, parked in the staff and visitors' lot. They did not talk. Amanda was thinking of going to early mass on Sunday and lighting a candle for Chris. Flynn, as he often did, was thinking of what had gone wrong.

By Flynn's reckoning, he had begun to lose his son somewhere in Chris's freshman year of high school. At the time, Chris was playing football and CYO basketball, getting decent grades, attending Sunday school and mass. He was also smoking marijuana, shoplifting, fighting other boys, and breaking into cars and lockers. This was all happening at the same time, when Chris was about fifteen. To Amanda, Flynn began to refer to his son as if he were two people: Good Chris and Bad Chris. By the time Chris was sixteen, only Bad Chris remained.

As a teenager and into his twenties, Flynn had blown his share of marijuana, so he detected Chris's use right away. Flynn could see the high in Chris's eyes, the way he would laugh inappropriately at violent images on the television screen, or his sudden interest in their Lab mix, Darby, playing tug-of-war or wrestling him to the ground, things he would never do while straight. Of course, there was the smell that always hung in Chris's clothing and, when he had copped, that unmistakable skunky odor of fresh bud in his bedroom.

It didn't bother Flynn horribly that his son smoked marijuana. In fact, he told Chris that he had no moral objection to it but felt that it was, basically, a waste of time. That for an already marginal student like Chris, it could impede his progress. What bothered Flynn, what became alarming, was that Chris began to smoke marijuana to the exclusion of everything else. He stopped playing sports. He stopped going to mass and hanging out with his church friends. He quit his job at the coffee shop in Friendship Heights. His grades edged toward failure. He seemed not to care about the loss or what his degeneration was doing to his parents.

Amanda still thought of Chris as her little boy and couldn't bring herself to discipline him like a young man. Plus, she was certain that the Lord would step in and, when He deemed it appropriate, blow the black clouds away and give Chris the wisdom to get back on the righteous path. Flynn's response was elemental and not carefully considered. He believed in Darwin over fairy tales and aimed to reinforce his position as the alpha dog of the house. He put Chris up against the wall more than once, raised his closed fist, and walked away before punching him. So Chris knew that his father was willing to cross the line and kick his ass, but the knowledge did nothing to alter his behavior. He didn't care.

Chris was charged with possession of marijuana. The arresting officer did not show up for court, and the charge was dropped. Chris got in a fight at school and was suspended. He strong-armed a fellow student for his Walkman on school property and was arrested and expelled for the remainder of the year. He received community service time. Chris and his friend Jason were caught on camera looting the lockers of their high school basketball team while the players were at practice, and were arrested and charged. An adjudicatory hearing was scheduled. Chris was videotaped vandalizing and stealing from cars in the back lot of a Mexican restaurant. His father paid off the owners of the restaurant and the owners of the vehicles, thereby avoiding the involvement of police. And then there were the final charges and the conviction that led to his incarceration: assault, possession with intent to distribute, leaving the scene of an accident, reckless driving, driving on the sidewalk, fleeing and eluding police. With each succeeding "incident," with each visit to the Second District station on Idaho Avenue to pick up his son, Flynn grew more angry and distant.

Kate would be eighteen now. We'd be looking at colleges. We'd be taking photos of her, dressed up for the senior prom. Instead of visiting that little shit with his prison uniform and his pride in knowing "how to jail."

Christopher Flynn was the only surviving offspring of Thomas and Amanda Flynn. Their first child, Kate, died two days after she was born. The death certificate listed the cause as "respiratory distress syndrome," which meant that she had suffocated. She was a preemie, and her lungs had not fully developed.

At the time of Kate's birth, Thomas Flynn was a young uniformed police officer in D.C.'s Fourth District. He had signed up impulsively, successfully passed through the academy, and upon his graduation he almost immediately realized he had made a mistake. He was dispassionate about the job and did not want to lock up kids, making him unsuited to be a soldier in the drug war. Flynn resigned and took a position as an account representative for a carpet-and-flooring wholesaler whose sales manager, not coincidentally, was his former high school basketball coach. Flynn's intention was to learn the business, establish contacts, and eventually go out on his own.

Soon after Kate died, Amanda became pregnant but lost the baby in the first trimester. Despite assurances from her obstetrician that she was healthy, Amanda, who along with Flynn had dabbled in cocaine in her youth, blamed her past drug use for Kate's premature birth and death. She believed that she had permanently damaged her "insides" and could no longer carry a child to term. "My eggs are dirty," she told Flynn, who only nodded, preferring not to argue with her, in the way that one does not try to reason with a loved one who has begun to mentally slip away. Amanda had by then welcomed Jesus into their lives, and Flynn found it increasingly difficult for the three of them to coexist.

Kate's death did not ruin their marriage, but it killed a piece of it. Flynn barely recognized in the humorless, saved Amanda the funny, spirited woman he had married. Despite the emotional gulf between them, they continued to have sex frequently. Amanda still secretly hoped to have a healthy child, and, born again or not, she had a body on her, and Thomas Flynn liked to have it. Chris was born in 1982.

As the problems with Chris progressed, Flynn found himself thinking more and more of Kate. She was with them for only two days and had no discernible personality, but he was haunted by her and obsessed with what she might have become had she lived. Chris was real, a stained reminder of Flynn's failings as a father. The Kate he imagined was a charmer, lovely, well mannered, and successful. Kate would surely have looked upon Flynn with loving eyes. He fantasized about the daughter he would never have, and it made him feel optimistic and right. Knowing all the while, from the evidence of his business and his everyday life, that reality was usually far less intriguing than the dream.

"Tommy?" said Amanda, now seated beside him in the SUV, Thomas Flynn in the driver's bucket and fitting his key to the ignition.

"What."

"We should schedule a meeting with our attorney. I want him to keep in contact with the warden."

"You want to help him, huh?" Flynn glared at his wife. "I saw you slip Chris that money."

"He might need it."

"I told you not to do that, didn't I?"

"Yes, but —"

"*Didn't* I."

"Yes."

"He's going to buy marijuana with it. They get it from the guards."

"I can't just leave him in there with no resources. He's our son."

Flynn held his tongue.

TWO

THE FIRST time Chris took a charge, for loitering and possession of marijuana, he was all nerves, standing in this room they had at the 2D station, waiting for his father to come and take him home. He was expecting his pops to spaz on him, put a finger up in his face, give him the lecture about responsibility and choices, maybe make some threats. But his father entered that room and, first thing, hugged him and kissed him on the cheek. It surprised Chris and, because there was a police officer in the room, embarrassed him. If his father was soft like that, someone might get the idea that Chris was soft, too.

"I told you not to touch him, sir," said the police officer, but Thomas Flynn did not apologize.

Chris should have expected his father to support him. If he had thought about it, he would have realized that his father had always taken his side against teachers and school administrators in the past, including those times when Chris had been in the wrong. Thomas Flynn had even physically challenged a security guy at Chris's middle school back when Chris started getting in trouble. The security guard had said, "Your boy needs to see a psychiatrist, somethin. He's not right." And his father said, "If I want your opinion, young man, I'll kick it out your ass." His father had a temper, and he was also in denial about who Chris was. But Chris knew who he was, even then.

It came to him one morning, lying in bed, after his mother had woken him up to go to school. He was in the seventh grade, thirteen years old. It occurred to him that he didn't have to get up and go to school if he didn't want to. That his parents couldn't force him to go. They couldn't, in fact, force him to do anything. Most kids would do what their parents said because they were the parents and that was how it worked, but Chris did not feel the way those other kids felt, not anymore. It was like something in his brain got switched off at the same time that something else, something more exciting, had been ignited. He still thought of his mom and dad as his parents, but he was no longer interested in pleasing them or doing what they thought was right. He didn't care.

His father's attitude changed after Chris began to get in trouble time and time again. It was partly the repetition of the incidents that wore his father down, but it was also the nature of them.

Chris liked to fight. He wasn't an honors or AP kid, and being good at fighting was a way of showing that he was someone, too. If it was a fair fight, meaning he wasn't picking on a retard or a weakling, then it was on, and someone was about to get hurt.

He rationalized robbery, too. If someone was stupid enough to leave cash in a locker, or have designer shades or a cell phone visible inside a parked car, then he was going to break into that locker or car and help his self.

He had bad luck, though, and he got caught. His old man would come to pick him up from the school office or the police station, and each time, his father's face was more disappointed and less forgiving. Chris wasn't trying to hurt his parents, exactly. But in his mind it was written like this: They have unreasonable expectations for me. They don't realize who I am. I am hard and I like to get high. I don't want to be their good boy and I don't want the things they want for me. If they can't face that, it's their problem, not mine.

"Why, Chris?" said his father, driving him back from the Mexican restaurant, Tuco's, where he'd been caught vandalizing and stealing from cars. "Why?"

"Why what?"

"Why are you doing this?" His father's voice was hoarse, and it looked to Chris that he was close to desperation.

"I don't know. I can't help it, I guess."

"You're throwing it all away. You've quit on everything, and you get high all the time. You've got a police record, and your grades are . . . they're *shit*, Chris. Other kids are studying for the SATs and looking at colleges, and you're breaking into cars. For *what?* What could you possibly need that I haven't given you? I *bought* you a car; why in the world would you want to damage someone else's?" Flynn's fingers were white on the steering wheel. "You live in one of the most upscale neighborhoods in Washington, in a nice house. You're trying to act like someone you're not. Why? What's *wrong* with you?"

"Nothing's wrong with me. I'm me. That SUV you bought me, it's fine and all that, but I didn't ask you for it. Far as my grades go, what's the point? I'm not going to college. Let's be real."

"Oh, so now you're not considering college?"

"I'm not *going*. I don't see any reason to go, because I'm not smart enough. Look, accept me like this or don't. Either way, I'm going to be who I am."

This was before the final incident, which started in the lot behind the drugstore on the west side of Connecticut Avenue, up by the Avalon Theater.

It was a midsummer night, and Chris and his friend Jason Berg, whom everyone but Jason's parents and teachers called Country, were walking out of the drugstore with a vial of Visine they had purchased and a bunch of candy and gum packs they had stuffed in their pockets and stolen. They had been drinking beer and smoking some bud, and were laughing at something that struck them as funny because they were high.

A pound of weed was stashed in the back of Chris's vehicle, under a blanket. They had bought it earlier in the evening from a connection on the D.C. side of Takoma and were planning to sell most of it off to their peers and keep an ounce for themselves. Jason had an electronic scale, and their intention was to bag out the marijuana the next day at his house while his parents were at work.

Jason was a big kid, tall and muscled up. He had a buzz cut and still wore braces. People thought he was stupid. He had the mouth-breathing, shallow-eyed look of an idiot, a lumbering walk, a stoner's chuckle, and he was into NASCAR and professional wrestling. Because of those interests and because he was white, the black kids at school had dubbed him Country.

Jason did nothing to discourage the impression others had formed of him. Truth was, he wasn't stupid in the least. His grades were middling because he didn't try during tests or turn in homework, but he had scored very high on his SATs, despite the fact that he had gotten massively baked the night before the exams. He was the son of a Jewish attorney who was a partner in one of the most prominent firms in the District, but he kept this and his intelligence hidden from the kids at school. The hard yahoo stoner was a preferable costume to him over the smart, privileged Jew.

Chris Flynn was of Irish Catholic extraction, shorter than Jason but not by much, and broad in the chest. He too wore his blond hair close to the scalp. He was fair skinned, green eyed, and had a lazy, charming smile. His one physical flaw was the vertical scar creasing the right side of his upper lip, acquired when he walked into an elbow during a pickup game that had gotten out of hand at the Hamilton Rec in 16th Street Heights. Chris liked the scar, and so did the females. He was handsome, but the scar told anyone who suspected it that he was no pretty boy. It made him look tough.

He *was* tough. He and Jason had proven it on the basketball courts and in situations involving hands. They did not hang with other white kids, the skateboarders and punk rockers and intellectuals who populated their high school, and were proud of the fact that they had earned respect, mostly, from the young black men who were bused in from the other side of town. Whether they were liked or not was beside the point to them. Everyone knew that Chris and Jason were on the edge, and that they could ball and fight.

"I think that Chinese girl behind the counter saw us pocket this stuff," said Chris, as he and Jason headed for Chris's SUV.

"What's Ling Ho gonna do? Get up after us?"

As they neared the Isuzu, Chris saw a group of three boys getting into a late-model Volvo station wagon parked down the row of spaces. One of them gave Chris a look, glancing at the old Trooper with the safari roof rack, and smiled in an arrogant way.

"Is he muggin me?" said Chris.

Jason stopped and hard-eyed the kid, who was now slipping behind the wheel of the Volvo. "I'll drop him if he does, son."

"They must be private school," said Chris. "You know those bitches can't go."

Chris and Jason, public-school kids, imagined themselves to be more blue-collar than the many kids in Ward 3 who attended private high schools. For Jason Berg it was an affectation, as his father was in the top 1 percent of earners. Chris, too, was living in a financially comfortable home environment, but he'd inherited the chip on his shoulder from Thomas Flynn.

Chris and Jason got into the SUV. Chris turned the ignition while Country messed with the radio. Despite his moniker, Country listened exclusively to hip-hop and go-go, and found something he could tolerate on KYS. It was a Destiny's Child thing that was popular and bogus, and they talked about that for a minute, and then Chris pulled down on the transmission arm, still talking to Jason and looking at him, and reversed the SUV. Both of them were jolted by a collision. They heard and felt the impact at the same time, and Chris said, "Shit."

He looked over his shoulder. They had hit the Volvo, passing behind them, and the three boys were getting out of the right-side doors because the Isuzu was up against the driver's side. Chris cut the engine and took a deep breath.

"You hit the right car, at least," said Jason with a grin.

"My father's gonna go off."

"What now?"

"'Bout to see what the damage is," said Chris. "You stay in here."

"Sure?"

"Positive. I don't want no trouble tonight. Remember, we got some weight in the back. I'm serious."

"Holler if you need me."

"Right." Chris left the keys in the ignition and got out of the SUV.

He walked toward the boys, now grouped in front of the Volvo. The largest of them was wide and strong, a football player from the looks of him, bulked up in the weight room, but he had nonthreatening eyes. The driver was Chris's size, prep school definitely from the square-hair, clean-shaved looks of him, and standing with his chest puffed out, which meant he was insecure and probably scared. The third kid, small and unformed, had pulled out a cell phone and was talking into it as he walked away. After sizing them all up quickly, the way boys and men do, Chris decided with some satisfaction that there wasn't one of them he could not take. Knowing this chilled him some and allowed him, for the moment, to stay even and cool.

"My bad," said Chris, facing the driver, the boy who'd given him the look. "Guess I wasn't payin attention."

"You *guess,*" said the driver. "Look what you did to my car." Annoyed, not giving Chris any slack, not giving him a "That's all right" or an "It happens."

Chris shrugged and his eyes were dead as he looked at the driver. "Said it was my bad."

Chris checked out the Volvo, saw that the left front quarter panel and the edge of the driver's door carried a dent. He then looked at the bumper of the Isuzu, which was not scratched but showed a bit of gold paint that had come off the Volvo's body.

Chris thought of his old man, and the day he had brought the used SUV home and presented it to Chris. It was a corny-looking vehicle, the old, boxy Trooper, which his father said had style and looked "cool." Nerdy was more like it, but whatever. Chris would have preferred an Impala SS or Buick Grand National, but he took it. One thing his father was right about, the Isuzu was a tank. Shoot, it had put a hurtin on a Volvo.

"Somethin funny?" said the driver.

"Nah. I was just . . . look, let me give you my *in*surance card."

"My *in*surance caahd," said the small one, having rejoined the group and slipped his cell into his pocket. The football player looked down at his feet.

Chris's jaw tightened as he drew his wallet and found the card in his father's name. He held it out for the driver, but the driver did not take it.

"Show it to the police," said the driver. "They're on the way."

"That's who your boy called on his cell?" said Chris.

"Yeah."

"Wasn't no need to do that." Chris replaced the card in his wallet, feeling his heart tick up a beat. "We supposed to exchange information."

"We *'posed* to," said the small one. "Look at him. His eyes are glassy, Alex. He's fucked up."

"How do I know if that card is real?" said the driver, with that same smart look he had given Chris when he'd mugged him and his vehicle.

"Leave it alone, Alex," said the football player to the driver.

"See, why you got to say that?" said Chris, staring at the driver, regretting that he had asked the question, not wanting the boy to speak, not trusting what he would do if the boy kept pushing it.

Adults were now standing in the lot, watching.

You want to see some drama? I'll give you something to look at.

Chris felt himself move his weight to his back foot, as his father had taught him to do long ago.

Punch with your shoulder, not your arm. Pivot your hip into the punch. Punch through your target, Chris.

"I don't have to tell you anything, Ace," said the driver. "Just talk to the police."

"*Alex,*" said the football player.

"Okay," said Chris, his face hot as fire. "I guess there's no need for words."

He threw a deep punch and it connected. The driver's nose felt spongy at the point of contact, and it shot blood as he fell to the ground.

Chris did not look at the football player but turned to the small one who had jumped back a step. Chris almost laughed. He said, "You're too little," and turned and walked back to his vehicle. A couple of the adults were shouting at him but not moving to stop him, and he did not turn his head.

He got behind the wheel. He turned the key in the ignition. Jason was laughing. Colored lights had begun to strobe the parking lot, and Chris looked left and saw the 2D cruiser enter the lot from Morrison Street, and then another one behind it.

There was no right or reason. Chris's head was a riot of energy.

THREE

W HERE YOU about to *go*, dawg?" said Jason. His face showed no fear or care, and it amped Chris further. "We blocked in behind us."

"Not on the right," said Chris.

"That's one-way to the right, comin in. You'll be going against traffic."

"I can deal with that." Watching as a uniformed officer in the lead car stepped out of his vehicle. "*Fuck* this."

Chris pulled the console's transmission arm toward him and locked it into drive. He cut the wheel right and gave the Trooper hard gas. The SUV went up the driveway, toward a car coming in, and Chris took the Trooper up onto the sidewalk. People shouted out behind them, and Chris swerved and drove across the sidewalk, behind the bus shelter on McKinley Street. A panicked pedestrian leaped away from their path, and then they were off the curb and straight onto the street.

"Red light," said Jason, indicating the signal at Connecticut.

"I see it," said Chris, and he blew the red. A sedan crossing north on the green braked wildly and three-sixtied, its tail end sweeping and missing them, and Chris punched the gas and blew up McKinley's rise going east.

"Ho, shit!" said Jason.

"They're comin," said Chris.

One of the squad cars had hit its sirens and light bar and was maneuvering through the intersection, which had been blocked by the car that had spun and stalled.

Chris stepped on the pedal and kept it pinned to the floor. The gas flooded into the carb, and the Isuzu wound up and took the hill fast, sailing over the crest. It was a narrow street, and a boxy sedan was headed straight for them. Jason said, "Chris," and the sedan swerved to the right and swiped a parked vehicle, sparks illuminating Chris's side vision as they passed. He ran a four-way stop and in the rearview saw the squad car gaining on them, and the one behind it doing the same. The sirens grew louder.

"They about to be on us," said Jason.

"Hold on," said Chris.

He made a right on Broad Branch Road, barely braking. The first squad car squealed a right and fell in behind them. As they neared the Morrison Street intersection, Chris saw a car coming in from the east and Jason gasped as they jetted through the four-way and the oncoming car braked into a ninety-degree skid. They heard a metallic explosion as the skidding car pancaked the squad car behind them, and Chris made a crazy sharp right onto Legation Street. The top-heavy Isuzu went up on two wheels, and Jason's face turned white as milk as he raised his arm to grip the handle mounted on the headliner. Chris kept the wheel steady and put the Trooper back on four, then quickly turned into an alley that he knew elbowed off to the left. He followed the angle of the elbow and when he felt they

were out of the sight line of Legation, he put the Trooper beside a wooden fence and cut the lights and engine.

Chris and Jason laughed. They stopped and got their breath,
looked at each other, and laughed some more.

"You *dusted* 'em," said Jason.

"They don't live here, man. They don't know these streets
like we do."

"The po-po gonna be angry like hornets," said Jason.

"Word."

"When you ran that red on Connecticut . . . shit, I thought
that car was gonna do us."

"That car had brakes, too."

"We gonna be legends, son."

"Yeah," said Chris.

Colored lights faintly lit the alley as one of the squad cars
slowly passed by on Legation. The boys sat there, hearing sirens that were different than police sirens, closer to those on
fire trucks or ambulances, and voices coming from speakers,
and they speculated on that. After a long while it was quiet and
Chris decided to risk it and make their way from the alley,
which had been a good hiding place but was also a trap. He did
not hit the headlights until they were back on Legation.

Carefully, Chris crossed Connecticut Avenue and then took
39th Street south. Down near Fessenden, Jason claimed he
saw a stripped-down Crown Vic, which could have been a police vehicle, creeping a nearby street, and because of this, and
because they still felt invincible, Chris put the Isuzu into four-
wheel drive and jumped off-road and onto a hill. They caught
air going over the hilltop, and with exuberance Jason said, "Rat
Patrol!" and then they were down the hill and rolling across
the wide expanse of Fort Reno Park, where Chris and Jason

had seen Fugazi and others perform in the summer, and where Chris's father, Thomas Flynn, had come as a teenager in the seventies to see hard rock bands do Deep Purple and Spanish bands try to do Santana. Satisfied that they had not been followed, they dropped back down onto asphalt at Chesapeake and took it east, back across Connecticut and into the beautiful upscale neighborhood of Forest Hills.

It was a section of Northwest whose residents were wealthy in a living-off-the-interest way. Large homes of brick and stone, deep and wide, lushly landscaped lots, Frank Lloyd Wright knockoffs, many embassies, and, down Brandywine toward Rock Creek Park, towering contemporaries housing gyms and indoor movie theaters. In the past, Forest Hills had been the exclusive base for Washington's most wealthy Jewish residents, so for many years D.C.'s less enlightened had called it Hanukkah Hills. Chris and Country knew it as a good place to get high.

Chris pulled into their usual spot at the dead end of Albemarle, where it ran into a striped barrier at the woods of Rock Creek, and cut the engine. Their place was past the light of the last streetlamp on the road. It was dark here and very quiet. Unless they turned around, there was no exit, but they weren't worried; they had never been hassled here before, not even by embassy police.

Chris pulled a couple of beers from the brown paper bag resting on the floorboards behind his seat and opened them both. Jason rolled a tight joint, sealed and dried it with fire, then lit it. They passed it back and forth, drank warm beer, and listened to the radio turned low.

"You used to come here with your mom and pops, didn't you?" said Jason, when they had smoked the joint down. Both of their heads were up, but without the new-high joy of the first smoke of the night.

"Once a year, in the spring," said Chris. "Darby, too, back when he was a puppy. We'd hike that trail they got. You get onto it back up Albemarle, near Connecticut."

He meant the Soapstone Valley Trail, a one-mile hike up and down hills, through an arm of Rock Creek Park. It was one of those city secrets, a wonderful green place, old-growth trees and sun glinting off running water. Chris had thought of it as his family's place when he was a kid, because they rarely saw anyone else on the trail, and because they had claimed ownership on a tree. There was a big oak down there, rooted in the valley floor, on whose trunk his father had carved their names with his buck knife. Thomas and Amanda in a heart when they'd been married, and then, in another heart, Chris when he was born. His father had put Darby's name in a smaller heart as well. When they were down there, Chris and his father would throw rocks and try to skip them in the creek, and sometimes his father would pick up a stick that was shaped like a gun and Chris would find one, too, and they would play war, his father coming from behind a tree and pretending the stick was a machine pistol or some such thing, his mouth making the sound of it spitting bullets. In his mind he could see his father doing this, younger, without that disappointment on his face. But it was just a memory. It didn't make Chris feel anything at all.

"Chris?"

"Huh?"

"What are we gonna do?"

"Go home, I guess."

Jason stubbed out the roach in the ashtray and put it inside a matchbook, which he stowed in his jeans. "What if Johnny Law's waitin on us?"

"Why would they be waitin on *you*? No one even saw you, Country. You stayed in the car the whole time."

"True."

Chris stared out the windshield. "You think someone wrote down my plate numbers?"

"Not the way you shot out that parking lot," said Jason with an unconvincing smile. "I don't see how they could."

Chris sat there, stoned, hoping and wishing that this were true.

"I can't take the weed home," said Jason. "This funk is potent. It stinks."

"I'll stash it under the deck of my house," said Chris. "We can bag it up at your place tomorrow, after your parents go to work."

Chris took a circuitous route back to their neighborhood and stopped the Trooper a couple of blocks away from Jason's house, a Dutch colonial on the corner of 38th and Kanawha. Jason and Chris shook hands and said good-bye.

Jason walked down the street. When he turned the corner, Chris drove off, but not in the direction of his own house. He had too much energy, and he needed to work it off. He headed south, where his girl, Taylor, stayed with her mother, on Woodley Avenue, a street of modest row houses in Woodley Park, between Connecticut Avenue and the zoo. Taylor's mother would be sleeping now, but Taylor would be up and ready. She'd let him in.

TAYLOR DUGAN had put Chris's two remaining beers in the freezer to rechill them quickly, then brought them back down to the

basement, where Chris was sprawled out shoeless on the couch.
Taylor's mother, a divorcée who worked as a lawyer for a trade
association downtown, was in her bed and snoring, two floors
above. Though it was tempting, Chris and Taylor never raided
the mother's liquor cabinet while Chris was visiting late at
night. Taylor's mother, like many alcoholics, counted her
drinks and memorized the levels of the bottles, no matter how
trashed she got, and Taylor did not care to get busted by her
mom.

Taylor was a slim young woman with short dyed-black hair,
a nose ring, freckles, and blue eyes. She had changed into boxer
shorts and a V-neck white T-shirt after going upstairs to get
the beer.

Taylor handed Chris his beer and put hers next to a 35 mm
camera that was on an old table set before the couch. She went
to a bookshelf, removed a paperback, and found a stash pipe
with a hole in each end, one to light, one to draw from. In the
middle, a small amount of marijuana was fitted in a screened
chamber.

"You want some?" she said.

"Sure," said Chris.

He got up on a chair and cranked open a casement window,
and then she joined him. The chair wobbled beneath them and
they giggled as they each took a couple of deep hits and blew
the exhale out into the night.

"Whew," she said, as she stepped down onto the carpet.

"You need some more?" said Chris.

"No, I'm good."

"Because I copped tonight. I got a pound out in my truck."

"That's not all you did tonight."

"Oh, man. You should have seen me."

"Were you scared?" said Taylor, flopping down onto the couch. Chris had already told the general story, but she was buzzed now and wanted to hear the details.

"Nah, not really," said Chris, walking to the table to get his beer, careful not to step on the sketchbooks scattered about the carpet. "I mean, I didn't think on it all that much. It's like that shrink said to me, the one my parents made me go to? 'It's all about choices, Chris.' Well, I made one."

Taylor picked the camera up off the table, framed Chris through the lens, and snapped a photograph. "Why'd you take off?"

"I dunno. That boy practically begged me to hit him. I mean, what, I was supposed to take the weight for *that?* I hate the police. I don't like explaining myself to them. I don't even like to speak to them if I don't have to." Chris took off his T-shirt and dropped it on the floor. "Hot in here."

"Uh-huh," said Taylor.

Chris tipped his head back, took a long swig of beer, and let her have a look at his flat stomach. Taylor took several more photographs of him like that and placed the camera back on the table.

"How far did they chase you?"

"A good long while," said Chris. "It was like *Cops*, only they didn't get me. Shit *was* sick, Taylor. I blew a red light on Connecticut Avenue at McKinley, and cars were spinning out in the intersection."

"Bad Chris," said Taylor.

"That's me."

Taylor was at that public arts school, Duke Ellington, and liked to paint and stuff. Chris had met her at a Blessed Sacrament dance when they were both in middle school. She had come over to *him*. Told him later that she'd noticed him straight off, that he looked different from the other boys, that he wasn't trying too hard and that she liked his aloof manner, whatever that meant. They had been together, friends and lovers, for a couple of years. He wasn't worried about the other boys at her school, who she said were "fey." He guessed that meant they were faggies or something, 'cause it rhymed with *gay*.

"I'm just a bad boy," said Chris, smiling slowly.

"Did you bring any protection?"

"Didn't know I'd be seein you, girl."

"We'll improvise," said Taylor.

Chris said he was good with that, and Taylor laughed and opened her arms.

Chris put his beer down and went to the couch. His jeans were tight before their mouths met. She stroked his belly, and her breath was hot and smoky as they kissed. She moaned as they made out, and Chris thought, *God, this girl can do it*. Taylor pushed him away, crossed her arms, and drew her T-shirt over her head. She came back to him naked above the waist, and Chris ran his strong hands over her slim hips and up her ribcage, and he found her small breasts, circling her hardening nipples with his thumbs, and she took one of his hands and put it inside her boxer shorts. He did what she liked until Taylor couldn't stand it any longer and she climaxed under his touch. She finished him deftly the same way.

It would be a long time before he would get with a female again. Later, when he was masturbating at night in his cell, bitter because she had stopped taking his calls, but still, wanting Taylor again so badly he thought he would shout out her name, he would regret settling for a hand job in her basement the last time he saw her. He should have put it in her. So what if he didn't have a condom? Okay, she could have got pregnant. What difference would that have made to him then?

"Are they going to get you, Chris?" Taylor was in his arms on the couch, on top of him, her breasts crushed against his chest.

"Nah, I'm straight. I can get the Volvo's paint off my bumper, and there's plenty of Troopers out there the same color as mine. Long as they didn't read my plates, I'll be fine."

"Maybe you got lucky."

"I could have."

"Why'd you hit that boy?"

"I was really tryin not to. Used to be I'd get angry and just fight, but this time was different. I tried to hold back, Taylor. If he hadn't pushed me so hard, run his mouth like he did, all this shit tonight, it wouldn't have happened."

"It's over now."

"No doubt."

"I don't want you to get hurt."

"They can't hurt steel," said Chris with a weak smile.

Taylor hugged him tightly. "I applied to a college I want, Chris. I'm trying to get into the Rhode Island School of Design."

"That's the art school, right?"

"My counselor says it's one of the best."

"I hope you get in."

"What are *you* going to do?"

"Don't know. First thing, I need to get out my house. I can't take livin with my father. When I turn eighteen I figure I'll get a job. Me and Country will find an apartment somewhere. Maybe sell weed on the side, but do it real quiet."

"That's your plan?"

"For now," said Chris. "Yeah."

Taylor said nothing else and soon fell asleep in his arms. Chris untangled himself without waking her and covered her with a blanket. He dressed and left the house quietly, went to his Trooper, and drove toward his house through backstreets. There were few cars out. It was very late.

He drove west on Livingston, the street where he lived, and a car turned off 41st and fell in behind him. The car was a big square sedan, and it was then that he knew. Several squad cars were parked on his block, and their light bars were activated as he neared his house. The air had gone out of him, and he simply put the Isuzu in park in the middle of the street and let them come to him. They leaned him over the hood of his Trooper and cuffed him, and one of the uniformed men said, almost in admiration, "That was some real fancy driving, son." Chris said, "I guess someone got my plate numbers," and the uniform said, "*Oh*, yeah," and Chris remembered that he had a pound of marijuana in the back of his vehicle and he idly wondered what that would do to compound the charges. "You don't even know the trouble you're in," said the uniform. "The woman who hit our cruiser at Morrison, where you blew that stop sign? Mother of three. She's in Sibley's emergency room with severe injuries. They collared her and taped her to a gurney. And that kid in the parking lot is gonna be breathing through his mouth for a while. You broke his nose."

Chris raised his head and squinted through the red and blue shafts of light coloring his yard. His father was standing outside their clapboard colonial, framed beneath the portico he'd built himself, his hands buried in his pockets, his eyes black and broken.

"You made your folks real proud tonight," said the police officer.

Chris didn't care.

FOUR

THOMAS FLYNN obtained a bond and made Chris's bail, twenty-seven hours after he'd been booked. At the arraignment, in a courtroom down in the Indiana Avenue corridor of Judiciary Square, Chris was released to the custody of his parents until the date of his trial. He was represented by Bob Moskowitz, a boyhood friend of Thomas Flynn's who was a private-practice attorney. The *Washington Post* court beat reporter, interested and aggressive because Chris was a white kid and his "night of crime" had made the TV news, tried to ask Chris questions, but Chris made no comment by order of Moskowitz and was hustled out of the building by his father, who held him roughly by the elbow.

Moskowitz followed them to their house, where he met with Thomas, Amanda, and Chris to discuss the status of the case and their general plan. They sat in the living room, where Thomas had built shelves to hold his collection of history and other nonfiction books. Amanda served coffee that neither Moskowitz nor Thomas Flynn touched.

"I've been contacted by Jason Berg's father." Moskowitz wore a caterpillar mustache and was forty pounds too heavy for his height. "After questioning Jason, the police and prose-cutors are satisfied that Jason was not significantly involved in the night's events to the degree that he should be charged."

"You mean," said Flynn, "his father's wired down at the courthouse, and he got his son off."

"There's no doubt that Mr. Berg has some suction. But more likely the prosecutors feel they can't make any charges on Jason stick. Jason never got out of the SUV, so there was no contact or conversation between him and the boys in that parking lot. And of course he wasn't the driver. They're going to focus on Chris."

"What about the pound of marijuana?" said Flynn. "Jason had nothing to do with that, either?"

"He says it wasn't his."

"It was mine," said Chris.

"Shut up," said Flynn.

"Tommy," said Amanda.

"So, what, they're gonna let that idiot off in exchange for his testimony against Chris?"

"Country's my boy," said Chris. "He wouldn't do that."

"I told you to shut the fuck up," said Flynn.

"*Tommy.*"

"I don't think they're going to compel Jason to testify," said Moskowitz with deliberate calm. "His father told me that he had no such indication from his contacts down there. They feel as if they have enough evidence and witnesses to make their case without Jason's testimony."

"What's going to happen to my son?" said Amanda.

"I'm going to give him the best representation possible," said Moskowitz. "Chris?"

"Yes."

"We'll speak in more detail, obviously. But what I want to

ask you now concerns your alleged assault on Alexander Flem-
ing, the boy in the parking lot. It's important, because this is
the act that triggered everything that followed. If you had reason to hit him, if you felt threatened or were defending yourself —"

"He didn't threaten me or nothin like that," said Chris. "I
can't even say that I was defending myself."

"Why did you hit him, then?" said Moskowitz.

"I was angry," said Chris. "It wasn't what he said so much as
how he said it. Actin like he was smarter than me."

"And what did he say to you?"

Chris shook his head. "I don't remember."

"God," said his father.

"Unfortunately," said Moskowitz, making a show of glancing at his watch, "I've got to get to an appointment. Will you
walk me out, Tom?"

"Let's go."

"Amanda," said Moskowitz, taking her hand and squeezing
it as he rose off the couch. "Chris. You're to stay here in the
house unless otherwise directed. You understand that, don't
you?"

"Yes."

"Okay. Don't worry. We'll get through this."

Bob Moskowitz and Thomas Flynn walked to a Mercedes
sedan parked on Livingston. Moskowitz stowed his briefcase
in the trunk, shut the lid, and leaned against his car.

"Talk to me, Bobby," said Flynn.

"Honestly?" said Moskowitz. "This is going to be a chal-
lenge, to say the least. Individually, a few of the charges are
minor, but compounded they are significant. That, together
with the fact that Chris has a history, will give the impression
that the incident follows a pattern of violent, reckless behavior.

There's the robbery of the locker room, the fights at the school. He has that assault-and-strong-arm arrest and the possession charge on his record as well."

"That was a while back."

"It's there. You have to remember, people were seriously injured because of his alleged aggression and negligence on the night in question. That woman's back injuries alone appear to be the kind that will plague her for the rest of her life. The boy whose nose Chris broke? His father was a major donor to our own D.C. Council member. Unfortunately, the events made the news and now Chris will be tried, in effect, in the public eye."

"What are you getting at?"

"We'll aim to get some of the charges reduced or thrown out. But I'm almost certain that something's going to stick. What I'm going to recommend to you . . . Well, hear me out. You're going to need to keep an open mind."

"Go ahead."

"The US attorney is making a hard push on this one because of all the publicity. Chris is *not* going to walk. The best thing we can do for him is plead guilty on some of the charges. I mean, we can roll the dice and go to trial, but a conviction in court can result in a stay in an adult prison. Juvenile jail is not the worst that can happen to him."

"My boy's going to jail?"

"Possibly. If so, I'd say that it would be for a relatively short period of time."

"You're talking about that place for juvenile offenders the District's got."

"Pine Ridge," said Moskowitz. "I'm telling you it's *possible.* Of course, I'm going to try to prevent it."

"That's all black kids out there, isn't it?"

"I'm guessing it's about ninety-eight percent, yes. The rest are Hispanics."

"They wouldn't send a white kid from this neighborhood to that place, would they?"

"It's rare. But it has happened. There's only one facility that houses D.C. juveniles who habitually commit these kinds of crimes. He's not exempt from serving time there because he's comfortable and white."

"I can't . . ." said Thomas Flynn, his voice trailing off.

"There's something else you need to prepare for," said Moskowitz. "We've only discussed the criminal aspect of this. There will probably be some litigation in civil court as well."

"Meaning?"

"You're going to be sued, Tommy. Your insurance company, sure, but probably you as well. All those people who got hurt or whose cars were wrecked because of Chris's actions? They're going to claim negligence on your part for letting a boy with Chris's history get behind the wheel of an SUV that you bought for him. It's convoluted, but there it is."

"Can they do that?"

"My brethren are probably lining up to feed at the trough as we speak. They'll certainly try."

Flynn opened his mouth to speak but said nothing. Instead he shook his head.

"I know this is rough," said Moskowitz, putting a hand on his friend's arm. "It all seems insurmountable right now. But look, I see this kind of trouble in families all the time. They get through it eventually. You will, too."

"Let me ask you something, Bob. Your oldest son, how's he doin?"

"He's fine," said Moskowitz.

"I'm asking you, where is he in life right now?"

Moskowitz looked away. "He graduated high school a couple of months ago. He's headed to Haverford in the fall."

"Don't tell me to look on the bright side."

"Tommy —"

"Everything's fucked," said Flynn.

AMANDA FLYNN made Chris a sandwich while her husband and Bob Moskowitz stood talking outside the house. She did it quickly, so as not to annoy Tommy. Tommy would say that Chris, who could take a vehicle his father had bought him and use it to lead police on a high-speed chase, who could punch out a kid in a parking lot for no reason, who could cause a woman to go to the hospital taped to a stretcher, who could carry around a pound of marijuana in his car, who could manage to get kicked out of public high school in the District, who could quit church and sports and everything else, could certainly manage to make a sandwich for himself.

Amanda did not see it that way. She looked at Chris, knowing all that he had done, and saw a young man who had been locked up for a day and night, who was confused and ashamed, who had to be hungry, who needed to be fed. Thomas looked at Chris and saw failure and an insurmountable problem. She saw her little boy. Amanda thinking, *With everything he's done, he's still my son.*

"Here, honey," she said, putting a turkey and Swiss on white down in front of him, mayonnaise, lettuce, no tomatoes, his sandwich, how he liked it. A glass of apple juice, Chris's preferred drink, set beside the plate.

"Thanks, Mom."

As Chris ate, Amanda looked through the living-room window and watched Bob Moskowitz drive away. Thomas Flynn stood on the lawn momentarily, checking the beeper hung on his belt line, replacing it, rubbing at his face. Then wheeling around and walking heavily back toward the house, sullen, his eyes to the ground. Amanda saying a wordless prayer that he would not enter their home and immediately explode.

Flynn came through the door. He looked at Chris, eating a sandwich off a TV tray, and shook his head in disgust. He looked at Amanda and sharply pointed his chin toward the center hall stairway. She followed him up the stairs.

It came to Amanda, when she was trying to "understand" Tom in moments of tension and conflict such as these, that it must be odd for her husband to have to act like an adult and deal with adult problems in the home in which he had grown up. Walking behind him up the stairs, she imagined him as a little boy, taking the steps two at a time, going up to his room to play or to wrestle with his big brother, Sean, now a Boeing executive in Chicago with whom he had little communication. She wondered if Tom, alone at night with his private demons, talked to his parents, whose spirits surely were in this house, and in his desperation sought their help.

It wasn't difficult to imagine him as a child. She had known him since their days at Blessed Sacrament, the Catholic school at Chevy Chase Circle that went from K through eighth. They were boyfriend and girlfriend through high school, and had married against her parents' wishes when Thomas was twenty and she was nineteen. Her father was dismayed that she was making this decision at so young an age and openly discouraged her from marrying a young man who had no intention of going to college.

"He wants to *work*, Dad," said Amanda. "He's ready to make money now."

"And what about you, Amanda? You're going to throw away a chance to go to college, to have that experience?"

"I'm with Tommy," she said.

Amanda had known he was the one as soon as she'd seen him, a black-haired, green-eyed Irish boy, walking cocky through the halls of BS. He was a tough kid, quick to fight, a basketball player who haunted the courts at Friendship, Lafayette, the Chevy Chase Library, and Candy Cane City, and later was point guard and the sole white player on his Interhigh team. He was not a good student, and, with the exception of American history, a subject that fascinated him, he had no interest in books. He liked to have fun, fucked off in class, drank Budweiser from cans, and smoked any kind of weed that was offered to him. His father, an Irish immigrant complete with brogue, worked for the Government Printing Office. His mother was of Irish stock, American born, and proud to be called a housewife. They bought the clapboard house on Livingston on the cheap, when nonprofessionals still lived in Friendship Heights and Chevy Chase, D.C., and upper Northwest neighborhoods were heavy with Irish Catholics. Thomas Flynn delivered the *Washington Post* all through high school, even during basketball season. On his route lived Red Auerbach, whose Celtic-green Mercury Cougar was usually parked in the driveway of his home, two blocks off Nebraska Avenue. Tommy Flynn always put Mr. Auerbach's newspaper at the top of his stoop, just outside the door.

Amanda had grown up on 31st Place in Barnaby Woods, on the east side of Connecticut Avenue, in a brick colonial that looked like several others on her street. Her father worked for an unidentified government agency, traveled frequently, and never talked about his job. Friends and neighbors assumed correctly that he was CIA.

Flynn had his buddies but spent most of his time with Amanda, a full-figured girl with strawberry blonde hair and fair skin, physically mature and sexually precocious at the age of fifteen. The two of them enjoyed their marijuana, alcohol, mushrooms, and downs, and, when they were in the company of kids with money, finger-thick lines of cocaine. They were faithful to each other and made it everywhere, in the front and backseats of Flynn's 442 Cutlass, on a blanket in the high-grass field at Glover and Military, and on the green of Rock Creek Golf Course on summer nights. Tommy couldn't get enough of her lush figure, and Amanda liked the wheel.

After high school, they married and rented a row home in pregentrified Shaw, still dirt cheap at the time. Flynn took retail jobs, then entered the MPD Academy and briefly worked as a police officer. Kate was born and died. Flynn's father dropped dead of a heart attack, and soon after that his mother, Tara, was diagnosed with pancreatic cancer and was gone in six weeks. His parents had willed the house on Livingston to Thomas, leaving their pitifully meager savings to their elder son, Sean, causing a rift between the brothers that would never heal. Flynn quit the MPD and moved with his wife into the Friendship Heights house in which he'd been raised. Amanda found Jesus, had a failed pregnancy, then carried Chris successfully to term. All of this occurred in the space of two and one half years.

Thomas Flynn walked into their bedroom, waited for Amanda to join him, and closed the door behind her. He used his right hand to pop the knuckles of his left. When he started the mangling of his joints, Amanda knew he was attempting to control himself and also that he would fail.

A shock of black hair had fallen over his forehead. He didn't look all that different than he had as a teenager. A little thicker and some lines around his eyes, but that was all right. She still found him handsome and often wanted him and his touch. Because of fatigue, and because their differences on the handling of Chris had put something impenetrable between them, they made love infrequently. Sometimes it was good, and occasionally it was eye-popping, but when it was over, Tommy's black mood would always return.

"What is it?" said Amanda. "You're not going to lecture me, are you?"

"I see you made Chris a sandwich."

"And?"

"Did you serve it to him on his Star Wars plate?"

"I fixed him some lunch. You think I should let him starve?"

"Let the kid make his own lunch. He's old enough to stick a knife in our hearts. He can build a sandwich by himself."

"Okay, Tom. Okay."

"You're not helping him, Amanda. He doesn't need an enabler or a personal chef. It's pretty obvious that the gentle way doesn't get results with him."

"I'm keeping the lines of communication open."

"I tried that and it doesn't work."

"You tell him to shut up. Then you tell him to shut the *fuck* up. That's not communication."

"It's what he deserves."

"He deserves our support. And I don't want to lose him."

"We've already lost him."

"I don't believe that. Look, I know you're angry. But he needs to know that we still love him."

"Fine." Flynn's beeper sounded. He checked the number on the display and took a deep breath. "My mailbox is so full it's not taking any more messages. I can't keep ignoring the business."

"Go to work," said Amanda. "You need to."

"I will. But listen, don't let Chris leave the house. He's going to tell you he's only going up to the store, or he's *only* going out to see his girlfriend. It's a violation of his terms of release. Don't let him play you, do you understand?"

"I *get* it, Tommy."

Flynn looked her in the eyes. He dropped his hands to his sides and softened his tone. "Amanda."

"What?" Now he was going to apologize.

"I'm sorry. This stuff with Chris has knocked me down, obviously. I'm all messed up."

"I know. Go to work. It's all right."

She *wanted* him to go. It was better here when he was not around.

Flynn left without touching her. He left the house without speaking to his son.

THOMAS AND Chris Flynn had little communication over the next few months. Chris continued to see the same psychiatrist that Thomas and Amanda saw as a couple, but Chris refused to meet as a family. At home, Amanda and Chris spoke regularly and cordially, and she cooked for him and did his laundry. Thomas and Chris spoke to each other only if necessary. Often they were in a room together and did not speak at all.

Thomas Flynn kept busy with his carpet-and-floor business and met Bob Moskowitz occasionally to discuss Chris's upcoming hearing. Fall arrived, and as other students returned to their high schools, Chris remained home, sleeping late, watching television, and killing time. He spoke often with Taylor on the phone but had infrequent conversations with his friend Jason Berg, and finally had none at all.

When Chris's case came up on the court's docket, everything seemed to accelerate. Chris pled guilty, and Moskowitz made a well-reasoned and passionate plea for lenience. But the judge was well aware of the criticism he would receive if he were to show mercy to the white kid from upper Northwest who had made the print and broadcast news, especially in light of the boy's history of theft, reckless acts, and violence. In accordance with D.C. juvenile justice procedure, he committed Chris Flynn to the custody of the District of Columbia. It was decided that society and the District would be best served if Chris were to be incarcerated with other young men until it was determined that he had achieved an acceptable degree of reform. And that was it. Chris kissed his mother, said nothing to his father, and was led away, shackled in handcuffs and leg irons, to a van that would transport him to the juvenile detention facility at Pine Ridge, in Anne Arundel County, Maryland.

That night, Flynn and Amanda ate a meal at home and turned in early. Amanda slipped under the covers and turned her back to her husband. He listened to her sob quietly and when her breathing evened out he knew she had fallen asleep. But he couldn't sleep or even close his eyes. He got off the bed and, in his boxers, went downstairs to the dining room, poured bourbon into a tumbler, and drank it down neat. He poured two more fingers from the bottle and took it out to the living room and stood by the mantel over the fireplace, where Amanda had set up framed photographs, the usual array of family and friends.

Thomas Flynn looked at an old photo, taken at the annual St. Patrick's Day parade down on Constitution Avenue, when Chris was two years old. Thomas had put Chris up on his shoulders so he could see above the crowd, and Chris's tiny hands were wrapped around his father's thick index fingers. And then there were those days that Flynn would ride his old

Nishiki ten-speed on the bike path of Rock Creek Park, Chris strapped into a seat mounted over the rear tire, a smile on his chubby face as the wind hit it and blew back his hair, Flynn reaching behind him and squeezing Chris's hand. Flynn could feel the warmth of those hands, the way they clung to him, even now. He remembered how proud he had been the day of the parade, how proud he was to have people see him and his son together on that bike, how certain he was then of his role as provider, protector, and father.

It was no longer about Chris's disturbing behavior, or his indifference to fitting into society, or his trouble with the law, or his marijuana use, or the embarrassment Flynn felt around the friends and acquaintances whose sons and daughters had stayed on track and were heading for college.

Chris was in prison. It felt final and irreversible, and Flynn did not know what to do.

He placed his empty tumbler on the mantel and listened to the tick of the clock mounted on the wall. It was very quiet in the house.

Chris Flynn had spent nearly every night of his life here on Livingston Street. Now it was as if he had never lived here at all. There would be no muffled sounds of the television behind his closed bedroom door, no floor-rumbling bass of his stereo, no low chuckle as he talked on the phone with his girl, no heavy, clumsy footsteps on the stairs. Chris was gone, and the silence he had left behind was a scream in his father's ears.

It was 1999. Chris was seventeen the day he entered juvenile prison. Thomas Flynn was thirty-nine years old.

PART TWO
UNIT 5

FIVE

THE GUARDS called it a room, but it was a cell. To name it anything else was a lie.

It was a six-by-nine-foot space containing a floor-bolted cot
and thin mattress, a particleboard desk and chair, and a steel
shitter and piss hole. There was a barred window giving to a
view of a dirt-and-mud field, leading to a twelve-foot-high fence
topped with razor wire. Beyond the fence was a forest of oak,
maple, wild dogwood, and weed trees, but no pines. The door
to the cell held Plexiglas in its cutout. Comically large Joliet
keys, so named because they were originally manufactured for
use in Illinois's Joliet prison, unlocked the steel doors.

Wake-up was at 6:30 a.m., then group showers, check-in,
and breakfast. Then school, 8:30 to 2:00, Monday through
Friday. Regularly scheduled recreation, canceled as often as it
occurred, dinner, visiting hours, and psychiatric counseling
with staff who barely spoke English. The intended illusion was
of routine, just like for boys on the outside.

There were a dozen units housing offenders of various de-
grees of criminality. The most violent boys, those convicted of
second-degree murder and manslaughter, and sexual offend-

ers, who were few, were housed together in Unit 12. That they were designated with the highest number, putting them by implication at the top of the pecking order, was a distinction not lost on the other inmates.

Chris Flynn lived in Unit 5, an L-shaped, low-slung brick building, with fourteen other young men. The residents of each unit wore the same color polo shirts, short sleeves in the summer, long in the winter, and system-issue khakis. They were allowed to wear lace-up shoes and sneaks. Their shirts had distinct colors so that an inmate could quickly be identified by his unit. The boys from Unit 5 wore maroon.

Classes were held in a building the size of a small-town elementary school. It was set apart from the housing units, close to another building that held a cafeteria that sometimes doubled as an auditorium, complete with stage. The warden and other administrators, including the central guard detail, kept offices in a separate structure.

The classrooms looked like the classrooms at Chris's former high school, each with a blackboard, a cluster of old chairs, an opaque projector that only one kid admitted knowing how to operate, and the usual silhouette cutouts of Frederick Douglass and George Washington Carver that the boys spit on and occasionally ripped off the wall. Teachers came to work every day, same as any other teachers, but faced more resistance and saw less progress or success. Chris could not imagine why anyone would want that job and guessed that these folks were do-good types, people his father called "crunchy granolas." What he didn't know was that Pine Ridge was a dumping ground for teachers who could barely cut it in the D.C. public school system.

"Does anyone know who the president of the United States was at the time of Martin Luther King's assassination?" said the teacher, Mr. Brown, a young black dude the boys called Mr. Beige, on account of he talked white. Mr. Brown's clothes were threadbare, further lowering his status in the boys' eyes.

"Roosevelt," said Luther, a boy who talked incessantly to hear his own voice and always gave the wrong answers.

"That's incorrect, Luther."

"Coolidge, then."

"Gump," said a boy wearing blue in the back of the room.

"Boy, you just naming high schools."

They were in history class, the maroon shirts of Unit 5 mixed in with the navy blue shirts from Unit 9.

"No, it's not Calvin Coolidge, either. But nice try, Luther. Anyone else?"

Chris thought he knew the answer. He was *certain* Ali knew. Sure enough, when Chris turned his head and looked at him, Ali Carter, seated at the desk-chair beside him, was staring down at the floor, mouthing the word *Johnson*.

Ali was smooth skinned, handsome, with a swollen upper body built by doing push-ups in his cell and dips wherever he could. He wore eyeglasses, which somewhat lessened the effect of his bulldog chest, and at five-foot-six was one of the shorter boys at the facility. Ali was in on an armed-robbery conviction.

"Nobody?" said Mr. Brown. "Okay. It was President Johnson, also known as LBJ. Who knows what those initials stand for?"

"Lonnie's Big Johnson," said Lonnie Wilson, a horn dog who tended to turn any conversation toward pussy or his dick.

"It ain't near as big as mine," said a boy.

A seated guard, one of two stationed in the room, chuckled, his fat moving gelatinously on the action. The other guard, a tall older man named Lattimer, who the boys called Shawshank because he looked like the graybeard in that movie, told Lonnie to watch his mouth and show respect.

"President Johnson and Martin Luther King had a cordial but sometimes rocky relationship during the civil rights era," said Mr. Brown.

"A sex relationship?" said one of the boys, and several of the others laughed.

"That's enough," said Lattimer.

"Perhaps 'rocky' is too strong a term. It's probably more accurate to say that their relationship was one of guarded respect," said Mr. Brown, gamely plowing ahead. "Understandably, Dr. King became increasingly frustrated with the slow progress in achieving his goal of racial equality in America, and was also frustrated with the escalation of the Vietnam War. . . ."

Many of the boys sat slumped in their chairs, some with their arms crossed, some looking away from the teacher, a couple with their eyes closed, stealing sleep. Understandable, as the most blatantly inattentive of them could neither read nor write. Ali, by far the smartest boy in the class, understood what Mr. Beige was saying, but the majority of the other boys did not. Just as many did not have any interest in the subject matter and felt that it had no relevance to the reality of their lives. All of this stuff with Dr. King and Lonnie's Big Johnson had happened before they were born, and wasn't no Dr. Anyone coming to save them and pull them up out of this jail.

". . . Ironically, it was Lyndon Johnson, a product of the South and its racist environment, who signed the Civil Rights Act of 1964, which gave all citizens in this country, regardless of their color, the right to vote."

"He was a leader," said Chris, not intending to speak but recalling something his father had said about Johnson at the dinner table one night. His old man was a history buff. The living room of their home was full of books on presidents and war.

"Black folk couldn't vote before then?" said Ben Braswell, a big dark-skinned boy with soulful eyes who lived in Chris's unit. Ben had stolen many cars and had been caught one too many times.

"Until then," said Mr. Brown, "some white people in power found loopholes and obstacles to prevent African Americans from participating in the process. The Civil Rights Act made any kind of racial discrimination illegal."

"What you think about that, White Boy?" said a husky voice behind Chris.

Chris did not turn his head, knowing that it was Lawrence Newhouse, who some called Bughouse, doing the talking. He did not feel threatened by Lawrence, nor slighted by the tag, which had been given to him his first day in. Everyone had another name in here, the same way soldiers did on the battlefield, and White Boy, though a supremely uncreative moniker, was as good as any other. Lawrence was stupid running to illiterate, unnecessarily abrasive at times, but not considered dangerous unless he was off his meds, though everyone knew he had shot a boy on Wade Road, which had been his ticket in. He was thin and had almond-shaped eyes and skin that in certain lights looked yellow.

"Asked you a question," said Lawrence.

Chris shrugged, the rise and fall of his shoulders his response.

"What, you can't speak?"

"You mind?" said Ali, turning his head to glare at Lawrence. "I'm tryin to hear this shit."

Ali had no intention of defending Chris, but Lawrence annoyed him. Plus, there was that old thing between them. Ali had grown up in Barry Farms, a Section 8 complex in South-east, and Lawrence had come up in the Parkchester Apart-ments, a neighboring housing unit. Neither of them were crew members, but there was a rivalry between the young men of the dwellings, a long-standing beef that no one, if pressed, could dissect or explain. Nonetheless, Ali Carter and Lawrence Newhouse had been assigned to the same unit. Boys with a history of animosity, gang related or otherwise, were mixed in with one another and were expected to work out their differ-ences.

"I say somethin to you, Holly?" said Lawrence.

"My name is *Ali.*"

"There a problem?" said the old man, Lattimer.

"I'm about to see you outside, little man," said Lawrence under his breath.

But instead, when the class was done and the boys filed out, Lawrence Newhouse took a wild swing at a guard for no ap-parent reason and was subdued by several other guards and hustled down the hall into an empty room, from which the boys could hear shouts and sounds of struggle. The next time the boys from Unit 5 saw Lawrence, just before lockdown that night, his cheek and upper lip were swollen. He and Ali passed each other in the recreation room but said nothing and made no hard eye contact. A couple of the young men, who did not particularly care for Lawrence, dapped him up. Fights between inmates were inevitable and sometimes necessary, but they bought you nothing. When you swung on a guard, you were going to take a beatdown for sure, but you earned a little piece of respect. Even from your enemies.

CHRIS HAD been inside for several weeks and had been in no fights yet. He had been the recipient of many shoulder bumps and hard brushes, and given out a few, but they had come to nothing. As for his color, he absorbed the usual comments and chose not to respond. Truth was, it didn't bother him to be described as a cracker. Had he called someone a nigger, there would have been immediate go, but there was no corresponding word for whites that would automatically start a fight. Because of Chris's indifference, the other young men grew tired of using his race as a launching pad for aggression and dropped it.

Not that he was feared. He was on the big and strong side, but this did not deter anyone. In fact, it made the smaller boys more eager to drop him. But the deliberate bumps were perfunctory and did not escalate to anything approaching real violence.

The nature of Chris's crimes gave him a certain mystique that was useful on the inside. He was the crazy white boy who had cold-cocked a kid for no reason, led the police on a high-speed chase, and outrun them. When asked, Chris told the story true, but in its telling it did sound as if he had no regard for consequences or respect for the law, when in fact, on the night in question he had just acted impulsively. Chris believed it was wise to take this rep as a gift and did nothing to dispel the notion that he was a little bit off.

The other thing that served him well was his ability to play and sometimes excel at basketball. The Pine Ridge half court, out in the field, was an asphalt surface land-mined with fissures and weeds, equipped with a slightly bent rim with chain netting. The rim was unforgiving, but once Chris learned its idiosyncrasies, he was good with it, and word quickly got around that he could ball. At first he wasn't chosen for pickup because of his color, but the guards forced the issue, and soon he was out there, getting hacked and bumped like everyone else. Playing those games on Saturday afternoons, and holding the court and bragging rights with what would become his team, which included the tall and athletically gifted Ben Braswell, was the high point of his week.

There were no other peaks. The boys were indoors most of the time, and the atmosphere in the unit buildings fostered depression. With clouded Plexiglas substituting for glass, little light entered the structures, so even on sunny days, their world seemed gray, colorless, and grim.

By design, the boys did not have a say in the rules or conditions at Pine Ridge. There was no suggestion box. The boys took orders or they didn't. They were ordered to go from one place to another, to keep in line, to get out of bed, to get in and out of the showers, to get to the cafeteria and to leave the cafeteria, to hurry into class and to leave class, to move into their cells. The guards didn't ask. They shouted and they commanded, often with obscenity-laced language.

Chris found himself bored with the sameness of his life inside. He was smart enough to know that he was being punished, that the boredom, the attitude of the guards, the tasteless food, the scratchy old blanket on his cot, all of it was intended to make him want to act right so he could be released and not return. But still, the treatment and surroundings didn't have to be so harsh all the time. The boys *got* it, they knew they weren't on some field trip, but it seemed counterproductive to get shit on day after day. After a while, the way they got treated felt less like punishment and more like cruelty.

So with bitterness they acted out and broke rules. They talked out of turn in class and swung on guards and one another. Many smoked marijuana when they could get it. It was brought in by a guard who walked it through the gatehouse by taping it under his balls, and it got paid for by money the boys'

relatives gave them on visiting days. The weed, stashed in ceiling tiles, was occasionally potent but frequently was not, and
most times it produced headaches over highs, but it was something to do.

Because the scent of marijuana was often in the air at Pine
Ridge, and because the high was evident in the boys' eyes, this
indiscretion was not a secret and the boys were piss-tested and
strip-searched at random. They knew they would most likely
be caught and that a drug offense would potentially increase
their time inside, but most of them didn't care. The warden
ordered urine tests on the guards, too, and some of them came
up positive. The guard who was selling, a man who arrogantly
drove his BMW 5-series to work and thereby generated suspi-
cion, was eventually served a warrant at his residence, where a
search turned up several pounds. He was fired and prosecuted,
but another guard saw an opportunity and stepped into his
shoes. Wisely, this guard continued to drive his old Hyundai.

It was said by some that the juvenile prison system tainted
everyone, employees and inmates alike.

Not all succumbed to the atmosphere. There were guards
who did their jobs straight and felt they were achieving some
kind of good.

Pine Ridge's superintendent, Rick Colvin, was one authority
figure most of the boys liked. He managed to remember their
names and ask after their well-being and their families. He was
decent, and the boys felt better when he was on campus. But
Colvin was not always around. His was a nine-to-five job, and
his absence was felt at night. The regular guards went home in
the evening, leaving duties to the crew of the midnight shift,
who the boys considered to be the scrub members of the security team. Ali said, "The low end of the gene pool get the shit
hours," and it seemed to be so. These were also the men and

women who woke them up in their cells at 6:30 in the morning. They rarely did so with empathy or kindness.

THE NIGHT after Chris assured his dad he knew how to jail, he was in the common room of Unit 5, hanging out on an old couch, reading a paperback novel, not paying attention to what he was reading because as usual the boys in what was called the media room next door were arguing about what they were watching and what they would be watching next on the scarred television mounted high on the wall. Also in the common room was an old Ping-Pong table, looked like a dog had been chewing on its corners, where two boys played. One of the boys liked to slam the ball and then ridicule his opponent about his inability to return the slam. It was hard for Chris to concentrate.

Ali Carter was seated in a fake-leather chair with riveted arms, ripped in spots. It was comfortable and he had commandeered it. Most of the other furniture here had been purchased out of a correctional facility catalogue, items made of hard plastic, indestructible and impossible to sit in for long periods of time. Ali, like Chris, was reading a book, but he did not seem bothered by the noise.

Chris had been given his book by the reading teacher, a young woman named Miss Jacqueline who wore white shirts with black brassieres underneath and tight pinstripe pants to their school. Miss Jacqueline came to school twice a week and worked with the boys individually, and after she visited she was the subject of much talk in the units and fantasies that led to masturbation when the boys got into their cells. Chris had heard Shawshank, the old guard, talking to Superintendent Colvin one day, complaining about Miss Jacqueline's style of dress, and how she "oughtn't be looking like that in here," and how she was driving all the boys crazy, walking around with her behind "all tight and full in them pinstripes." Chris agreed, but he liked looking at her just the same, and he liked the way she smelled of lavender when she leaned toward him. It was nice of her to give him the book, too.

"All right," said Ben Braswell, entering the room, tapping Chris's fist, and sitting down beside him. "Those pieces took my head up, man."

Chris had bought some marijuana with the money his mother had slipped into his pocket and had passed a couple of buds on to Ben.

"What I owe you?" said Ben.

"Nothin."

"I'll get you later, hear?"

"We're straight," said Chris. Ben never had money and had no way to get it. No one visited him, ever.

"We gonna ball this weekend, son?"

"No doubt," said Chris. "Better play while we can. It's startin to get cold out."

"Cool weather means gobble time," said Ben. "They'll be servin a special dinner on that day, too. Turkey and stuffing, cranberry sauce, everything. They did last year, anyway. It was tight."

Thanksgiving was just another day to Chris. But he said, "Sounds good."

He didn't want to taint Ben Braswell's vision of the upcoming holiday. More than any other boy Chris had met at Pine Ridge, Ben saw the brightness in things. His attitude was positive, he was never cruel to be cruel, and he didn't bully anyone out of boredom. Ben kept stealing cars, though, and the court kept putting him back inside.

"Hey, Ali, what you reading, man?" said Ben. "That book looks thick."

An open hardback book rested in Ali's lap. He took his eyes off the page and looked over the top of his specs at Ben. "Called *Pillar of Fire*. Miss Jacqueline gave it to me, said it came out just last year."

"That's a big-ass book."

"You can read it when I'm done, you want to."

"I ain't gonna read shit, Ali. You know that."

Because you can't read, thought Chris.

"It's about that time Mr. Beige was speakin on," said Ali. "The Civil Rights Act, Dr. King, LBJ, all that stuff. You know, that president Chris called a leader."

"He was," said Chris.

"Yeah?" said Ali.

Chris concentrated, tried to arrange his thoughts in a logical manner so he'd sound as if he knew what he was speaking on. For some reason, he wanted to please Ali.

"He did good, even though he wasn't all pure inside. My father told me that Johnson was . . . he was a product of his environment."

"Your pops meant that Johnson was racist," said Ali.

"More like, he couldn't really help what he was."

"Way I heard it, the man told nigger jokes at the dinner table," said Ali.

"Maybe he did," said Chris. "But he signed that act because it was the right thing to do, even though he might not have been feelin it in here." Chris tapped his chest. "That's what I meant when I said he was a leader."

"Okay," said Ali. "You're right. Not only that, he lost the South for his party when he did that, and they ain't never got it back."

"What the fuck are y'all talking about?" said Ben.

"You ain't all that stupid," said Ali, looking directly at Chris for the first time. "You just tryin to act like you are."

Chris blushed. "My father told me that, is all."

"Your father read books?" said Ben.

"History books and shit. He's got a library, like, in our living room."

"Your father," said Ali with a small smile. "Your living room. Books. A library."

"*What?*" said Chris.

"How you end up in this piece?" Ali shook his head and lowered his eyes back to his book. "You don't belong here, man."

IN HIS cell that night, Chris lay on his side on his cot and looked at a charcoal sketch that Taylor Dugan had done of him, taped to the wall. It was made from a photograph she had taken of him in her mother's basement, the night he was arrested. The sketch showed him shirtless, drinking a beer, with a cocky, invincible smile on his face. It had come to him through the prison mail, along with a note that simply said, "Thinking of you and miss you." On the bottom of the sketch, Taylor had put her signature. Underneath his figure she had printed the words "Bad Chris."

That's me.

It was *me. And now I'm here.*

The smile in the sketch seemed to mock him, and Chris turned his back to it. He stared at cinder blocks and felt nothing at all.

SIX

THOMAS FLYNN'S business was called Flynn's Floors. Despite the name, which he'd chosen because of its alliterative effect, the majority of his work was actually in carpet. He avoided wood flooring jobs, which were prone to costly error, and for the same reason he turned down work that involved ceramics. "I prefer not to deal with that," he'd tell customers. "It's outside my comfort level in terms of expertise." To builders and sub-contractors, he'd simply say, "I don't fuck with tiles. You can fix a carpet mistake. With ceramics, you screw up, you've got to eat it."

He catered primarily to the residential trade, with a smatter-ing of commercial work in the mix. Much of his business came from referrals, so he spent a good portion of his day calling on potential clients in their homes, checking work that his instal-lation crew had already done, and putting out any attendant fires. Amanda handled the paperwork end of the business — inventory, bills, receivables, payroll, insurance, and taxes — from the office they had set up in the basement of their house. Flynn was a good closer and could mother his crew and talk dissatis-fied clients down, but he had no interest in the clerical aspect of the business, while Amanda was efficient in paperwork and the collection of moneys. Their talents were complementary and they knew their roles well. Take one of them out of the equation and Flynn's Floors would not have been a success.

Flynn drove a white Ford Econoline van with a removable magnetic sign on its side, advertising the company name and phone number. His crew, headed by a hardworking El Salvadoran named Isaac, rode around in an identical van that Isaac drove home at night and parked on the grass of his Wheaton home off Veirs Mill Road. Chris, when he was still speaking to his father, called the vans the Flynn's Floors fleet.

Like many salesmen, Flynn did not believe in showing up at a client's house looking like he made more money than he needed. He felt that it was prudent to look humble and hungry. His work clothing was plain and square, Dockers from Hecht's, polo shirts bearing the company patch when it was warm enough, long-sleeved cotton-poly blends in the winter and fall, Rocksports on his feet. For a while he had gone through the Vandyke phase, in the rebel yell manner of a white Major League baseball player, but he saw too many guys with double chins doing the same thing, and it screamed middle-age desperation when in fact he wasn't there yet. Amanda said it made him look pleased with himself rather than honest or smart. He shaved it off.

Flynn looked in the mirror and saw what others saw, a guy who went to work every day, who took care of his family, who made what would always be a modest living, and who would pass on, eventually, without having made a significant mark.

He had been fine with this in the past. His aim was to instill values, work ethic, and character in his son, and to see him through to adulthood, when he would become a productive member of society and in turn pass this along to his own children. That was what he felt he was here for. That was how all of this "worked." But when Chris jumped the tracks, Flynn's belief in the system failed. There just didn't seem to be a point to anything anymore. He knew that this attitude, this inability to find purpose in his daily routine, was a sign of depression, but knowing it did not restore any sense of meaning to his life.

It was true what some folks said: When your kid is a failure, your life has been a failure, too.

Still, he continued to go to work. He had bills and real estate taxes, and the responsibility of maintaining employment for Isaac and his crew, who had families they were supporting here and family members they took care of in Central America as well. "It" hadn't worked out for Flynn, but that didn't mean these men and their loved ones had to suffer, too.

And then there was Amanda. Flynn loved her deeply, though he often spoke to her dismissively and they were no longer the friends they had once been. They communicated, and occasionally they came together in bed, but for Flynn the dying of their friendship was the most awful result of the troubles with Chris.

"I got a call from the superintendent," said Bob Moskowitz.

"Yeah?" said Flynn. "What'd he have to say?"

Flynn and Moskowitz were at the bar of the Chevy Chase Lounge on Connecticut Avenue, Flynn's neighborhood local. Flynn was drinking a Budweiser. Moskowitz was kidding himself with a Bud Light.

"He said that Amanda has been calling him fairly frequently."

"And what, he doesn't like it?"

"Colvin's a good guy. But he's got, like, two hundred and seventy-five boys he's responsible for in that facility."

"He's busy."

"Yes. The thing is, Amanda's not calling him with any significant problems or queries. After visitation, she calls Colvin and says stuff like 'I saw Chris and he looked a little thin,' or 'Chris sounded congested.' I mean, they're feeding them out there, Tom. If those boys get sick, they care for them. Guarantee it."

"You're saying Amanda has to stop with the bullshit calls."

"They're not going to release Chris just to get his mom off their back. And it's not helping his case."

"Colvin and them aren't used to parents who give a shit."

"They aren't used to parents who nitpick everything," said Moskowitz. "I understand she's scared for Chris. Outraged, too. But I think she needs to, you know, deal with this in a more internal way."

"Okay. I'll talk to her." Flynn had a pull off his beer and placed the bottle back on the stick. "Did Colvin say how Chris is doing? Or did he just phone you to crap on my wife?"

"Colvin's all right. And Chris is doing okay, too. Maybe too resigned to his incarceration, if you know what I mean."

"I do."

"He doesn't seem to care one way or another about his situation, and that's problematic, because he's got a level meeting coming up. I'm going to advise him to, like, sit up straight in his chair. Tell the review board that he recognizes and regrets his mistakes and that he wants to better himself. That he *will* better himself and is looking forward to the day he'll be released."

"That's good, Bob."

"You could do the same when you see him next."

"He doesn't really speak to me much. Mostly he communicates with his mom."

"I'm saying, you could speak to *him*."

"Right," said Flynn.

Speak to him. That's what the shrink, Dr. Peterman, said in their weekly meeting. And Flynn would nod and say, "You're right. I should try."

Dr. Peterman's office was in Tenleytown, on the corner of Brandywine and Wisconsin, over a beauty parlor, where Mitchell's, the sporting-goods store where as a teenager Flynn had bought his Adidas Superstars, used to be. Flynn wondered if the high rent was added into his tab. Like many men, Flynn did not care to talk about himself or, God forbid, his feelings. He continued to go to their sessions because it made Amanda happy, but as a concession he made sure that he complained about the impending visit on the drive to the man's office. Predictably, he called the shrink "Dr. Peterhead" when speaking of him around Amanda, and brought up more than once the fact that the doctor had a copy of *I'm Okay, You're Okay* displayed on the bookshelf behind his desk. "What," said Flynn, "is that the fountain of knowledge from which Dr. Peterhead drinks?" And Amanda would say, "Please don't be sarcastic when we get there, Tommy."

Flynn was polite in the man's presence, and not unduly sarcastic. Dr. Peterman was a pleasant young guy with a prematurely receding hairline, seemed pretty normal for a head doctor, and not overly analytical or mommy obsessed. Flynn looked around the office, at the usual pedestrian watercolors hung on the wall, at the beanbag chairs for those who liked to get comfy on the floor, at the self-help books on the bookshelf, at *that* book, and he was silently amused.

One day Dr. Peterman set up an easel and on it was a poster showing an imaging photograph of a brain shot from several angles. The man liked his props. The doctor pointed at a section of the brain, seen from a bird's-eye view, that was colored green.

"What are we looking at?" said Dr. Peterman.

"From that overhead angle?" said Flynn. "It looks like a set of nuts."

"*Thomas.*"

Dr. Peterman smiled charitably. "You're looking at a brain, of course. Specifically, the brain of a sixteen-year-old boy. This area in green is the limbic system, which regulates emotion. You can see that it is dominant in terms of geography. Now this blue area, representing the prefrontal cortex, is for reasoning. You can see that it's much smaller. That's because it develops more slowly than the limbic system." Dr. Peterman removed the poster to reveal another poster beneath it with similar imaging photographs. "Now, here is the brain of the same boy, but the photos were taken several years later. The boy is now a man in his twenties. And you can see here that the blue and green areas are represented equitably, more or less. Reasoning has, in effect, caught up with emotion."

"The kid matured," said Flynn.

"In layman's terms, yes. Teenage boys act with emotion more frequently than they do with reason. There's a physiological reason for that."

"But this thing with the brain must be true for all boys," said Flynn.

"I know what you're getting at. Why does someone like Chris find so much trouble and another boy find none at all?"

"Environment," said Amanda.

"Right," said Flynn. "But why Chris? You could understand some kid born into poverty, who comes from a broken home, who's around thugs and drug dealers; I mean, that kid's got problems coming out of the gate. You might not *excuse* it, but you can understand why a young man like that finds trouble. But a boy like Chris . . . why?"

"That's one of the things we're here to talk about. But I bring it up to show you that this is not a permanent state of mind for your son. It's going to improve."

Amanda reached over and squeezed Flynn's hand. The doctor had made her feel better, and Flynn supposed that in this regard, the session had been worthwhile.

THE HOLIDAYS came and were difficult. Then New Year's Eve, the turn of the century, which was supposed to be the biggest party of their lifetimes but which they did not celebrate, and then a return to routine. Low interest rates had encouraged folks to buy homes or take out second mortgages and remodel, which was good for Flynn's business. He and Amanda were kept busy, and Flynn's crew had steady work. The greater profit they experienced, however, was offset by the extreme increases in Flynn's insurance rates. As Moskowitz had predicted, Flynn had been the target of civil suits. The settlements, in total, had been costly.

Amanda visited Chris weekly, sometimes with Flynn, sometimes alone. She thought Chris had grown more receptive to their visits, but Flynn found him sullen and unchanged. On joint visits, it was Amanda who generated conversation and kept things moving along. Chris and Flynn continued to keep each other at arm's length.

Chris had advanced several levels since he had arrived at Pine Ridge. The monthly level meetings consisted of a kind of informal review where the opinions and testimony of administrators and guards came into play. An inmate was required to achieve Level 6 before he would be considered for release. Chris was now at Level 4. His progress was encouraging to Amanda, and the news of it seemed to brighten her outlook. To Flynn, she looked younger than she had in a long while.

Thomas and Amanda continued to see Dr. Peterman. One cool day in late March they made the familiar drive to his office, complete with Flynn's running commentary on Dr. Peterhead, the watercolors, the books in his office, and his fees. Amanda did not mind. She was just happy that Flynn was cooperative and coming along.

As he did with every visit, the doctor returned to the issue of the gulf between father and son. For his part, Flynn contended that Amanda was too soft on Chris. Flynn said that while he disagreed with her, he understood Amanda's approach and that someone, he supposed, had to continue to nurture their son, but he could not bring himself to do it. Eventually he admitted that he was too wounded by Chris's attitude and actions to speak to him in a loving way. And then, perhaps because he was embarrassed by this admission, Flynn claimed that his hard-line stance was part of a larger strategy.

"Somebody's got to show him the iron fist," said Flynn. "Let him know that what he's done has been unacceptable. Amanda can be the one to pour juice into his sippy cup and give him hugs."

"Oh, please," said Amanda.

"I'm saying, you've got your role, Amanda, and I've got mine."

"Why don't you switch roles?" said Dr. Peterman. "Amanda can adapt a bit of a tougher stance and you can do the nurturing."

"What," said Flynn, "you want me to wear a skirt?"

Dr. Peterman smirked nervously and blushed a little. "Well, I wouldn't put it quite that way."

Flynn looked at his watch. A quiet settled in the office and they all knew the session was done.

Flynn and Amanda walked over to the Dancing Crab and had lunch and a few beers. Amanda called Flynn a Neanderthal but laughed about his comments in Dr. Peterman's office, and in her eyes he saw light and youth. That afternoon, they made love in the quiet of their bedroom. She fell asleep as the sun streamed in through the parted curtains. Flynn stepped over their Lab, Darby, who was sprawled out and napping on his cushion, and got dressed and left the house.

He drove down Bingham Drive into Rock Creek Park and stopped at a turnoff lot, where he cut the engine, his van facing the water. He and Amanda had come here one day as teenagers after they had eaten mushrooms from a plastic bag. Their spot was a beach of fine pebbles and sand, and they had lain down upon it. Tommy Flynn had taken Amanda's shoes off and massaged the balls of her feet and her toes, and as the psilocybin kicked in, they laughed without reason and uncontrollably for what seemed like a long time. Flynn could barely imagine having so little responsibility again, so little weight on his shoulders. To look up and see no clouds blocking the sun.

I'm just disappointed, thought Flynn. *That's all it is. I've been a failure as a father, and there's nothing ahead of me that looks promising or new.*

In one of their sessions, Dr. Peterman had looked straight at him and said, "Why do *you* think Chris has gone down this road, Thomas?" And: "Is it possible that Chris was trying to please you or emulate you in some way? By your admission, you were a pretty tough kid. Did Chris feel he had to be that way, too, in order to garner your respect and your love?"

Flynn had taken no offense. Peterman was smart and he was onto something. The doctor *knew*.

Flynn tried to think on his early years with his son. How he had continually emphasized the physical over the intellectual with Chris. John Wayned him up with instructions to never show weakness and "step aside for no man." He had taught his son how to fight but never shown him the value in walking away from one.

Pivot your hip, Chris. Aim for two feet behind your target and punch through till you get there. If you're going to throw it, make sure it counts.

While other fathers were reading books to their sons and pointing out countries on the globe, Flynn was showing Chris how to shoot a gun in the woods and teaching him the police ten codes. It became a kind of shorthand between them. Chris would fall down and scrape his knee, and he would reassure his father that he was 10-4. Or Chris would call his father on the car phone, wondering where he was, and ask, "What's your ten-twenty?" The code 10-7 meant out of service, but Chris learned from Flynn that to cops it also meant dead. So when Flynn buried Chris's deceased hamster in the backyard, Chris said, "Mr. Louie is ten-seven."

Flynn had taught his son that an off-the-ten code for an officer in serious trouble was a Signal 13. In elementary school, when Chris was just beginning to act up, he would come home and tell his father that he had been sent to the office, but that the offense was minor and nothing to worry about.

"It was no Signal Thirteen, Dad."

"That's good, Chris," said Flynn with a smile.

The boy had spirit and fire, character traits that annoyed teachers but would serve Chris well as an adult. That's what Flynn had always believed. But in this, and in everything else pertaining to the raising of his son, he now felt that he'd been wrong. Chris had been headed for serious trouble for a long time, and Flynn had missed the signals. It was as if he had been watching his kid drive a car, in slow motion, straight into a brick wall. Watching it, letting it happen, without so much as a shouted warning.

It's not Amanda's fault that Chris is what he is. It's mine.

Speak to him.

I should try.

SEVEN

"HOW'S IT going?" said Thomas Flynn.

"It's goin all right," said Chris.

Chris had just seated himself at the table across from Flynn. Chris's eyes were cool and he sat low in his chair.

"Where's Mom at?"

"She wanted to come."

"Why didn't she?"

"I talked her into staying home today. Thought it might be good for you and me to see each other alone."

Chris sat back and crossed his arms. "What are we supposed to do now?"

"Talk, I guess."

Chris looked around the room. A couple of other boys, one in a black polo, one in a forest green, were being visited as well. The boy in black had a male visitor. Chris took mental note of this because it was rare. He returned his attention to his father.

"I'm not trying to be hurtful," said Chris. "But, really, I don't have all that much to say."

"You say things to Mom."

"Honestly? Mom doesn't tell me to shut the fuck up. Mom never called me a piece of shit."

"I shouldn't have said those things," said Flynn. "I was wrong."

"How did you expect me to respond to that, Dad?"

"I didn't think it through."

"It sure didn't make me want to change the way I was."

"I know it."

"It didn't make me want to put my arm around you or get on my knees and beg you to forgive me. It just made me feel nothing. It was like you weren't trying to be my father anymore and you didn't want me as your son. I felt like, *so be it*. You know?"

"Yes, I do," said Flynn. He looked down at his hands, tented on the table. "I took everything that happened . . . I took it too personally, I guess. I let my emotions get the better of me."

"So what you tryin to tell me now?"

What are *you trying to tell me?* thought Flynn. He bit down on his lower lip. "I'm trying to tell you that I'm sorry about the way I reacted."

Chris did not comment. A silence settled between them.

"Your mother said you called her last week."

"Yeah?"

"I'm saying, she was pleasantly surprised. Normally you don't call us at home."

"They only give me ten minutes a week on the phone. Before, I was using that time to call my friends."

"Why'd you change up?"

"My friends stopped taking my calls."

"Jason, too?"

"I haven't spoke to Country in a long time."

"What about your girlfriend?"

Chris shrugged and shook his head. But Flynn could see that he was wounded.

"You'll make new friends," said Flynn.

"I got friends in here."

"That's good, Chris. But I'm saying, when you get out, it'll be a new start. New friends, everything."

Chris looked away.

Flynn breathed out slowly and said, "Mom told me you're doing well in school."

"I'm gonna graduate. A real high school degree, not some GED."

"Excellent. With a degree in hand you could test into a community college."

"That's not gonna happen."

"What, then? What will you do?"

"Work, I guess. I don't know."

Flynn used one hand to crack the knuckles of the other.

"Don't get frustrated, Dad."

"I just don't want you to make that kind of crucial decision without thinking about it."

"I don't want to go to college. You didn't go, and you turned out all right."

"*Don't* . . . don't compare yourself to me. Back in my day, with only a high school degree, you could still make something of yourself. But now there are two distinct societies, Chris, plainly separated. The educated and the uneducated. You don't just go to college to learn. You go to mingle and forge a permanent network with people who all move up the chain together. Don't go to college and there's going to be a ceiling on your earnings. The pool will be limited on who you date and marry. Not only will you probably live in a lower-income neighborhood, but so will your children, and their peers will be lower income, too. Don't you see how it works? There are people who strive to make it to the upper level of society and then there are the other people who stay down below."

"It was you who was always cracking on the lawyers and doctors in our neighborhood. Saying how they came from privilege and money, and how they had a leg up. Being all sarcastic about how they never got their hands dirty or broke a sweat. Like how you sweated every day."

"Chris—"

"You don't want me to be like you?"

"You're not listening to me."

"I guess I'm just one of those other people. The ones who stay down below."

"God*damn* it, Chris."

"Anyway. All this talk about the future? It doesn't mean nothin to me. I mean, I'm in *here*. This is what I got to deal with now." Chris swept his arm around the room as if he were showing his father something grand. He pushed his chair back and stood away from the table. "Thanks for coming by. Tell Mom I was askin about her, hear?"

Flynn put his hand on his son's forearm and held him a bit too hard. He knew that he should tell Chris he loved him and that now was the time. He tried to say the words but he could not.

"Sir?" said the guard on duty. "There's no physical contact allowed."

Chris pulled his arm free. He stared at his father for a moment, then made a chin motion to the guard, who let him out the door of the visitation room. Flynn watched his son walk back into jail.

*   *   *

THE BOYS were sitting around in the common room on a cold night in early spring, cracking on one another, talking random shit, and killing time until lights-out. None of them were anxious to go to their cells, where a few would study, fewer would read books for pleasure, many others would masturbate, and most would simply go to sleep as their bodies wound down and the shield they felt they had to carry fell away. Though cell time was the one truly quiet, introspective time of their day, it was also the loneliest, and the most difficult to face.

Ali Carter and Chris Flynn were seated on the couch, and Ben Braswell was in the fake-leather chair with the rivets in the arms. Luther Moore and Lonnie Wilson were playing Ping-Pong. Lattimer, the old graybeard guard they called Shawshank, was in a hard-back chair too small for him. The boys liked him well enough for what he was, but they would not defer to him and give up a seat more suited to his age, size, and authority.

They could hear Lawrence Newhouse in the media room, arguing with a boy, trying to get time on the computer, an old, slow machine with a blinking cursor that sat next to a dot matrix printer. Lawrence's tone was becoming more threatening by the sentence, but Lattimer was not moving from his chair.

"You better get in there, Shawshank," said Luther. "Lawrence sound like he ready to blow."

"Scott's in there," said Lattimer. Scott Stewart, a fellow guard, was built like a Minotaur. "He can handle it."

"Scott's swole," said Ben.

"They need to get Bughouse out this unit," said Ali. "Put him in Unit Twelve."

"He ain't that kind of bad," said Lattimer. "Lawrence just be talkin, mostly."

"Either get him out or put me somewhere else," said Ali. " 'Cause I cannot stand to be around that fool anymore."

"Won't be long till you're gone anyway, young man," said Lattimer, trying to make eye contact with Ali. "Stay focused on those books and walk that straight line. You keep doing what you been doing, you'll be all right."

"They can put *me* somewhere else," said Lonnie Wilson, laying down his paddle, signaling to Luther that their game of table tennis was done. Both of them came to join the group but remained standing, as no one was about to move over and make room for them to sit.

"Where you want to go?" said Ben.

"Unit Six," said Lonnie, running a hand across the crotch of his khakis. "What you think?"

Lattimer rolled his eyes. Unit 6 was the girls' building, out in the woods somewhere, out of sight from the boys' camp. It was on Pine Ridge acreage, surrounded by its own razor wire–topped fence. The conversation was about to go where it usually went this time of night.

"Boy," said Lonnie, "I would punish the *shit* out them girls in Unit Six. I would be like a bull in one of them Chinese shops."

"Don't be runnin your fingers through their hair, though," said Luther.

"I know it," said Lonnie.

"They put razor blades in their braids!" said Luther.

"You don't know nothin, Luther," said Ali.

"I know enough not to touch their braids."

"It's a lot of gray girls they got out there, too," said Lonnie.

"White Boy would like it out in Unit Six," said Luther, and Chris felt warmth in his face.

"Them pale skins are runaways and hos, mostly," said Lonnie. "But I got love for all the girls. I don't care what they did to get locked up or what color their skin is. Shoot, I'll even get with a Mexican. They pink to me, too."

"What about, like, Asia girls?" said Luther.

"*'Specially* them. I'm all about equal opportunity."

"If they got to squat to pee, you gonna take the opportunity," said Luther, and he and Lonnie Wilson smiled and dapped each other up.

"Do they let those girls have dogs out there, Shawshank?" said Ben.

"Hell, no," said Lattimer.

"Warden Colvin said we might get puppies," said Ben.

"For real?" said Chris. He missed Darby.

"I saw Colvin today and he said we might. Every unit could have their own."

"We could have us a pit," said Luther. "Or a rot with a head big as a horse. Five would have a fierce-ass dog."

"Nah," said Ben. "It wouldn't be a dog we'd use to fight. It would be like a pet."

"Ya'll ain't getting *no* kind of dog," said Lattimer. "Some of these boys in here, they'd torture those poor animals. And a lot of you are allergic to dogs and don't even know it. You'd be surprised how many."

"'Nother words, your people gonna try to stop it," said Ali, looking hard at Lattimer.

"They'd be *right* to stop it. It's not in my contract to pick up dog shit."

"It's not about dog shit," said Ali. "It's about keeping us low. Any time the superintendent try to do somethin nice for us, the guard union blocks him."

"That's not true."

"Sure it is. You know it, too."

"You're a smart young man," said Lattimer. "So I'm gonna tell you something, because I believe you can understand it. This ain't no country club out here. Y'all are here for a reason. You've done wrong and now you here to learn and be reformed. You know what re-formed means? It means you were one thing, and then you get formed into something new. What the superintendent don't seem to understand is, you boys need to learn consequences, not get rewarded for what you done. And that means you don't get served ice cream sundaes after dinner or get to talk to fine young women during your reading class. And you sure don't get the right to have no pets. You see your way out of here? You can eat all the ice cream and have all the women and dogs you want. That's what law-abiding citizens get to do. But you ain't that. Not yet. You got to *earn* that."

A crashing sound came from the media room, and all turned their heads. Lawrence Newhouse was cursing, and struggling from the sound of it, and though they did not say it, the boys assumed his conflict was with the big guard, Scott. And then Lawrence came airborne out of the media room, with Scott moving strong toward him, and Lawrence was falling, and before he hit the ground Scott had grabbed his shirt and lifted him back up to give him more of what he'd already had. Scott threw him against a wall of shellacked cinder block. His face hit it pretty hard. Scott put Lawrence's right arm behind his back and twisted it up, getting control of the young man.

"Boy, you just had to get on my last nerve," said Scott, and he began to push Lawrence out toward the cells.

Most of the boys had lowered their eyes. None of them liked Lawrence, but when the guards won, it was like they had been robbed of a piece of their manhood, too.

As Lawrence passed he looked at Ali, who had not looked away, and said, "What the fuck you staring at, Holly?"

Ali said nothing. Lawrence spit a mouthful of blood in the direction of Ali and Chris. Scott hustled him down the hall.

"Bughouse always be tweakin," said Luther Moore.

"That boy just angry," said Lattimer.

Ben Braswell looked at Chris. "You think we might get a puppy, man?"

"We might," said Chris, though he knew Ali was correct. The guards' arm of the FOP union, which tended to fight any reforms the superintendent proposed, would find a way to stop the boys from having pets.

"You got a dog at home, right?" said Ben.

"Yeah," said Chris.

"You're *lucky*," said Ben. Chris could feel Ali's knowing stare but did not look his way.

"Time for y'all to get to your bedrooms," said Lattimer.

The boys got up from their seats without objection and headed to their cells.

As they walked, they could hear the old man still speaking to them, giving them his parting words of inspiration. "Another good day for you fellas. Another day closer to your goal. You get right with God, you gonna get right with yourselves."

The boys went down the narrow hall, where Lattimer would wait until they entered their six-by-nine spaces, then use his Joliet key to lock the steel doors behind them. From his own cell, Lawrence Newhouse was alternately screaming and laughing. His anguished wail echoed in the hall.

"Ain't no God in here," said Ali.

Chris walked into his cell.

THE NEXT day, while Chris and Ali were walking in the hall between classes, Ali took a fist in the back of the head, for no apparent reason, from a boy named Maximus Dukes. Ali tripped and fell to the floor, severing the bridge of his glasses. Without even thinking of himself, Chris was on Maximus, throwing him up against the wall and delivering several body blows and one solid uppercut to the jaw before Maximus could return fire. He was a big boy and Chris's rain had not hurt him, and he came back strong. Chris took a glancing temple shot and one deep right to the solar plexus that blew half the wind out of him, but he kept his feet, and several more punches were thrown before the guards charged in and stopped the fight. It had been meaningless, and there was no rancor between any of them again. Because neither Chris nor Maximus had gone down, their reps had been elevated. The fight cost Chris his Level 5, but he would achieve it at a later date.

Of the many things Chris learned at Pine Ridge, one would be embedded in his mind for years after his release: When you or one of your own is attacked, retaliation is mandatory, no matter the consequences or repercussions. It has to be on.

The guards had seen Maximus blind-punch Ali. Wasn't any need for Chris to step in. But it wouldn't have been as satisfying to see the guards strong-arm Maximus and lead him down the hall. When Chris swung on the boy, his blood got up in a righteous way, and he felt like a man. He wished his father had been there to see that he'd stood tall.

EIGHT

For SECURITY reasons, doors had been removed in the bathroom stalls, so the boys voided their bowels in full view of the other inmates. It was something Chris had to get used to quickly. Let it bother you, you'd have to hold your shits till you got back in your cell. That wasn't natural, and no one liked to stink up their rooms.

On the same level of indignity was the morning ritual of group showers. There were no privacy curtains or barriers of any kind, and if someone was modest or ashamed, he had to get over it, that is if he wanted to be clean. The open area was meant to discourage violence, and perhaps it had been a wise idea, as there were rarely serious altercations in the showers. The best Chris could say about the experience was that it was fast. If you lingered in the shower more than a little bit, the tepid water would go cold.

Chris and the other boys did not worry about nonconsensual homosexuality in the showers or anywhere else inside the walls. It was the most dreaded aspect of prison for a boy on the outside looking in, but the truth was, oral and anal rape were extremely rare at Pine Ridge. The boys in juvenile had not yet gone to that level of degradation that occurred in adult male prisons. There were scattered consensual homosexual relations here, but, somewhat surprisingly, it was not an issue of derision among the boys who were straight. They knew who among them had gone that way, but didn't berate them to their faces or, for the most part, behind their backs. Those boys were just as tough as the other boys, and no one was going out of their way to find a fight.

What took away their dignity was the presence of the guards, who watched the boys shower though a Plexiglas window. The fact that they, fully clothed and outfitted with security gear, could stare at the inmates, naked and completely vulnerable, seemed wrong. Thing of it was, you didn't know what they were thinking while they were looking at you. Chris was reminded of that one summer when his mother had persuaded his father to vacation with a wealthy neighborhood family, the Rubinos, who had invited them to their house on Martha's Vineyard. The house was steps away from a nude beach, and from the start, even though the Flynns had been assured that they did not have to "participate," his father had been annoyed. Many families went naked, including their prepubescent sons and daughters, and there were also grown men on the same beach, naked and alone, and Thomas Flynn said, "Why would a father let his little boy or girl go nude in front of those men? You don't know what's going on behind their sunglasses." Amanda had said, "Don't be rude, honey; we're guests here," and his dad muttered something about "bored rich people" and left it at that. That was their first and last vacation with the Rubinos. Years later, when Steve Rubino cashed out of his law firm and left his wife and kids for a twenty-two-year-old GW student, Thomas Flynn said, "You know what Rubino was doing up on that beach? He was *shopping*. I told you that guy wasn't right."

Chris smiled, thinking of his old man. They had a word for the way he was. Crum-something. Always complaining but doing it in a funny way.

"What you grinnin on, White Boy?" said Lawrence Newhouse, standing beside Chris in the shower.

Chris shrugged, giving Lawrence nothing.

"Thinkin about your home?" said Lawrence. "Bet you got a nice one. A real nice family, too."

Chris recognized the mention of his family as some kind of threat, but it had no weight or meaning. For a moment, but only for a moment, he thought, *Bughouse is right*. But to let himself dwell on what he'd had, and on his mistakes, was not productive. He was here now, and it didn't matter where he'd come from; he was the same as everyone else inside Pine Ridge. Locked up and low.

"Why you never speak to me, man?" said Lawrence. "You too good?"

Chris did not answer. He stepped out of the spray and reached for a towel smelling of body odor that hung on a plastic knob.

"We gonna talk, *Christina*," said Lawrence.

Chris dried himself off and walked away.

A MAN who had done time at Lorton, and who had written poetry there and eventually a series of popular street-lit message novels aimed at juveniles, came to speak to the inmates of Pine Ridge late in April. The residents of Unit 5, wearing maroon, and Unit 8, wearing gray, were ushered into the auditorium, having walked from the school building through a cold rain.

Many of them were soaked and shivering as they sat in their too-small chairs and half-listened to the speaker, who started his talk with the usual I-came-from-the-same-streets-as-you, I-made-it-and-you-can-too platitudes that went through them faster than the greasy Chinese food they used to eat in the neighborhoods they'd come up in.

Ali Carter and Chris Flynn sat in the row of chairs farthest back in the room. Ali was wearing his glasses, a piece of surgical tape holding them together at the bridge, and a kufi skull cap, finely knitted. The cap was allowed for religious reasons, despite the facility's no-hat policy. Ali had confessed to Chris that he had been named by his mother after the boxer and held no Muslim beliefs. He wore the skull cap just to mess with the guards, who didn't like the boys asserting their individuality, and to take a minor victory where he could.

"When I wrote *Payback Time*," said the writer, whose nom de plume was J. Paul Sampson, "I was thinking of young men just like you. Because I was once where you are now, and I understand that revenge is a natural impulse. I understand that you *think* it's going to make you feel good."

"Not as good as gettin a nut," said Lonnie Wilson from somewhere in the crowd, and a few of the boys laughed.

J. Paul Sampson, immaculate in a custom-tailored suit, plowed on. "But revenge, my young brothers, is a dead-end street."

Ben Braswell was a row ahead, seated among gray shirts. He was listening to the book writer and nodding his head. In the front row sat Lawrence Newhouse, defiantly slumped in his chair, arms crossed. A half-dozen guards, including Lattimer, and a few teachers, including the school's earnest, bearded young English teacher, Mr. McNamara, were standing around the perimeter.

"Where I was," said J. Paul Sampson, "in lockup? It was full of men who felt they'd been disrespected, and because of that, they acted on impulse and got violent. With the passage of time, as the years went by in prison, they couldn't even tell you why they'd killed. Because what they did was unreasonable. You know what that means, don't you, gentlemen? There was no *reason*."

In one of the rows ahead, a young man in a gray polo shirt had turned his chair slightly so that he could look to the back of the room. His gaze was focused steadily on Ali.

"Why's that dude eye-fuckin you?" said Chris, keeping his voice low.

"Calvin Cooke," said Ali, leaning in close to Chris. "Boy's from Langdon Park, over there off Rhode Island Avenue. It's a Northeast-Southeast thing. I guess he feel the need to stare."

"So?"

"He just bein unreasonable," said Ali with a small smile.

Ali often got singled out for intimidation because of his short stature and, due to his eyeglasses, his studious appearance. Some called him Urkel as he passed. The ones who said nothing had taken note of his big chest.

"I'm here to tell you that the life I have now is better than the one I had," said J. Paul Sampson. "I made a choice when I got out of prison, and I'm a successful and productive member of society today. You can make the same kind of choice."

Luther raised his hand. "Do you get paid?"

J. Paul Sampson chuckled nervously. "Yes, of course."

"Do you get pussy?" said another boy, and the auditorium erupted with laughter. A guard pulled that boy roughly out of his chair and led him from the room.

"Show respect to Mr. Sampson," said the English teacher, McNamara. "He took valuable time out of his day to come here and talk to you. Listen to what he has to say."

There were murmurs in the room, and the boys' posture slackened further.

"I got a question," said Lattimer, stepping forward from the back of the room. "I knew you were coming to speak, so I read one of your books. You know that one, *Brothers in Blood*?"

"Yes?"

"The boy in that book is bad, almost all the way through. He's in a crew, he gives other kids beat downs, he drops out of school. To him, all the authority figures, including the police, is hypocrites and fools. Then in the last chapter, the boy comes to his senses and turns his self around."

"That's right. The message is, you can make many mistakes, but it's never too late to change."

"See," said Lattimer, "I kinda figured out what you're doing. What they call the formula. You're getting kids all jacked up on one hundred and eighty pages of violence and disrespect, and then you add ten pages of redemption in the end that they not even gonna read. What I'd like to see is a whole book about a kid who doesn't do any wrong at all. Who stays on the straight even though he may be living in a bad environment, because that's the right thing to do. Because he knows the *consequences* of being wrong."

Scattered mumblings came from the crowd: "You stupid, Shawshank," and "Why you got to talk?" and "Sit down, Mr. Huxtable."

"I try to tell the truth, sir," said the author amiably. "My books reflect the reality of the street."

"A little more respect for authority is all I'm looking for," said Lattimer. "That's what these boys need to read about and learn."

"I appreciate your comments."

"Got to give Shawshank credit," said Ali, staring at the boy from Langdon Park, who was still staring at him. "Man believe what he believe, and you can't move him off it."

"Shawshank's a rock," said Chris.

Luther raised his hand. "Can I be a book writer, too?"

"You can be whatever you want to be," said J. Paul Sampson. "If there's one thing I want you gentlemen to take away from this today, it's that."

"I want to be one now," said Luther.

"It's a goal to strive for," said J. Paul Sampson, exasperation replacing the fading brightness in his eyes. "But it takes time. Like anything worth having, you need to work for it. Being an author is like having any other job."

"I don't want no job," said Luther. "*Fuck* that."

LAWRENCE NEWHOUSE had been put on heavier meds, rumored to be in the lithium family, and when his behavior improved it became contagious. Unit 5 was more peaceful when Lawrence was subdued, and at times the atmosphere was nearly congenial. There were arguments, but the fire in them died quickly, and people laughed at Luther's dumb jokes and listened patiently to Lonnie Wilson's boasts and three-way fantasies though they had heard them many times before.

Ali and Chris were in the common room one night, Chris sprawled out on the couch. A guard was nearby, but he was sleeping. Many of the boys from the unit were in media, watching television, Joneing on one another, cackling at whatever was onscreen, debating whether the male actors were real or soft, talking about the girl actors and what they'd do to them if they had the chance. Someone was riffing on an actress, twisting her name, predictably, into something obscene, and Ben Braswell was laughing. Also laughing, in baritone, was Scott, the big guard.

"You high?" said Ali, putting the book he was reading down on the floor beside the ripped fake-leather chair where he sat.

"Nah," said Chris. "Just chillin."

"You look like you're high."

"I'm not."

" 'Cause you need to stop doin that shit."

"I *been* stopped," said Chris.

"You know they gonna make you drop a urine. And you got that level meeting comin up. Ben does, too."

"I haven't given Ben any weed," said Chris. "Not for a while."

"That's good. Ben needs to drop a positive so he can get out this piece. Just like you do."

"Ben gets out," said Chris, "he's just gonna steal a car again and come right back in. That's who he is."

"Ben wants y'all to think that. He tells everyone how he was born to hot-wire, how he loves to get behind the wheel of a vehicle, how he can't stop himself, all that. Truth is, it's a crime he can do where he doesn't have to hurt no one. All he wants is to get his self put back inside these walls."

"Why would he want that?"

"Because this is the only place where he feels right. I'm not talkin about that three-hots-and-a-cot bullshit you hear all the time. You notice nobody ever comes to visit him? I mean, we all got *some*one, right? Ben got nobody. His crackhead mother died young and then he got moved to foster homes, and everywhere he lived was shit. In here, at least he got friends. In the classroom, he listens, even though he doesn't understand half the stuff the teachers be sayin, and you know he can't read. The fact that anyone notices that boy or calls him by his name is good to him. Bad as it is, this here is his home."

"He can't stay, though."

"No," said Ali. "Neither can you. Won't be long before I'm out, too."

"You're always saying how I don't belong here—"

"You don't."

"What about you? How'd someone smart like you fuck up so bad?"

"Which time?" said Ali.

"I hear you," said Chris, thinking on his many mistakes, how he'd piled them on top of one another without consideration or even a glancing thought.

"The last time, though," said Ali, shaking his head, "with my uncle? That's what got me put away."

"Talkin about the armed-robbery thing."

"Yeah. My mom's half brother, he ain't but five years older than me. He's ignorant and weak, I see it now, but me bein a dumb-ass kid, I looked up to him at the time. He was more like a father to me than an uncle. I'm sayin, when he put his eyes on me, I wanted him to see a man. So when he asked me to come along with him, and told me I had to hold the gun and do the thing, on account of I didn't know how to drive the car, I did it. You think I'm smart and maybe I am. But I wasn't smart that day."

"So now you got yourself a Pine Ridge education. You learned."

"Not the way they wanted, though. They tryin to break us down to nothing, so we can get reborn. But all their commands and speeches don't mean shit to me. I learned on my own. I'm not what they think I am and I'm not gonna be what they expect me to be. Once I'm out, I'm not coming back, but not because of anything they did to me in here. I'm gonna be right because I *want* to be." Ali jabbed a finger at his own chest. "For me."

"Nuff 'a that high-and-mighty talk," said the guard, who had awakened. "You boys need to get to bed."

Later, in his cell, Chris lay atop his scratchy wool blanket with his forearm covering his eyes. The unit grew dead quiet as one by one the boys fell asleep. Chris was not tired. His head was full of contemplation and, for once, regret. He sat up on the edge of his cot.

Chris stood and went to the wall where he'd taped Taylor Dugan's drawing. He looked at his image, shirtless, eyebrow arched, mouth in a bold smile, his hand holding a beer, and it did not make him feel proud or amused.

Bad Chris. He was not sure who he was, but he was certain that he was no longer the boy in the drawing. Nor did he wish to be.

Chris peeled the paper off the wall, ripped it apart, and dropped the pieces in the trash. He went back to bed and fell asleep.

NINE

O N A cool, cloudy Saturday in May, a three-on-three basketball game was in progress on the asphalt court out in the middle of Pine Ridge's muddy field. Chris Flynn, Ali Carter, and
Ben Braswell were in maroon, up against Calvin Cooke, Milton "the Monster" Dickerson, and Lamar Brooks, all wearing
gray. Lawrence Newhouse stood out of bounds, as did a boy
named Clarence Wheeler, wearing navy blue. They had called
next and would choose one from the losers of this game to
round out their team. A rotund guard, Mr. Green, stood on a
weedy patch of dirt, observing, a two-way radio in hand.

Chris had the ball up top. He was being covered by Lamar
Brooks, a quiet boy who had no offense but whose darting hands
were quick. Lamar was trying to slap the ball away, but Chris
had turned his hip and was protecting the pill. Down below, Ben
had boxed out Milton, a kid in on multiple drug charges, who
was Ben's size. Ben had his hand up and was calling for the ball.

Out beyond the imaginary three stood Ali, loosely matched
with Calvin Cooke, the Langdon Park boy who had lately been
mugging and shoulder-brushing him in the auditorium and
cafeteria. Cooke wore his hair in small twists and had flat eyes

and a smile of pain. He was in on a firearm conviction, having beaten a murder charge in court. The prosecution's witness, too frightened to testify, had muted up on the stand.

Chris faked a chest pass to Ali, then bounced one around Lamar and in to Ben, who caught it, turned, and hooked it up. On a normal hoop it would have dropped, but this iron granted no favors, and the ball bounced off the back of the rim. Ben threw his ass out on Milton, got his own rebound, and passed it to Ali. Ali was the shortest man on the court but had the greatest vertical leap. He went up, way over the outstretched hand of Calvin, and put one through the chains.

"All right," said Chris.

"You gonna play defense on that retard?" said Calvin to Milton. "Or you gonna let him pick apart your candy ass?"

"Wasn't my man made that bucket," said Milton.

"Mini Me lucky," said Calvin.

Chris walked the ball to the top of the key and looked at Lamar.

"Checked," said Lamar.

Chris bounced the ball over to Ali. Chris clapped, and Ali tossed it back. Lamar was three feet away, playing him loose, so Chris went up and gunned it. From out here, he knew it had to be all net or a kiss off the backboard. It felt right as it left his fingers, and the chains danced.

"Splash," said Ben.

"Luck," said Calvin. "None 'a these bitches can play."

"Six-nothin," said Ali, and Ben grinned.

Mr. Green's radio crackled. He listened to its message and his face told the boys that it was urgent. He said, "Copy that," and turned to the inmates. "Ya'll play on. I got an emergency situation I got to attend to. I'm gonna be right back, hear?"

The boys watched the overweight guard jog laboriously

across the field toward one of the unit buildings. They could see heightened activity there. Guards streaming in, a guard posted at the door. It meant that there had been some kind of violence.

"Now that Tubby the Tuba gone," said Calvin, "we can play for real."

"Look to me like they *been* playin," said Lawrence Newhouse.

"I ask you somethin?" said Calvin. "Take a pill and dream you a man, Bughouse."

Lawrence, his eyes glassy from his meds, smiled at Calvin Cooke. A wind came up and whipped at the boys' shirts and cooled their sweat.

"Ball up top," said Chris.

"Checked," said Lamar.

"Cover that Gump," said Calvin to Milton.

"I got him. Get your mans, too."

"He too scared to come inside," said Calvin.

Chris dribbled and faked a move to the left. In his side vision he saw Ali slashing into the lane and he put English on the rock and bounced it in. Ali took it and put the ball down on the asphalt and made his move, driving toward the basket with Calvin in front of him. Ali did a jump-step thing and elevated, and as he went up, Calvin threw a forearm into Ali's shoulder. Ali released a shot as he fell back. He landed hard, and the ball clanged off the back of the iron.

"Don't even walk past the front of my house," said Calvin.

Milton pounded his fist. "Eastside."

"Ball," said Chris.

"That wasn't no foul, White Boy," said Calvin. "Your boy flopped like Reggie Miller."

Ben reached down, grasped Ali's hand, and pulled him up off the asphalt.

"You all right?" said Ben.

"I'm straight," said Ali. "Play it."

"See?" said Calvin. "Your own man say that shit was clean."

"Don't matter what Holly say," said Lawrence. "You fouled his ass."

Lamar Brooks quietly stepped off the court. Clarence Wheeler, the boy in the navy blue polo shirt, took a few steps back and separated himself from the group.

"What you say?" said Calvin, stepping up to Lawrence.

"I said you got him. You throwin forearms 'cause you can't fuck with Unit Five."

Calvin smiled. "And you a stone faggot."

"Then *do* somethin," said Lawrence.

Calvin Cooke's right fist whipped out and connected. Lawrence's head snapped back and he lost his legs and dropped to the ground.

Calvin grunted with effort as he kicked Lawrence in the ribs. He pulled back his foot to kick him again.

"Don't," said Ben, moving quickly and wrapping his arms around Calvin from behind. Calvin struggled wildly in his grasp. Ben lifted him off his feet. "Don't!" he said in an imploring way.

Milton Dickerson charged Ben, and Chris stepped in front of him. Dickerson hit Chris like a nose tackle, and it knocked the wind from both of them as they went down.

Chris broke free and rolled away. He caught his breath and got to his feet.

Ben had Calvin in a hug and was swinging him, attempting to gain some kind of control but stumbling back.

Ali shouted, "Let him go, Ben!"

Ben whipped Calvin around, and Calvin's head caught the steel pole of the backboard. When it hit, it sounded like a bell.

Ben released him.

Calvin fell to the ground, landed on his back, and for a moment was motionless. Blood began to flow from one of his ears and bubbly saliva poured out the side of his mouth. His eyes were open and crossed, and his body began to spasm.

"Help," said Ben, horrified, his voice soft and low.

Several guards ran across the field toward them. Chris looked at Ali, and Ali lowered his eyes and shook his head.

Chris lay down on his stomach and waited. He felt his arm twist up violently behind him. He felt a knee grind into his back.

IT SEEMED as if it took a long time for the emergency medical technicians to arrive. When they came, the ambulance driver drove the vehicle very slowly across the muddy field, as if he were wary of getting stuck. The boys were being led toward the guards' building then, and they watched the ambo pass.

They were taken to separate rooms and interrogated by Pine Ridge authorities and police. Warden Colvin and a visibly agitated Glenn Hill, the director of the Department of Youth Rehabilitation Services, were in attendance. When the interviews were done, Chris and the others were taken to their cells, where their dinners were brought to them. Chris did not touch his food.

They found out later that Calvin Cooke had suffered what one of the guards called "a cerebral hemorrhage caused by trauma." It was said that the slow response time by the emergency people had allowed Calvin's brain to swell up and that was why his condition would not improve.

In a J. Paul Sampson novel, the boys from Calvin's unit would have been out for revenge on the boys of Unit 5. There would have been eye-mugging, shoulder brushes, talk of getback, and maybe another minor tragedy of some kind, but in the last chapter the boys of the two units would have met in another contest on the same court where Calvin got his dome crushed, and the game of basketball would have united them. They would have agreed that revenge was a dead-end street and decided to honor the spirit of Calvin and shake hands and walk away as comrades rather than enemies.

The reality was, no one thought to avenge Calvin. The boys in his unit understood that what happened to him was an accident he'd brought upon himself, the cost of boasting and stepping to someone, and anyway, they never did like him much. Calvin did not return to Pine Ridge, and no one spoke of him. When he died two years later, of infection brought on by bedsores, he had been forgotten.

In his cell, Chris lay on his stomach, his arms dangling over the sides of his cot. On the floor in front of him was an open notebook, a pen resting on a blank white sheet of paper. Chris could hear Ben Braswell, speaking to himself and crying, from his cell down the hall. He could hear the guards out there in the hall, walking back and forth, talking and chuckling, making one another laugh to try and cut the boredom of their suicide watch.

In his mind, Chris saw a spring day down on the Soapstone Valley Trail in Rock Creek Park. Darby galloping clumsily though a carpet of leaves, Chris's mom in a new down vest, a shade of green that was her favorite color. His father swinging out from behind the trunk of a tree, a stick in his hand, making machine gun noises, a lock of black hair fallen across his forehead. Chris jumping from rock to rock across the creek, the sun dancing off the water.

Chris picked up his pen. Across the paper he wrote: "Signal 13."

In his bedroom on Livingston Street, Thomas Flynn woke suddenly, startled from a dream.

PART THREE
SIGNAL 13

TEN

THE JOB was north of Logan Circle and south of U Street, in a section of the city that people in the past had broadly called Shaw, but now got called Logan by many real estate agents and some residents. In midtown the homes were row houses, mostly, some topped with D.C.-signature turrets, all backed by alleys. There were houses here and there whose disrepair went back generations, but the majority had been restored and remodeled, and the general impression was one of transformation.

A white Ford cargo van rolled down U Street, its two occupants in matching blue polo shirts, taking note of the sidewalk parade, people strolling past restaurants, bars, and boutiques. Different skin colors, a mash-up of straight and gay, non-flash money and hipsters, heads, hustlers, and intellectuals, young couples, bike messengers, old folks who remembered the fires of '68, everyone trying this new thing together. It wasn't perfect because nothing is, but down here it seemed as good as Washington had ever been, and for some, it was a dream realized.

To Chris Flynn, it just looked like a nice place to live. But he figured that he would never be able to afford to buy a place in this zip code. Weren't any carpet installers who owned property here. The ones who carried mortgages here, he reckoned, had gone to college.

"Dag, boy, it sure is different than it was," said Ben Braswell, his big frame sprawled on the bench, his arm on the lip of the open passenger window.

"It was the Metro system did it," said Chris, thinking on something his father had once said, explaining the positive changes in the city. "Every place where they opened subway stations, the neighborhoods improved around them. Public transportation got all this shit going again."

"Took, like, twenty-five years to happen."

"Point is, it happened."

"Yo, man, pull over," said Ben, rubbernecking the diner that bore his name. "I need a half-smoke *now*."

"After this job, maybe," said Chris.

"Chili, mustard, onions," said Ben, his gentle eyes gone dreamy. "Sweet tea. Maze on the juke . . ."

"We don't do this installation, we don't get paid."

"How we supposed to work if we don't eat?"

"How you supposed to pay for your half-smoke if you don't work?" said Chris.

"True," said Ben.

Chris was going to have to disappoint him. There wasn't time to stop anywhere because they were already behind. After this install they'd have to drive back out to Beltsville in Maryland to pick up the roll for the next job, then head over to a home in Bethesda to complete it. Ben would understand.

Chris turned left off U into the residential section of the neighborhood. "If we get done quick, we'll have time for lunch."

They found a spot on the street close to the job site. A real estate agent was standing outside the row house, talking on her cell, a look of annoyance on her face as she spotted the van, recognizing the magnetic sign on its side that read "Flynn's Floors."

"Wait here," said Chris. "Let me get up with this woman before we unload."

Chris got out of the van and approached her. She continued to talk on her cell and did not acknowledge him. She was in her midfifties, with a short, spiky, gelled hairdo. She was blond, heavily made up, and had crinkle-bunny lines from age and too much sun. Her petite figure seemed shapeless under her loose, sleeveless purple dress.

The "For Sale" sign mounted on a post behind her had her photograph on it, arms crossed, smiling, with two young people, also smiling, standing behind her. In big letters, the sign said, "Mindy Kramer," and below it, in smaller script, "The Kramer Dream Team."

"I've got to go," said Mindy Kramer into her phone. "They finally got here." She shut the cell's lid with an audible snap and looked at Chris. "You are?"

"Chris." He did not use his last name unless asked.

"I expected you earlier."

"We got hung up on another job—"

"And now I have to leave and meet a client on Capitol Hill. I'll let you in and then I'll come back and lock up when the job is done." She looked past him to Ben, seated in the van, slouched, his blue Nationals W cap worn sideways on his head. "Mr. Flynn said his crews were bonded and insured. I assume that includes you and your partner."

"Yes, ma'am."

"Let's take a look at the room."

She marched up the granite steps that led to the front door. Chris turned to the van and did the darting-tongue thing, and Ben smiled. Chris followed Mindy Kramer into the house.

Chris admired the structure and its craftsmanship as soon as he walked inside. Chair rail molding in the dining room, wide-plank hardwood floors in the center hall, plaster walls. No furniture, though. Whoever once lived here was gone.

"This way." Mindy Kramer cut a right through open French doors.

Chris stepped in, rapping his knuckles on the door frame out of habit and curiosity. As he expected, it was solid wood, not the Masonite he saw in so much new construction. The space was about fourteen by twelve, he guessed, and would be called a library on the listing, as it held a wall of built-in book-shelves. He looked down at the worn carpet that covered the floor.

"It should be a pretty straightforward job," said Mindy Kramer. "I went with the cable. Mr. Flynn said the loop pile would be fine for a medium-traffic space."

"It'll work," said Chris, pulling his Stanley tape measure off the belt line of his Dickies where he kept it clipped. He laid down the tape and measured the length and width of the room, which was close to his estimation, and mentally noted that his father had ordered a larger roll than was needed to do the job. This meant that he hadn't liked Mindy Kramer or that he foresaw complaints from her or multiple post-job visits. When the customer showed arrogance or attitude up front, they tended to pay extra. Chris's father called this the "person-ality defect tax."

"Is what you brought sufficient?"

"Oh, yeah," said Chris. "It's gonna be fine."

"There's a walnut floor under this carpet, but it needs sand-ing and refinishing. Nice hardwood is preferable to carpet when you're selling a home, of course, especially to younger clients, but I don't have the time or inclination to go that route. I just want to get some carpet down and bring in a few pieces of furniture here and there so I can flip the property. I bought it at auction for a song. The previous owner was a gay gentleman who had no surviving heirs. . . ."

Chris nodded, trying to keep eye contact with her. All she was doing was bragging on how savvy she had been and how much money she was going to make. Telling a stranger this because she was insecure. He was not impressed.

"We'll get started," said Chris. "It shouldn't take us long."

"Here's my card," said Mindy Kramer, handing him one. "Call me on my cell when you're almost done and I'll shoot back over and give it a look. Tell me your number, Chris."

Chris gave her his cell number. She punched it into the contacts file of her phone and typed in a name.

"I'm going to call you Chris Carpet," she said, proud of her cleverness, "so I can remember who you are when I scan through my contacts."

Whatever, thought Chris. But he said, "That's fine."

Mindy Kramer hit "save" and glanced at her watch. "Any questions?"

"That'll do 'er," said Chris, giving her the redneck inflection that she no doubt expected.

Ben had already slipped his kneepads over his jeans and was tying a leather multipocket tool belt around his waist when Chris emerged from the house. Ben and Chris wore the same type of belts and in their pouches they kept their pro-shop razor knives. As Ben finished tying his belt off, Mindy Kramer got into her C-series and, cell phone to her ear, sped away.

Chris put his pads on, and he and Ben went around to the

back of the van. They untied a red towel from the end of the out-hanging carpet and removed the roll and its sister roll of padding. They carried the carpet inside, came back and got the padding, took it up the steps, and placed it beside the roll they had stowed in the hall. It was hotter in the house than it was outside, and both of them began to perspire. They had done one job already, so it was the second time they were sweating into their polo shirts that day.

"In here," said Chris, and Ben followed him into the library.

Ben sized up the job, liking that there was no furniture to move and that the space was virtually square. "Looks easy."

"Can you take up the old carpet?"

"What, you too busy to help?"

"I gotta check in with my father. I'll only be like a minute. I'm sayin, get started, is all."

Ben commenced taking up the old carpet in the library. He started in a corner as Chris walked from the room and reached into a pocket of his Dickies for his phone. He wandered down the hall to what had been a living room and punched in his father's number.

"Hey," said Thomas Flynn. "Where are you?"

"Down at that job off U Street."

"The Dream Team there, too?"

"Just Mindy. She had to bolt, but she's coming back. We were late gettin down here. That job in Laurel set us back about an hour."

"I'm in the warehouse. My guy says you were late getting *started* this morning."

"A little." Chris was a bit annoyed that his father was still checking up on him so closely. At the same time, he told himself that it was business, only business.

"Ben sleep in again?"

"Wasn't Ben, Dad. We were just a *little* late. We did the job in Laurel quick, but the guy had a problem with the bubbles. I had to talk to him for a while. Explain why it looked that way."

"They all belch about the bubbles, son. Did you tell him they'll flatten out after he walks on it?"

"Yeah, I told him."

"The bubbles go away. They do flatten."

"I know. So that's done, and now me and Ben are gonna knock this out."

"And then that job in Bethesda, right?"

"Yes. We'll get that done, too."

"It's money for all of us," said Flynn.

"Right," said Chris.

He walked down the hall, slipping the phone back into the pocket of his work pants. He could hear Ben chuckling, saying, "Chris, come *in* here, man," and then, almost in wonder, "Oh, *shit*." For a moment, it reminded Chris of Ben's voice coming from his cell down the hall at Pine Ridge, how Ben had talked to himself at night, how his talking had bothered others, how it had been a comforting sound for Chris.

Chris stepped into the library. Ben was sitting on the faded, scuffed walnut-plank floor, the worn carpet and corroded padding peeled back. A piece of the floor, a cutout, had been removed and was propped up against the wall.

There was an old Adidas gym bag, the kind with the stiff handles that was popular before Chris and Ben's time, on the floor beside Ben. It had been zipped open.

Chris could see cash. Green money in stacks, held together by bands.

"Oh, *shit*," said Ben, grinning up at Chris.

Chris felt a rush of excitement. Found money did that to a man, even a rich one.

But Chris did not smile.

THOMAS FLYNN warehoused his inventory at a space on Sunnyside Avenue, a long loop of road holding cinder-block and concrete structures in an industrial park in Beltsville, Maryland, north of College Park. Flynn didn't own the space, called Top Carpet and Floor Install, but paid in-and-out charges to keep his goods there. TCFI's main business was installation, subbed out from one of two big-box retailers serving the PG County do-it-yourself trade.

Flynn stood before a large wooden stage at the head of the warehouse. The stage had holes in it and air was blown up through the holes, a hovercraft effect that allowed one worker to handle a large piece of carpet and spin it around while he laminated or cut it.

Beside Flynn was one of Isaac's crew, a young curly-haired man named Hector who wore a blue polo shirt displaying a breast patch company logo, the L's in "Flynn's Floors" depicted as vertical, slightly bent carpet rolls. Amanda had come up with the design, along with the idea that the employees wear the shirts. She said that with the shirts the installers looked as if they worked for a "real" company. Flynn agreed to it, with the childish condition that his polo shirt be red, to separate him from the others. Also, with his black hair, he felt that red looked good.

"You gonna take that Berber roll with you, right?" said Flynn.

"That job is not today," said Hector.

"I need to get it out of here. Otherwise I've got to pay, like, rent for it. You've got Isaac's van, haven't you?"

"Yes."

"C'mon, I'll help you put it in."

They found the roll in Flynn's section. He checked its tag, on which was written the customer's name, and he motioned for Hector to grab an end.

"The Berber popular," said Hector, grunting as he lifted.

"I can move as much as they give me," said Flynn.

He was, and always had been, a good salesman. He sold like a factory rep, not an untrained retail salesman with an eye on the clock or a better job. He was a professional carpet-and-floor man. He knew the product thoroughly, explained its advantages, and, because he was a good listener rather than a fast talker, made many deals.

The problem was not with sales. Through referrals and his own acumen at closing, Flynn had as much business as he could handle. The problem was with installations and installers.

Flynn still had Isaac and his crew, and they were golden. Isaac had been with him for many years and would be with him as long as Flynn had work. Isaac had built on to his house in Wheaton, one of the many unconventional "Spanish mansions" seen in the area around Veirs Mill and Randolph roads, had a daughter in college and a son who was learning the installation trade. He would never live in El Salvador again. Isaac's crew came and went, usually leaving the country due to unpaid taxes or immigration complications, but even though the faces changed, to a man they did quality, responsible work. No wonder Flynn's mantra was Thank God for Hispanic workers.

Flynn and Hector loaded the roll into the van.

Hector looked at Flynn sorrowfully and said, "No more job today."

"We didn't make much money today," said Flynn, always

careful to use the inclusive pronoun. "But we will tomorrow. I've got something for you every day this week."

"Okay, boss."

Hector drove the van out of the lot, Flynn thinking, *Yeah, these Spanish guys like to work. Not like Chris and his crews of parolees.*

There were plenty of installers with tough pasts. Ex-offenders, bulls, and badasses of various colors and ethnicities, all on the young side. None had gone to college. This wasn't the place for students looking for summer jobs. Flynn had tried one or two out, and they hadn't been able to cut it. It was hard, demanding work. The goods were heavy and bulky, and much of the job time was spent on one's knees.

Many of the installers drank heavily at night and used marijuana and other drugs. Flynn could smell the alcohol in their sweat, could see the misery in their eyes nearly every morning. Unhealthy skin pallor was another giveaway. When Flynn interviewed a potential worker, he took note of his teeth. A guy had fucked-up teeth, it meant he came from little means or was raised by people who didn't care enough about their own kid to see to his dental hygiene. Whites from East Baltimore had the worst choppers.

Because it was hard work, and because the success of his business depended on their diligence and conscientious manner, Flynn compensated his installers relatively well. A sharp, hard-charging bull could make fifty, sixty grand a year installing carpets, but guys like that were rare. Chris's guys were lucky to make twenty-five to thirty thousand. Flynn put a little extra on Chris's check, due to the fact that he was a crew chief, so Chris made about thirty-five.

Thirty-five tops, thought Flynn, as he walked into the TCFI offices to drop off a check.

"Hey, Tommy," said a young woman behind one of two computers in the office.

Flynn couldn't remember her name. She was usually outside smoking in the morning when he came by, a gregarious Laurel girl, chubby, with a Route 1 hairstyle, one of those burn perm things.

"How's it going, sweetheart?" said Flynn.

"It's Susie."

"I knew that. Sweetheart suits you better, though." Susie smiled, and Flynn dropped an envelope on her desk. "Give that to the boss, will you? I don't want him to send the cavalry out after me."

"Your son was in this morning," said Susie.

Susie made eye contact with the girl seated behind the other computer, a pretty, fair-skinned strawberry blonde, voluptuous for her thin bone structure, couldn't have been more than two or three years out of high school. Flynn had noticed her before but had never heard her speak.

"Say hello to Katherine," said Susie. The girl looked down at her desk in a self-conscious gesture and smiled.

"Nice to meet you, darling," said Flynn.

"And you," said Katherine.

"Chris never says more than a couple of words to me," said Susie, once again glancing at her office mate. "Course, I'm spoken for. But he doesn't mind talking to Kate."

"It's Katherine," said the woman, gently correcting her co-worker.

Kate would be twenty-seven now.

"Chris is just shy around girls named Susie," said Flynn, forcing a grin. "Not like me."

"He doesn't even look like you," said Susie. "All that blond hair."

Again the girl named Katherine looked down at her desk.

"He got that from his mom," said Flynn, then comically puffed out his chest and made a bodybuilder's pose. "But he got the beef from me."

"Get out of here, Tommy!" said Susie, her boisterous, wheezy, Marlboro Light–inflected laughter trailing Flynn as he left the office.

Out in the hot sun, he put on his shades and walked to his van.

Kate would be twenty-seven. Amanda and me would be getting her ready for a wedding, or visiting her where she works, some professional job in New York City, maybe, or Chicago.

Flynn passed a guy he knew in the parking lot but did not say hello.

Chris is twenty-six. No college, time in prison, his days spent on his knees, laying carpet.

Flynn opened the van's driver's-side door.

Thirty-five grand a year, tops.

He got into the van and fitted his key to the ignition.

What's going to happen to my son?

ELEVEN

"SHOULD WE count it?" said Ben Braswell.

"No," said Chris, staring at the money, shaking his head slowly. "I don't even want to touch it."

"You don't want to know how much it is?"

"Zip up the bag and put it back in that hole," said Chris. "Then seal it up again with that cutout piece. We'll get this new carpet down and move on to the next job."

"You're serious."

"I am."

Ben stood up, went to the window that gave to a view of the street, and opened it. He meant to cool the room, but the air outside was still, and there was no discernible relief from the heat.

"Why?" said Ben, walking back to join Chris. "Why you don't even want to talk about this?"

"It's stealing."

"You just told me yourself, the dude who lived here died, and he had no kin. You can *see* how old this bag is. Prob'ly the man who lived here last wasn't even the one who buried it. And you *know* that real estate lady didn't bury no money. Whoever put it under this floor got to be buried now, too. So how is this stealing? From *who?*"

"It's not ours," said Chris.

"It ain't nobody's, far as I can tell."

Chris ran his hand through his longish blond hair.

"Forget this," said Ben, and he got down on his haunches and reached into the bag. "I gotta know."

Without removing the band, he slowly counted one of the stacks of money, bill by bill. His lips moved as he mentally tabulated the sum.

I've seen this movie, thought Chris. Innocent, basically good people found some money and decided to keep it, rationalizing their act because the cash belonged to no one. The money corrupted them, and they betrayed one another and were ultimately brought down by their own greed, a basic component of their human nature that they thought they would overcome. It always ended up bad.

Ben finished counting the one stack, then counted the number of stacks in the bag and multiplied.

"It's damn near fifty thousand in here," said Ben.

"Now you know," said Chris. "Zip up the bag and put it back."

Ben pointed a finger at the money. "That's two times what I make in one year, Chris. Working on my knees. I could buy something nice for my girl, take her out to dinner to one of those restaurants got white tablecloths. I could have some real clothes, and not the off-brand shit I got now. A pair of designer shades—"

"Put it back."

Ben stood up and faced Chris. He was going for confrontational, but he couldn't get there. There wasn't anything like that inside him. Instead, he looked hurt.

"How you gonna *do* this to me, man?"

"I'm doing you a favor."

"Nobody would know, so what's the harm? You can't tell me I'm wrong."

"My father gave us a chance here," said Chris. "Wasn't anybody else looking to hand us a decent job, was there? Someone does find out, it's his reputation we'd be messin with. That's *his* name on the truck."

"And yours," said Ben.

"What's that supposed to mean?"

"Means that I got nothin. Someday, whatever your father's got, whatever he built up, it's gonna come to you."

Chris moved his eyes from Ben's. "I've never taken anything from him but a paycheck."

"Comes a time, you will." Ben's features softened. "You *know* I appreciate what your pops did for me. But this thing we're talkin about here, it could change my life."

"It's already changed," said Chris. "You don't see it yet, is all. I'm sayin, there's no shortcut to where we're trying to get to. Just work, every day. Same as how it is for everyone else."

"Don't you want more?"

Chris stared at Ben. "Put the bag back in the hole. Let's finish the job."

"Damn, you just *stubborn*."

While they were laying down the new carpet, Mindy Kramer called and said she was on her way to the row house. She arrived shortly thereafter, just as they were finishing the installation. Mindy eyeballed the work, walked on it, questioned the bubbles, and carefully inspected the line where the carpet met the bead at the edge of the wall.

"I guess it's fine," said Mindy Kramer, constitutionally incapable of telling them that their work was satisfactory. "I need a little time to let it marinate. If I have any problems, I'll call Mr. Flynn."

"Any concerns you got," said Chris, "he'll take care of it."

They cleaned up the work site and packed the old carpet and padding in the back of the van. On the way out the door, Ben looked for an indication of an alarm system and saw none. He and Chris climbed into the van and took off.

Driving down U Street, Chris said, "Hungry?"

"You *know* I am."

"I'll buy."

"That's gonna make us late to our next job."

"I'll handle my dad," said Chris. "You earned lunch."

Ben adjusted his W cap on his head and slouched in the bucket. "I coulda bought a whole restaurant with what I left back there. I had what was in that bag, I could eat a hundred half-smokes every day for the rest of my life."

"You'd get sick of half-smokes," said Chris. "You'd shit like a horse."

"In my gold bathroom."

"Okay."

"And I'd have a butler to wipe my ass."

"Every man should have a dream," said Chris. He pulled the van to the side of the road and locked it down.

They walked toward the diner on U.

"I don't like wearing these things," said Ben with petulance, fingering the short sleeve of his Flynn's Floors polo shirt.

"Neither do I," said Chris.

"You *know* what it reminds me of," said Ben.

"I'll talk to my dad."

Ben Braswell pushed on the door of the eat house. He was hot and tired, and still thinking about the money. Chris was, too.

ALI CARTER sat in a rickety chair behind an old metal desk, manufactured and used by federal government workers before he was born. On the other side of the desk, in a chair just as suspect as Ali's, sat a young man named William Richards. He wore a Bulls cap, Guess jeans, a We R One T-shirt, and Nike boots. Richards was seventeen, full nosed, slightly bug-eyed, and annoyed.

"Mr. Masters said you been fighting him on the uniform shirt," said Ali.

"That shirt stupid," said William.

"It says you work for the company. It identifies you so when you do those events, the clients and the kids know who you are."

"That shirt got a picture of a clown on it. *And* balloons. I can't be walkin down the street wearin that mess."

"The clown's part of the logo," said Ali with patience. "You work for a company that sets up parties for kids. That logo is what makes people remember the business."

"The younguns where I stay at be laughin at me, Mr. Ali."

"So put the Party Land shirt in a bag and wear another shirt to the job. When you get to the site, change up. That'll work, right?"

William Richards nodded without conviction and looked away.

They were seated in a storefront office situated on a commercial stretch of Alabama Avenue, in the Garfield Heights section of Southeast. Ali was a junior staff member of Men Movin on Up, a nonprofit funded by the District, local charities, and private donors. Though there were many such organizations, set up in churches, rec centers, and storefronts, to help young men find their way and stay on track, Men Movin on Up was specifically designed to work with offenders, boys on parole or probation and boys awaiting trial. Its director, Coleman Wallace, was a career social worker and activist

Christian who had grown up poor and fatherless in Ward 8. A lifelong Washingtonian, he stayed in contact with many locals from his generation, and he put his hand out to those who had made it and asked them without shame to donate their money and volunteer their time to help young men who, like them, had come up disadvantaged. This group occasionally brought the boys to their places of work, counseled them, coached them in rec basketball, and took them on day trips to ball games and amusement parks.

Occasionally they made a difference in the boys' lives. There were many disappointments, failures, and setbacks, but Wallace and his friends had long ago stopped laboring under the illusion that they were going to save the collective youth of the city. If they could reach one kid, plant a seed that by example might grow into something right, they felt they had achieved success.

Ali was the sole staff member on the payroll. Coleman Wallace had hired him right out of Howard, where Ali had earned a bachelor's degree at the age of twenty-five. Coleman was attracted to Ali's intelligence and commitment, and also to the fact that Ali had done time at Pine Ridge and made the complete turnaround from incarcerated youth to productive member of society. He was smart and accomplished but also had the cachet of the real. His history bought him respect from the clients.

Also, Ali's relative youth was an attraction. Coleman Wallace was well aware that many of the boys he counseled could not relate to him, a middle-aged man. Most of them didn't even know that the organization's name, Men Movin on Up, referred to the Curtis Mayfield lyric. Or that the hand-lettered lyrics framed and hung on the office wall were from Coleman's favorite Curtis composition. Nine out of ten in this current crop didn't even know who Mayfield was. To these young men,

Ali Carter was go-go and hip-hop, and Coleman Wallace was slo-jam, tight basketball shorts, and way past old-school. Coleman needed an Ali Carter to help him connect.

Ali's focus was on getting the young men jobs and making sure they held them. To do this he communicated with parole officers, defense attorneys and prosecutors, and the staff of Ken Young, the recently hired reform-minded director of the District's Department of Youth Rehabilitation Services. He dealt with the members of the District's Absconding Unit, who tracked down kids who had skipped supervision, and he reached out to potential employers throughout the area, in particular those who had seen some trouble in their own youth and were willing to give his kids a try.

Without realizing it or having it in mind, Ali Carter was becoming connected and making a name for himself in the city. He liked his work and tried to forget that he was earning little more than minimum wage, which left him close to the poverty line.

"Any other problems?" said Ali.

"That man just aggravate the shit out of me, man," said William Richards.

"Mr. Masters?"

"Mr. *Slave*master. He *al*ways tryin to tell me what to do."

"He's paying you ten dollars an hour. It's his right to tell you what to do."

"I don't need that job."

"He's trying to introduce you to the culture of work."

"Huh?"

"Mr. Masters knows how hard it is to come back from jail time. He doesn't want you to have to go through that. He's trying to teach you how to work so that work becomes routine for you."

"I don't need him to teach me that. I know how to work and I damn sure can make some money. That's one thing I can do."

"Listen to me. It's important that you have a legitimate job right now and keep it, so that when you go to your hearing, you can stand before the judge and say that you're gainfully employed. Do you understand, William?"

"Yeah." But his slack posture and lack of eye contact said that he did not.

"Did you get your paycheck?"

"Here in my pocket."

"What are you going to do with it?"

"Take it that check-cash place round my way."

"They charge you big for that, don't they?"

"So?"

"I been tellin you, you should open a checking account at the bank. They charge much less than that store does. And they'll give you an ATM card. You can manage your money better and get to it any time."

"My mother got to take me to that bank, right?"

"To open the account? Yes."

"She too busy."

"You asked her?"

"No, but I'm about to. Next week." William stood abruptly out of his chair. He drew his cell from his jeans, opened it, and checked it for text messages.

"We straight?" said Ali.

"Huh?"

"Look at me, William." Ali stared into his eyes. "You're good with this job, right?"

"Yeah," said William. "But I'm not wearin no clown shirt. That ain't me."

Ali watched William slip out of his office. He didn't reflect on William or strategize on what to do with him next. At seventeen, William was at a point in his life where he had to choose a path for himself. Ali would be there for him if need be, but he wouldn't spend an inordinate amount of time on him if he continued to display his current level of resistance. Ali had many boys, and though they rarely expressed it verbally, some of them recognized the value in the hand that was being offered to them. It was unproductive for Ali to focus on one who was not willing to meet him halfway.

For the next hour, Ali made some phone calls. One was to a midlevel manager at the new baseball stadium, where Ali had been trying to get a couple of his boys put on. He knew that there were plenty of workers needed at the concession stands as well as less-desirable positions of the janitorial variety. Thus far the stadium officials had been unresponsive. The manager had said something about the need to present a more polished face to the public. Ali actually understood this from a business standpoint, but he vowed to be persistent. He'd call Ken Young. Young had direct dealings with stadium officials and the ear of the mayor, who had hired him from out of town.

There was a cursory knock on the glass storefront door, and a man pushed through it. Almond-shaped eyes, skin that in some lights looked yellow. He now wore his hair in braids. He was twenty-six but looked ten years older. Ali could see that he was high.

" 'Sup, *Holly?*" he said.

"Lawrence."

"Can't your boy visit a minute?"

Ali nodded warily as Lawrence Newhouse crossed the room.

TWELVE

——

"DAMN, BOY," said Lawrence Newhouse, looking around the office. "You oughta fix this joint up some."

"We got no money to speak of," said Ali. "None extra, anyway."

"Still," said Lawrence.

The space consisted of two desks, one for Ali, one for Coleman Wallace; a computer with slow dial-up service that they shared; and file cabinets. Also in the room were a foosball table with a cracked leg, a television set with no remote, a roll-in blackboard, several chairs, and a ripped-fabric couch. Ali did his best to make it a place where the boys would feel comfortable hanging out. Everything had been donated. It wasn't nice, but it was good enough.

"What can I do for you, Lawrence?"

"Wonderin why I stopped in, huh."

"Been a while."

"Bet you think I'm lookin for work, somethin."

"No, I didn't think that."

"I *got* work, man. Got this thing where I detail cars."

"That's good."

"What you doin here, it's for young men at risk. You know I'm not at risk."

"And you're not that young," said Ali.

Lawrence chuckled and pointed a finger at Ali. "That's right."

"So what can I do for you?"

"It's about my nephew. Marquis Gilman?"

Ali knew him, a nonviolent boy of average intelligence, funny, with lively eyes. Marquis was sixteen, up on drug charges, a recent dropout of Anacostia High School. He had been picked up several times for loitering and possession. His heart wasn't in his work. He was a low-level runner who didn't care to run.

"Marquis is one of my clients," said Ali. "I'm tryin to help him out."

"He told me. Want you to know, I appreciate it. He stays over there at Parkchester, with my sister and me. She's havin a little trouble containing him. You know how that is. Boys that age just don't think right. They wired up stupid in their heads."

Ali nodded. He wouldn't have put it that way, but Lawrence had the general idea. No one knew more about teenage brain scramble and bad decisions than Lawrence Newhouse.

"I'm lookin out for him, though," said Lawrence. "I got no kids myself, so he as close to one as there is."

For a moment, Ali thought of his own uncle and shook his head.

"What's wrong?" said Lawrence.

"Nothin," said Ali.

"So let me tell you why I'm here. Marquis said you tryin to hook him up with a job."

"I'm trying. So far we haven't had much luck."

"What, you tryin to put him in a Wendy's, sumshit like that?"

"At this point, we need to find him a job anywhere. Then, if he doesn't want to return to school, I'll get him started on earning his GED. Get him used to work and study. Change his habits. Marquis has all the necessary tools."

"That's what I'm sayin. He's better than some fast-food job. I mean, he could do better right now. I been talkin to Ben Braswell. You know I still stay in contact with my man."

"And?"

"Ben workin with White Boy, laying carpet. Both of them make good money at it. That's the kind of thing I'd like to see Marquis get into. Learn a trade, and I'm not talkin about operatin no deep fryer."

"I don't think Marquis is ready for that right now. It's a man's job, for one. Heavy lifting and hard work. And it's a trade that requires experience. You have to know what you're doing."

"White Boy's father got the business, right?"

"Chris's father owns it," said Ali. "That's right."

"Then he could put Marquis on. I mean, shit, he put Ben on, and you know Ben ain't no genius."

"Chris's father already hired some guys from our old unit. Remember Lonnie and Luther? Plus Milton Dickerson and that boy we used to ball with, Lamar Brooks. Lamar's the only one who worked out, and he left to start his own thing. It was me who asked Mr. Flynn to give them a try, so I can't go back to that well right now."

"Marquis ain't never been incarcerated. He was in that pre-trial jail at Mount Olivet, but no hard lockup."

"Marquis isn't ready," said Ali, holding Lawrence's gaze.

Lawrence smiled. "All right. Maybe I'll just talk to Ben. See what he got to say."

Ali rose from his chair, telling Lawrence it was time to go. Lawrence stood, and the two of them walked toward the door.

"Damn, you all swole," said Lawrence, looking Ali over. "I remember when you was one step off a midget. You always did have a chest on you, though."

"I got one of those late growth spurts," said Ali. He was now a man of average height with a fireplug build.

Above the door, where boys who were exiting the office could read them, were framed, hand-lettered lyrics:

We people who are darker than blue
Don't let us hang around this town
And let what others say come true.

"What's that mean?" said Lawrence, pointing at the lyrics.

"Means, don't become what society expects you to become. Be better than that."

"Damn, boy, you like Crusader Rabbit and shit."

"Not really."

"What you gonna do after you save all these young niggas down here? Run for president?"

"I think I'll just stay here and work."

Ali held the door open for Lawrence, who walked down the sidewalk toward his vehicle, an old Chevy, parked on Alabama Avenue. Two young men stood outside the storefront, talking loudly, laughing.

"Y'all want to come inside?" said Ali.

"What for?" said one young man.

"You can watch television."

"Ya'll ain't even got cable. Or a remote."

"Play foosball if you want," said Ali.

"That shit broke," said the other young man, and he and his friend laughed.

Ali went back into the office, thinking, *He's right, it is broke.* He made a mental note to get some duct tape and fix it, when he found the time.

THOMAS FLYNN'S last stop of the day was at a Ford dealership in the Route 29 corridor of Silver Spring. It was where he bought his E-250 cargo vans and had them serviced. He dealt with the manager, Paul Nicolopoulos, a good-looking silver-maned guy in his fifties taken to double-breasted blazers and crisp white oxfords. Nicolopoulos always introduced himself as Paul Nichols to his clients, just to make his life easier. Increasingly, many of his customers were Hispanics and other types of immigrants, and they had trouble with his name, which his proud Greek immigrant grandfather had refused to change.

"Just give me the cheap stuff," said Nicolopoulos, watching Flynn measure the space with his Craftsman tape. They were in the used-car office, set up in a trailer. Nothing about it was plush.

"I'm gonna sell you the olefin," said Flynn. "Twenty-six-ounce commercial, level loop."

"The service guys walk through here all day with their boots on, and they're not delicate. It's like they got hooves."

"The olefin's made for high traffic. It's not pretty, but it's plenty tough."

Flynn drew the tape back into the dispenser and clipped it onto his belt. He produced a pocket calculator and began to punch in numbers. He typically took the cost, added his profit, then tacked on the personality defect tax or, if he liked the client or owed him something, gave him a discount. In this way he arrived at a final figure.

"Don't hurt me," said Nicolopoulos, watching Flynn calculate.

"I'll only put the head in," said Flynn.

"Pretend that I'm a virgin," said Nicolopoulos.

"I'll be tender and kind," said Flynn.

"Afterward, will you brush the tears off my face?"

"I'll take you to McDonald's and buy you a Happy Meal."

"Thank you, Tom."

Flynn closed the calculator and replaced it in his breast pocket. "Twenty dollars a square yard, including installation and takeaway."

"Is that good?"

"I dunno. Did you give me a good price on my vans?"

"I did the best I could."

"Me, too," said Flynn.

"When can you put it in?"

"Early next week."

"Perfect," said Nicolopoulos.

Out in his van, Flynn called in the order to the mill. He phoned Chris, who was still in Bethesda with Ben, and checked on the status of the job. The two of them were slow, but Chris was conscientious and did decent work. Flynn tried not to lose patience with Chris, though sometimes, depending on his mood, he did become agitated. The trick was to avoid comparing Chris and Ben's work to that of Isaac and his crew. No one was as fast or efficient as Isaac, but in general Chris and Ben were fine.

Which wasn't the case with some of the other ex-offenders Flynn had tried to help. At the urging of Chris's friend Ali, he had hired, at various times, several men who had once been incarcerated at Pine Ridge. A couple of them, genial guys named Lonnie and Luther who had been in Chris and Ali's unit, had issues with drugs and alcohol, rarely reported to work at an acceptable time, and dressed inappropriately. Another, a large man named Milton, could not grasp the mechanics of installation. Flynn ran a business that grew and was perpetuated by referrals, and who he sent into his clients' homes made or broke his reputation. He had to let them go.

There was one guy, a quiet, polite Pine Ridge alumnus named Lamar Brooks, who Flynn had hired and who had acquitted himself well. Lamar was ambitious, had his eyes wide open, and quickly learned the trade. After six months he bought a van and tools, went out on his own, and started an installation service, subcontracting for small carpet retailers in the Northeast and Southeast quadrants of the city. Flynn saw the failure of Lonnie, Luther, and Milton as insignificant in the face of Lamar's success. And though Chris did not verbalize it, Flynn sensed that Chris appreciated his efforts on behalf of his friends, and that alone had been worth the aggravation a few of these young men had caused.

"So you guys are almost done?" said Flynn into his cell.

"Should be out of here in a half hour," said Chris.

"What are you doing tonight? You want to come to dinner?"

"Can't."

"You have plans?"

"Yeah."

"I met a young lady named Katherine today," said Flynn. "Works over at TCFI?"

"Uh-huh."

"Are you seeing her?"

"A little."

"Don't be so effusive," said Flynn.

"I'm busy here."

"What's her story?"

"I gotta get back to work, Dad."

"All right. Come by for dinner sometime; your mom misses you. I've got a book to give you, too. Guy named Paul Fussell."

"I've read Fussell."

"Have fun tonight," said Flynn.

"I need to finish this job. . . ."

"Go."

Flynn headed home. It had been a decent day. No serious fires, no major mistakes. Not too busy, but he had closed a couple of deals, and there would be steady work for all his people in the coming week.

Inside his house, he greeted Django, an adult Lab-pit mix they had adopted fully grown from the Humane Society at Georgia and Geranium after Darby's death. Django had gotten off his circular cushioned bed that sat beside the couch in the den, and met Flynn at the door after hearing Flynn's van pulling into the driveway, the distinctive sound of its Triton V-8 jacking up the beast's ears. Django's tail was spinning like a prop, and Flynn rubbed behind his ears and stroked his neck and chin. Django weighed eighty pounds and was heavily muscled. The pit in him was most visible in his blockish head.

Amanda's car was out on the street, so Flynn knew she was home, despite the utter quiet in the house. In the early evening she liked to pray the rosary in their bedroom. She would be up there now, making the sign of the cross, reciting the Apostles'

Creed, touching the crucifix and then the beads as she proceeded into the Our Father, the three Hail Marys, and the Glory Be.

He had come to accept Amanda's devotion to Catholicism and Christ. He no longer thought it was square or weird, or a Stepford wife phase she was going through, as he had when she became deeply religious in the early days of their marriage. He was thankful for the comfort that religion gave her, even as he was unable to buy into it himself. He had learned to share her with the one he had once called "Uncle Jesus," whom he thought of as an unwanted relative who had camped out in his home, and in turn Amanda had stopped trying to convert him.

Flynn grabbed the plastic wrapper from that morning's *Washington Post*, which Amanda saved daily, off the kitchen counter. Django began to bark, knowing that the plastic container was no longer a protective cover for the newspaper but was now a shit bag for his nightly walk.

"Let's go, boy," said Flynn, and ecstatically the dog followed him down the hall to where Flynn grabbed his harness and leash off a peg.

They walked their usual route through Friendship Heights, Django stopping at the houses where he knew other dogs lived, barking excitedly at the canine faces that were barking at him through doors and windowpanes. When Amanda walked Django, she stopped to talk to neighbors and occasionally strangers, but Flynn was not gregarious that way and politely nodded or said hello but kept up his pace. He was a workingman in a neighborhood of what he thought of, rather archaically, as professionals and yuppies, and as an adult he felt he did not fit in here, despite the fact that this had been his home almost his entire life. Sure, he ran a successful business and cleared six figures every year, but to his knowledge he was the only homeowner in Friendship Heights who drove a cargo van to work, and he believed that people looked at him and saw a guy who was not as educated as they were, not as accomplished, and, on some level, not in their class.

This was largely in Flynn's mind. In reality, most of the neighbors liked Thomas and Amanda Flynn and had never been anything but friendly and inclusive. Flynn knew this, yet he could not keep those feelings at bay.

He stopped, as always, at the rec center and playground near their house. There in the grass Django sniffed about, found a spot he liked, and commenced to take a crap. Flynn looked at the playground, where young parents stood talking to one another while their children played. "I'm going to en-roll Emily in the French-immersion program," and "Skyler loves science; we're taking him to the Smithsonian tomorrow," and "Dylan is strong at soccer; we're looking at a sleepaway camp for him this summer. Maybe he'll get an athletic scholarship someday!"

Enjoy it now, thought Flynn. *There's nothing but heartache ahead. Okay, some of you will be luckier than I was. But not all of you. So enjoy your dreams.*

Flynn made a glove of the plastic bag and scooped up Django's shit.

Amanda was standing over the granite kitchen counter, chopping a red onion for a salad, when they returned. Beside the cutting board sat a ziplock bag containing chicken breasts in a marinade of salad dressing. Flynn guessed he would be grilling the chicken shortly. His plan was to pour himself a bourbon over ice and take it out on the deck while he worked.

"Good day today?" said Amanda. Django pressed his nose into her thigh by way of hello.

"Not bad," said Flynn, going to the sink. He pushed down on the plunger of a liquid-soap dispenser, turned on the faucet, and began to wash his hands. "You?"

"I had to pay the insurance for our guys. But a couple of receivables came in, too."

Flynn ripped a paper towel from a roll and dried off. "Our son's got a girlfriend, I think."

"Yeah?"

"She works in the office at the warehouse. Nice-looking girl. I doubt she's educated. . . ."

"Don't be such a snob."

"I'm not."

"I didn't go to college. You saying you have regrets?"

"Hell, no."

Amanda stopped chopping momentarily as Flynn walked behind her and placed his hands on her waist. She was twenty pounds heavier than she had been as a teenager but carried it naturally. She had kept her curves, and the thought of her naked still excited him. He pulled her shoulder-length hair away from her neck and kissed her there and took in a clean smell of soap and lotion.

"How do you know she's his girlfriend and not just a girl?"

"Just a feeling I had," said Flynn. "She has your hair color and build. You know what they say about boys trying to date their moms."

"Stop."

Flynn saw the lines at the corners of her eyes deepen and knew that she was pleased. "I don't blame him." Flynn cupped her breasts and kissed the side of her mouth.

She turned in to him. They kissed and in no time it went from love to passion. Finally her skin became flushed, and she chuckled low and gently pushed him away.

"That was nice," she said.

"We're done?"

"Why does every kiss have to lead to sex?"

"Because I'm a man?"

"A caveman, you mean."

"They don't bother with kisses."

"Go pour yourself a drink."

"Trying to get rid of me?"

"Not entirely," said Amanda.

"So, later on tonight . . ."

"Perhaps."

Flynn walked toward the dining room, where he kept a small bar.

"What's her name?" said Amanda to his back.

Flynn said, "Kate."

He made a drink. He drank it rather quickly, and reached for the bottle on the cart.

THIRTEEN

B EN LIVED in a one-bedroom unit in a group of boxy red brick apartment houses set near the Rock Creek Cemetery in upper Northwest, steps away from Northeast. The neighborhood was not dangerous, nor did it carry an air of tension like the foster homes in which he'd been raised. After the rush hour traffic died down on close-by North Capitol Street, a commuter route in and out of the city, the atmosphere was fairly quiet. His apartment got little sun, was furnished with Goodwill and Salvation Army stuff, and roaches scattered when he turned on the kitchen light.

Ben's place was nothing to brag about, but it was the first living quarters he'd ever had to his self outside lockup. It was his and it was fine. Only bad thing was, the management didn't allow pets. He wanted a dog.

Ben didn't own a car or possess a driver's license. He hadn't been behind the wheel of a vehicle since his days of joyriding and grand theft. For a while he'd been barred from getting a license, but he was clear to obtain one now. Chris had been urging him to take the test. It would be easier on Chris, and make Ben more valuable to Mr. Flynn, if he could drive the vans. He supposed he would do so eventually, but he was not in a hurry. He preferred to take small steps.

Other than for work, Ben had no need for a car. He was on a bus line, and he was not far from the Fort Totten Metro station. You stayed in the District, it was easy to get around.

He liked to take walks in the cemetery, eighty-some acres of hills, trees, monuments, and headstones, some of the nicest green space in D.C. He entered at the main gate, at Rock Creek Church Road and Webster Street, and walked up past the church to the high ground, where the finest, most ornate monuments were located, and down a road so narrow it did not look like a proper road, to the Adams Memorial, his favorite spot. A marble bench faced the statue, the monument shielded by a wall of evergreens. On his weekends off, he'd sit on the bench and try to write poetry. Or open a paperback novel he had slipped into the pocket of his jeans.

Ben could read.

He had been at Pine Ridge until the age of twenty-one. The incident with Calvin Cooke had kept him behind the fence and razor wire, even as his friends had been set free. At eighteen, Ali and Chris had rotated out when they'd achieved Level 6. Lawrence Newhouse had been released, violated the conditions of his parole, was reincarcerated at the Ridge, and went on to do adult time for gun charges, first at Lorton before it closed, and then at a penitentiary in Ohio. By the time Ben had walked free, he was the old man of the facility. The guards had clapped him out, the way faculty did for kids graduating elementary school.

Under supervision, he lived in several halfway houses with other men. He stayed to himself, kept his appointments with his parole officer, walked by unlocked cars without stopping, was piss-tested regularly, and always dropped negatives. Chris, by then employed by his father, put him on as an assistant and taught him the carpet-and-floor-installation trade. Ali, then a student at Howard but already working the system, found out about a special night program at UDC, funded by the District and local charities, set up to educate ex-offenders. Ali got Ben enrolled.

There he met his teacher, a kind and patient young woman named Cecelia Lewis. In the schools of his youth, and his high school classes at Pine Ridge, he had worked with instructors who tried to get him to read, and corrected him, always corrected him, when he could not make out words, and he became ashamed and got to where he hated to look at books. Miss Lewis read *to* him, which no one had ever done. She read from newspapers, comic books, books written for teenagers, and then from adult novels, not fancy ones, but clearly written books with good characters that anyone could appreciate and understand. She would read from a book, and he would hold a copy of that same book and follow along, and after months of this, twice a week at night, the words and sentences connected and became pictures in his head. He was reading, and a door opened, and when he went through it he felt as if things were possible now that had not been possible before. It was like putting on a pair of prescription eyeglasses for the first time. The world looked new.

Of course, he fell in love with Cecelia Lewis. He picked flowers from people's gardens and window boxes on his walk to the Red Line train, handing them to her when he arrived at her classroom, and he wrote poems, sensing they were awful but giving them to her anyway to let her know that she had reached him deep.

They never did make it to bed. They never even kissed. When he finally expressed his feelings to her, she told him that it would be inappropriate for a teacher to have that kind of relationship with her student, that it was certainly not him, that she did care about him as a person, whatever that meant, and that they should remain friends. Her eyes told him something different, they said she was into him, but he understood her reticence and didn't press it further. When the semester was over, he never saw her again. No matter. Cecelia Lewis had changed his life, and there would always be a place for her in his heart.

Ben had a girl now, nice woman named Renee, built low to the ground, lived over in Hyattsville and worked at a nail salon. She was easy to get along with. They stayed in mostly, had pizza delivered, sat together, and laughed. She didn't complain about Ben watching his basketball on the TV, didn't ask why he seldom took her to restaurants or clubs. Maybe she knew that he was uncomfortable in such places and, in general, out in the world. Renee was just cool with it. She was all right.

Ben's cell sounded. Its ring tone was that old Rare Essence "Overnight Scenario" joint that Ben loved. He checked the ID and answered.

"Wha'sup, Chris?"

"Checkin up on you."

"I'm fine."

"You're not cryin over that bag of money, are you?"

"I wished I had it. But I'm not blown by it."

"So what're you doin?"

"'Bout to take a walk. You seein your redhead tonight?"

"Uh-huh."

"Should I call you in the morning and wake your ass up?"

"No need. I'll swing by and get you, same time as usual."

Ben ended the call. He slipped *Of Mice and Men*, a worn Penguin edition he had bought used, into the rear pocket of

136 • GEORGE PELECANOS

his jeans and headed out the door in the direction of the cemetery. There was still an hour or so of summer light, enough for him to sit and read in peace.

CHRIS LIVED in a house that had been converted into three apartments on a street of single-family homes in downtown Silver Spring, just over the District line in Maryland. He had chosen it when he'd seen the built-in bookshelves in its living-room area, a place to house the many biography and US history titles that he read and collected. Ali had gotten him hooked with the Taylor Branch books on Dr. King and the civil rights movement, which were two volumes when Chris was incarcerated and had grown to a trilogy after his release. He liked anything by Halberstam, the unconventional takes on the world wars by Paul Fussell, David McCullough's entire body of work, and war memoirs like E. B. Sledge's *With the Old Breed*, which he felt was the finest book of its kind ever written. He was inspired by these extraordinary writers and their subjects, even as he was aware of and resigned to his own very ordinary life.

His place was small but entirely adequate for his needs. He did not have many possessions other than his books, and he kept a neat and uncluttered apartment. He lined his shoes up in pairs under his bed, heels out, as he had done beneath his cot at Pine Ridge. He had a small television set and bought the most basic cable package so that he could watch sports. Every morning, before he went to work, he made his bed.

The other tenants of the house were the Gibsons, a young punkish couple, the husband a rock musician, the wife a private music teacher, and Andy Ladas, a middle-aged man who kept to himself and smoked cigarettes on the porch at night as he slowly drank bottled beer. The four of them took turns mowing the lawn with regularity, and the couple went beyond the call and landscaped the yard, keeping the property in better shape than many of the homeowners on the block did. Despite this, there were rumblings on the neighborhood Listserve about keeping future renters off the street. If they wanted him gone, fine, he'd go. He'd had the sense that he'd be moving around frequently, anyway. That his would be that kind of nomadic life.

But he was feeling different lately, since he'd been going out with Katherine. Yeah, she meant more to him than the other young women he'd been with since coming out. If pressed, because he was not one to talk about such things, he'd even admit that he was in love with her. But also, he felt that this change in outlook had to do with his age. Just as it felt normal to rebel as a teenager, settling into something more permanent felt natural as he moved into the tail end of his twenties.

After a long shower, Chris dressed in Levi's and an Ecko Unlimited button-down shirt, which he had purchased from the Macy's up in Wheaton. Most of his peers from the neighborhood he'd grown up in shopped at Bloomingdale's and Saks in Friendship Heights, or the Rodeo Drive–like stores that lined a block of Wisconsin Avenue across the Maryland line. Chris did not have the money to shop in those places, nor was he particularly cognizant of trendy fashion. The Macy's where he shopped seemed to market to their black and Hispanic base in the Wheaton location, and he was cool with that. More accurately, he made do with what they offered. He could afford to shop there.

Chris drove the van over to PG County. It still held the old roll and padding, fitted between the buckets so that the rear doors would close, from the Bethesda job. He was headed to pick up Katherine at her parents' home in University Park, a township of colonials and restored bungalows south of College Park.

Katherine's father, James Murphy, was a tenured professor in arts and humanities at the University of Maryland. Her mother, Colleen, worked at a downtown think tank specializing in energy policy. Both were brilliant and perhaps overeducated to the point of social retardation. Their son had earned a bachelor's degree but had no desire to go to graduate school and was working in New York as a boom operator on feature films. He was respected in his field, but his parents felt he had underachieved.

Their daughter, Katherine, had disappointed them completely. After graduating in low standing from Elizabeth Seaton, the Catholic girls' high school in their area, she had floundered in PG Community College, dropped out, and had been working in the office of a warehouse for the past year. And now she was dating a man who installed carpet for a living and apparently had been incarcerated in his youth.

Chris understood their negativity. They were basically good people and in other circumstances they might have welcomed him into their home, but they wanted the best for their daughter. Admittedly he was not an exemplary prospect, but he cared for Katherine, respected her, and would protect her. He worked with his hands, but he worked hard and honestly. None of this was reassuring to her parents, but he was who he was, and for now it was the best he could do.

He stood on the stoop of their house and rang the doorbell.

Colleen Murphy answered. She was a tall brunette whose perpetually serious nature had taken a toll on her looks and spirit. Katherine had gotten her fair complexion and reddish hair from her father.

"Hey, Mrs. Murphy. How you doin?"

"I'm fine, Chris."

"Is my friend ready?"

"Yes, just about. Would you like to come in?"

"Nah, this is fine."

Chris had called Katherine from his cell when he was a few minutes away from the house, hoping she'd be waiting when he arrived, hoping to avoid this.

Colleen Murphy stared at him, looking down on him slightly because she was up a step in the door frame. He moved his eyes away from hers and looked around at the old-growth trees on the property, the azaleas framing the stoop, and a large triple-trunk crepe myrtle with scarlet blossoms. A Sunfish sailboat, covered by a tarp, was set on a trailer beside the house.

"Nice yard," said Chris lamely.

"Yes," said Colleen Murphy.

"Does Mr. Murphy sail?"

"Occasionally."

Thankfully, Katherine came down the center hall stairs. She wore a green-and-rust shift with green T-strap sandals, and she had one of those black band things in her strawberry blonde hair. She brushed past her mother and met Chris outside the door.

"See you, Mom," said Katherine.

"Take care, Mrs. Murphy," said Chris, saluting stupidly, immediately wishing he hadn't. Katherine kissed him on the cheek and took his hand, and they walked across the yard to his van. Chris thinking, *Her mom hates me.*

Colleen Murphy watched as her daughter and Chris Flynn got into the van. At that moment, she had no animosity in her at all. She was thinking of a time when her boyfriend, Jimmy Murphy, had picked her up from her own parents' house in

Burke, Virginia, back in the midseventies. How they had laughed and held hands on the way to his car, a gold Ford Pinto station wagon with synthetic wood-paneled sides. How tall he was, how strong his hand felt in hers, how she couldn't wait to have those hands on her breasts and ribcage.

She turned and went back inside her house. James Murphy would be in his office, working. They would have a quiet dinner with little conversation. She would turn in early, and he would come to bed after she had gone to sleep.

In the van, around the corner from her house, Katherine told Chris to pull over to the side of the road.

"Where?" said Chris.

"Here. That house has been unoccupied for the last six months."

"So?"

"Just do it."

"Okay."

When he put it in park, she leaned across the carpet and padding and kissed him deeply.

"What's that for?" said Chris.

"My apologies. For keeping you waiting."

She rubbed the crotch of his jeans. He placed his hand on her muscled thighs, and she opened her legs as she unzipped him and pulled him free.

Chris laughed. "Right here?"

"There a problem?" she said, working him until he could take it no longer. He moved her hand away.

"*Damn*, girl."

"What?"

"I'm about to bust."

"You afraid you're gonna mess up the seats?"

"More like your hair."

"Quit boasting."

"I'm sayin, I'm a young man. I got velocity."

"C'mon, let's get in the back."

"For real?"

She kissed him. "Come on, Chris."

Afterward, they went to dinner at a pho house in Wheaton, because they liked the soup and it was cheap. The restaurant was in a commercial strip of Laundromats and Kosher and Chinese grocers. The diners sat communally at tables similar to those found in school cafeterias. Except for Chris and Katherine, all of the customers were Vietnamese. No one talked to them, or seemed to notice the sweat rings on Chris's shirt or Katherine's unkempt hair. At the end of the meal, Chris bought an inexpensive bottle of Chilean red at the deli next door, and they drove back to his place in Silver Spring.

They made love properly, but no less energetically, in his bed. Chris had lit votive candles around the room, with his small stereo set on WHUR, playing the old EWF tune "Can't Hide Love." The candles and the music were on the corny side, but Chris was a D.C. boy all the way, and Quiet Storm was in his blood. His parents had listened to Melvin Lindsay, the originator, spin Norman Connors and Major Harris when Thomas and Amanda Flynn were young and making love on hot summer nights just like this one.

Katherine, lying naked atop the sheets beside Chris, reached over and traced her finger down the vertical scar above his lip.

"Your dad finally talked to me today," said Katherine. "Susie sort of made him. In her own sloppy way, she let him know that you and I were together."

"Did he call you honey or sweetheart?"

"I think it was 'darling.' "

"That's my pops. He has trouble remembering names. Odd for a salesman, but there it is. He'll remember yours now, though."

"Why's that?"

"My parents had a baby named Kate who died before I was born. Dad still talks about her. Like she's going to come back and be everything that I'm not."

"Your father cares about you, Chris."

"Like you care for a lame dog. You know Champ is never gonna win a show or a race. But you look after him anyway, out of the kindness of your heart."

"It's not attractive when you feel sorry for yourself."

"I'm not. I *never* do. I'm sayin, this is how I think it is from his eyes. I don't have a problem with who I am. Far as I'm concerned, I'm doing fine. But my pops looks at me like I'm some kind of cripple. My past still eats at him, Katherine. There's got to be a reason for the troubles I had, and he needs to know why. Look, my parents didn't cause me to jump the tracks, and I never meant to hurt them. I was selfish and full of fire, and I wasn't thinkin right. That's the best way I know how to explain it. Truth is, my fuckups were mine and mine alone."

"When I dropped out of college," said Katherine, "I could hear my parents whispering, and then arguing, behind their bedroom door. It was all about the bad decisions they thought they had made along the way. How they should have moved out of PG County, or put me in a better high school, got me away from my friends and other bad influences. How they should have pushed me harder to get better grades. But I just plain didn't *like* school, Chris. I didn't like it when I was a little kid. Not everybody goes to college. Not everybody can get more education than their parents, or make more money than them, or live in a nicer house than the one they grew up in."

"I hear you. But they want it for you anyway."

"It's natural for them to feel like that."

"Way your mom looks at me, seems like she's made her mind up that I'm not the right one for you."

"My mom'll come around," said Katherine. She moved beside him and pressed her flat belly against him. "You know, if you weren't an installer, if I hadn't dropped out of school and taken that dumb job in the office . . ."

"We wouldn't have met."

"So everything's been to the good, far as I'm concerned."

They kissed.

"This is right," said Chris, holding her close.

"You can feel it, can't you. We're supposed to be together, Chris."

"Yes."

He told her about the bag of money that Ben had found earlier in the day. He told her that he'd convinced Ben to put it back in the space under the floor.

"You made a good decision," said Katherine. "I guess."

Chris chuckled. "You're not so sure, either."

"Who wouldn't think twice about keeping it? But it seems like it would come to bad if you took it. I mean, it's not yours. Technically . . ."

"It's stealing. What I'm worried about is, did I do right by Ben. At the time, I *thought* I did. I felt like I was tryin to protect him by leaving that money there."

"But you're not positive now."

"Back in Pine Ridge, Ali told me that I was always going to be taken care of in some way, 'cause of my father and mother. And he was right. But Ben, he's got nothin. No family and no kinda breaks. To him, fifty grand in a gym bag is a gift from heaven."

"He's not angry with you, right?"

"No, we're straight."

"So why are you stressed about it?"

Chris stroked Katherine's arm. "I'm just worried about my friend."

FOURTEEN

BEN BRASWELL heard a knock on his apartment door. He got up from his chair, walked barefoot and softly to the peep, and bent his tall frame to look through the glass in the hole. He sighed audibly, stood to his full height, and considered his next move.

There was little chance that Lawrence could know that Ben was home. If Ben stood here quietly, eventually Lawrence would give it up and go. Ben knew that a drop-in by Lawrence meant that Lawrence's hand was going to be outstretched in some way. But Ben could not just stand behind the door like a coward, and it wasn't in him to be deceitful. Lawrence, low as he was and could be, was a man. He deserved respect until it was no longer warranted. Ben unlocked the deadbolt and opened the door.

"My boy," said Lawrence Newhouse.

Ben raised his hand warily and they touched fists. Lawrence's eyes were pink and the smell of weed was on him.

"What you doin here, man?"

"Can't a friend visit?"

"It's late."

"Night owl like you? Shit. You was always the last one asleep at the Ridge. Talkin to yourself in your cell at all hours. Remember?"

"Come on."

Lawrence walked in. Ben closed the door behind him, leaned his back against it, and crossed his arms. Lawrence went to a chair that had been new in the 1970s and had a seat. Ben dropped his arms to his sides and spread himself out on a worn sofa near the chair.

"I got work tomorrow," said Ben.

"That's good," said Lawrence. "Wished I did, too."

"Thought you had a detailing thing."

"I do, but it's slow. Gas prices go up, people don't be drivin their cars. They don't take 'em out the garage, they don't feel the need to clean 'em. You know how that is."

"You got a place of business?"

"Nah, my shit is portable, man. I bring my supplies in a grocery cart and wash and detail the whips right at the places where people stay at. Most everybody got a hose. If they don't, I carry one with me. All my, you know, transactions are in cash, so I don't have to fuck with no taxes. Don't pay rent, either. I got a good thing. But like I say, right now it's slow."

Some business, thought Ben. *But at least Lawrence is doing something halfway straight. Least he's not shootin at anyone. Or getting his ass beat regular.*

"Why you come to see me?" said Ben.

"Damn, boy, you just short and to the point, ain't you?"

"Told you, it's late."

Lawrence rubbed sweat theatrically from his yellowish forehead. He head-tossed his braids back off his face. "Hot in this piece."

"Air's on. Maybe it's you."

"Hot and small. Feel like I'm in a coffin in here and shit. You know I don't like these small spaces. Reminds me of when I was inside."

"You free to roll out."

"Let's both go out. Have a drink. Little bit of vodka on a nice summer night like this?"

"I got no extra for that."

"I got you. Bottle's sittin out in my car. All's we need to do is stop and get some ice-cold juice."

Ben looked down at his bare feet. It was warm in the room, and a cool vodka drink sounded good. Might be a way to get Lawrence out of this apartment and out of his world. Drive around and sip some, find out what he wanted, then say good-bye.

"What say you, Big Man?" said Lawrence.

"Let me get my shoes," said Ben.

As Ben went into his bedroom, Lawrence inspected the leather tool belt hanging on a hook by the front door. In one of its pouches he found a razor knife with a hooked end. He replaced it as he heard Ben's heavy footsteps heading back into the room.

"Let's get that drink," said Lawrence.

They bought a large bottle of cold grapefruit juice at the 7-Eleven on Kansas Avenue and emptied half of it out in the parking lot. Lawrence drove back down Blair and then North Capitol while Ben filled the bottle from a fifth of Popov vodka. He closed the lid of the juice bottle tightly and shook it, mixing the vodka and grapefruit.

They passed the bottle back and forth. Lawrence turned left on H Street and drove east. Ben relaxed and sat low in the seat. He kept his arm on the lip of the window and held his hand palm-out to catch the air. The car was an old Chevy Cavalier and it barely contained him. But he felt good. The vodka was working pleasantly on his head.

"I got this nephew," said Lawrence Newhouse.

"Uh-huh."

"Name of Marquis. My sister's boy."

"Okay."

"Sixteen years old. Had a few problems here and there. Loitering, possession, like that. He's up on charges right now, but they gonna slap his wrist, most likely. He's not cut out for that business no how. I tried to tell him, you gonna be in the game, at least show some heart. But the boy didn't listen. Police came up on him and he said, 'Here.'" In illustration, Lawrence touched his wrists together so that they were cuff-ready. "He's thick like that."

Maybe he took a look at you and saw what the life would get him, thought Ben.

"Kids be hardheaded sometimes," said Ben.

"Exactly." Lawrence looked over at Ben. "Gimme that bottle, man. You hoggin that shit."

Ben handed him the bottle. Lawrence drank sloppily, and some of the vodka and juice rolled down his chin. He fitted the bottle between his legs and made a sweeping gesture with his hand toward the street.

"City don't look like it did," said Lawrence. "Got bars and clubs for white people now in Northeast. On *H* Street. You believe it? Graybeards down by my way talk about H Street burning down during those riots they had, what, forty years ago. Took a while, but now the white folk got their hands in this, too. They were waitin on it to hit bottom all along so they could buy it up cheap. Just like they did on U."

As usual, Lawrence had oversimplified the situation and taken the conversation into the realm of conspiracy. There were all kinds of people, owners and customers, in these new bars and restaurants, not just whites. They were young and they dressed better than Lawrence and Ben, and probably had more school. They had a little money and they wanted nice places to sit and hang with their dates and friends. One or two of these nightspots had opened up, and then they started to multiply. It was progress, and people got displaced because of it, and that was a shame, but Ben didn't feel it was all to the bad. On this street here, there were lights on in windows that had once been dark, and jobs for people who needed work, and folks spending money to keep it going. Anyway, once the ball started to roll, wasn't anyone could stop it.

"No Metro on H Street," said Ben, recalling what Chris had told him earlier in the day. "That's why it took so long to turn."

At 8th, near the bus shelter that was always crowded with locals, a group of young men were running across the street, stopping traffic, yelling at the occupants of cars.

"It ain't turned all the way yet," said Lawrence.

"What about your nephew?"

"Right. Ali Carter's trying to help him out. Ali's at that place down on Alabama Avenue, Men Move Upstairs, or whatever they call it. He's workin with at-risk kids, finding them jobs and stuff. I *respect* that, you know?"

"So?"

"He means well, but I feel like he selling my nephew short. Tryin to put Marquis into a *Mac*-Donald's or a Wendy's."

"It's somethin."

"But he's better than that. Boy needs a real job. Like the kind of work you and White Boy do."

"What about it?"

"I was thinking, you know, White Boy's father could maybe

put Marquis on. Teach him so he learns a trade. So Marquis doesn't have to take some dumb-ass job where he got to wear a paper hat and get laughed at."

"Lawrence, I don't know. I mean, we got our crews set. I don't see Mr. Flynn hiring anybody new right now."

"You can ask, can't you? This for my nephew, man."

"Yeah, I can ask."

"You my boy, B. You know this."

They drove down to the new baseball stadium on South Capitol Street. Ben had not yet seen it except in photographs. There was no game that night, but the stadium was lit up and they parked and admired it, and finished what was in the bottle. A security vehicle drove by, and its occupant shone a light in their car, accelerated, and turned a corner up ahead.

"He gonna come around again," said Lawrence, cranking the ignition of the Cavalier. "They always got to be funny."

Lawrence drove east on M Street and they went past a corporate headquarters of some kind. The road wound and dipped down along the old marinas, where modest powerboats were docked, some sitting beneath colorful Christmas lights strung overhead, tucked in along the banks of the Anacostia River. Lawrence kept on cruising and pulled over near a land leg of the Sousa Bridge, in a spot where old men and kids sat on overturned plastic buckets and fished during the day; it was deserted now.

Lawrence reached under his seat and found a joint of weed he had freaked in a Black & Mild wrapper, and he slipped it into the breast pocket of his oversize shirt.

"Let's walk," he said.

They got out of the car and crossed the road. Lawrence used a lighter to fire up the blunt, and by the time they had made it to the railroad tracks it was live. The road down here dead-ended eventually, so if the police were to roll through, which they did often, it would be trouble. But Lawrence only carried enough weed to eat and be done with if need be. The police could make out that you were high, they could smell it on you, they could even see the smoke coming out your mouth, but they couldn't do shit if you had none on you. Lawrence knew the law, or so he told anyone who would listen. He felt that he was slick like that.

He offered the blunt to Ben, who took it and drew on it deep. Ben loved to get after it, but he only smoked occasionally with Chris outside work, and sometimes with his girl, Renee. He was careful to get his head right in places where he was comfortable and around people he trusted and felt safe with. Tonight, though, he made an exception. Lawrence was all right. He *could* be, sometimes. It would be bad manners to turn him down. Also, Ben was near gone on the alcohol. When he got like that, he craved a little marijuana to take him up further and, at the same time, even out his high.

They walked the tracks and smoked the joint down. Laughing and wasted, they returned to the car. Lawrence got the bottle of Popov from the Cavalier, and the two of them sat on the hood, facing Anacostia Park across the river, watching the lights from the bridge lamps play on the water, passing the alcohol back and forth, drinking warm vodka and feeling its burn.

"Pretty from here," said Ben.

"East of the river?" said Lawrence. "Nicest part of town, you ask me. That's the high point of D.C. High and green. You ever been on the grounds of Saint Elizabeth's?"

"Can't say I have."

"They got a bench on the top of a hill where you can sit and look down at the whole damn city. I mean, it's nice."

"Why were you there?"

"I got sent there. Understand, I wasn't crazy or nothin like that." Lawrence looked at Ben, then looked away. "I just didn't want to be in regular lockup no more. I'm talkin about when I was incarcerated in the *a*dult facility. People always muggin you and, you know, *challenging* you. I got tired of it. So I acted all messed up."

"What'd you do?"

"It ain't all that important what I did. Point is, I got moved. They transferred me over to Saint E's for a little bit. Had some good-ass meds in there, too."

Ben reached for the bottle. The lights on the water had blurred, and the bridge split apart and kind of flew off and came back together.

"Sounds tough," said Ben.

"Well, it was better than the joint. But I could only fool them white coats for so long."

"Anyway, it's all behind us."

"Yeah, it's past," said Lawrence. "I ain't goin back to none 'a that."

"Neither am I."

"I just wish shit was easier." Lawrence took the bottle from Ben's hand and swigged from it. He wiped vodka from his chin. "I guess I'll be workin the rest of my damn life. Ain't gonna be no money tree growin in my yard."

"There is such a thing, though. For real."

"*Shit.*"

"I saw one. Wasn't no tree, though. It was a bag."

"Fuck you talkin about, man?"

"I found a bag of cash today," said Ben. "Me and Chris did, on the job."

"How you gonna lie like that?"

"I'm not. I counted it myself. And I put it back where it was my own self, too."

"What, you just left it there?"

"Uh-huh."

"For what reason?"

"There were fifty thousand reasons to take it. Right now, I can't say why I didn't. But that ship sailed out the harbor. Can't do anything about it now."

Lawrence handed Ben the bottle. "Where was that at, B?"

Ben told him the story, and the row house address, and, because Lawrence deftly and gently prodded him, every other detail that he could remember. And when he was done talking, realizing that he was too drunk and high, and that he had to be up for work early in the morning, he asked Lawrence to drive him home.

Lawrence grinned and said he would.

FIFTEEN

C OME DOWN here," said Thomas Flynn. "Dream with me."

Thomas Flynn was in the home of Eric and Linda Wasserman. He was on his knees in their living room, pitching carpet. A large book of samples was open beside him.

Linda Wasserman, a blonde in her midthirties, stood over Flynn, her arms crossed. Her husband was at work and their child was at sleepaway camp. She had a toned body, a perfect dye job, immaculately pedicured feet at rest in designer sandals, and lovely skin. Flynn reckoned she spent a great deal of time working out and getting worked on. He was in the presence of new Potomac money.

"Come on down here," said Flynn again.

"Should I?"

"Absolutely!"

Linda Wasserman got down on all fours. She was looking to replace her living-room carpet with something nicer. The Wassermans had recently bought the house and inherited its shag carpeting and scuffed-up floors.

Flynn was there to guide her and make a sale. He was trying not to concentrate on her tight, perfect ass, which was small enough to fit into one of his hands. It would be like palming a basketball. *You could actually carry her around the house,* thought Flynn. *She's light enough. Put her in one hand and rest her on your hip, hold a beer in the other, and walk her to the bedroom.*

What's wrong with me? thought Flynn. And in his head he heard a reply: *Nothing that isn't wrong with any other man.*

"Now what?" said Linda Wasserman.

Flynn had his fingers deep in one of the samples, and he was kneading it while looking into her eyes.

"Put your hand on this," said Flynn. Meaning the sample.

She reached out and stroked the carpet sample. As she leaned forward, her breasts became pendulous beneath her pullover blouse, one of those jobs with an oval cutout and a little string tied at the scoop of the neck.

"Plush pile," said Flynn. "It's sheared several times to give it a velvety sheen. Imagine walking on this. You're not going to want to wear shoes in this room, I can tell you that. Neither are your guests."

"We don't actually use the living room much."

"Perfect. This is low-traffic carpet."

"It is nice," she said. "Is it expensive?"

"Yes," said Flynn. With her, the high cost would be a positive. But not too high. They weren't stupid rich. "It's not over-extravagant, mind you. It's the Benz of carpet, rather than the Ferrari."

"Hmm." She caught him glancing at her breasts and quickly got to her feet. "I'm going to have to discuss this with my husband, Mr. Flynn."

"Of course," said Flynn, standing more slowly than she because of his aging knees. "My wife and I always talk about these kinds of purchases before we come to a decision. Let me just size this out and give you an estimate."

While he was measuring the room, his cell rang. He read the caller ID, prepared himself mentally, and answered. With one finger he made an "excuse me" sign to Linda Wasserman, then he walked out of the room.

"Thomas Flynn speaking."

"Mr. Flynn, this is Mindy Kramer."

"Hello, Mindy—"

"I need to see you down at the job site right away."

Clearly she was agitated. But with these aggressive, hard-charging types, it could be nothing more than a few drops of soda spilled on a hardwood floor by a worker, or a piece of the old carpet left behind on the site. A negotiating ploy to get the price of the job down.

"Is there a problem?" said Flynn.

"A *very* serious problem."

"With the product or the installation?"

"The installation. Maybe the product. *I* don't know."

"So I should send my guys down."

"I'd like you here, too. Frankly, I have no faith in them at this point."

"Can you just elaborate a little bit so I know what we're talking about here?"

"I don't have *time*. The police are here, Mr. Flynn, and I have to go. On top of the subpar work that was done by your men, this house was broken into last night."

"I'm sorry to hear that. Okay. I've got to finish up here, but it won't be long."

"I'll see you shortly."

Flynn phoned Chris and asked him if he knew the nature of Mindy Kramer's malfunction. Chris, on a Northwest job with Ben, told him that the install at her row house had been clean and error free. Flynn caught a bit of hesitation in Chris's voice that did not comfort him.

"Finish up what you're doing," said Flynn, "and meet me down at the house."

Flynn gave Linda Wasserman her estimate, deliberately not allowing his eyes to drop below her chin as he explained the pricing and terms. He shook her hand and headed back down into the city.

FLYNN SPOTTED a Third District cruiser on the street as he pulled up near Mindy Kramer's row house. He went through the unlocked front door and followed the sound of Mindy Kramer's distinctive voice to the kitchen at the rear.

The kitchen door opened to a small deck whose steps led down to the alley. Mindy Kramer and two young uniformed officers, a woman and a man, were standing on the deck. Mindy was smoking a long, thin white cigarette, gesturing with it as she spoke to the two rather uninterested-looking police.

"I don't have an alarm system," Mindy Kramer was saying, as Flynn joined the group. "I'm flipping this place, so I'm not going to invest in one. And you don't want to try and sell a home with bars on its windows. I mean, the house is unfurnished, so what's there to steal?"

"Whoever broke in didn't know that till he got inside," said the female officer.

"That's right," said Flynn, just to inject himself into the conversation.

The female police officer looked at Flynn. "And you are?"

"He's here for something else," said Mindy Kramer, by way of both introduction and dismissal, waving at him with her cigarette, waving him away.

The male officer drifted and eyed the severely splintered doorjamb. It looked to Flynn as if a jimmy or crowbar had been taken to it. It had been an unprofessional and successful effort.

"It could have been kids," said Mindy Kramer. "Or a junkie. I don't care who it was. But you'd think the neighbors would have heard something. A couple of people on this block have dogs, for God's sake."

"We'll knock on some doors," said the female officer. "See what we can find out."

"Aren't you going to dust for prints?" said Mindy Kramer.

The female officer looked at Flynn for a moment and light danced in her eyes. They could "dust" the whole house, but, short of walking into the 3D station himself and confessing to the crime, this particular perpetrator, who apparently had stolen nothing, would not be brought to justice.

"First thing, I'm gonna need to fill out a report," she said.

"Ach," said Mindy Kramer, rolling her eyes. It was as if the officer had told her that she was about to be strip-searched.

"Excuse me," said Flynn. "About that problem."

"Go have a look at it," said Mindy Kramer. "You'll see what I'm talking about right away. I have to stay here and help her *fill out* a report."

Flynn exchanged another commiserating look with the officer before moving away.

He was not in love with the police, but he was empathetic about the job they did and the people they had to deal with every day. He had never once regretted his decision to leave the MPD, but he was glad he had experienced that life, if only for less than a year. The brevity of his tenure aside, the man in blue had never left his blood entirely.

He owned a .38 Special, which had been the MPD sidearm

in his day, before the force switched over to the Glock 17. Though it probably wasn't true that all police felt naked without a gun after their retirement, it happened to be true for Flynn. Despite the District handgun ban, recently lifted, he had bought the revolver hot from one of his installers and kept it loaded in the nightstand beside his bed. He liked knowing that there was a firearm within reach. Given the relative safety of his neighborhood, his decision to own an illegal gun was emotional rather than rational. He realized he'd pay a heavy price if he was caught with it, but he was willing to take the risk.

"Pardon me," said Flynn to the male officer, as he stepped around him and went through the open kitchen door.

Flynn went toward the front of the house, into the center hallway, and cut left into the library. He inspected the work that Chris and Ben had done. It had simply been a sloppy performance. One side of the carpet was misaligned with the wall and slanted away from the bead. On that side, nearest the built-in bookshelves, the corner of the carpet had not been laid properly and appeared to have been pulled up and hastily put back down.

"Chris," said Flynn, shaking his head. Flynn knew that he had measured correctly and he had double-checked the size of the roll when it had come into the warehouse. This was on Chris and his friend Ben. They just hadn't done the job with conscience or care.

He went to the spot that looked worse and got down on his knees. He lifted the corner to check on the padding and saw that a cutout had been made in the hardwood floor. With one knee holding down the bent-back carpet, he got his fingers under a notch in the cutout and lifted it away from the floor.

A kind of basket, fashioned with wood slats, had been built

in beneath the floor. It was meant to hold something, but it held nothing now. Flynn actually scratched his head. The concealed cutout and basket were nothing to him, and asking Mindy Kramer about them would only be a further complication. He replaced the panel, put the carpet back down, and phoned his son. Chris and Ben were headed south on 16th Street, just five minutes away.

When they arrived, they came straight to the job site where Flynn was waiting.

"Hey," said Chris.

"Chris," said Flynn, "what's this?"

Chris breathed through his mouth, his eyes darting nervously as he revisited the work they'd done. What Flynn used to call his "what the fuck did I do" look. Ben stood beside him, silent, not able or willing to look at Flynn. Flynn smelled the alcohol sweat coming off Ben and could see a hard night and shame in his eyes. He wondered how long he could carry this man. When poor performance began to affect Flynn's business, he had to reconsider the hire. Even if it was his own son.

"That's not how we left it," said Chris.

"C'mon, Chris. Don't play me like that."

"Listen to me, Dad. We did this job right."

"Yeah, okay."

Chris thumb-stroked the scar above his lip, something he did unconsciously when he was struggling with a problem. "What are the police doing here? We saw 'em in the back of the house when we came down the hall."

"Somebody broke in last night," said Flynn. "It's got nothing to do with this."

Flynn noticed Chris glance at Ben, and he saw Ben stare

down at his shoes, his posture slackening. Something wasn't right.

"Maybe whoever broke in came in here and messed up our work," said Chris.

"Please," said Flynn.

"I'm *tell*ing you. We did the job correctly."

"I don't have time for this right now," said Flynn. "You two get to work and correct it. I've got to go back out there and make some sort of price adjustment for the customer. It's gonna cost me, but hey, what's a few hundred dollars."

"Take it out my check," said Chris.

"You know I don't do that," said Flynn. "Go on, get to work."

Flynn left the room. Chris stared at Ben, who would not meet his eyes.

"You heard him," said Chris. "Let's fix this shit."

CHRIS AND Ben refinished the job properly while Thomas Flynn dealt with Mindy Kramer and adjusted her bill. When they were almost done, two young police officers came into the room where they were working and had a look around. The female officer asked Chris what he was doing, and he told her that they were correcting a new-carpet install that had been done the day before. Chris and Ben said nothing further. If they had been asked other questions, their responses would have been similarly to-the-point and minimal. They did not hate police, but neither did they trust them or have any desire to cooperate or fraternize with them.

The day had cooled little by early evening, when Chris pulled into the small parking lot behind Ben's apartment house, finding a spot shaded, somewhat, by a thin-armed maple. Chris pushed the transmission arm up into park and let the motor run. Ben had his elbow resting on the lip of the window and was staring out toward the cemetery. They had spoken very little on the ride uptown.

"You gonna talk to me now?" said Chris.

Ben turned his head and looked into his friend's eyes. "I didn't take the money, Chris."

"You told me that already."

"You believe me, right?"

"I do. But you know who took it."

Ben nodded slowly. "Had to be Lawrence Newhouse."

"*Shit.* You told Lawrence?"

"Uh-huh."

"Why him?"

Ben briefly shut his eyes, as if that could erase what he had done. "Lawrence came past my spot last night."

"He just dropped in for no reason."

"Nah, he wanted something. *You* know that. Ali's been tryin to help his nephew out. Young man's up on charges, I expect. So Ali's lookin to, you know, help him get a job at a McDonald's, someplace like that. Lawrence don't think that's good enough for his nephew. He wanted to see if your father could put him on."

"I'm not doing that," said Chris. "I'm not getting involved with Lawrence or anyone in his family. I wouldn't do that to my old man."

"I told Lawrence the same. In a different way, but I told him. And then I went for a drive with him, just to get him out my apartment."

"I would've shown him the door."

"That's what I should've done, but I didn't. We ended up down by the river, and Lawrence got me all fucked up on weed and alcohol. You know I can't hold my drink. I started to talk behind the vodka. I'm not making an excuse. I'm just sayin, I was trippin and that's what I did. I can't even tell you what I said to him. I mean, I was that far gone. But I woke up this morning and I knew I had told him enough and that I had messed up bad."

"Shit, Ben."

"I know, man. I'm sorry."

"Sorry don't fix this."

"I could talk to Lawrence. He still stays down there at Parkchester. Ali could get up with him through his nephew."

"What for?" said Chris.

They sat there for a while without speaking. They thought about what to do, and it came to Chris that there was nothing to do. There was no one to return the money to. There was simply a basket, now empty, underneath a floor in an unoccupied row house. No one would miss the money or know that it had been there or that it was gone.

Naturally, their thoughts drifted toward regret and then resentment. Why hadn't they gone ahead and taken the money themselves when they had come upon it the day before? If taking it had no consequences, and it appeared that there would be none, then what had been the wrong in it? Now Lawrence Newhouse had the money, and he didn't deserve to have it. Lawrence would blow it on bad clothing, strippers, potent weed, and stepped-on cocaine. And Chris and Ben would be ass-broke and back at work at seven in the morning, sweating through polo shirts they hated to wear.

"Bughouse," said Chris under his breath. He managed a small incredulous smile.

"Stupid," said Ben, shaking his head. "*Stupid*."

"Anyway," said Chris.

Chris and Ben shook hands.

"Same time tomorrow?" said Ben.

"I'll pick you up."

Ben left his tool belt in the back of the van and shut the doors. Chris watched his friend go into the stairwell of his building, then pulled from the lot and headed out of the city. By the time North Capitol became Blair Road, his bitterness had dissipated. He was thinking of a cool shower, a cold beer, and Katherine.

In his apartment, Ben Braswell washed up and changed his clothing. He phoned Renee to see if she wanted to hook up that night, and she said she did. She'd come by with a pizza and a Blockbuster movie when she got off work, around ten o'clock.

"See you then, girl," said Ben.

"That's a bet," said Renee.

He took a catnap on his sofa. When he woke, the room had darkened. He got up, went to the window, and parted the blinds. There was still light left in the day.

Ben slipped a paperback into the back pocket of his jeans, left his place, went along the black iron fence to the open gate at Rock Creek Church and Webster, and entered the cemetery grounds. He was headed toward the Adams Memorial, where he would sit on the marble bench shielded by evergreens and read until dark.

He stepped down a road so narrow it was no kind of road, then went off it, taking a shortcut across a stand of graves. The dying sun settled on the headstones and threw shadows at his feet.

SIXTEEN

MINDY KRAMER ate in the same place most every weekday. It was a Thai restaurant up in Wheaton, off University Boulevard, in an area heavy with Hispanics and Orthodox Jews, where nothing was upscale and fast-food wrappers and cigarette butts littered the streets.

The restaurant itself had little ambience, holding eight four-tops and a half-dozen deuces, with the standard royal family portraits hung on plain blue walls. But the food was clean, the service mostly efficient, and the specials went for four dollars and ninety-five cents, including a choice of spring rolls or watered-down lemongrass soup.

Thai Feast was out of the way from Mindy's core business, which was down in Dupont, Capitol Hill, and that broad area of Shaw that included the neighborhood she and her fellow real estate professionals called Logan. Mindy made the half-hour trek out to Wheaton because Thai Feast had become her base camp. The girl who always served her, Toi, gave her the same deuce by the window, leaving it unoccupied until her arrival, and had her ice water and iced coffee on the table shortly after Mindy had taken her seat. As Mindy made her calls and answered e-mails from her BlackBerry, Toi was busy fetching the spring rolls that came with the special and making sure the main dish that Mindy had chosen would come out right behind it. The bill was always seven forty-nine, and Mindy always left one forty-nine in the tip column of the check, exactly 20 percent.

Mindy Kramer was all about routine and organization. She had married at twenty-two, had one daughter, Lisa, and divorced her layabout husband at twenty-five. She had raised and supported Lisa by herself as she got her license and grew her business. Now she had an office in Northwest, where "a girl" handled the phones and paperwork. Mindy had trained and polished two young sales protégés who, along with her, made up the Dream Team. Unfortunately, Lisa had made the same mistake as her mother and married a young man who had no energy or ambition outside the bedroom. She was now single with two little girls, ages six and four, of her own. Because she felt that Lisa was not emotionally equipped to be a proper mother to them, Mindy often took the children, Michelle and Lauren, with her to the office or dropped them off at summer day camp.

She handled all of this because she was efficient. *And* she looked good. At fifty-five, she was toned, well-dressed, and properly made up and manicured. There wasn't one gelled, spiked, highlighted hair out of place on her head.

"How is your family, Toi?" said Mindy Kramer, as she added the tip and signed the credit card voucher before her.

"They are well," said Toi with a smile.

"I'll see you tomorrow," said Mindy.

"Thank you so much," said Toi, her smile frozen in place.

Mindy Kramer got up and, smoothing her sleeveless lavender shift down her thighs, her purse in hand, left the restaurant, donning her oversize sunglasses as she walked toward her C-class, parked in the lot.

Watching Mindy through the plate glass window of Thai Feast, Toi let her smile fade. She couldn't stand this weathered shrew with the stupid haircut, who would never round up the tip one penny to an even one fifty, who asked about her family but never really listened to the reply or looked into her eyes. But this was what you put up with every day. It was work.

Mindy got into her Mercedes and turned the ignition. She glanced at the Anne Klein watch on her tan, lightly freckled wrist. She was exactly on schedule to make her meeting down at the row house in Logan. She had gotten a call from a gentleman that morning, telling her he was interested in taking a look at the house. It had been a week since the break-in, and several months since she had bought the home at auction. The market was extremely soft, her interest rate had not been optimum, and the clock was ticking. But, like all good sales professionals, she was an optimist. Perhaps this would be the client she had been waiting for. It could very well be Mindy's day.

THERE WERE two men standing at the top of her row house steps as Mindy Kramer pulled into a nearby space on the street. Her immediate impression, looking at them through the windshield of her sedan, was that these men could not be her potential buyers. They looked more like workmen than clients.

She got out of her car, smile in place, and walked across the sidewalk and up the steps to greet them. She kept her smile rigid as she got a good look at them, thinking, *God, why are they wasting my time?* She would qualify them quickly and let them know with diplomacy that this was too much house for them and that perhaps she could find them someplace else, in a neighborhood, say, where trailer trash was more welcome.

"Mindy Kramer," she said, extending her hand to the larger of the two men.

"Ralph Cotter," he said, vise-gripping her hand, showing her a row of grayish, cheaply capped teeth. "This is my friend Nat Harbin."

"Pleasure," said Nat Harbin. Tattoos of some kind showed on his veined biceps beneath the rolled-up edges of his T-shirt, and tattoos sleeved his forearms. He wore black ring-strap boots.

Cotter had not released her hand. She looked at his and saw a tattoo, like a four-leaf clover, on the crook of it. Cotter let go of her, stepped back, and smiled.

Both were in their late thirties and both wore jeans. Harbin in a black T-shirt and Cotter in a windbreaker with a white oxford underneath. Harbin had some sort of chain going from his wallet pocket to his belt loop. He was short and wiry, with a bushy mustache that appeared to originate in his nose. His eyes were flat and brown. His long brown hair was parted in the middle and it was unclean.

Cotter was tall, broad, and strong, with a big chest and an unchecked gut. His black hair was also on the long side and swept back behind his ears. He wore a dark walrus mustache on a face with high, pronounced cheekbones. His eyes were black, mostly pupil, and did not appear to be threatening or unkind.

Mindy prided herself on reading people. She was in a business that required such a talent, after all. These two were strange, stuck in a time warp, perhaps new to the city, and uninterested in current fashions. But they weren't here to do her any harm. In any event, there had never been a situation that she couldn't handle.

Mustaches, wallet chains, boots . . . costume macho. *Gay*

bikers, thought Mindy Kramer. *Okay, I'm projecting. Gay would fit fine here, though. But do they have the dosh to buy this house?*

"You gentlemen are both interested in the property?" she said. "You're considering it . . . together?"

"Yeah," said Ralph Cotter. "Can we have a look inside?"

"Of course!"

Mindy opened her small purse, where she kept her Black-Berry and keys, and negotiated the lockbox hung on the door-knob.

"No alarm system?" said Cotter.

"No need," she said, looking over her shoulder and up because he was so tall.

"Street looks peaceful enough."

"You notice no bars on the windows, either. We really don't have those kinds of problems in this neighborhood. It was dicey at one time, but" . . . she opened the door . . . "no longer."

They stepped into a foyer, where a staircase led up to the third-floor bedrooms and a hall went straight back to the body of the house. The little one, Nat Harbin, shut the door behind them. The closing of it darkened the foyer, and Mindy switched on a light.

"Where did you find out about this home?" said Mindy. "I always like to know if my advertising dollars are well spent."

"Drove by it and saw the sign," said Cotter. "Then we got on the Internet and learned the particulars."

"So you've read the entire listing."

"We know the price," said Cotter patiently. "We can handle it."

"You gentlemen are in what business?"

"Don't worry, we qualify," said Cotter. Not annoyed, just matter-of-fact. "Let's see the house."

"Okay," said Mindy. "We'll start with the kitchen."

They went down the hall. The one named Nat eyed the layout and various rooms as they went along, but Cotter kept his focus on Mindy. He looked down at her head, noticing her scalp showing through all the clumps of hair glued together and sticking up straight. There didn't seem to be much to her under that dress. She had an ass but not enough of one. She had small cans and she was old. He didn't mind the old part, but he liked a woman with big tits.

"Here's the kitchen," she said, casually sliding a dimmer switch mounted on the wall and bathing the room in a yellow-ish glow. "Granite countertops and stainless steel appliances, as you can see."

Granite countertops were now as remarkable as toilet paper holders in bathrooms, and stainless steel surfaces had no bearing on the quality of the appliances themselves, but the public was gullible. Who was Mindy Kramer to educate them when she was merely trying to move a house?

"Nice," said Cotter, nodding his head.

"And all new," said Mindy. She placed her purse on the granite counter. "Do you two like to cook?" Neither of them answered, and Mindy said, "This is a very diverse neighborhood, you know."

Cotter and Harbin looked at each other and laughed.

Mindy scratched at her neck. It was something she did when she became a bit self-conscious and insecure, and she hated herself for succumbing to the reflex now. These two were vulgarians. They were not going to buy this house, nor could they afford to. They were wasting her time.

"Internet said this place had a library slash den," said Nat Harbin. "Can you take us to it?"

"Yes, but . . . please understand, I have a very busy schedule today."

"We'd like to see it," said Cotter, still smiling, his capped teeth perfect and ugly in the yellow light. "If you don't mind."

She led them back down the hall. She stumbled, catching the toe of one Stuart Weitzman sandal on the walnut floor, and Cotter grabbed her elbow with his big hand and steadied her.

"Easy now," he said, and as he held her elbow with one hand, he lightly stroked her bare arm with the other. Bumps rose on her flesh.

She went into the library and they followed her. She crossed her arms and looked out the window that gave to a view of the street, and then back at the men. The one who called himself Ralph Cotter stood blocking the door. The little one, Nat Harbin, was looking at Cotter expectantly, waiting for a signal or direction.

"Get to it," said Cotter.

Harbin bent forward, hiked up the left leg of his jeans, and pulled a knife from a tie-down sheath inside his boot. The knife was hardwood handled, with a heavy-duty pommel and a spine-cut surgical-steel blade.

Mindy Kramer hugged herself and looked down at her feet.

"That's right, honey," said Cotter. "You just stand there and mind your own."

Harbin went to a corner of the room, lifted a bit of the carpet, and cut cleanly beneath it in a filleting motion. He pulled back a triangle of the Berber and with his knee kept it pinned down. He found the notch in the cutout of wood floor and lifted the piece away, and when he saw there was nothing in the basket that had been fashioned beneath it, he said, "Shit."

"Nothin, huh," said Cotter.

"It's empty," said Harbin.

Cotter shook his head. "That's a problem."

"Where is it, lady?" said Harbin.

"Where is what?" said Mindy Kramer in a small voice, keeping her eyes to the floor.

"I had somethin in that hole," said Cotter. "It belonged to me."

"I don't know anything about it," said Mindy.

"Look at me," said Cotter.

Mindy willed herself to raise her eyes and face him. "I swear to you. I don't know what you're talking about. I bought this house to flip it. I've never lived here. I've never even looked under that carpet, not once."

"Rug looks brand-new to me."

"I replaced it, just a week ago. Not me, of course . . ."

"Who?"

"I used a local company."

"Who *exactly?*"

"I've got the information. I keep a file on all the work I've done here. Warranties and such."

"Where?"

"It's in the kitchen."

"Let's go."

Cotter stepped out of the room to let her pass, Harbin close behind her, knife in hand. They all went back down the hall, and in the kitchen Mindy maxed out the dimmer switch and pulled open a drawer near a stainless steel gas cooktop. On top of a stack of use-and-care manuals was a manila file folder, and she withdrew it. She opened the file on the granite countertop, her hand visibly shaking as she rooted through papers and found the one she was looking for.

"Here it is," she said, handing it to Cotter.

He examined the piece of paper. The name of the company and the billing address were at the top of the page. The cost of goods and the labor were line-itemed in the body of the bill. At the bottom, in the total slot, the number had been changed and initialed.

"Flynn's Floors," said Cotter. "And you dealt with . . ."

"The owner. Thomas Flynn."

"Looks like he gave you some kind of break on the price."

"It was an adjustment. His installers did a poor job. They had to come back and redo the work."

Cotter and Harbin exchanged a look.

"You wouldn't recall the names of the *in*-stallers, would you?" said Cotter.

"I . . ."

"C'mon, honey. You're doing good so far."

Mindy Kramer chewed on her lower lip. "I'm going to reach into my purse. I need to get my BlackBerry."

"Do it," said Cotter.

She took her purse off the counter, opened it, and retrieved her phone. She scrolled through her contacts and found the one she was looking for. She had entered it using a memory device so that she could recall it easily.

"Here's one of them," said Mindy, handing him the phone.

"Chris Carpet," said Cotter, squinting to read it.

"I didn't get his last name."

"Describe him for me."

"Young. Big, with blond hair."

"You said there was two of them."

"The other installer was black. Young and strong, like his partner. Tall. That's all I can remember about him. I'm sorry—"

"That'll be fine. Write down Chris Carpet's phone number on the back of the bill for me, will you?"

Mindy found a pen in her purse and did as she was told. Cotter took the bill of sale, folded it, and slipped it into the pocket of his windbreaker. Then he stepped forward and pressed himself against her. His cock grew hard. Because of his height and her lack of it, he pushed it against her belly. She turned her head to the side. A tear sprung loose from one eye and rolled down her cheek. He felt her body shiver against his.

"Don't cry, honey," said Cotter.

"I can't . . . help it."

"You wanna know what I had in that hole?"

"No."

"I had money."

"No . . ."

"How about our real names? Wanna know what they are? Bet you're curious."

A string of mucus dropped from Mindy's nose and came to rest on her lip. "I'm not."

"Course you're not. You think if I tell you my name I'm gonna go ahead and kill you. Ain't that right?"

Mindy's tears flowed freely and she closed her eyes and shook her head. Cotter stepped back. A triangle of urine had darkened the crotch of her dress.

"Look at that," said Harbin. "She tinkled."

"I'm not gonna kill you, Mindy," said Cotter. "Not you. I don't need to." Cotter put his hand into the pocket of his jeans and pulled free a cell phone. He flipped it open and punched buttons clumsily with his thick thumb. "I got a phone, too. Not as fancy as yours, but hey. Here we go."

Cotter handed her the phone. She looked at the screen and made a small choking sound from deep in her throat.

"You recognize those little girls, right? Kinda hard to see 'em, I know, 'cause I was far away. But that's them. That would be your granddaughters, right?"

Mindy did not answer.

"Say it's them," said Harbin.

"It's my granddaughters," said Mindy Kramer.

"Okay," said Cotter. He pointed to the ink on the crook of his hand. "Now, do you know what this is?"

"A clover?"

"It's a shamrock, honey. Means I'm part of something, kind of like a club. We got members in prisons all across the country. We *run* the prisons, matter of fact. Got a lotta members who are out and in the world now, too. All of us, in this club, forever. When you ride with the rock, you're protected. And if anything bad does happen to you, you're avenged. Families, children . . . we'll kill 'em all and not even think on it twice. It's part of the blood oath we take to get in. Do you understand?"

"I think so."

"I hope you do. You know what we were doing this morning? We were parked outside your office, watching you bring in your granddaughters, watching you bring them back out. After, we followed you to where you dropped them off, at that rec center outside the elementary school. What was that, Thirty-third Street? Yeah, that's where it was. Where I snapped these pictures from my phone."

Cotter reached out and took his cell from Mindy Kramer's hand.

"You never met us today," said Cotter.

Mindy Kramer nodded.

"You ain't gonna talk about this to your priest or rabbi, or your shrink, or nobody else. You're not gonna warn Chris Carpet that we're looking to speak to him, either."

"I won't."

"Because if you do, my little friend here will visit your grand-daughters."

"Please, don't—"

"He'll cut their heads off and skull-fuck 'em both, *Mindy*. Do you get it?"

Mindy Kramer nodded.

"Say you do," said Harbin.

"I get it," said Mindy.

"I think she does," said Cotter. "C'mon."

Harbin sheathed his knife. He and Cotter walked down the hall, straight out of the house, closing the door behind them and taking the steps to the sidewalk, not caring if they were seen.

When Mindy Kramer heard the shut of the door, she dropped to the kitchen floor and sat with her back to the cabinets, weeping, her head between her knees, chest heaving, mascara running down her face. She made no move to phone the police or anyone else. She sat there and waited for the fear to leave her. She sat there for a long while. What they had taken from her would not come back soon. Maybe it would never come back at all.

THE MEN walked to their car, a 1988 Mercury Marquis they had picked up from a cancer-ridden old man in West Virginia. From the long-term lot at Dulles Airport they had switched out plates, and the car now bore D.C. tags. The sedan was boxy and black, with a landau roof and red velour interior, a fake-fur-covered steering wheel, and a V-8 under the hood.

Ralph Cotter and Nat Harbin were not their names. The big man with the walrus mustache was Sonny Wade. He had chosen the fake names from two of the many novels he had read while incarcerated at the federal prison in Lewisburg, Pennsylvania. In those books, Cotter had been a stone killer and Harbin had been a career burglar. It was at Lewisburg that Sonny Wade had met the little man, Wayne Minors, who had been his cell mate. Wayne did not read books.

Sonny got himself positioned in the driver's seat and turned the key in the ignition. Wayne looked tiny beside him, as if he were Sonny's child, if Sonny could have had a son his own age. Wayne's features were compressed toward the middle of his face, folding into one another, so he looked like a piece of fruit that had begun to rot. Wayne drank and used speed, but his longtime cigarette smoking had done the bulk of the damage to his looks.

Wayne lit a Marlboro off a butane flame as Sonny pulled out of the spot on S Street. They were headed toward New York Avenue, where they had a room in a flophouse motel populated by unwitting tourists, assorted losers, prostitutes, alcoholics, drug addicts, and people on the government tit.

"She wasn't so full of herself when we got finished with her," said Wayne.

"She won't speak on this to anyone," said Sonny.

"She pissed her panties."

"That she did."

"Kramer's a Jewish name."

"Uh-huh."

"You hear what she said about us being together? And askin, do we like to cook?" Wayne's eyes crossed slightly as he considered this. "It was like she thought we was faggots."

"She thought *you* was," said Sonny.

"Your daddy was," said Wayne.

They were silent as Sonny wheeled the radio dial, trying to find something he liked, settling on a station playing a Rascal

Flatts song. Wayne smoked and studied the city as they passed through it, looking at the whites and the blacks together in these neighborhoods, wondering how a father could let his daughter live among these low coloreds in a shithole such as this.

"Those installers took my money," said Sonny after a while. "Had to be them."

"We'll get it back." Wayne pitched his cigarette out the open window. "Sonny?"

"Huh."

"Why'd you tell that woman I'd fuck those little girls and cut their heads off? You know I wouldn't do no such thing. I wouldn't kill a kid. I'm a gentleman. I ain't like that."

"And I'm no AB. I was just puttin the fear into her, is all."

"I'd kill a nigger," offered Wayne.

"You might could get your chance," said Sonny. "But we're gonna talk to Chris Carpet first."

SEVENTEEN

CHRIS, ALI, and several younger men were in a Saturday after-noon game on the basketball courts at the Hamilton Rec Center between 13th and 14th in Northwest, in an area known as 16th Street Heights. When he was available, Ali liked to have Chris hang out with his boys, so that they could see by example an ex–juvenile offender who had managed to reenter society in a positive way. Chris wasn't about giving speeches or deep advice, but if it meant simply showing up to ball, he was there.

Chris had asked Ali to bring the boys to Hamilton, as the fenced-in courts were in good shape, and the red, white, and blue nets were kept intact. He'd been playing there since his teens and found the quality of players fairly high. It was here where an errant elbow had split his lip and given him his scar, which Katherine later told him was the second thing she'd no-ticed about him and liked, after his eyes. Ham Rec now held value to him for that alone.

Ali had driven out from Southeast in his mother's beat-up Saturn with William Richards and Marquis Gilman, Law-rence's nephew, in tow. They had invited in two young men who lived on Farragut Street and gone three-on-three for a few games. Chris had bulk and a jumper, and Ali still had his vertical leap, but the teenagers had them on speed. The games had been hard fought but without major conflict, the players evenly matched, and all had been sweated out and satisfied when it was agreed that they were done.

Chris stayed on the court and worked with Marquis, showing him his box-out move and telling him to watch the extra step on his drive to the bucket. Marquis, still gangly in his youth, looked Chris in the eye when spoken to but disagreed that his pretty move was a violation.

"That's a jump step, Mr. Chris," said Marquis.

"It's an *extra* step," said Chris. "Just 'cause they don't call it in the NBA doesn't mean you can do it out here."

"I'll do it when I go pro, then."

"You're not goin pro, Marquis. But you *could* be a good pickup man. If you didn't travel with the ball every time you drove."

"Okay," said Marquis. "I hear you."

Ali returned with some bottles of water he had gotten out of the Saturn's trunk. William Richards, who had been sitting by himself near the playground, got up and joined them. Ali offered him a bottle, but he waved it away.

"I don't want it," said William, his Bulls cap cocked sideways on his head. "That water's hot."

"Wet, too," said Ali.

"I'm gonna walk down to Kennedy and Georgia, get somethin to drink at the Wings n Things."

"They closed that place," said Chris.

"Whateva they call it now, they still got cold sodas," said William. "You comin, Marquis?"

"Is it all right, Mr. Ali?" said Marquis.

"Yeah, go ahead. Keep to yourselves, hear? I'll come by and pick you two up on my way out."

The two young men walked east on Hamilton, then cut north on 13th. Ali and Chris went to the black Saturn, parked behind Chris's van. Ali sat on the hood and took a swig of warm water.

"Marquis is all right," said Chris.

"Ain't nothin wrong with him," said Ali. "He got some issues at home and with his peers at those apartments, is all. Marquis only did dirt 'cause his friends did. He's just tryin to belong to something, man."

"You get him legit work?"

"I'm about to hook him up at a Wendy's, if the manager ever calls me back."

"Ben said Lawrence came to see you."

"He wanted me to put Marquis up with your pops. I wouldn't even ask. Wendy's is a better start for him at this point. That boy's gonna be one of my success stories."

"No doubt," said Chris.

"You seen Lawrence lately?"

"No. Ben and him were together one night recently. But I wasn't with 'em."

Chris hadn't told Ali about Lawrence and the bag of cash. Lawrence had been putting that money up his nose, most likely, or watching it bounce on his dick since he'd broke into the Kramer house to take it. Chris was trying to forget about the money, and for the most part he had.

"Man looks old," said Ali. "But he's the same Lawrence."

"Bughouse is Bughouse," said Chris, repeating something that had been said often in their unit, many years back.

Ali took a long drink. Chris bunched up his shirt and wiped sweat from his face.

"Appreciate you coming out today," said Ali.

"I just came to play basketball."

"It's more than that. The boys like seeing you. You got a nice way with them, man."

"I don't mind hangin with them, when I have the time."

"You ever think of changing up? Doing something different?"

"What, you asking me to come work with you?"

"I make less than you do," said Ali. "So I wouldn't suggest that. I'm talking about switching careers. You love reading those books of yours so much, why don't you use it? Good as you are with kids, you could be a history teacher, somethin like that."

"You mean like Mr. Beige? He didn't look all that prosperous to me."

"Teachers make decent money now, Chris, and it's getting better all the time. In some cities schoolteachers make six figures, they hang with it long enough."

"But I can't be one," said Chris.

"Sure you can."

"Armed with a high school degree?"

"So get yourself enrolled in a community college, then transfer to a university or state school when you make grades."

"How would I support myself?"

"You'd work, just like you do now. Work during the day and go to your classes at night."

"That would take forever."

"Those years would go by quick. You could earn your teaching certificate and get out there and do some good. They got this Teach For America program, where people come fresh out of college and go to work in disadvantaged school districts—"

"Nah, man."

"Why not?"

"That's not who I am," said Chris. "I'm a carpet installer, Ali."

"You could be more."

"Okay, Shawshank."

Ali chuckled. "Shit. That old man just didn't know when to quit, did he."

"Like you," said Chris, eyeing his friend and tapping his water bottle to Ali's.

"Well, let me go pick up those knuckleheads," said Ali, getting off the hood of his mother's car.

"My father's having his employee barbecue tonight at his house," said Chris, retrieving the van keys from the pocket of his shorts. "You gonna come past?"

"Your pops walks backward when he sees me," said Ali.

"He asked me to tell you to come by. Even though you made him put Lonnie and Luther on the payroll."

"Don't forget Milton."

"Yeah, Milton couldn't operate the tape measure. But my old man does like you. Not that I can figure out why. Prob'ly cause, out of me and my friends, you're the only one who's had any success."

"You're doin all right, too, man."

"Right." Chris walked toward the white van. "Come by, hear?"

Ali said, "I will."

LAWRENCE NEWHOUSE walked up the road in his long T-shirt, along the Barry Farms dwellings, this particular block a two-story strip of tan motel-style structures with chocolate doorways and arches. Time was, in his youth, he and his boys at

184 • George Pelecanos

Parkchester would have been beefing with those at the Farms, and he supposed the young ones still did the same, but that was past for him. People looked at him as he went along, eyeing him but not hard, like he wasn't worth the time it took to fix a stare. At twenty-six, Lawrence was old. He had not taken care of himself, what with his poor diet, drinking, all manner of smoke, and powder when he could get it. He looked close to forty.

He had a plastic bottle of fruit punch in his hand. He had bought it at the local Korean place, having woken up, still in his club clothes atop the sheets of his bed, with a vicious thirst. He'd spent a bunch of money the night before in that strip club he liked on New York Avenue. He'd spent it on hard liquor and dancers, the usual shove-the-bills-in-the-string thing, and on a gram of coke he'd copped in the bathroom from a young man he'd met at the bar. The freeze had made him shit soon as he'd taken his first bite of it off the end of a key. That's what he got for buying coke from someone he didn't know. Wasn't much more than laxative, but it kept him awake. And it got one of the dancers interested enough to come outside with him and swallow his manhood in the backseat of her man's car. Which had cost him another hundred. He didn't remember driving his Cavalier back to Southeast, but it was parked in his spot, so he supposed that this is what he had done.

Money went quick.

Lawrence walked across a small dusty playground with monkey bars and the rusted, spidery frame of a swing set. At the edge of the playground a steel pole with no backboard was set in concrete. Around the pole was a tribute to a boy named Beanie, a loose arrangement of teddy bears, ribbons and banners, empty Hennessey bottles, and photographs, a commemoration of Beanie's short, fast life and death by gun.

Then Lawrence was on Wade and heading toward the Parkchester Apartments, stepping around boys he recognized but did not speak to who were grouped at one of the entranceways, and going into a stairwell holding the usual stagnant smells of things that were fried, eaten, or smoked.

He went into his place.

It wasn't his place, exactly. It was Dorita's, his half-sister. Dorita was on government assistance, had three children by two different men, and let him stay here. When she was short on food or needed Nikes for the kids, he gave her cash, if he had it. He had it now, but Dorita didn't know.

Her two younger kids, Terrence and Loquatia, were on the carpet, watching a show on a widescreen plasma television Dorita had bought on time. Loquatia, eleven and already running to fat like her mother, had her hand in a bowl of Skittles, running her fingers through the colored bits. Long as Loquatia was touching food, she was cool. Her little brother was staring at the cartoon lobster on the screen but daydreaming, thinking on something called a galaxy, which he had learned about in school. He had an active imagination, and his teacher suspected he was highly intelligent. The teacher had phoned Dorita to tell her about an accelerated program available at his elementary, but Dorita had yet to call her back.

Dorita sat on the living-room sofa, her feet up on it, cell phone in hand. There was no man currently in her life. She was thirty-two, and her stretch-marked belly spilled out from beneath her tight shirt. At two fifty, she had eighty pounds on Lawrence. They had the same mother but looked nothing alike.

"Where you been at?" said Dorita.

"I went down to the Chang's," said Lawrence.

"And you ain't get me nothin?"

"Wasn't like I went to the grocery store." Lawrence head-shook his braids away from his face. "Where's Marquis at?"

"Mr. Carter came past and picked him up. Before you woke up. Marquis said they were going to play basketball."

"Okay," said Lawrence, annoyed but not fully understanding why. He appreciated that Ali was trying to help the boy, and he also resented it.

"You snored last night," said Terrence, and Dorita laughed.

"So?" said Lawrence. "You farted."

Terrence and Loquatia laughed.

"If you goin to the Chang's, you need to tell me," said Dorita. "We could use some soda in this house."

"I ain't no shopping service."

"You could contribute," said Dorita. 'Stead of just taking all the time."

"Least my mother didn't name me after a corn chip," said Lawrence, saying the same tired thing he had been saying to his sister since they were kids.

Dorita did not respond, and Lawrence went to his room.

It wasn't his room, exactly. He shared it with the two younger kids. He had strung up a sheet between their beds and his single bed to give him some privacy. Didn't leave much space, but this was what he had. Free rent, you couldn't complain. Anyway, he was about to be out of here.

About to be.

He pulled aside the sheet, flopped down on his bed, and draped his forearm over his eyes. Underneath the bed, the bag of money. He felt he had to keep it close. But what was he going to do with it? That was the thing that was fucking with his head.

He knew he should be looking for a nice place of his own. Maybe go to one of the Eastern Motors and trade up off that hooptie he had. But then he'd be in an apartment by himself, no one to talk to, no one to Jone on, and driving a car that was newer, that's all. He'd already spent a couple of thousand on women and fun. Beyond that, wasn't anything that he could see to buy that would make him happy.

What he wanted, what he'd always craved, was to have friends and pride. He'd thought that money would help him get those things. But to get it, he'd tricked the one dude who'd *been* his friend, the only boy who'd stepped in and stood tall for him back when he was getting his ass beat regular at Pine Ridge. And now he, Lawrence, had gone and done him dirt.

Sometimes, no lie, he hated the sight of his own self in the mirror.

Lawrence rolled over onto his side. In the heat of the room, sweat dampening his long T-shirt, he went to sleep.

ALI CARTER lived with his mother, Juanita Carter, in a vinyl-sided duplex town home on Alabama Avenue in Garfield Heights, across the road from the offices of Men Movin on Up. The development was on the new side, the yards were still clean, and the several hundred homes that had been constructed here had replaced some problem-ridden projects that had been good for no one. Houses here were still being sold for about three hundred thousand dollars, with low-interest loans and no-money-down offers in effect. A chain grocery store, the Seventh District Police Station, and Fort Stanton Park were within walking distance. Communities such as this one, housing longtime residents and newcomers alike, had been appearing in several spots in Southeast. Only those who were unreasonably resistant to change could say that this was not a positive development. For Ali, it was a huge step up, and a world away from where he'd been raised.

Juanita Carter had not been a bad mother to Ali and his sisters in any way; she had merely been born poor. Her start at the back of the line had crippled her, and by the time she had made a family, her lack of higher education and unfortunate choices in men had put her at a severe disadvantage. She and her kids lived in the Barry Farms dwellings, and she had no choice but to raise them in that rough-and-tumble and occasionally toxic atmosphere. After earning her GED, she started taking health care classes while working on the cleaning crew at the old D.C. General Hospital. But while she was bettering herself in order to move her family out of the Farms, Ali was entering his teens, a dangerous time for a boy to have little supervision at home. Juanita blamed herself to this day for the trouble Ali and one of his sisters, who eventually was lost to the streets, had found. But Ali knew it wasn't her. It was him, and the fact that some young men just had to touch their hand to the flame to see for themselves that fire was hot.

"Where you off to?" said Juanita, as her son entered the kitchen in his pressed jeans and a sky blue Lacoste shirt, picking a pair of sunglasses out of a bowl on the counter that held his things.

"Chris Flynn's father is having a cookout," said Ali. "For his employees."

"You don't work for him."

"No, but he's been good to some fellas I know. At least, he tried to be."

"So you gonna, what, show your appreciation to this man by eating his burgers and potato salad?"

"I'll prob'ly ask him for some more favors, too." Ali put his hand in Juanita's bowl of things, set beside his, and looked at her sheepishly. "Can I get your car?"

"If you say you're not gonna drink."

"You know I don't even like it."

Ali took the keys and kissed his mother on the cheek. She was a small woman of forty-two with big brown eyes and a pretty smile. It was from her that he had acquired his modest height and handsome features.

In the past, they had experienced conflicts, but as adults, they made a good team. They had cosigned for the loan on the house and together they had made it work. She was an attendant at a dialysis center on 8th Street on Capitol Hill, and had learned to budget herself, watch her purchases, and still walk down the street in relative style. He stayed with her to pay her back, in some way, for the trouble he'd caused her as a youth. Both knew he'd be gone when he found someone special and started having kids of his own. She seemed to want it more than he did.

"Any girls gonna be at this barbecue?"

"Nah, Mama. We're all members of the He-Men Women Hater's Club."

"I wonder sometimes."

"Huh," said Ali. He had his eye on this one girl he'd met at church, but his mother didn't need to know that yet.

"Don't drink tonight," said Juanita, as her son headed out the door, her car keys in hand.

"I won't," said Ali.

She watched him go, thinking, *I'm not trying to get on you or nag. I don't want anything to happen to you. That's all it is.*

You've come so far.

EIGHTEEN

CHRIS CAME down into Rock Creek Park on the winding Sherrill Drive, took Beach for a piece, and came up out of the park on Bingham, the east-west cut-through his father had showed him as a child. He drove the van up the long hill of Nebraska Avenue and headed west on McKinley. Katherine was beside him in the shotgun bucket, and Ben was on the collapsible second-row bench. As he tended to do when he reentered his old neighborhood, Chris grew quiet.

They stopped at the red light at McKinley and Connecticut Avenue. To their right were the fenced-in courts of the Chevy Chase Rec Center, where Chris had played under the lights and stars in various summer leagues. Across the avenue, to the north, was the Avalon, the theater where he had smoked weed in the men's room with his friends before movies, now an independent operation showing art films.

"See those blocks of concrete?" said Ben, pointing a long finger between Chris and Katherine at the planters on the sidewalk past the bus shelter, lined along the sloping driveway entrance to the drugstore at the southwest corner of Connecticut.

"Yes?" said Katherine, suspecting what was coming, having heard the story of Chris's night of crime.

"Those are, like, monuments to Chris," said Ben. "They put 'em up there after he drove his truck 'cross the sidewalk."

"That wasn't me. That was some other dude."

Chris accelerated through the intersection on the green and glanced at the concrete barriers as he drove past.

"My legacy," said Chris, and Katherine reached over and squeezed his hand.

Driving west on McKinley, Chris pulled to the right as far as he could to allow a late-model Audi to pass. The coupe came alongside him, and Chris looked to the driver for the courtesy nod. Their eyes met. The driver, a good-looking man around Chris's age with a salon haircut and a clean open-necked white shirt, smiled nervously in recognition.

"Hey," said the driver, with a finger wave.

"How's it goin, man?" said Chris, returning the smile.

Neither of them stopped. Chris's heavy foot gave the van a bit too much gas.

"Who was that?" said Katherine.

"A kid I ran with from the neighborhood," said Chris.

"Looks like he prosperin, whoever he is," said Ben.

"He got out of law school last year," said Chris. "My father says he's with a downtown firm now."

"You never mentioned him to me," said Katherine.

"Yes, I did," said Chris.

"I guess I don't remember."

"No big deal," said Chris. "He's just a guy I used to know."

THE COOKOUT was in the backyard of the Flynns' clapboard colonial on Livingston. Depending on the level of business, Thomas Flynn employed six to eight men, but they came to this annual event with children, wives, girlfriends, and one or two uninvited friends. The yard was not large to begin with, and it was full.

Amanda Flynn had laid out a food spread on a table set on their screened-in porch, which led to an uncovered deck, where Flynn was busy barbecuing burgers, chorizo sausages, half-smokes, and chicken breasts on his commercial-grade gas grill. Amanda and Isaac's wife, Maria, were moving back and forth from the kitchen to the porch, putting out sides, paper plates, napkins, and utensils, catching up with conversation as they worked. Flynn had a spatula in one hand and a bottle of Bud in the other. Within reach, on the rail of the deck, was a party ball of Jim Beam and shot glasses for anyone who cared to join him. Nearby were two iced-down coolers, one stocked with beer and white wine, the other holding sodas and water.

Music was coming from outdoor speakers mounted on the ceiling of the screened-in porch. It was a mix of Spanish-language pop with dramatic vocals, which everyone enjoyed to some degree but would become a bone of contention and discussion as the night wore on. Ben had brought his Rare Essence and Backyard Band tapes, Maze's greatest hits, and the new Wale to drop in later, when folks got loose. One of Amanda's jobs was to keep her husband away from the stereo, especially after he'd had a few drinks. This was not the crowd for Thin Lizzy or Lynyrd Skynyrd, and no one here, with the exception of Thomas Flynn, was into Bruce.

Renee, Ben's girlfriend, had joined them late, after she came off work at the nail salon. In her evening clothes and heels, she was overdressed for a cookout, but she looked good. Katherine, in a sundress, her hair down, was in conversation with Renee, as Ben was spending much of his time playing with Django, the Flynns' dog.

Also in attendance was Lonnie Wilson. Though he had not worked for Flynn's Floors for several years, and his employment had been short-lived, Lonnie liked a party and could not pass up free food and drink. He had brought along his wife, Yolanda, and their two children. Pussy-crazy Lonnie, who had talked incessantly about all the women he was going to slay when he left Pine Ridge, had married Yolanda, the first girl he got with when he came out. Despite the fact that Lonnie had been unable to hold a job and their money problems were deep, Lonnie and his family were a tight unit.

Darkness had settled on the yard. Chris, Ali, Ben, and Lonnie stood around an outdoor fire pit, drinking beer from bottles, talking, and looking into the fire that Chris had lit using wood stacked beside the alley garage. Thomas Flynn had built the pit years ago. Flynn had leveled the dirt, constructed the base and walls with cinder block and mortar, covered it with decorative stone veneer, grouted it, and capped it with concrete he cut and mitered himself.

Chris could not have constructed such a fine piece of work. He was not a natural handyman like his father. He was not even a particularly good carpet man, though he had learned enough to do satisfactory installations. Truth was, he wasn't suited to his current job, but it had been made available to him and was what he had.

"Look at this dog, man," said a gleeful Ben, holding a rubber toy by its U-shaped handle, the other end death-clenched in Django's powerful jaws, the dog pulling furiously, his rear legs dug in, his eyes rolled back in his square head. "You see pit when he's got somethin in his mouth."

"The ID card at the shelter said 'Labrador mix,'" said Chris. "They put that tag on all the dogs, even the beagles. People want to adopt Labs."

Ben let go of the toy. Django dropped it at Ben's feet, sat, looked up at him, and smiled.

"He wants to play more," said Ali.

"If I had a dog like this, I'd play with him all the time," said Ben. "But it wouldn't be right for me to keep him in my apartment all day while I was at work."

"Dog's all ass," said Lonnie.

"That's the pit in him," said Ben.

"All that power in his ass, I bet he can fuck like a machine, too," said Lonnie.

"Not anymore," said Chris. "My parents had him fixed."

"See, man, why they have to do that?" said Lonnie.

"Someone should do it to you," said Ali.

"I'm not done, though," said Lonnie. "I'm gonna have a big family. I'm into kids, see, and I got the means to make 'em. Also, Yolanda is fertile as mess. I'm like one of them sperm banks you read about, and Yolanda's the vault. Couple times a day, I got to make a deposit."

"That doesn't even make sense," said Ali.

Chris looked up to the deck, where Isaac was talking intently with his father. Chris felt a slight pang of jealousy. Isaac was a better worker than Chris, more skilled, more diligent, and more conscientious. Isaac deserved to get a shot at running Flynn's Floors someday, more so than Chris. What hurt Chris was the realization that his father had to know this, too, and would be torn by his loyalty to his son and this exemplary employee.

"Hey," said Hector. "I was wondering where all the women was."

Hector, the young, curly-haired worker from Isaac's crew, stepped into the circle, playfully elbowing Ben to move him aside. Hector tapped Chris's beer bottle with his own.

"If it ain't Hector the Dick Inspector," said Ben.

"You inspect the *vergas*," said Hector pleasantly. "I will work. And faster than you, my friend." In the light of the fire, with his glassy eyes and wide grin, he looked a bit drunk.

"Ali, Lonnie," said Chris, "this is Hector."

Hector nodded, then gave them a small bow. "Nice to meet you."

"You, too," said Ali.

"Hector works on one of our crews," said Chris.

"The *best* crew," said Hector. He was a competitive type and could back up his boasts.

"I thought your name was Mary," said Ben.

"My name is not Mary," said Hector.

"Sure it is," said Ben. "Mary Cone."

Hector's face contorted as he figured it out. Then he smiled with delight and pointed his finger at Ben. "*You* are *maricone!*"

They laughed and drank more beer. Katherine and Renee joined them, and the circle enlarged. Everyone took a step back from the fire. They were all sweating, and the alcohol was not cooling them down. Kids ran through the yard, and one of Isaac's crew was dancing with a young woman in the light of a torch to a Tejano ballad playing on the stereo.

"Where's your shadow tonight?" said Chris to Lonnie. "He usually comes to this thing."

"Luther?" said Lonnie. He shook his head. "I don't get up with Luther too much anymore. Luther *lost*, man."

"He druggin?" said Ali

"Luther's doin everything wrong," said Lonnie. "Just runnin with the wrong people, basically. One of 'em he met at the Ridge originally. Remember DeMarco Hines?"

"From Twelve," said Ali, naming the unit housing the most violent boys.

"Last time I seen Luther, I told him, it's time to get away from those kinds of people and stop all that nonsense. You too old to be in that game. But he wouldn't listen. Thing is, Luther isn't bad, not like DeMarco."

"Luther had no business being in Pine Ridge to begin with," said Ali. "You put someone in with boys who got sickness for real, he's gonna catch a virus."

"Luther got arrested as a runner one too many times," said Lonnie. "Police would jump out their cars and grab him, and then he kept violating his parole. That's all it was."

"Imagine the law, on foot, catchin a young kid like that," said Ben.

"We used to look back and laugh at the police while we was runnin from 'em," said Lonnie. "But that boy was just too slow."

"Bad luck," said Hector, trying to contribute to the conversation.

"There's the other kind of luck, too," said Chris. "I saw an old friend of mine, earlier tonight. Eight, nine years ago, he was your basic fuckup, just like me. Now Jason's a lawyer, looks like fresh money. And I'm . . ."

"Chris," said Katherine.

"All because he stayed in the SUV," said Chris, "and I got out."

"Who you talkin about, man?" said Lonnie.

"My boy Country." Chris raised his bottle in weak salute. "The one who didn't get out of the Trooper."

No one commented. Chris tipped his head back and killed his beer. Katherine looped her arm though his and touched her thigh to his.

"I'm gonna get something to eat," said Ali, pouring the rest of his beer out onto the grass. "I already broke a promise to my mother. I gotta put some food in my stomach before I drive home."

He walked across the lawn and up the steps to the deck. Thomas Flynn stood before the grill, flipping the last of the burgers. Ali went to him and put a hand on his shoulder, and Flynn took a couple of steps back in mock retreat.

"Don't worry, Mr. Flynn. I don't want anything."

"Not tonight."

"I'm not working tonight. But you know I'm gonna have to come back *to* you."

"That's what you do."

"I can't accomplish anything without folks like you," said Ali. "Anyway, want you to know, I appreciate your patience."

They looked at each other with respect, and Ali reached out and shook Flynn's hand.

"Do a shot with me," said Flynn.

"Nah, I don't mess with that stuff. But thanks."

Flynn pointed his chin out into the yard. "I see Lonnie and his brood made it."

"Lonnie went forth and multiplied."

"What was his friend's name? The one who could never show up for work on time."

"Luther. He's not doing so good."

"They can't all be success stories."

"I know it."

"Last time I saw Luther, I spotted him ten dollars until payday."

"You never want to see Luther again, just give him ten dollars."

Flynn waved his spatula toward the screened-in porch. "Go on, get something to eat."

"Thank you."

Ali headed for the food table, and Flynn poured a shot of Beam. He sipped it, watching his son, his friend Ben, and their girlfriends standing by the fire pit out in the yard. Chris and Ben looked older than their years. He had seen them wearing the shirts they had on tonight many times before. Chris had missed the experience of high school sports, the senior prom, cap-and-gown day, and so much more, and now he was a man too weathered to enjoy his own time. Flynn lowered his head in regret.

"What are you brooding about, Tommy?"

Amanda had appeared at his side.

"Nothin, Amanda."

"I had a nice talk with Katherine earlier."

"Pretty girl."

"Smart, too," said Amanda. "It's obvious she and Chris are in love."

"I'm happy for him."

"You don't look too happy to me."

Flynn drained his shot and placed the glass on the railing. "I was having a quiet moment, is all. Until you interrupted."

"Stop focusing on what Chris isn't and be thankful for the good in him. He's doing fine, Tommy."

"Okay. I'm okay, you're okay."

"And ease up on that bourbon. You still have to make your little speech, remember?"

Flynn picked up the oversize bottle of Beam, still capped, and pretended to swig from it. Then he stumbled broadly across the deck.

"Quit screwin around, Tommy."

"I love you guys," said Flynn, his eyes comically unfocused. "I really fuckin . . . *love* you guys, man."

"Stop it."

"You mean *that* speech?"

"Just stop." Amanda stepped forward and shouted out to the adults and children in the yard. "C'mon, everybody! Come eat before it gets cold!"

Flynn reached out and touched her ass. She swatted his hand away deftly, turned, and quick-stepped toward the screened-in porch.

"WHEN YOU start a company," said Flynn, "you're thinking about yourself. Your wife and kids, maybe, if you're lucky enough to have them. But my point is, you open a business to make money. That's your goal."

Flynn was on the deck, a shot of bourbon in hand. He was no longer acting, but in fact was now half drunk. Amanda stood beside him, concerned, loving, patient, and somewhat proud. He had built the business and earned the floor. For his troubles, he could be sentimental and smashed for one night.

Below them on the grass stood the employees and their companions, looking up at Flynn. Whatever they were feeling, and it ranged from loyalty to indifference, they were paying attention and respect. Some were finishing up their plates of food, some were still drinking, and others were completely sober. Isaac had Maria and his kids close by. The other children were running and playing in the yard.

"What you don't expect, when you get yourself into this, is the feeling of responsibility and affection you get for the people you employ and have the privilege of working with every day. Now, I've had many employees over the years. For most of them, they and their wives and children have been better off and had better lives after coming to work for me. That's quite an accomplishment. It's the one I'm most proud of, you want the truth.

"I'm also very fortunate to be able to work with my family. You know my lovely and extremely capable wife, Amanda." Flynn reached to his side and squeezed Amanda's arm. "And my son, Chris, is an integral part of our installation team. But they're not the only ones I've come to think of as family. I'm thinking of Isaac, of course, who has been with me for a long time. Isaac, you know this company doesn't work without you."

"Thank you, boss," said Isaac, his posture erect.

"But it's all of you, really," said Flynn. "Friends and family are what we're about. Together, we are gonna prosper. When we do a job and do it right . . ."

"It's money for all of us," said Chris under his breath, a rush of affection for his old man washing over his chest.

"It's money for all of us," said Flynn. "I know we've had a little downturn in business this summer. Hell, everybody's taking gas in this economy. That's nothing but a blip on the radar screen. So we didn't make much money this month. But I promise you . . ." Flynn paused dramatically ". . . we will tomorrow."

"Yes!" said Hector, too emphatically.

"Easy, Mary," said Ben.

"*You* Mary," said Hector, with a lopsided smile.

"That's it," said Flynn. "See you at work on Monday."

There was some mild applause as Amanda turned to him, put her hand around his waist, and kissed him on the mouth.

"Damn, I'm good," said Flynn, a lock of black hair falling across his forehead. "Henry at Agincourt had nothin on me."

"Save some of that bravado for the bedroom."

"For real?"

"Yes."

Chris said, "We're taking off." He was standing at the foot of the stairs, watching his parents, waiting for them to finish.

"You're not driving, are you?" said Amanda.

"Katherine is," said Chris. "Don't worry, she barely drank."

"That's one lovely young woman," said Flynn.

Chris nodded. They watched him join his group, saying good-bye to Ali, who was still talking to Lonnie.

"He's the effusive type," said Flynn.

"Come on," said Amanda. "Help me clean up."

Chris, Ben, and their girlfriends walked out of the backyard.

TWO MEN, one large and one small, sat in a black Marquis, parked down Livingston, a good distance from the Flynn home. The old Mercury, though well maintained, was out of place among the late-model imports of Friendship Heights. Sonny Wade and Wayne Minors had not been here long and did not intend to stick around. They had come to check out the business address for Flynn's Floors and were surprised to discover that it was a residential location.

"Party's endin," said Sonny.

"For them it is," said Wayne.

A young white couple and a young black couple moved across the front yard of the colonial and came to a stop near a white work van. It looked like they were about to split up.

"By God, look at the titties on that redhead," said Sonny.

"I'd make a tunnel outta them bad boys," said Wayne.

"And what would you drive through the tunnel?"

"You know what they say about little dudes."

"They got little pricks?"

"Ho," said Wayne.

Sonny picked up a cheap 8 x 21 monocular he had purchased at a surplus store and put it to one eye. "Our gal Mindy said it was a black and a blond, large and young. They're both big. Could be them."

"What you gonna do, walk up and ask 'em?"

"Keep your eyes on the white boy." Sonny handed the monocular to Wayne, picked up his cell from the red velour seat, found the number he was looking for in his contacts, and punched it into the keyboard.

They waited.

"He's answering," said Wayne with a short giggle.

"Hello," said Sonny. "Is Chris Carpet there?"

"Who is this?" Chris's annoyed voice came through the speaker.

Sonny hit "end" and took the monocular back. Looking through it, he said, "Boy's staring at his phone like it's gonna tell him somethin."

"But now he's got your number on the caller ID."

"Why would I give a fuck? He's the thief. He stole from *me*. What's he gonna do, go to the law?"

"Should we follow him to where he's goin?"

"I'm thinking," said Sonny, stroking his walrus mustache.

Katherine took Chris's keys and the two of them got into the white van. Ben and Renee walked toward her black Hyundai, parked up by 41st Street.

"That coon's really got some size on him," said Wayne.

"The white boy looks like a tougher nut, though," said Sonny, squinting. "The way the other one walks, all loose . . . somethin about him says soft to me."

"You know what they say: Cut a tall boofer, he falls like a big tree."

"I got Mr. Carpet's number," said Sonny. "We can get hold of him anytime. Let's follow the black one and see where he goes."

NINETEEN

BEN AND Renee woke up late on Sunday and spent most of the day indoors, lounging, ordering in, and making love. They watched a Martin Lawrence movie that Renee had brought with her and several innings of a Nationals game on cable. Ben walked her to the parking lot in the early evening and kissed her good-bye through the open window of her Hyundai. They had laughed all day and were right for each other in the bedroom. He was thinking that she might be the one.

Ben went back to his apartment. On his nightstand he found a paperback novel, *Blood on the Forge*, that he had been struggling with at first but getting into of late. He rubbed his fingers over the handsome cover. To him, it was like touching gold.

He was challenging himself these days to take on reading material that was a bit more difficult. Ben knew who he was and where he wanted to go. He was never going to be accomplished by society's standards, or rich by anyone's, but he was comfortable with his limitations. For many, life was about the pursuit of status, but it was not so for him. Ben's was all about the quest for knowledge, and his vehicle was books.

He thought of work as a means to acquire food and shelter. Friends and Renee kept him socialized and sane. He tried not to stress on his broken childhood or troubled teens, and mostly managed to steer his mind clear of dark places. He was past that, and looked forward to learning something new every day.

Ben sniffed the short-sleeved Timberland button-down he'd worn the night before, decided that it did not stink, and put it on. He went to the front door and took his keys off a peg bar mounted on the wall. He had his cell, his wallet, and his book, which he had slipped into the back pocket of his jeans.

He left the apartment, crossed the street, and walked along a black iron fence. In the apartment house parking lot, from inside an aging sedan, two men watched.

Ben entered the cemetery gate at Rock Creek Church and Webster, walked down the wide road around the church, and took the very narrow road to the Adams Memorial. As it was a weekend, the memorial had visitors, an elderly couple whose car was parked nearby. Ben moved on, finding a spot atop a stone retaining wall near a large pond. He began to read.

Shadows lengthened as the sun dropped. A Hispanic groundsman finished his edging and, his day done, drove a motorized utility cart up the slope toward the physical plant. A little while later, a security car rolled by, and its driver, a middle-aged gentleman who knew Ben on sight, tapped the face of his wristwatch, telling Ben by signal that it would soon be time to go.

Ben waved at him and held up five fingers. The driver nodded and drove on.

Ben stayed longer than he intended. Though the light was dying, he was at a point in the novel that he could not walk away from. In the book, three black brothers, country boys from the South, had come north to work in the steel mills, and now their fates were being laid bare. Ben was transfixed.

An old black car drove slowly down the road. It came to a

stop near Ben and sat idling like a crow at rest. Ben looked down at the pages of his book. He looked back at the car. The engine had cut off. A big man with a walrus mustache got out of the driver's side, and a small man with wiry tattooed arms and a bushy mustache stepped from the passenger side. The big man, wearing a windbreaker and jeans, looked around, saw no one, and walked toward Ben. Ben put the book down and eased off the stone wall. He stood with discomfort, unsure of what to do or where to put his hands.

As the big man neared him, Ben said, "Somethin I can help you with?"

"I sure hope so." The man drew a semiautomatic pistol from where it was holstered beneath his windbreaker. He pointed the gun at Ben, then waved its barrel toward the old sedan. "In the car."

"I didn't do nothin," said Ben.

"Yes, you did." He waved the barrel in the same direction once again. "Do what I say. Quick."

Ben looked around. It was near dark and no one, visitor or employee, was in sight.

The big man locked back the pistol's hammer. "Run, you got a mind to."

Ben willed himself to walk toward the vehicle. The man with the gun was behind him as the little man opened the passenger door to let Ben in.

"Up front," said the big man.

Ben got in and the door shut after him. In his side vision he saw the big man hand the little man the gun. He heard the little man get into the backseat as the other one settled into the driver's seat.

"Remember this," said the big man. "My friend will shoot you dead."

Ben couldn't speak. He felt the car lurch forward. His fingers dented the red velour seat. They drove slowly through the cemetery, up the hill and around the church. The security vehicle came just as slowly in their direction as the big man deftly went through the gate and pulled out onto Webster Street.

"We just made it," said the little man.

"Yeah, they're about to close that gate." The big man with the high cheekbones looked over at Ben. "What's your name, fella?"

"Ben."

"You can call me Sonny." His smile showed perfect gray teeth.

THEY DROVE around without apparent destination until it was full dark. Ben listened to the random, pointless banter between the two men, much of it concerning female singers, the discussion starting with the merits of their talent and quickly veering off toward cup size. The little one smoked and commented frequently on what he saw out the window. The city and its residents did not please him.

Ben tried to think of the reason for his abduction, and he could not. He had no enemies that he knew of. He'd been straight for a long time, and in his recollection had done no one wrong.

The car stank. His abductors had awful body odor, and Ben suspected that he did, too. He had sweated into his shirt.

At several stoplights he considered jumping out of the Mercury but decided against it, fearing that the little one with the stove-in face would shoot him. He would have to sit here and hope that these two would not harm him. There was nothing else he could see to do.

Sonny caught Ben noticing the shamrock tattoo on the

crook of his hand, wrapped around the fake-fur-covered steering wheel.

"You dig my ink?" said Sonny.

Ben did not answer.

"C'mon, fella. Ain't no need to be silent. We gonna converse, eventually."

They drove south on a downward slope of North Capitol and traveled under the New York Avenue overpass.

"You know what my tattoo is?" said Sonny.

"It's a four-leaf clover," said Ben.

"Why don't no one ever get that?" said the little man.

"It's a shamrock," said Sonny. "Means I'm part of a club."

"He's talkin about the Aryan Brotherhood," said the little man.

"Shut up, stupid," said Sonny. "Let me tell it how I want to."

"My name is not Stupid."

"Shut up, *Wayne*."

Sonny stopped at the red light on K. A panhandling drunk came across the street from the east corner of North Capitol, out of the shadows of a shuttered church. As he neared the driver's side of the Marquis, Sonny turned his head to him and said, "Get your dirty ass gone." The man retreated without a word.

On the green, Sonny turned left onto K Street. They entered an old tunnel with water-stained walls, lit by globe-topped streetlamps. From above, Ben could hear the clomping sound of a train moving on tracks.

"I hope you're not frightened," said Sonny.

"I'm not," said Ben quickly.

"I'm glad you're not," said Sonny. "I want you thinkin clear. We gonna go someplace now and have a quiet conversation. Okay?"

Sonny drove several blocks, hooked a left onto 6th Street, and parked along the curb. They were beside an old, boxy, three-story building surrounded by a chain-link fence, standing out in a residential neighborhood of row homes. Metal security screens and plywood were fitted in its large windows, and a sign announcing the coming of the Ward Six Senior Wellness Center was posted on the south face. Ben had seen buildings such as this, shuttered or laced with creeping ivy, around the city. He guessed that this one, like the others, had once been a school.

"Wait," said Sonny. Two young men were walking down the sidewalk in their direction, talking loudly, and when they had passed, Sonny tossed the keys over the seat to Wayne and said, "Get the things."

Wayne handed Sonny his gun and got out of the car. Sonny kept the gun low and pointed at Ben. The trunk opened, and Ben could hear Wayne ratfucking through it.

Wayne returned and opened the passenger door. He was wearing latex gloves and tossed a pair to Sonny.

"Don't worry," said Sonny, noticing a twitch in Ben's lip and the sweat bulleting his forehead.

"Put your hands behind your back," said Wayne.

Ben looked at Sonny.

"It's all just a pre-caution," said Sonny, fitting the gloves on his hands.

Ben allowed the little man to cuff him. When Sonny was satisfied that the street was clear, Wayne pulled on Ben's arm and brought him out of the car. Wayne locked the Mercury, and the three of them went north on the sidewalk, along the school, whose main entrance faced 6th. Ben made out a naked flagpole mounted over the wide front doors, and big letters that spelled out "Hayes School."

"Round the side," said Sonny. Wayne pushed on a gate that had been padlocked but was open because its chain had been severed by a pair of cutters, now in the Mercury's trunk. Ben moved off the sidewalk and walked onto the asphalt and weeds of the property.

"Hey," said Ben. He was encouraged by the sound of his own voice, and he screamed, "Hey!"

Wayne jumped up and punched him behind the ear. Ben stumbled, and Sonny grabbed his left arm and righted him.

"That wasn't smart," said Sonny. "Now, you just relax."

From a nearby porch, out front of one of the houses on 6th, Ben heard someone laugh.

They went to the north face of the school, out of the glow of streetlamps. There were two windows on the ground floor covered by heavy wire screen, and one in the center holding a square of plywood painted white. Wayne removed the plywood, which he had kicked in earlier that day. Ben saw only complete darkness there and in fear he turned away from it, but Sonny spun him and pushed him from behind. As Ben fell into the room, it was illuminated, slightly, by the beam of a mini Maglite held in Wayne's hand. Wayne moved the flashlight beam and it hit on eyes that glowed. Ben heard the fluttering of clawed feet and saw animals, big as cats, scatter back into the shadows. His stomach dropped.

"Rats gotta live someplace, too," said Sonny.

Wayne used his butane lighter to put fire to candles pushed into the necks of beer bottles placed in a circular shape on the concrete floor. A child's chair with a plastic seat and steel legs was set in the center of the circle. As the old classroom revealed itself, Sonny gestured to the chair and said, "That's for you."

Wayne refitted the plywood to the frame as Sonny helped

Ben down into the chair. Its seat was small, and Ben had to rest on the edge of it to accommodate his arms, cuffed behind his back. His rolled his shoulders to alleviate the ache in his neck. He saw a bottle of water standing on the floor and he licked his parched lips.

"I know it's uncomfortable," said Sonny, standing before him. Sonny picked up the bottle, drank from it, then placed the bottle back on the floor. "So let's get this over with and we'll all go home."

Wayne moved through the light and crouched down on one knee, half of him in darkness. Then he stood and moved beside the chair. Ben did not look at him. He focused on the big man. He seemed to be reasonable and he was the one in charge.

"You know that thing I told you 'bout my tat?" said Sonny. "You ride with the rock, you take a blood oath to the Aryan Brotherhood. Well, I didn't take no oath. I put this ink on after I got out the federal joint. If any genuine AB saw me carryin it, he'd cut my throat. I just put it on my hand to make an impression with folks that need to get a certain message. Like Mindy Kramer. You know her, don't you, Ben?"

Ben's eyes betrayed him, and Sonny chuckled low.

"Course you do." Sonny shifted his weight from one foot to the other. "I wasn't bad enough to be Aryan Brotherhood. I'm not ashamed to say it. I don't even *sub*-scribe to their notions of race. I don't hate African American people. Want you to know that. This here ain't got nothin to do with the color of your skin. Truth is, the modern Aryan Brotherhood ain't even about hatin blacks, Mexicans, or Jews. It's about power, money, and control. Now, Wayne here, he does have a bit of a problem with, what's that they call it, *people of color*. Wayne wanted to get in, but they don't let itty-bitty boys like him into the club. I'm a big man, as you can see, but I look like queer bait next to them ABs. They are some big specimens. They're honest-to-god animals, Ben."

"Can I get a drink of water?" said Ben.

"Not just yet," said Sonny. "To finish my point: Me and Wayne were just cogs in the machine at Lewisburg. We did favors for the bad boys. Runnin errands and such. They called our kind peckerwoods."

"They called *you* it," said Wayne.

"Not that I wasn't capable of doing bad things," said Sonny. "Wayne, too. Got to give it to my little friend, because he can be fierce. But I wasn't interested in that power thing. I only wanted to have what I worked for. I like a roll of folding money in my pocket, and when I get it I expect to keep it. Do you understand?"

"Yes."

"I *had* some money," said Sonny. "Fifty thousand dollars, give or take. Me and an associate, fella named Leslie Hawkins, took off four jewelry stores in the Baltimore area over the course of, I don't know, five or six months. Wasn't any kind of trick to it. You put a gun up in someone's face, they gonna give you what you askin for. I was a young man at the time, about your age, and I had a kind of energy comin off me that was very convincing. The Jews and the slopes who we were robbin, they knew we meant business. Me and Hawk, we made over a hundred grand on those jobs after we fenced it out. I gave him half, even though the only thing he did was drive a car. And it was all clean. I wore a mask when I was workin, a hood with cutout eyes, like a hangman's bag. So the cameras didn't pick up on shit. The problem wasn't that the law knew who I was. The problem was Leslie Hawkins. I should have known better than to partner up with a man had a girl's name."

"Please," said Ben, sweat stinging his eyes. "Can I get some water?"

"When I'm done," said Sonny. "Hawkins got pulled over one night by a state trooper for a busted taillight. Leslie panicked and booked, thinking they had made his vehicle from the robberies. Led the police on one of those high-speed chases you see on the tee-vee, and of course he got caught. Dumbass had his share of the money in the trunk of the car. He spilled soon as they got him into a room. Hawkins put me in for the robberies. That wasn't no surprise. Through the underworld telegraph, I'd heard he got picked up, and I figured it was just a matter of time before the law got around to me. So I went to visit my uncle, who lived here in D.C."

"Hot in here, ain't it?" said Wayne.

"It is stuffy," said Sonny, and he removed his windbreaker and tossed it aside. The semiautomatic was holstered in a leather rig looped over his shoulder and chest.

"I need a drink," said Ben, desperation entering his voice.

"My uncle came from the same place I do," said Sonny, ignoring the request. "What passes for mountain country, way up in Maryland. Ever been there, Ben?"

"No."

"Well, my uncle had one of those alternative lifestyles, and they don't exactly tolerate that kind of thing up there. So he moved down here to the city, got a job managing a fancy furniture store, had a partner for a while, bought a house. Carved out a nice life for himself. I never had no problem with him or who he was. Matter of fact, I loved him. Now that he's gone, makes me feel a little bad that I buried my money without his knowledge in that library-slash-den of his before I got arrested. He died while I was in the joint, and then his home went to auction. But I won't go on about it. You know the rest. *Don't you, fella.*"

"I didn't take that money," said Ben.

Sonny drew the gun from its holster. It was an S&W .45 with a black grip and a stainless steel slide and body. Sonny worked the slide and dropped a round into the chamber. He squinted as he inspected the gun.

"Shaved numbers," said Sonny. "I reckon I'm in big trouble if they pick me up."

Wayne laughed.

"Plus, I'm a parole violator," said Sonny. "I haven't reported to my supervisor but one time since I got out. Never did pee in no cup. I just left and picked up Wayne, my old cell mate, and came straight down to War-shington via West Virginia to get my money. Imagine my surprise when I found out that my money is gone."

"I didn't take it."

"Yeah, I'm in a world of trouble if I cross paths with the law." Sonny stepped close to Ben. The flames from the candles reflected in his black, empty eyes. "But I don't care. I want you to know it. I plain don't give a fuck."

"I saw it," said Ben. "It was in an old gym bag. But I didn't take it."

"'Scuse me if I can't believe that."

"We left it there."

"You mean, you and your partner, Chris. The both of you."

"That's right," said Ben, holding Sonny's stare. "We saw it, but we left it where it was at. Someone broke into that house after and took it. I know because we had to go back and fix the carpet."

"It wasn't you. It was someone else."

"Yes."

"So you told someone 'bout the money."

"No," said Ben.

Sonny cocked back the hammer of the gun and locked it in place. He touched the barrel to the corner of Ben's eye. Ben turned his head, and Sonny pressed the tip of the barrel tighter to his flesh.

"Liar," said Sonny. "I'm only gonna ask you one more time. Who took my money?"

"I . . . don't know."

Sonny held the gun in place. Ben heard clawed feet gaining purchase on concrete, and a scampering sound. He closed his eyes.

"I was wrong about you," said Sonny, standing straight, dropping the gun to his side. He took several steps back. "I thought you was a soft one. I guess now I'll have to talk to your friend Chris. 'Cause you damn sure ain't gonna talk. Makes me think you got the code of the jailhouse in you. You ever done time, Ben?"

"Juvenile," said Ben softly.

"Me, too," said Sonny. "They had me up in that boy's reformatory in Sabillasville. I wasn't so bad when I went in. But they cured me of any goodness I had by the time I came out. That's what that place did for me. It made me well."

"I'm thirsty."

"I know it, fella." Sonny holstered his gun. "Wayne?"

Wayne's tattooed arm arced into the light. Ben gasped as he saw the blade swing toward him, and his eyes crossed as the knife pierced his chest and entered his heart.

The force of the blow knocked Ben off the chair. Wayne stood over him and with his face contorted, he grunted and came down with the knife, rabbit-punching, stabbing Ben's torso, his abdomen, his neck. Ben writhed and cried out, and Wayne did not stop. Ben went into shock, and chopping sounds filled the room as Wayne worked on.

"Wayne," said Sonny.

Wayne stood, spent with exhaustion. His latex gloves and forearms were dark with blood. The front of his T-shirt was soaked with it. Bloodied hair had fallen about his face.

"He ain't nothin now," said Wayne, his eyes bright. "Is he, Sonny? *Is* he."

"You did end him," said Sonny. "Get his wallet and cell if he has one. Seal this shithole up and I'll meet you out at the car."

Ten minutes later, Wayne Minors crept out of the shadows of the school property, opened the gate, and looped its padlock and chain through the links of the fence so that it appeared to have been undisturbed.

On the street, Sonny Wade sat patiently behind the wheel of his Mercury, waiting for his little friend.

TWENTY

CHRIS FLYNN stopped by Ben's apartment house on Monday morning, as he usually did, to pick him up for work. Normally, as Chris neared Ben's place, he gave him a heads-up via cell or, if they couldn't connect in that manner, through a text message. But Ben had replied to neither, so Chris got out of the van, walked into the building, and knocked on Ben's door. He tried it the soft way and even gave it the cop knock, but there was no response.

Heading back to the parking lot, he phoned Renee.

"Ben over there?" he said.

"Uh-uh," said Renee. Her voice was raspy, and Chris assumed that he had woken her up. "He stayed at his place last night. We were together all afternoon."

"You haven't spoke to him since?"

"I called him late to say good night, but he didn't pick up."

"Well, he's not in his apartment," said Chris. "Either that or he's in bed and not answering the door. Not answering his cell, either."

"Ben wouldn't do you like that." After a pause Renee said, "Now you got me worried."

"He'll turn up," said Chris.

"Call me when you hook up with him. I'll text him soon as we cut off, and if he gets back to me I'll hit you up."

"Okay, Renee. Thanks."

Chris called his father. He briefly considered telling him that Ben had phoned in sick, but he decided to be truthful, take the hit, and say that Ben was MIA.

"This is bad," said Thomas Flynn. "You've got two jobs today."

"I know."

"Why would he do this to us? To *you*."

"We don't know that he's done anything. You should wait to speak to him before you pass judgment."

"Thanks for the lecture. But see, I'm trying to run a business. If he went out and overdid it, and now he's got the Irish flu, that's not something I can excuse."

"You don't know that. He could have taken a walk and got hit by a car. Could be he's lying in a hospital bed right now, somethin like that."

"If you think so, then maybe you ought to call the police."

"No," said Chris, too quickly. "I don't think we need to go there just yet."

"Fine. You better get on out to the warehouse, then. I'll pull Hector off Isaac's crew, and the two of you can work today's jobs."

"Okay, Dad. Okay."

Chris stood by the white cargo van but didn't get in right away. Ben had no relatives that Chris knew of, and a small circle of friends. It was possible that Lawrence Newhouse had got up with him and they had been clubbing, drinking, or drugging, spending some of the money Lawrence had stolen. Chris would be disappointed in Ben if that were the case, but it was understandable. Ben was a young man, and maybe he was still bitter about having left the cash in the row house and wanted to try some of it out. Chris didn't know how to get up with Lawrence and he really didn't care to. But Ali would find a way to reach Lawrence. And it could be that Ali had heard from Ben.

Chris phoned Ali and had a brief conversation. Later in the day, while Chris was doing an install, Ali reached him on his cell and told him that he had spoken to Lawrence, who claimed he hadn't seen or heard from Ben.

Chris and Hector finished the job. Hector was animated as always, moving quickly while he talked, humming and making jokes. Chris worked quietly, with a gathering sense of dread.

THAT EVENING, Amanda stood in the kitchen and listened as Flynn spoke to their son from their house phone. Amanda could hear the impatience in her husband's voice, and noted the way he cradled the receiver a little too roughly at the end of the conversation.

"He went by Ben's apartment with Renee," said Flynn. "She's got a key. Ben's stuff is intact. Doesn't look like he packed up anything or took a trip."

"Chris is worried," said Amanda.

"Yeah, he's worried. But he doesn't want to call the police. It's partly because he doesn't know what Ben is into. Could be, you involve the law, you're gonna get the young man in trouble. But there's that other thing, too. These guys, with their histories, they've got that code. They don't like to give up information, and the last person they want to talk to is a police officer."

"Do you think Ben's done something wrong?"

"I don't think of him as a guy who holes up in a motel room

with an eight-ball and a couple of whores, if that's what you mean."

"I don't think of him that way, either."

"So I should probably call the police myself. Report him as a missing person."

"That means they're going to come here and take a statement. His past might come up in the course of the conversation. Chris's, too."

"It might. If they've done nothing wrong, then it's not a problem, right?"

"Right," said Amanda, without conviction.

"Look, Ben is my responsibility. More than anyone else who works for me, this company is his only family. Do you get that?"

"Yes."

"Do me a favor and go down to the office and pull his file, okay? I'm gonna need the information at hand."

Flynn punched a number into the phone as she left the room.

MONDAY HAD brought tension, but Tuesday was worse. Renee called in sick to the nail salon, and Chris's installations were completed in a satisfactory but perfunctory manner. Even Hector, for a change, was subdued.

Flynn had reported Ben as a missing person to the MPD, but he knew from his brief experience that they would be busy with crimes of the here-and-now and would not actively investigate his disappearance, which, after all, could be nothing more than a young man gone out of town. Ben would be just another name added to a database, the daily sheets, and eventually the missing persons Web site.

From Chris, Flynn learned that Ben often haunted the

Adams Memorial in Rock Creek Cemetery. Because he had been in Brookland doing an estimate on his last call of the day, Flynn decided to stop by the cemetery grounds on his way home on the chance that he might speak to someone who was on duty Sunday or find something of importance.

In the main office, near the front gate, he was directed to the office of security, where he found a middle-aged man who had been on patrol Sunday evening past. This man, a Mr. Mallory, said that he knew Ben as described by sight but not to name, and that he had seen him sitting on the retaining wall near the pond, reading, and that he had indicated by signal that the cemetery would be closing and that Ben should prepare to leave. Mr. Mallory had not seen him go and could recall no suspicious visitors or unlawful activity for the remainder of the night.

Flynn thanked him and drove down to the pond. There he found a copy of a book called *Blood on the Forge*, still wet from a late-afternoon thunderstorm typical to Washington summers, face-up on the stone wall. Inside the cover, Ben had printed his full name.

Flynn called the police, used the case number as reference, and reported his discovery to a nameless listener with an uninterested voice. He then phoned Chris and told him what he had found. Chris agreed that Ben would not have left his book behind, even if he were done with it. Chris did not tell his father that he was certain now that something bad had come to Ben. That night, Chris drove the streets, looking for his friend.

ON WEDNESDAY morning, three brothers, Yohance, Ade, and Baba Brown, residents of the neighborhood of Trinidad and all under twelve years old, were walking south from their row house with a bat, one mitt, and a tennis ball, looking for someplace to play, when they came upon the old Hayes School at 6th and K, Northeast, now fenced in and shuttered. They saw the possibilities in the broad north face of the building and its weeded blacktop, and went to the gate to see if they could find a way to dismantle its Master padlock. To their delight they found that the chain had been severed and by unthreading it through the links of the fence, they could simply walk onto the school grounds.

They played stickball against a wall where a rusted sign reading "No Ball Playing" was anchored into brick. They commented on the putrid smell of the area around the school, accusing one another of incomplete wipes and dirty asses, but played on because they had found a spot where they could throw hard, swing freely, and enjoy a summer day.

Around eleven o'clock, the youngest of the brothers, Yohance Brown, noticed that the white-painted square of plywood covering the middle window of the first floor was fitted poorly and askew. He used the bat to push the plywood and watched it fall into the dark of the room beyond. Immediately the awful smell that they had been commenting on hit them full force. Because they were boys, the three of them had to know, and they stepped into the space, now faintly illuminated by sunlight, and, holding the bat as a club, the oldest brother, Baba, led them to where hundreds of flies buzzed deeply and furry rodents scrambled back into the shadows, leaving a thing that had once been a man lying in the center of the concrete floor. What they saw would trouble them into adulthood and haunt the youngest for the rest of his life.

Five minutes later, a 1D patrolman named Jack Harris drove his cruiser east on K and saw a boy run into the street, his arms waving, horror and excitement in his eyes.

*   *   *

SERGEANT SONDRA Bryant, a homicide detective in her midforties with almost twenty in, was on the bubble when the body was found, and caught the case. She did not jump up from the seat behind her desk, located in the offices of the Violent Crime Branch behind a shopping center in Southeast. She was a slow, deliberate mover anyway, what with the extra weight she was carrying these days in her hips, belly, and behind. Sondra Bryant was known as a good detective, intuitive and conscientious, as she liked to put down cases for the white shirts and her own pride. But she was in no hurry to get to the crime scene. The victim had been dead for a couple of days. Her thought was to let the techs do their scene work, and meet them on the tail end of their task.

After speaking to two of her children on the phone and attending to a personal item, she got up out of her chair and headed out to find a car in the back lot that she could use. She went by a medium-size detective with a black mustache and a good chest, who was standing in his cubicle, a dead telephone receiver in his hand, staring down at his desk.

"Your kids again?" said Bryant.

"My son," said the detective. "My wife found some marijuana in his bedroom. A package of Black and Milds, too."

"No stroke mags?"

"Those are under my bed."

"Could be worse. She could have found a gun or a kilo of somethin white."

"I know that. I'm just disappointed, I guess."

"It'll pass."

The detective looked at Bryant, carrying her oversize purse, her badge on a chain around her neck. "You caught one?"

"I'm the primary. Kids came up on a body in the old Hayes School. Wanna ride along?"

"No, thanks. I'll send DeSchlong down when he comes back."

"You busy with something?"

"I'm gonna go to the boys' room and practice looking hard in the mirror, so I'm ready to talk to my son when I get home."

"Good luck, Gus."

"You, too."

Detective Bryant drove a maroon Impala to the school in Northeast. She ducked the crime tape, then spoke briefly to Jack Harris, the first officer on the scene, and to the three young brothers, who had been detained for her arrival. She entered the opening in the north wall of the school and held a handkerchief to her face as she had a look at the body, which was being attended to by a Mobile Crime Lab tech named Karen Krissoff, wearing a surgical mask and a smudge of Vaseline under her nose. Portable lights had been set up in the room, and flies buzzed and moved through the blasts of white.

"Karen."

"Sondra."

"How long's he been here?"

"Won't know till we get him back to the ME. The heat and the rats didn't do us any favors. Neither did the flies."

"Cause of death?"

"Multiple stab wounds, so far. Marks on the wrists indicate he was bound or cuffed."

"Any identification?"

"No wallet, no cell, no business cards."

"I need prints on the deceased."

"I already got 'em and sent them out."

"Thanks, Karen."

"Go get some fresh air."

Sondra Bryant went back outside and met up with Detective Joseph DeLong, who had come to assist her. DeLong, known as "DeSchlong" in the unit just because, was an affable fellow who worked many overtime hours after a divorce had left him lonely and rather helpless. Bryant and DeLong split the east and west sides of the street between K and L and canvassed the residents of the houses. This took a couple of hours. Bryant then drove over to the 3500 block of V Street, NE, to the Crime Scene Examination complex. Because of Ben Braswell's priors, there had been a hit on his prints.

Bryant sat at a computer station and typed Ben's name into the WACIES program, which brought up his profile. His father was unknown and his mother had been dead since he was two years old. He had no known relatives or known accomplices. She read his charges, convictions, and history of juvenile incarceration. She then switched programs and searched the missing-persons database, and her hunch came up aces. The man who had reported him missing, a Thomas Flynn, was identified as his employer.

Sondra Bryant picked up the phone.

THOMAS FLYNN took the call. He listened intently, asked a few questions, and told the detective that his son, Chris, was the person closest to Ben. He mentioned Ali Carter and told her the name of the place where Ali worked and the nature of his business. He told her that Ben had a girlfriend named Renee. He agreed to meet with Sondra Bryant later that night and have Chris in attendance. Flynn would supply Renee's full name and contact information, which he could get from Chris, when Bryant arrived. He was trying to be as cooperative as possible.

Amanda stood beside him, tears streaming down her face, when Flynn phoned Chris at his apartment. After he gave his son the news and told him the few details he knew, there was a long pause on the other end of the line. When he spoke, Chris's voice was even.

"I'll call Ali," said Chris. "Me and Katherine will go over to Renee's place. I think we should tell her in person. Then I'll swing by your house and talk to the detective."

"You okay?"

"Yeah."

"Chris, I need to ask you . . . I promise I'm only going to ask you this one time."

"I don't know anything, Dad. I don't know why Ben was killed."

"I'll see you in a little while. Take care."

When Flynn hung up, Amanda said, "How is he?"

"Same as ever," said Flynn unhappily. "Tough."

Flynn phoned his friend, the attorney Bob Moskowitz.

AFTER CHRIS spoke with Ali and Katherine, they agreed to go to-gether to Renee's apartment on Queens Chapel Road, not far from the District line. Chris and Katherine met Ali in the park-ing lot, and they steeled themselves before going inside. Pre-dictably, Renee became hysterical upon hearing the news of Ben's violent death. Thankfully, her mother was there, so Chris, Ali, and Katherine were not entirely helpless in the face of the young woman's loud outbursts of emotion. Her mother, a de-voted churchgoer with a quiet manner, had sedatives in her purse for whatever reason, and gave one to Renee. Chris hugged her on the living-room couch for a long while, Renee sobbing and shaking in his arms. After a while her breathing evened out and she lay down there, her mother sitting by her side. Chris, Katherine, and Ali quietly left the apartment house.

"I gotta go speak to the homicide detective," said Chris to Ali, standing by their cars in the lot. "Lady named Bryant. I expect she's gonna get up with you, too."

"She already called me," said Ali. "I'm hooking up with her first thing in the morning."

"You might want to put her up with Lawrence."

"You think—"

"I don't think anything. Lawrence was with Ben recently. That's all."

"Listen," said Ali, "I've got to go to a funeral tomorrow in Northeast. Boy I was working with who didn't make it. I figure you're not going in. . . ."

"I'm not."

"Come with me, Chris. I don't feel like being alone tomorrow."

"All right. Swing past when you're done with the detective."

They gave each other backward glances as they walked to their vehicles. Chris joined Katherine, waiting for him in the van.

THOMAS AND Chris Flynn sat in the living room of the Flynns' home with Detective Sondra Bryant and Bob Moskowitz. Bryant had a small notebook in hand and was making notes in it with a Parker pen. Amanda and Katherine were in the kitchen, quietly talking. Django was asleep at Chris's feet.

Bryant had remarked that it was unusual for an interviewee

who was not a suspect to ask for the presence of a lawyer at this point in the process. Thomas Flynn was forthright and told her that his son and Ben had been incarcerated together as juveniles at Pine Ridge, that both had led straight and productive lives since, but that the scars of the experience made Chris extremely cautious about speaking with police.

"I get it," said Bryant. "All right, Mr. Moskowitz. Is it okay for me to speak with your client?"

"Chris will answer any questions you have," said Moskowitz, who had found diet religion and was now a slim bald man nearing fifty whose suit was too large for his frame.

Bryant asked Chris a series of questions. He answered a bit robotically and with little eye contact but did so to her satisfaction. He had a hard exterior, but she could see from his red-rimmed eyes that he had cried at some point in the evening and was grieving. He obviously came from a good family, or at least one that was intact. She believed that he had no direct involvement in his friend's murder and felt, with a lesser degree of certainty, that he had no knowledge of the causes or circumstances surrounding Ben Braswell's death. But she was unconvinced by Chris's repeated claim that Ben had no enemies and had done nothing wrong.

"I had a look at Ben's record," said Sondra Bryant. "There was an incidence of violence at Pine Ridge that kept him incarcerated for a longer period time than was indicated by his original conviction."

"That was an accident," said Chris. "Ben was just defending someone. He wasn't trying to hurt anybody. That kind of thing wasn't in him."

"Maybe the boy he hurt had relatives or friends who didn't see it that way."

"No," said Chris. "This wasn't a revenge thing. Everybody liked Ben."

"Somebody didn't." Bryant had a sip of water and placed her glass back on the table. She looked at Thomas Flynn. "I know this is difficult. May I speak freely?"

"Go ahead," said Flynn.

"We have a saying in our offices. A gun murder is often business. Killing by knife is almost always personal. This victim was stabbed, many, many times. He had been cuffed or had his hands tied. It's possible he was tortured."

"Ben didn't do anything to anybody," said Chris very quietly.

"I believe he's answered the question, Detective Bryant," said Moskowitz.

"Right." Bryant closed her notebook and dropped it into her purse. "We'll speak again. In the meantime, I'll leave you good people and let you have some peace. Have a blessed evening."

"You do the same," said Thomas Flynn.

He and Moskowitz walked her outside. Moskowitz was seeking a few words with her away from Chris, and Flynn intended to ask about the procedure involved in the release of Ben's body. He wanted to know how he could get authorization to gain possession of it.

Chris stayed in the living room, rubbing behind Django's ear. Soon Katherine joined him, kissed his mouth, and sat close to him on the couch.

When Flynn reentered the house, he went to his bar cart in the dining room and poured himself several fingers of Jim Beam. He killed the drink quickly and poured another. He saw Amanda looking at him from the kitchen.

"What?"

"Easy with that," said Amanda.

Flynn tipped his head back and drank.

Out on the street, far down Livingston from the Flynn home, two men sat in an old black Mercury. They were waiting for the man called Chris to emerge from the house that doubled as the business office for Flynn's Floors. They intended to follow him. They wanted to see where he lived.

TWENTY-ONE

THE FUNERAL service for Royalle Foreman, nineteen, was held at a large Baptist church on Nannie Helen Burroughs Avenue in Burrville, in the 50s in far Northeast. Ali and Chris arrived early, pulled into the parking lot, and sat in Juanita Carter's black Saturn, letting the air conditioner run. They talked about Ali's conversation with Detective Bryant earlier that morning, and they spoke fondly and bitterly about Ben. They were in no hurry to get out and stand in the summer heat by the front door of the church, where a line had already formed.

"Looks like it's gonna be full," said Chris.

"Royalle touched a lot of people," said Ali. "He played football for Ballou before he dropped out, and he shined. That right there gets you some positive notoriety. He had a charming smile on him, and he was funny. People *liked* Royalle."

"What happened?"

"The usual. Peers pulling him down. No one at home strong enough to keep his head in the books or tell him to stay indoors at night. He was a repeat offender. Possession first, then sales. Nonviolent stuff, but after multiples they're gonna lock you up. He did a little time with the hard boys out at Pine

Ridge. Did a second jolt on a parole violation, and that set him up with new contacts and problems. I was tryin to work with him, and I did find him some employment. I had him with this auto body dude I know, as an apprentice. But Royalle couldn't stay out his own way. He had some kind of long-standing beef with someone, over a girl. Last Saturday night a car, three deep, rolled up on him in while he was walkin to his aunt's house, where he stayed. He took one in the neck and bled out right on the sidewalk. Another bullet had eyes for a row house window. Kids in there had the presence of mind to get down on the floor when they heard the first pops."

"City kids learn young," said Chris. "The police know who did it?"

"No witnesses. I'm guessing that some of the young men at this funeral know who was in that car, and who the shooter was. But they won't talk to the police."

"They're gonna settle it themselves."

"No doubt," said Ali. "You know, I went to court and pled for lenience on behalf of Royalle before they sent him back to the Ridge a second time. I was tryin to get him into this charter high school they have now, where the kids eat and sleep on the premises."

"Like a boarding school?"

"Exactly. Gets the boys out of their environment but doesn't put them into a prison environment. Judge wouldn't listen. I guess he was reading those editorials in the newspaper about how the juvenile justice system is letting too many bad kids back out on the street. You know, 'I grew up black and poor, and now I'm a professional journalist. You have to be extra tough on these boys and keep them locked up. I made it; why can't they?' All that bullshit. No question, some boys, the gunmen and killers, they do need to be jailed and off the street.

But Royalle wasn't one of those boys. Juvenile prison just kept him low."

"They're letting them in," said Chris, watching the line move.

"Yeah, let's go."

They walked across the parking lot, now nearly full. Chris and Ali wore sport jackets over open-necked shirts and jeans, in the medium range of dress for those who had come to the funeral. The majority of the attendees were young, some in suits, others in T-shirts bearing Royalle Foreman's likeness with mentions of love, the Lord, heaven, and RIP.

In the lobby, Chris took a program and looked up at the memorial wall adorned with more than a hundred photographs of deceased teenagers and young adults from across the city, victims of shootings and other violent acts. Ali tugged on Chris's jacket, and the two of them walked into the sanctuary, where female ushers were handing out Kleenex and paper fans to sweating mourners. A large video screen was set up behind the pulpit and altar, and on it was the image of Royalle Foreman lying in an open casket. Gospel music played through a PA system. A receiving line had formed, and a woman in it was crying loudly.

A minister stood in the pulpit and leaned into a lectern's microphone. "Please turn off your cell phones. And please, let me remind you, there is no drinking in the parking lot."

Chris stood in a pew beside Ali. He closed his eyes and said a silent prayer. He was not religious, but he felt, in an uncomplicated way, that there had to be something higher, some reason that he and the people he loved were here and alive, and others had been taken. In his mind he saw Ben, a dog beside him, both of them walking in a field, the dog's tail switching back and forth, Ben smiling. It should have made Chris happy to envision his friend this way. But instead his thoughts went to violence, and he found that he was no longer speaking to God but fantasizing about murdering the men who had murdered Ben.

"No," said Chris very softly.

Not in church.

ALI HAD an appointment to meet with Ken Young, the most recent director of the District's Department of Youth Rehabilitation Services, and Reginald Roberts, the superintendent of Pine Ridge. Because it was Young's day to visit Pine Ridge, Ali had planned to meet them both out there. Chris, after a bit of prodding from Ali, agreed to come along. He knew that Ali wanted company. Also, he did not want to go back to his apartment and be alone with his thoughts.

They drove out to Anne Arundel County in Maryland. The facility was less than thirty miles from the city, but it was country, with stretches of highway running past woods, the occasional new housing community, warehouses, government agencies, and company headquarters. It felt a world away.

Ali turned off the two-lane and went down a long road that wound back into more country and dense stands of trees. Chris felt a sense of dread creep up on him. He wondered if Ali, who made the trek out here regularly, still felt it, too.

"No pines," said Chris.

"None that I ever seen," said Ali.

They passed the site of the new facility, which was close to completion. A Democratic senator from Maryland had fought the building of it, as had representatives of neighboring residential communities, arguing that the D.C. jail for youths should be located in the District of Columbia, but they had failed, and construction had gone on as planned.

"Ken Young put some of the boys to work on the crews here," said Ali. "A lot of it was straight labor, but a few of them apprenticed with tradesmen and carpenters. When they get out, they'll have skills. The new facility is gonna have a wood-working shop in it."

"What about private showers?"

"That, too. The housing units are gonna be more like dorms than bunkers."

"Where'd this guy Young come from?"

"Some big city with problems like ours. The mayor found him. He had years of experience implementing what they call the 'Missouri model' for juvenile rehabilitation. Basically, it stresses nurturing over hard punishment. Preparing these boys to succeed, playing to their strengths and interests rather than keeping them low. Bunch of states have picked up on it. It's not cheap, but it pays off later on, when you've got fewer boys graduating to adult prisons."

"Young must have enemies."

"They talk about the negative impact on the community when you let jailed boys out and put them under supervision. But when you lock up kids without looking at other alterna-tives, you *destroy* communities. There's gonna be some failures, naturally. But there's gonna be some success stories, too."

Ali parked in the lot among cars belonging to guards and administration. They walked along the link-and-razor-wire fence to the gatehouse. As if on cue, clouds had moved in, and inside the fence the palette was gray. *This is how I remember it,* thought Chris. *This is how it always seemed to me.*

They passed through the security office of the gatehouse. Ali had called ahead and had Chris's name added to the visitors list. Then they were inside the fence and moving toward the ad-ministrative offices, weeds and dirt beneath their feet. A group of boys were walking from one building to another, accompanied by a couple of guards. One of the boys chopped another in the back of the neck while the guards weren't looking.

"Knuckleheads," said Chris.

"That ain't never gonna change," said Ali.

"They don't make them walk with one hand grabbing their wrist behind their back anymore."

"Young stopped that, too. I mean, shoot, they're caged up in here. Where they supposed to go?"

They met Reginald Roberts, Pine Ridge's latest superintendent, in his office. Roberts had modest height, a bodybuilder's physique, and wore his hair in braids. He was a reform warden, handpicked by Ken Young. Young was tall, thin, middle-aged, and shaggy haired, unable to stay seated, with the kind of nervous energy that kept him standing next to the wall. Roberts took a seat behind his desk, and Chris and Ali settled into chairs before him.

"Chris here is a Pine Ridge alumnus," said Ali. "I've spoken of him before."

"Good to finally meet you, Chris," said Young. "Ali also told me that your father has employed some of our graduates."

"He's tried," said Chris.

"We appreciate it," said Roberts.

"I'm sorry for the loss of your friend," said Young. "Ali mentioned this morning that the two of you were tight. I read about his death in the paper."

"The whole paragraph?" said Chris.

"Ali says that all three of y'all were together out here," said Roberts.

"Unit Five," said Ali.

"I closed that one," said Young.

"Anyway," said Roberts. He pushed a manila folder across

the desk toward Ali, who picked it up. "Let's talk about these boys right here."

For the next half hour they discussed inmates who were about to come out, either released to their families or to residential treatment centers. Ali reported on the progress of several young men and talked about others who were struggling and might be headed back into the facility.

"You might want to make a bed up for William Richards," said Ali.

"When he was in he talked about culinary school," said Roberts.

"Half the boys say that," said Young. "When you ask them what they're gonna do, it's the most popular response. 'I'm about to go to culinary school.' "

"We're gonna graduate a lot of chefs," said Roberts.

"There's always McDonald's," said Ali. "That's one way to start."

"Coupla years ago the big thing was barber college," said Young. "I had this one kid, Morris Weeks, said in his last level meeting that he wanted to go to 'haircut academy.' He had just got off punishment for cold-cocking a guard. I said to him, 'Morris, who's gonna put a scissors in your hand when you're always acting so violent?' "

"Boy learned, though," said Roberts.

"He did," said Young. "Morris got a chair in a shop on Georgia and Piney Branch Road."

When they were done, Ali and Chris shook hands with Reginald Roberts.

"Walk with me, guys," said Ken Young.

They left the building and headed toward another. Chris could see the basketball court, its pole and backboard standing out in the field.

"That rusted old hoop," said Chris.

"We're gonna have a nice court in the new place," said Young.

They entered the school building and walked through its halls. Guards were standing outside the doors of the classrooms, all with handsets. Many nodded perfunctorily at Young and a few gave him more genuine greetings as they passed. Down the hall, an inmate, his arm pinned up behind him, was being pushed out the exit door by two guards.

"Who's that?" said Young to a burly guard wearing a Cowboys ball cap. "Is it Jerome?"

"Yeah, that boy swung on Bobby."

"Take him out and let him cool down."

"That's what we're doin, Mr. Young." Chris saw the guard roll his eyes slightly at the guard beside him.

They walked on. The colors of the walls were brighter than Chris remembered. Paintings done by inmates were pinned up on bulletin boards.

"We've got a new foundation running the school," said Young, seeing surprise on Chris's face. "New teachers. The classes are smaller because I have fewer numbers in lockup. Almost sixty percent of the boys here are Tier One, the high-security youth. Only about ten percent are low security. The majority of the kids committed to the DYRS are in their homes or in residential treatment. They don't belong in cells."

"I see you got them doin art," said Ali.

"Yeah, and there's a literary magazine. We even put on a Shakespeare play for officials at city hall. And I had some boys hook up with AmeriCorps, went down to Mississippi to rebuild some homes after Katrina. I'm trying everything."

"Some of those guards didn't look too happy to see you."

"We call them youth development specialists now," said

Young. "They don't like that, either. Matter of fact, a lot of them wouldn't piss on me if I was running down the street on fire. The union reps gave me and Reginald a vote of no confidence, tried to have us fired. And they've fought to retain abusive or incompetent guards that I've let go."

"I read all that stuff on the op-ed page," said Ali. "Their solution is to, what, keep kids locked up?"

"Seems to be."

"What'd you do, forget to kiss that columnist's ring? You damn sure aren't gonna win a popularity contest with the press."

"I'm not looking to," said Young.

Outside the school, Young led them to Unit Five. He got a key from a chain hung on his belt loop and unlocked the building's door.

"I don't know," said Chris.

"Come on," said Young. "They're going to tear it down soon. You should see it one more time."

"I see it every day," said Chris, as he stepped inside.

The smell got him. He had forgotten that. It was unidentifiable, but it suggested stillness and decay. They went into the common room. The Ping-Pong table was gone, as was the fake-leather chair with the arms studded in nail heads. The old couch was all that was left. Its back was now nearly completely shredded, and a spring showed from beneath its worn seat. Beyond the common room sat the media room, now in complete darkness.

Young led them down the hall. Chris looked up at the tiled ceilings where he'd stashed marijuana many years before. Then they were along the rows of doors leading to the cells. Chris feared that if he closed his eyes he would hear Ben's voice, talking to himself the way he used to do at night.

Ali and Chris looked through clouded Plexiglas into one of the small cells. The gray blanket covering the bolted-down cot. The steel shitter and pisshole. The particleboard desk.

"I've got the Joliet," said Ken Young, touching the extra-large key hanging off the ring on his belt line. "If you want to go in."

"No," said Chris.

"I brought you in here so you wouldn't forget," said Young. "The more allies I have, the better it is for me. If people could see this, they wouldn't be so eager to put kids in cages."

"They *should* tear this building down," said Chris. "I'd drive the bulldozer if you'd let me."

Young nodded. "You'd have to get in line."

TWENTY-TWO

CHRIS WAS quiet on the ride back to the city. It was more than circumspection. There was something on his mind beyond Ben and the awful memories rekindled at Pine Ridge.

"What's going on with you, man?" said Ali.

"I'm thinking on something," said Chris. He thumb-stroked the vertical scar above his lip. "When you spoke to that detective this morning, did you tell her about Lawrence New-house?"

"No. I had a conversation with him last night. He said he didn't know anything about Ben's murder. He said he didn't want to talk to police. I expected that, and I had to respect his wishes."

"How was he when you gave him the news about Ben?"

"Bad," said Ali. "He cried, and he didn't care if I heard it. He was blown."

"I gotta tell you something, Ali. I didn't say it to you before because I didn't think it meant anything. But now I'm not so sure."

Chris told Ali about the money in the gym bag. He said that

they had left it in the row house, but that Lawrence had gotten Ben wasted and Ben had told him where it was. Chris and Ben believed that Lawrence had gone to the house and stolen the money. They had done nothing about it because they felt that there was nothing to do.

When Chris was done, Ali said, "And now you think there's something with that money that connects Lawrence to Ben's murder."

"I'm not sayin that."

"Lawrence loved Ben. When Lawrence was getting his ass beat by everyone and their brother at Pine Ridge, Ben stood up for him. He was the only one who did. If there was one dude who Lawrence considered a friend, it was Ben."

"I know that."

"*What*, then?"

"Maybe they went out together and were spending the money. Maybe they ran their mouths off at a club or during a card game. Lawrence could have been braggin on what he had. Or someone thought the cash was Ben's and tried to take him off."

"That's thin."

"Shit, Ali, I don't know *what* I'm talkin about. I'm sayin there might be some kind of connection."

"You're speculating."

"Yeah."

"Then you need to talk to Lawrence. I know you don't like to, but there it is. And if Lawrence does know something, he needs to tell it to the law."

"Right."

Ali looked at his friend. "What else you got on your mind?"

"I don't know," said Chris. "It's like a finger is tapping the side of my head, trying to remind me that . . . I *know* something, Ali. Damn if I can remember it."

"You will."

They came off the Beltway and headed down Colesville Road toward the District line, traffic gathering thickly around them. Oddly, the congestion made them both more comfortable.

"Any plans for Ben's funeral?" said Ali.

"My father is taking care of it," said Chris. "When the police release the body, my dad is gonna have Ben cremated over at Rapp. He's getting him a spot at Rock Creek Cemetery."

"That's where Ben got took, right?"

"Yeah. My father spoke to that homicide detective, and she said that the Rock Creek security guard recalled an old black sedan leaving out the place at the end of the night. He didn't happen to see if Ben was inside it. He didn't say that he found it suspicious at the time. He just remembered it 'cause it was the last car out."

"Safe to say that it started there, though."

"But it wouldn't have changed Ben's opinion of the cemetery. That was his spot. It's where he would have wanted to be buried."

"I thought you had to be rich or connected to get put in that place," said Ali.

"So did I. But my father looked into it and found something that was available. Like anything else, all it takes is money. It's not gonna be a fancy monument or in the prime section of the grounds. It'll prob'ly be a small marker, something like that. Important thing is, Ben will be there."

"That can't be cheap."

"It's thousands."

"Your father's a good man," said Ali.

"He's like most people," said Chris. "He's trying to be good, and most times he is."

"Like you."

"But he wanted me to be better than him. Turns out I was human, just like him."

"That's behind y'all."

"It is for me."

"YOU GONNA lie there all day?" said Marquis Gilman.

"I might," said Lawrence Newhouse. He was on his single bed, on his back, in the room he shared with Terrence and Loquatia. Marquis had entered the room, held aside the privacy sheet, and stood at the foot of Lawrence's bed.

"Let's go shoot around some."

"Nah, I'm too tired."

Marquis could see that Lawrence's eyes were pink. He hated to think that his uncle had been crying.

"Mama told me 'bout your friend."

"Uh."

"You know who did the thing?"

"No."

"Whoever did it needs to be got."

Lawrence turned his head sharply toward Marquis. "That ain't for you to speak on, boy."

Marquis looked down at his Nikes. "I didn't mean nothin."

Lawrence's eyes softened. "This is on me."

"You not workin today?"

"I'm done with it."

"'Cause I could help you."

"I don't want you washin cars. You better than that. I'm still tryin to get you hooked up with my mans. You could learn the carpet trade, 'stead of doin mule stuff."

"I'm sayin, I can work."

"Go on, Marquis. Go play ball."

Marquis left the room.

Lawrence Newhouse hadn't washed and detailed one car since he'd taken the money. The young man he worked with, Deon Miller, was upset with him, because together they'd built up a nice little business. But he couldn't tell Deon why he'd lost his ambition. He'd known Deon since he was a kid, growing up at Parkchester, and smoking weed one day on Stevens Road, they'd made grandiose plans about this thing they were going to do, starting small and ending, in their minds, with a string of locations in Southeast and PG. They'd be known as the entrepreneurs who owned the spots to get the nicest cars in D.C. cleaned and shined. They'd be to cars what Murray was to steaks.

It hadn't turned out so big, but they'd done all right.

Lawrence and Deon took their business to the car owners. They used grocery carts they'd stolen from the Giant, and stocked them with everything needed to impress. Lawrence would go to the big auto parts store, buy their cheap house brands of liquid detergent, wax, wheel cleaner, and tire shine, and pour them into empty bottles of recognizable brand names, like Armor All and Black Magic, that he'd found in the trash. They called their business Elite Shine. If they had a sign, it would have read, "Only the finest materials used to detail the very finest cars." Lawrence had thought of that when he was high.

They were getting a rep around Southeast. Seeing the same customers getting their cars done. What they called "repeat clientele." So it was natural that, just as they were beginning to lift off, Deon would be disturbed and disappointed when Lawrence told him that he didn't want to work no more.

"What, you just gonna give up on everything we built up?" said Deon.

Lawrence said, "I'm retired," and left it at that.

That was before Ben got done. Now that he was gone, nothing mattered. Not even the money.

Lawrence draped his forearm over his eyes. He was sweating and he could smell his own stink.

Why would someone do his boy like that?

Why? was the first question. Then came, Who?

Lawrence burned to know.

CHRIS FLYNN returned to his apartment, put his shoes neatly under his bed, changed his clothes, and went to sleep. When he woke, the bedroom had darkened. He went to the window and opened the blinds and saw that it was night. He had slept heavily for several hours and could not recall if he had dreamed.

Chris phoned Katherine. She asked if he wanted company, and he said that he preferred to be alone. It was not that he did not want to see her. He knew that he would not be good with anyone tonight.

"I'm worried about you," said Katherine.

"I'll call you tomorrow," said Chris.

He showered, microwaved a Celeste pizza, and ate it standing up. He thought of smoking some marijuana he kept in his nightstand but decided against it. His head would be up for a while, but then he'd get to that overthinking phase, and he didn't want that. He grabbed a few bottles of Budweiser out of the refrigerator and put them in a six-pack-sized cooler, along with some ice. He dropped his cell into the pocket of his shorts and left his apartment.

Out on the front porch of the bungalow, Andy Ladas, the black-haired, middle-aged tenant of the three-family home, was sitting in a high-backed chair, drinking an Anchor Steam and smoking a Winston. Beside him was a steel stand-up ashtray of the type once common in barbershops. This was Ladas's position and activity for a couple of hours every night.

"Hey, Andy."

"Chris."

"We alone?"

"The kids got a gig," said Ladas. He was referring to the musician couple, Tina and Doug Gibson, who had the top floor. They were older than Chris but did not look it.

"Case you fall asleep with that cigarette in your hand and catch fire, I'll be out back."

The house was on a corner of the street, at an intersection featuring a four-way stop that was frequently ignored. There was a police station nearby, and it seemed the main offenders were cops. They were the most aggressive speeders, too. Neighborhood activists had petitioned for road humps to slow the cruisers down, which had improved things slightly.

Chris walked through the side yard to the back, where he put down the cooler and took a seat in a green metal rocking chair beside a brick grill. The yard went deep and it had been landscaped by the Gibsons and maintained by all the tenants. It was a nice spot, and he frequently sat here on summer nights. With a view unencumbered by the branches of trees overhead, he could look up at the stars. The sky was clear, and the moon cast a pearl glow on the property.

Chris drank a beer. He thought of Ben and the day at Pine Ridge, and as the alcohol kissed him he felt his shoulders relax. He tossed the first bottle into the grass and reached into the cooler for another. He twisted off its top and emptied its neck.

Chris heard a vehicle come to a stop and looked to his right.

An old black sedan had parked on the street and its engine died.

Chris reached into his pocket, retrieved his cell, and flipped it open, its buttons and screen illuminated. Because he was of a generation that was dexterous with keyboards, he quickly found the contact he was searching for.

Two men, one large and one small, got out of the car, crossed the street, and walked toward him in the yard. Chris studied them and continued to text with his fingers.

He was not thinking of police. He was a boy, and he was calling his father.

He typed the words *I'm at home*.

And: *Signal 13*.

TWENTY-THREE

THE LARGE man wore a windbreaker over a T-shirt and jeans. The small man wore black. They stood before Chris Flynn, still seated in his chair. Chris had slipped his cell back into his pocket. He held a beer bottle loosely in his right hand.

"Get up," said Sonny. "Let's take a ride."

Chris slowly shook his head. "I don't think so."

"We need to have a talk."

"We're talking now."

"Not here," said Sonny.

Chris's eyes disconnected from Sonny's. He drank slowly from his bottle of beer.

"Get up," said Wayne.

Chris looked at him blankly. Wayne's brush mustache seemed to spring from inside his nostrils and lay beneath a flat nose in a deeply lined, imploding face. He appeared to be rotting. His wiry arms were dominated by ink.

"What do you want?" said Chris, returning his gaze to the big man with the walrus whiskers and high cheekbones.

"Somethin that's mine," said Sonny.

"What would that be?"

"Try to tell me you don't know."

"I'm not playing this game," said Chris.

"You will."

"You're trespassing."

"Fuck you, sweetheart. Let's go."

Chris looked at him with lazy green eyes.

The big man held one hand out to Chris and turned it into the shine of moonlight. Chris saw a tattoo on the crook of it.

"You know what this is?" said Sonny.

"Prison ink," said Chris.

"What, *specific?*"

"It's a four-leaf clover."

Sonny breathed out heavily in exasperation. Chris thought he saw the little one smile.

"It's a shamrock," said Sonny Wade. "You ride with the rock, means you're part of a special club. You know what that club is?"

"The dick suck club," said Chris.

Wayne grinned and giggled. Sonny's smile showed perfect ugly teeth, gray in the light.

A car drove by and they all went silent.

"Let's just get this done," said Sonny, and he reached into his windbreaker.

"I wouldn't," said Chris. "Whatever you got inside that jacket, you pull it out, it's a mistake."

Sonny kept his hand where it was but made no move to pull his gun. "I said, let's walk."

"I'm not goin anywhere with you."

"How 'bout I just murder your ass right here?"

"You'll lose what you're after."

"Chris Carpet," said Wayne. "Boy thinks he's a real tough nut."

Chris felt the blood leave his face.

"Shut up, stupid," said Sonny.

A Montgomery County police cruiser drove by on the road beside the house. No one spoke, and the car passed from sight. Sonny's black eyes flickered and he moved his hand. Chris saw the grip of a pistol inch out from the jacket.

"There a problem here?"

Andy Ladas emerged from the shadows of the side yard and stood well back from the two men. In his hand was a flipped-open cell.

"Chris," said Andy. "Is there a *problem?*"

"Is there?" said Chris, staring into Sonny's eyes.

Sonny's hand came empty out of his jacket and he dropped it to his side. He looked at Wayne and nodded shortly.

Sonny looked down at Chris. "See you around, fella."

Sonny walked out of the yard, his little partner creeping along beside him. Chris heard car doors open and slam, and the turn of an engine. He heard the creak of worn shocks and watched the old black sedan roll down the street.

"How long were you back there, Andy?"

"I came off the porch soon as I seen those two walk back into the yard. Those guys didn't look right."

"What did you hear?"

"Most of it. I was about to call nine-one-one."

"Wasn't any need for that. But thanks." Chris stood from his chair and killed the beer left in the bottle. He tossed it on the ground and noticed that his hand was shaking. He picked up the cooler and gripped its handle tight.

"You all right?" said Ladas.

"Yeah," said Chris. "When my dad comes, don't speak on any particulars. Just tell him I'm inside."

He walked toward the bungalow, using his damp T-shirt to wipe away the sweat that had broken on his face.

*   *   *

THOMAS FLYNN arrived shortly thereafter and parked Amanda's SUV sloppily on the road, one set of tires up on the curb. He jogged across the yard to the front porch of the bungalow, where Andy Ladas sat, working on another beer and a smoke. Flynn was winded and his color was up. His shirttails were out, covering the .38 he had holstered at the small of his back.

"Is Chris all right?"

"Yes," said Ladas.

"What's happening here?"

"Couple of guys were talkin to Chris outside." Ladas cut his eyes away from Flynn's. "That's all I know. They're gone and he's fine."

Flynn went into the house. He stepped to the door of Chris's apartment and turned the knob without knocking. It was a small place consisting of a bedroom, living room, kitchenette, and head. From behind the closed bathroom door he could hear the run of a shower. Flynn had a seat in a cushiony chair. He looked up at the crowded bookshelves. On the small table beside him lay a bookmarked copy of *Wartime* by Paul Fussell.

The shower shut off. Soon Chris stepped out of the bathroom, a towel around his waist.

"Dad."

"Everything all right?"

"I'm good."

"You're so *good*, why'd you send me that code?"

"Can I dry my hair off and put some pants on?"

"Go ahead."

"There's beer in the refrigerator, you want one."

Flynn found a bottle of Budweiser and uncapped it while Chris changed. He drank off a good piece of it standing up and finished it sitting in the same chair.

He's taking his time, thought Flynn. *He's figuring out his story and his lies.*

Flynn went back to the refrigerator and got another beer. He was drinking it when Chris stepped barefoot into the room, wearing jeans and a wife beater. His hair had been towel dried and left uncombed. The look on his face was clever and annoyed, as it had been when he was a teen. As if he was expecting a tongue-lashing from his father, was prepared to take it, and would give up nothing in return.

"Well?" said Flynn.

Chris pushed hair back behind his ears. "Couple of dudes came by to speak with me about somethin. I thought there was gonna be trouble, but I was wrong. I apologize for bothering you."

"What did they want?"

"I owe them money," said Chris. "I get into these card games sometimes. Texas hold 'em, like you see on ESPN. Only these are played in basements around town. I was into those two for a coupla thousand dollars."

"Bullshit."

"It was a card debt."

"No, it wasn't. You're lying. Don't forget who you're talking to, son. I had years and years of experience watching you lie to me. You don't look any different to me right now than you did when you were sixteen."

"I'm telling you how it was. I don't know what else to say."

"Say the truth. You sent me that signal. If it was nothing, you could have handled it yourself. If you needed just a little help you could have called the police. Shit, the station house is right up the street."

"I wouldn't call the police," said Chris.

"I forgot," said Flynn. "You don't talk to the *po*-leece."

"That's not necessary," said Chris, and he left the room to get himself a beer.

When he returned, his father was staring down at his shoes.

"I'm sorry," said Flynn. "I was out of line."

Chris dragged a chair beside his father and had a seat. Flynn popped the knuckles of his left hand with his right.

"Calm down, Dad."

"Okay."

"You know I'm tryin."

"I do."

"I go to work every day. I pretty much play by the rules. But you know, some things, some of the bad habits I picked up along the way, and especially the experience of being locked up—"

"I know. It's hard to shake."

"Me and Ali went out to Pine Ridge today. Ali had some work stuff to take care of out there, and I joined him. Bein back in my unit, looking into my cell, it hit me kinda hard. It's tough to get that monster off your back. Wasn't easy for Ben, either."

"You telling me that you and Ben slipped back into some criminal thing?"

"No. I already told you; Ben didn't do anything wrong."

"So those two men were here because of a card debt."

"Yes."

"Bullshit," said Flynn.

The two of them sat there and drank. Flynn finished his and went to the fridge and got another. He caught a look from Chris as he retook his seat.

"You should slow down," said Chris. "You gotta drive home."

"Fuck that," said Flynn. "I'm a grown man, and you sound like your mother."

Flynn took a long pull from his bottle.

"I'm not comin in for a few days," said Chris. "I need some time off."

"How you gonna pay your gambling debt if you don't work? What about the vig? Isn't that what you guys call it?"

"There is no vig."

"On account of there's no debt. 'Cause this card game thing is bullshit."

Chris chuckled. "You can't let it go, can you?"

"That's all right," said Flynn, his eyes a bit unfocused. He drank off more of his beer. "You'll tell me the truth when you're ready, I guess. I don't wanna pressure you or nothin like that."

"Can I say something else?"

"Go 'head."

"When I come back to work, I'm not wearing that polo shirt anymore. I'll wear anything you want, but not that. Me and Ben, we never liked those things. They reminded us of our uniforms at the Ridge. Is that all right?"

Flynn could not look at Chris. He said, "Yes, Chris. It's fine."

Chris cleared his throat. "I'm . . ."

"What?"

"I'm thinking of taking a class or two, spring semester, over at Montgomery College. American history."

"That's nice," said Flynn. And because he was his father, he added, "What would you do with that?"

"Just check it out and see what happens, I guess," said Chris. "Maybe work toward a teaching degree. I dunno. Things are gettin kind of serious between Katherine and me. If I'm gonna be, you know, responsible for someone else . . . I'm sayin, I don't want to be installing carpet all my life."

"I don't want that for you, either."

"Anyway."

"Yeah."

Flynn got up and went to the kitchenette and stood over its sink. He drank deeply of his beer, took a breath, and finished what was left. He placed the bottle along a row of empties on the counter and walked toward the front door.

"I'm outta here, Chris."

"Dad?"

Flynn stopped walking. "Yeah."

"Thanks for coming. When I called, I mean."

Flynn stared at Chris, his eyes sad and knowing. Now would be the time to say the words that needed to be said, but he could not. He waved and walked out the door.

Chris stared at the bottle in his hand. He drank from it, his chest heavy with emotion.

FLYNN STOOD at his bar cart and poured three fingers of Beam into a rocks glass. He sipped at the bourbon and felt it bite as Amanda came into the dining room. Her eyes traveled over him and flickered away.

"I'm just having one before bed," said Flynn.

"I didn't say a word."

"What would Jesus have done, Amanda? If he'd had a son like ours, I mean. Do you think Jesus might have a drink once in a while, just to take the edge off?"

Amanda hugged her arms. "What happened?"

"Nothing. I got there and whatever was going on was over. Chris says he's in a little trouble over a gambling debt."

"Chris doesn't gamble. Does he?"

"No idea. But he's lying about what went down tonight. Still lying to me, after everything we've been through."

"Maybe there's a reason."

"He was mixed up with Ben on something. Ben was killed because of it, and Chris won't tell me or anyone else what it's about. That's the reason, Manda. Chris fucked up again. He's into something wrong."

"You don't know that."

"And you're blind. You always have been."

"At least I didn't give up on him."

"Yes, you did. Call it nurturing if you want to put a sweet name to it, but to me, you just gave up. Because you stopped expecting anything from him. I never did."

"He's our child."

"He's a man. And I can't accept what he is. I won't."

"Give him a chance."

"I always have," said Flynn. "And I'm not the only one. You remember that time he broke into those cars in the parking lot of that Tex-Mex place on Wisconsin?"

"Tuco's," said Amanda. The owner of the restaurant had called them at home. His people had watched Chris do the crime on live camera. He'd been caught by a couple of employees and brought back into the kitchen. Her husband had told the owner he'd make restitution when he picked Chris up.

"When I got there," said Flynn, "I went up the stairs with these Mexicans, or whatever they were, to this little security room they had with video monitors in it, on the second floor. In the dining room of that restaurant the waitstaff was dressed in bright outfits, the music was festive, and everyone was smiling. Y'know, one of those happy ethnic eating experiences for white people in Ward Three. But up in that room these guys looked like some rough Spanish dudes who'd just had a well-to-do kid come to their business establishment and ruin that experience for their customers. I mean, these guys were hot. I had to beg them not to call the police. And I had to stand there with them and watch a tape of my son in that lot, looking around and hesitating before he made the decision to break into those cars. I was saying, 'Don't do it, Chris. *Please*, don't do it.' But he had al*ready* done it. I was watching a tape of something that had happened an hour earlier. Those Mexicans must have thought I was nuts."

"What difference does it make now?"

"The point is, I gave him plenty of chances. The guy who owned the restaurant, he gave the kid a chance that day, too. Chris just kept on screwing up."

"That was ten years ago."

"Right." Flynn swirled bourbon and looked into the glass. "You'll be happy to know that he's making plans, at least. Says he's going to take a couple of classes at Montgomery College in the spring. And apparently he's serious about Kate."

"That's wonderful," said Amanda.

"His blue area's finally catching up to his green area."

"What?"

"Reasoning and emotion. The limbic system and the pre-frontal cortex. Remember Dr. Peterhead's presentation on that easel? Chris's brain is evening out. Now if he can only stop himself from stumbling. Refrain from those criminal impulses he's got. I guess that's a different area of the, the *cortex*."

"You're drunk."

"So?"

"I'm going to bed."

Amanda left the dining room. Flynn listened to her footsteps ascend the stairs.

"I'll be up in a minute," he shouted.

There was no reply. He closed his eyes and drank.

IN HIS apartment, Chris sat in the dark and drank another beer. He had been thinking on something the little man with the thick mustache had said. As the pieces began to connect in his head, murder came to his heart.

TWENTY-FOUR

CHRIS FLYNN sat at a window deuce with Mindy Kramer in Thai Feast. Their view was of several painters' vans and pickups jumbled in a parking lot dominated by a green Dumpster. But neither of them was looking out the window. Before Mindy was her noodle special, a glass of water, iced coffee, and a full cup of chicken–lemon grass soup that had gone cold. Mindy was staring down at the table, her oversize sunglasses and BlackBerry neatly aligned beside the plates. Her hands were in her lap and her fingers were tightly entwined.

Chris had ordered nothing and was drinking water. Mindy had agreed to meet him after hearing the malice in his voice during an early-morning phone call. She knew what this was going to be about. She wanted the conversation to take place in public.

"How did you know?" said Mindy. Her hair was heavily gelled and her makeup was as thick as a cardboard mask.

"One of them called me Chris Carpet. It's the same stupid name you bragged about giving me when you entered it into your phone."

"I meant you no disrespect. It was just a mnemonic device I used."

"*And* I got an anonymous call on my cell last Saturday night. The caller addressed me as Chris Carpet. So it all goes back to you."

Toi, the house waitress, came to the table and refilled Chris's water glass. She looked at the untouched food and drink in front of Mindy.

"You are not hungry today, Miss Kramer? Something wrong with the noodles? You don't like?"

"Everything's fine," said Mindy, making a short, impatient chopping motion with one hand.

Toi smiled wanly and drifted to another table.

"Why'd you give up my name?"

"I was frightened," said Mindy. "I thought they'd murder me if I didn't give them a name. Can you understand that? I assumed that you and your partner—"

"His name was Ben."

"I assumed that the two of you found the money and took it. I certainly knew nothing about its existence until the day those animals came into my life."

"You were wrong," said Chris. "We didn't take anything."

Mindy used her thumb to rub at the corner of one eye and smudged mascara onto the side of her face. "I didn't know what else to do."

"Tell me what they looked like."

Mindy ran a hand up and down the goose bumps on her bare arm. "A large man with one of those mustaches that curve down around the mouth. It looked like he had false teeth to me. He had a small tattoo on his hand. A four-leaf clover."

"And the other," said Chris, his eyes losing their light.

"Much smaller. Bushy mustache. An awful, ugly face."

"Their names?"

"The big one called himself Ralph Cotter. He made the appointment and I wrote the name into my daybook. I don't remember what the little one went by. Cotter wasn't his real name. He told me as much."

"Any weapons?" said Chris, and Mindy looked at him quizzically. "You said you thought they were going to kill you. What would they have used?"

"The little man had a knife."

"What kind of a knife?" said Chris.

"He kept it in a sheath tied to his calf. It had a wood handle and teeth on the blade."

Chris mumbled something that she could not hear.

"What?"

"They killed my friend."

"I'm sorry," said Mindy.

"He didn't take their money. He never hurt anyone. He couldn't."

"I'm so sorry."

Chris said nothing and drank water from his glass.

"I have a daughter," said Mindy Kramer. "Lisa's about your age. She's been . . . I don't mind telling you, she's been a disappointment to me. It's not uncommon for a parent of my generation to feel that way, you know. We were so ambitious and hard-charging, and our children seem so, I don't know, unconcerned with what they are going to achieve in life." Mindy sipped her iced coffee and placed the glass gently on the table. "Lisa had two little girls. She's no longer married to the father, and I don't feel as if she's equipped to handle the responsibility of motherhood. So I'm practically raising Michelle and Lauren myself."

"I've gotta get going," said Chris.

Mindy reached across the table, put her hand on top of Chris's, and squeezed it. "They threatened my granddaughters. The big man said the little one would . . . he said the little man would cut their heads off. Do you understand what I went through that day?"

Chris gently pulled his hand free from hers. "Don't speak of this conversation to anyone. Ever. Not even if you get a sudden case of conscience. Especially not if you read something about these men in the paper or see it on the TV news. Don't ever speak on this again."

"I won't, Chris."

"And it's Chris Flynn."

He got up out of his seat and walked from the restaurant. She watched him cross the parking lot to the white work van with the magnetic sign that read "Flynn's Floors." Realizing now that he was the owner's son. She wondered if he was going to kill the men who had visited her and murdered his friend. She was not a violent person, but she found herself hoping that he would do just that.

"You finished?" said Toi, reaching for the main dish of uneaten food. "You want me to box it up for you?"

"No," said Mindy, wiping a tear that had threatened to break from her eye. "Just get me the check."

Toi went back to the waitress station, smiling to herself, thinking of the tall blond man who had humbled the bitch and made her cry.

SONNY WADE and Wayne Minors had moved out of the hotel in the badlands of the eastward strip of New York Avenue. In addition to the foreign tourists, who seemed shell-shocked to find themselves in such a place, the hotel was heavy with low-level criminals of various stripes, people drinking themselves to death, and one-night-stand women, both professional and amateur. Hence, a police car was often in the parking lot, either surveilling the premises or responding to a call. Sonny was aware that their old vehicle stood out, especially in Washington, where everyone, even those without the means, seemed to be driving late-model cars. Plus, their plates were certainly on the hot sheet now. It was not a good idea to stick around.

Sonny and Wayne were uncomfortable in cities, and in this one they felt particularly out of place. It wasn't just that they were among many blacks and Spanish. The white people made them feel different, too. Sonny and Wayne had been institutionalized for most of their lives, and they did not know how to dress, converse, or wear facial hair like straights. In an urban environment, they were socially inept.

After checking out of the hotel, Sonny and Wayne drove down to the bus depot near Union Station. Sonny had suggested it, as he had always had luck making friends in those kinds of places. They were looking for girls of a certain type, and they had what was needed to make their acquaintance: cash and drugs.

They had taken off a meth dealer at gun- and knifepoint in Wheeling, West Virginia, on the way to Washington, after they'd purchased the Mercury. Wayne enjoyed snorting the powder, and though Sonny did not partake, being a Jack-and-Coke man himself, he wanted his little friend to be happy. So they had gone to a bar to find a way to make a purchase. There they met a young dealer who had the distinct body odor and the pale, poorly complected look they were searching for, and when they followed him to his garden apartment to party and cop, they decided to relieve him of his money and premeasured, snow-sealed goods. Sonny ransacked the apartment while Wayne held his knife to the boy's throat. The threat of murder made it easy. Sonny didn't have to show the boy his tattoo.

At the bus station, they found what they were looking for, a girl named Ashley and her friend Cheyenne. Sonny had spotted them first and pegged them as runaways, hookers, or both. Neither had baggage or a backpack, and he guessed they were doing the traditional bus depot hustle. He approached both girls and engaged Ashley in conversation, choosing her because of her generous bosoms, a feature that had always closed the deal for him. Her face was plain, but she was young, and she had a belly on her like many young women did these days, but he didn't mind. While Sonny spoke to Ashley, Wayne stood back against a wall, tapping his foot nervously and head-shaking his long center-parted hair away from his face. Sonny waved him over. As Wayne neared the girls, the one named Cheyenne could not hide her look of revulsion, but she was no prize herself, bone skinny, dotted with acne, lank hair. Her features softened when Sonny mentioned the meth. Wayne added that it was "high-octane hillbilly coke" and didn't burn "too awful goin up the nose."

Sonny and Ashley quickly negotiated a fee.

"Let's do it," said Sonny. "Trouble is, Wayne and me don't have a place to throw no shindig."

"We know a spot," said Ashley. "You studs got a car?"

"A beauty," said Sonny.

Wayne, who figured himself a proper gentleman around the ladies, uncurled his fist and made a sweeping motion with his hand, as if he were pointing to a red carpet.

"Ladies," said Wayne. "After you."

On the way to their destination, they stopped at a liquor store for a big ball of Jack Daniel's, a liter of Coke, multiple cases of Coors Light, and, because Wayne thought they'd like it, a package of wine coolers for the girls.

*   *   *

CHRIS PHONED Ali down at his office and asked for Lawrence Newhouse's cell number.

"I'm ready to talk to Lawrence," said Chris. "I just wanna find out if he or Ben discussed the money with anyone. For my own peace of mind."

"Okay," said Ali.

Chris waited. "Well?"

"I'm gettin it."

"There a problem?"

"You sound different," said Ali. "Your voice got that hard thing to it. The way it used to when you had the need to show the world how tough you were."

"I'm still broke up about Ben. That's all."

"It's more than that. You sound like you got purpose."

"Give me the number, Ali."

"Here it is."

Chris wrote it down. "Thanks."

"You gonna get up with Lawrence, maybe I oughta come with you."

"I'd rather see him alone."

"Y'all could meet right here in my office."

"I'll hit you later," said Chris. "Tell you how it went."

Chris ended the call. Sitting on the edge of his bed, he stared at his cell awhile as if he were deciding, but it was theatrical hesitation. He had already made the decision, and he punched Lawrence's number into the grid.

"Who is this?" said Lawrence Newhouse, his voice raspy and low.

"Chris Flynn."

"What you want?"

"I know who killed Ben."

After a long silence, Lawrence said, "Who was it?"

"Two men. I met them last night."

"So?"

"The money you stole was theirs. They killed Ben over it. It's safe to say that Ben didn't give you up. If he had, you'd be dead now, too."

"Did *you* give me up, White Boy?"

"No."

"Why? All a sudden, you my friend?"

"I'm gonna need your help."

"I guess we should meet, then."

Chris said, "Where?"

TWENTY-FIVE

THE NATIONAL Arboretum was situated on four hundred acres of trees, fields, and landscaped plants bordered by New York Avenue to the north and the Anacostia River to the southeast. Thousands of cars drove along its black fence every day, and the park was open to the public, yet it seemed underutilized by Washingtonians, perhaps because of its ugly gateway and the overinflated reputation for violence of the neighborhoods around it.

Chris Flynn drove his van past the information center and gift shop, located near the New York Avenue entrance, noticing the many Jeep security vehicles parked in the lot. It was in his makeup to take note of such things, and to rank private cops in a low position on his police scale. Private security meant they must not have any serious trouble back here, beyond kids smoking weed.

Couples were hiking along the shoulder and on trails, and cyclists were taking their bikes off the racks of their cars. Chris went down Ellipse Road and saw the Corinthian columns, twenty-two sandstone structures that had once been located on the east portico of the Capitol, now standing in an open meadow. He remembered his parents taking him here as a child, water running under the shadows of the columns down a graduated channel to a reflecting pool, his father grabbing his collar as Chris had attempted to jump in.

He took another road, squeezing by a groundsman hauling hay in a motorized cart. He saw employees but fewer visitors as the van climbed up into more thickly forested areas, the Conifer and then the Dogwood collections. He followed the clearly marked signs and drove up the winding Hickory Hill Road, then parked beside a Chevy Cavalier in a shaded lot near a brick structure that he reckoned housed men's and women's bathrooms. He locked the van and headed toward a trail, passing a woman who was carrying a bucket and wearing an Arboretum shirt. He had arrived at the Asian Collection, a section boasting a variety of plants imported from China, Korea, and Japan, now thriving in the hilly woods.

Chris walked down a steeply graded wood-chip-and-dirt path lined by beveled railroad ties. At the bottom of the grade was a wooden bench in a clearing, where Lawrence Newhouse stood waiting. Lawrence wore an LRG T-shirt with a matching hat, and Nikes edged in red to pick up the red off the shirt. His cap sat high and cocked atop his braids.

They nodded at each other but didn't shake hands. Lawrence sat down on the bench and Chris joined him. Several feet before them was a ledge, and there the land dropped off precipitously. They could see the tops of trees and below, on the ridge floor, the brown ribbon of the Anacostia River, sun glinting off its water.

"This here's my spot," said Lawrence.

"I don't know this place," said Chris.

"That's what makes this shit so special. I used to ride my bike here all the way from Wade Road in Southeast. It's far, but I was young, and I had mad energy. I came all that way to look at this. To sit here and have that kind of peace, it was worth it to me. You ever see where me and Ali come up?"

"Ali drove me up Stanton once."

"Then you know. I was round the corner in Parkchester. Ali was down at the bottom of the Farms, near Firth Sterling Ave. What they called the dwellings. Not houses or apartments or homes . . . *dwellings*. Anyway, Ali and his mom got out. I'm proud of that boy."

"I am, too."

"He tryin to help all them young niggas who think they got to be one way. I thought he could help my nephew Marquis."

"I know Marquis. He's a decent kid."

"He's smart. Talented, too. He just needs to get out of that fucked-up environment he's in. Before it does to him what it did to me."

"Ali was gonna hook him up with a fast-food job, wasn't he?"

"But I wanted Ali to put him someplace better. A place where he could learn a trade. That's why I reached out to him and asked him to get up with you and your pops. But he wasn't willin to do it. Maybe 'cause it was me askin. So I contacted Ben. I thought Ben might speak to you about it. I didn't know nothin about no money until Ben's tongue got loose behind that Popov and weed. I wasn't tryin to do my boy dirt."

"But you did it anyway."

Lawrence narrowed his eyes. "That's right. I stole that money. What, you thought I was gonna let it sit there like you? I'm not that kind of sucker. But I didn't know Ben was gonna get done behind it. Ben was my boy."

They sat there and listened to the birds, and the wind moving the leaves on the trees.

"Who did this?" said Lawrence.

"Trash," said Chris. "Two white guys, older than us. Seemed

to me that they've been in the system a long time. No one who's lived on the outside looks like that. There was a little guy with a big mustache and heavy ink. Looks like he kissed a train. His partner's a beast. Clover tat on one hand. Big gut, big chest. The little guy's the blade man. I'm guessing he murdered Ben. The big one carries a gun."

"Then we gonna need to tool up, too. I can do that."

Chris nodded slowly.

"You know what you're fixin to do?" said Lawrence. "I'm sayin, are you up for it?"

"Are *you?*"

"I ain't never killed no one," said Lawrence. "But when they do one of your own, you got to come back hard."

"That's right," said Chris, with no enthusiasm.

"Unit Five," said Lawrence, and he held out his fist. Chris did not raise his hand. "You too good to dap me up?"

"I'm not about that anymore, Lawrence."

"You done put it all behind you, huh. But you here, though. Right?"

Chris looked away.

"Okay," said Lawrence. "How we gonna contact them?"

"I've got a cell number on my caller ID. I'll set up a meet. I'll tell them I'm ready to give up the money."

"Let *me* have the number. I'll make the call."

"Why?"

" 'Cause *I* took the money, White Boy. Like you said, it's on me. I'm runnin this shit or I'm out."

"I'll do it alone, then."

"No, you won't. You ain't hard enough, *Christina*. You just think you are. But you don't get to the kinda hard that me and them other boys at the Ridge were at, comin from where you did. With your home and your library and your pet dog."

"I did the same time you did."

"But you never did the real time. I'm talkin about the time I did as a child. All the beatings I took, from the men in my mother's apartment to the boys out on the street. The beatings I took in my heart from the teachers who told me I wasn't shit and never was gonna *be* shit. Then in Pine Ridge, feeding me meds just to make me normal." Lawrence shook his braids away from his face and stared down at the water. "I was in Lorton before they closed it. So crowded you were living on top of men who would punch you in the face for nothin. Know what I did to get out of there? I screamed like a baby. I smeared my own shit on myself and I ate it, too. They took me outta there. Put me in Saint E's for a while. They had me in one of them jackets with straps. I musta took everything they had in their medicine cabinet, boy. I couldn't tell the difference between who I was and who I was pretendin to be. When I got released? Wasn't nobody with their arms out and a smile on their face. But when you came out the Ridge, I bet there was someone there for you." Chris did not answer, and Lawrence said, "Bet your mother made you a real nice dinner, too."

She did, thought Chris. His father had put three New York strips out on the grill, and his mother had made onion rings and a big salad to go with the steaks. She had set the table in the dining room with candles, and for dessert had baked him his favorite cake, a rich German chocolate. The dog had flopped down under the table while they ate, resting against Chris's feet. They did not speak much during dinner, but it was not uncomfortable, and afterward Chris went up to his room and slept on clean sheets that smelled of spring.

"We about to do a murder, son," said Lawrence. "Who you want in charge of this shit? You or me?"

Chris reached into his pocket, retrieved his cell, and flipped it open. He scrolled through his contacts and found the number he had taken from caller ID and saved. He handed the phone to Lawrence, who transferred it into his own cell.

"Where they gonna put Ben?" said Lawrence.

"As soon as the police release his body, we're having his ashes buried at Rock Creek."

"That was Ben's thing," said Lawrence. "Me, I want to be right here."

"They don't bury people here, Lawrence. It's a park."

"I ain't say nothing about being buried. Why you always got to act so superior?"

"I wasn't—"

"Let's just go."

They walked up the path together. They crossed the road to the parking area, near the rest room structure. Chris's van was beside Lawrence's Cavalier.

Lawrence nodded to its rear doors. "Ben's tool belt in there?"

"Yeah."

"Let me see it."

Chris unlocked the van, opened its rear, and handed Lawrence the belt. From one of its pouches Lawrence took Ben's double-sided Crain razor knife and felt its weight and balance in his hand. The knife had a contoured wood handle and a heavy gauge three-inch blade that hooked at the end.

"Can I have it?" said Lawrence.

"Why?"

"Poet's justice," said Lawrence.

Chris nodded. "Hit me up."

"I plan to arrange this quick," said Lawrence. "We don't need to think on it too much."

"Right."

"Be ready, White Boy."

Lawrence back-pocketed the carpet knife and walked to his car. Chris's blood pounded in his ears as he watched him drive away.

SONNY AND Wayne had been partying all day in a white asbestos-shingled rambler on a generous piece of land bordering a community center in a place called Riverdale Park. Though the town was only a couple of miles off the District line in Maryland, there were trees and large lots as well as baseball and football fields visible from the backyard, and it felt familiar to both of them. They were comfortable here and relaxed. There were many Spanish in the neighborhood, and some blacks, but that didn't ruin it for them. It was as good a place as they'd been in since they had come to D.C.

The girls, Ashley and Cheyenne, had directed them out here via Kenilworth Boulevard, more miles of shit-laid road to their eyes, so it had been a nice surprise when they pulled into this neighborhood of quiet and green. Ashley said that she and Cheyenne were friendly with the boy, Chuck, who was renting the house. It was a group home for three undergraduates who attended the University of Maryland, and Chuck was the only one who'd stayed for the summer while his roommates had gone back to their hometowns. Chuck came from upstate New York money, had illegal habits, worked in a comic-book store, and was weak but sweet. He'd given them permission to crash there any time and told them where the key would be, under a flowerpot on the front stoop. They three-wayed him when he wanted it, and unlike most drug users, he shared, so it was a good arrangement. Chuck would be cool with them bringing their two new friends over for some fun. He wouldn't mind.

Sonny was outside the house, drinking a Jack and Coke from a plastic cup. Shadows had gathered and faded as night dark-

274 • GEORGE PELECANOS

ened the yard. Crickets rubbed their legs together, and the sound soothed him.

Sonny was high, maybe drunk, but in control. He had taken Ashley into one of the bedrooms as soon as they got there, asked her to strip for him, and told her to walk around. Predictably, she had a rose tattoo at the small of her back and one that matched just above her pubic line. She had cat eyes, freckles on her nose, and melon tits. It took a while, but he became aroused and he called her over to the bed, where he pushed the twins together, made them Siamese, and gave her a friction hump. It never took him long, and when he was done he was done for the day. He sat with her for a while as she snorted meth and he drank his cocktails, and he became bored, listening to her talk about bullshit, faster and faster, and listening to Wayne give it to Cheyenne in the adjoining room, the skinny girl making a whole mess of noise, Wayne showing off to his old cell mate, sending plaster chips off the wall, bottom-knocking that gal fierce, like he was hitting a pound of raw hamburger.

After, they all joined up back in the living room and commenced to partying group-style. The girls got down to panties and brassieres, which they no doubt thought was sexy, but to Sonny's mind just exposed Ashley's fat and Cheyenne's birdlike build and acned back. Wayne had his shirt off, showing off his wiry frame, not an ounce of body fat on that boy at all. They were all doing the crystal except for Sonny, with Wayne pounding Silver Bullets behind the speckled white. Wayne had no bottom for beer when he did meth. Ashley and Cheyenne found a colored station on the radio they liked, and both of them were rapping together to what passed for a song these days, and they got up and did some kind of jungle-jump to it as Wayne clapped out of time and shouted them on. Eventually Wayne and Cheyenne went back into the bedroom, and Ashley drifted off, lit some candles, and drew herself a bath. Sonny took a nap.

When he woke up, the house was quiet. He fixed a drink and went outside and saw that the Mercury was gone. He had a seat on the stoop and as night came he thought of his situation and what would come next.

He tried to envision his future, but nothing came to mind.

It occurred to him that he was where he wanted to be. A lifetime of incarceration, starting at the boys' detention center in Sabillasville, continuing on through several adult facilities, leading to the last, the federal joint in Lewisburg. All that schooling, and what he learned was: Live in the now. Take what you want, have no dreams, ride free. Like it said in the song by that wild country boy he loved: *There are those that break and bend / I'm the other kind.*

His cell phone rang. Sonny flipped it open and answered the call. When he was done talking, he put the cell back in his pocket and nodded tightly.

The Mercury pulled up in front of the house. Wayne got out, carrying a bunch of supermarket daisies, and crept across the yard. He stood in front of Sonny and head-shook his center-parted hair.

"You got that look," said Wayne. "Somethin's happenin."

"Outta the blue, I just got a call from some coon. Said he had my money and was lookin to give it back."

"I don't follow."

"Only Chris Carpet has my number. From the caller ID. So he's got a partner."

"You think it's a trap? Maybe he called the law."

"He didn't even call out for the patrol car when it passed by his yard last night, and that was life and death. He ain't that type."

Wayne grinned and his face folded in upon itself. "So it's on."

"I reckon. Whoever I spoke to is gonna phone me tomorrow and tell me when and where."

"Huh," said Wayne.

"What are the flowers for?"

"They're for my girl."

"Your girl? We paid that little heifer to fuck you, son."

"She's a nice young lady."

"She stinks."

"Watch what you say."

"She stinks like a menstruatin polecat."

"Your mother does," said Wayne.

Sonny snorted as Wayne slipped into the house.

Not much later, an old Honda coupe stopped on the street and a white boy got out of it. He walked gingerly toward Sonny. He was overweight and had long hair and a black T-shirt stretched tight over an hourglass figure. He stopped in front of the stoop where Sonny still sat.

"Who are you?" said the boy.

"Friend of Ashley's. You?"

"Chuck. I *live* here."

"So?"

The boy named Chuck tried to hold Sonny's gaze, but he could not. His shoulders slumped and he stepped carefully around the big man, opened the door to his place, and walked inside.

Sonny smiled.

TWENTY-SIX

CHRIS FLYNN sat shirtless on the edge of his bed and used one hand to pop the joints of the other. He had turned off his cell and had no landline, but now there was an incessant knocking on his apartment door. His van was on the street, so he couldn't pretend that he was not at home. He walked to the door and opened it. Katherine stood in the hall. She was lovely and agitated. Angry even, for her.

"You don't want to see me?"

"I do," said Chris. "Come in."

He stepped aside to let her pass. She came into the apartment and he followed her to the living room.

"You want a beer, somethin?"

"No, I don't want anything."

Chris pointed to a chair. "Sit down."

She sat, and Chris took a seat beside her.

"What's going on with you?" said Katherine.

"I need to be alone, is all."

"Your eyes are dead."

"It's because of Ben. I'm all fucked up behind it."

"Something's happening with you and it goes beyond Ben's

death. I need to know what it is. You've never shut me out like this before."

Chris stared down at the hardwood floor. Katherine had him. They were going to be together forever, and she was the one he could talk to. She was a piece of him and she wouldn't do him wrong. He looked her in the eyes.

"It *is* about Ben," said Chris. "I know who killed him."

"*How* do you know?" said Katherine carefully.

"It was two men. They came to visit me, right here in my backyard. They killed Ben over the money that we left in that house. It was theirs. They must have tried to get Ben to talk about who took it."

"Do you know who took it?"

"A guy named Lawrence. We were locked up with him at Pine Ridge. Ben got drunk and told Lawrence about the money, and Lawrence went back and stole it. The two men strong-armed the lady who owns the house. That led them to Ben, and me."

"And this Lawrence. He still has the money."

"Yes."

"If you know who these men are, why haven't you called the police?"

Chris looked away.

"*Chris.*"

"I'm not gonna do that," said Chris, his voice hoarse. "Me and Lawrence, we're gonna take care of this ourselves."

Katherine got up abruptly and went to the kitchen. She stood over the sink and cupped her hand and ran water into it, drank while the other hand held her strawberry blonde hair back behind her head. Chris watched her splash her face with water. She reentered the room, walking with purpose. Her cheeks were flushed and brightly freckled, and her green eyes were wildly flared. She sat beside him and grasped his hand.

"Say what you're going to do, Chris. Not that jailhouse bullshit talk, either. When you say you're going to take care of it, what are you talking about? Murder?"

"It's the only way."

"What about an arrest and conviction? The right way. The way that doesn't make you a killer and a candidate for prison."

"I can't. Ben didn't give me or Lawrence up. Ben stood tall—"

"*Stop* it." Katherine squeezed his hand tightly. "Listen to what you're saying. This isn't you, Chris."

"There's two of me," said Chris. "There's the person you think you know, and the one who's still inside me. The boy who did dirt and got schooled in that jail. The one you never met."

"I'm in love with the one I met. I could never love someone who deliberately took a life, not when there was a more reasonable option. I couldn't be with him or have his child. Do you understand that?"

"Yes. But I got to do this." He held her hand tightly. "Stay with me tonight."

Katherine pulled her hand back and stood out of the chair. She looked down at him and her lip quivered, but she held on and turned and stepped away. She headed for the door.

"Don't tell my father," said Chris.

Katherine left the apartment, shutting the door behind her without another word.

SHE DROVE straight to the Flynn home on Livingston Street. She cried on the way there but put herself back together before she arrived. After Flynn opened the door, Django bumped against her excitedly and followed her steps closely as she came into the house. Flynn was talking to her, but she was not responding, and he could only go with her, out the back door, onto the deck overlooking the yard. Flynn shut the door, leaving Django on the other side of the glass.

"What is it, honey?" said Flynn, joining Katherine at the rail. "Did you and Chris have a fight?"

She told him of their conversation in the apartment. By now Amanda had come downstairs, but as she moved toward the back door, Flynn raised his palm and she saw the look on his face and stayed inside.

"I knew he was mixed up in something," said Flynn, when Katherine was done.

"But he wasn't," said Katherine. "Someone else stole that money. A guy named Lawrence. Not Chris, and not Ben. The trouble came to them after. They were trying to do right and walk away from it. It came to *them*. Chris hasn't done anything wrong. Not yet."

Flynn pushed a shock of black hair off his forehead. He recalled the day at Mindy Kramer's house, when he'd accused Chris and Ben of botching the job. Whoever had taken the money, that Lawrence fellow, had messed up the good work they'd done. It wasn't them being lazy or sloppy. Chris had been telling the truth that day. As he tended to do, Flynn had assumed the worst about his son.

"Well, it's simple," said Flynn. "I've got to stop him. What he's saying he's gonna do, that's not him. It never was him. He was a stupid, selfish teenager, and he made mistakes. But he couldn't kill anyone. He won't."

"You should call the police, Mr. Flynn."

"I can't do that. Not until I speak to him. I don't know how far he's gone down the road. If anyone's going to call the police, it has to be him. I'll speak to him and talk him down. I can do that."

"If you think that's the way."

"I know it is. Yes."

Flynn hugged Katherine. He was perspiring, and she could smell the alcohol on his breath and in his sweat.

"He won't answer your phone call," said Katherine.

"I'm going to go over there," said Flynn, stepping back. "Stay here with Amanda for now."

"Okay."

"Thanks for coming here, Kate."

"It's Katherine," she said gently.

"Katherine. Right."

They walked into the house where Amanda was waiting.

"Chris is all right," said Flynn. "I just need to speak with him. Katherine will explain."

Amanda started to say something, but Flynn embraced her clumsily and kissed her on the mouth.

"Don't worry."

"Call me," said Amanda.

He nodded, grabbed his keys from a bowl on the kitchen counter, and headed out the door.

ROMARIO KNIGHT lived in a middle-class home in Hillcrest Heights, across Southern Avenue, which ran between the District and Prince George's County, Maryland. Knight's street was quiet and he kept to himself. He was a bachelor who occasionally brought women home and had friends over on Redskins Sundays. He looked like any man in his thirties who went to work and made a modest living. By day, Knight wore a uniform as a meter man for the gas company. He was also a gun dealer who serviced the Southeast trade. Knight's clients came to his place of residence after being screened by third parties.

Lawrence Newhouse stood with Knight in the downstairs rec room of the Hillcrest home. A huge television set, couches and chairs, and a wet bar filled the room, and Redskins memorabilia covered the walls. Knight wore a Sean Taylor jersey and he filled it out. He was a huge man who, even when in shape, had always been fat. In the years he played high school ball in PG, he was known, alternately and randomly, as Papa Doc and Baby Doc. He had the curious distinction of carrying the nicknames of both the father and the son.

Lawrence had put the word out with a boy at Parkchester he reckoned would have such connections, and soon Lawrence got a call on his cell and then was met by another young man, who checked him out, issued some barely veiled threats, and gave him instructions. In the course of a few hours, Lawrence was here, purchasing guns.

A large and a small revolver, a couple of semiautomatics, and boxes of ammunition were laid out on a card table. The weapons still had serial numbers and if confiscated would be traced back to legitimate gun stores in Virginia, where they had been originally purchased by straw buyers.

Lawrence stood beside Knight, looking down at the weapons, experiencing that curious sensation of excitement and dread some men feel in the presence of guns.

Lawrence had shot a boy many years ago. Had he killed the young man, Lawrence's punishment would have been more severe, but the wound was not fatal. Lawrence could barely remember why he had done the thing. Some slight, real or imagined, had sent him after the boy with a Taurus .38, a true

Saturday night special, because Lawrence knew he couldn't settle it with his hands.

"What's that?" said Lawrence, pointing to a small auto pistol with a chrome finish and a laminated wood stock.

"Davis thirty-two," said Knight.

"Does it work?"

"It ain't gonna blow up in your face, *I don't think*. I mean, shit, you said you wanted the cheapest thing I had."

"It's for my partner. I'm askin, will it stop a man?"

"I'm not even about to answer that. The Davis is a gun and it shoots bullets. That's all I can say."

"Okay. I'll take that."

"You said you wanted a revolver for yourself."

"Autos jam."

"They been known to."

"What you got?"

"I brought out a couple pieces you might like. S and W's, both. There goes a thirty-eight, right there." Knight pointed to a short-barreled Chief. "Smith and Wesson make a nice product. You can't go wrong with that."

Knight's voice was unenthusiastic. Lawrence knew he was about to be stepped up to the larger, more masculine-looking weapon set beside it. He knew, but he couldn't help asking the next question.

"What about that big boy right there?" said Lawrence.

"Go ahead and pick it up," said Knight.

Lawrence lifted the gun off the table. He hefted it and turned it in the light. It had a stainless finish, a six-inch barrel, and rubber, finger-molded grips. It felt right in his hand.

"Three fifty-seven combat magnum," said Knight. "That's a pup right there. You squeeze the trigger on that boy, it's like shootin a full can of beer at a thousand miles an hour. Make a nice hole goin in and a mess goin out. It's gonna kick, too. I don't know, you might want somethin more manageable for your body type. . . ."

"I'll take it," said Lawrence.

"You gonna need some bullets, right?"

"Not a whole box."

"I only sell bricks."

"What about a shoulder rig for this one? I can't be putting this monster down in my dip."

"I can sell you that, too."

"How about throwin it in?"

Knight laughed through his teeth and shook his head. They negotiated a price, and Lawrence paid him from a roll he had in his pocket, then stashed everything into a daypack he had brought with him.

Walking to the basement steps, Lawrence said, "Where you get all this Redskins shit, man?"

"Shows. The Internet."

"You go to the games?"

"Not anymore," said Knight. "I hate that stadium."

"We gonna do it this year?"

"Not this year. But we will." Knight put his hand on Lawrence's shoulder at the front door. "You don't know me, man. We ain't never met."

"I heard that," said Lawrence.

He walked to his Cavalier, parked on the street.

AFTER REPEATED knocks on Chris's door with no response, Flynn was let into the apartment by Andy Ladas, who had an extra key. There was nothing there, no note, no notepads to rub that would reveal the secret message, no telltale signs left behind to let Flynn know where Chris had gone. It occurred to Flynn that he knew little about Chris's life as an adult. He was not familiar with his hangouts, his haunts, or the locations of the homes or apartments of his closest friends.

He did have Ali's number logged into the address book of his cell. He phoned Ali, got him, and filled him in on the latest events. Ali said that he would try to contact Lawrence; he had his number and knew where he lived. While Flynn waited in the quiet of Chris's apartment, he helped himself to a beer, drank it quickly, and had another. By the time he was headed for a third, Ali phoned him back.

"Lawrence wasn't answering his cell," said Ali. "I went over to where he stays and talked to his sister. He's been out the apartment all night. She hasn't seen or heard from him."

"Can you get away for a while?" said Flynn. "I want to look for him. Two sets of eyes and all that."

"I can meet you," said Ali. He told Flynn where, a halfway point on Riggs Road, near South Dakota Avenue.

"Twenty minutes," said Flynn.

They drove the streets for hours, but they didn't find Chris.

HE HAD checked into a motel high on Georgia Avenue, in south Silver Spring, just over the line into Maryland. Though it was near the niceties of the new downtown, it had a Plexiglas reception area and the requisite male hooker, dressed and made up as a female, lounging in the lobby. It was not a plastic-sheet flophouse, but it was close.

What it did have was a covered garage. Chris had tucked the van far back inside, well out of view from the street, before he checked in.

He had a duffel bag with some clothes in it, and his shaving kit. He had not bought any alcohol or weed to smoke. He wanted his mind sharp and clear. His thoughts were grim and clouded, and he needed to see through them to some kind of light.

He had turned on his cell, and its ring tone sounded frequently. The calls were from his father, Ali, his mother, and Katherine. He let them go to message. Eventually the calls stopped.

He lay on the double bed of the stark room, watching television but not watching it, thinking. He had used the remote to get ESPN, and now there were highlights of a bicycle race, many men wearing tight shorts and colorful jerseys, navigating a twisting downhill road, and some sort of accident where several bicycles went down. He did not follow the sport, could not identify this particular race, and was uninterested. He had never been a fan of biking. As he reached his teens, he had thought it was nerdy and lame.

His father used to strap him into a seat on the back of his bike and ride him all the way down to the Potomac on the paved trails of Rock Creek Park. He had been very young and his memory was sketchy, and he had not thought of it at all in a long while. What he remembered, mostly, were flashes and sensations. Sun streaming down through the trees. The wind on his face and in his hair. The feel of his own smile. On those rides, when he got up a good amount of speed, his father would sometimes reach behind him and squeeze Chris's hand, reassure him, tell him that everything was going to be all right.

I am not someone who could kill a man. There is nothing in my past and nothing inside me that would allow me to do that. Ben couldn't, and neither can I.

Ben had tried to help Lawrence. Ben had seen something in him that others couldn't see. If Ben were alive, he'd stop Lawrence from what he had planned. Chris knew this. It was on him now to act for Ben.

He relaxed and fell asleep.

His ring tone woke him up. He looked at the caller ID on his cell and saw that it was Lawrence.

"Yeah," said Chris.

"It's me," said Lawrence, his voice gravelly. "We about to do this, son."

"All right."

"I set it up. Got us some iron, too." Lawrence listened to silence and said, "You still with me?"

"Where we supposed to meet 'em?"

"I'll tell you face-to-face. You and me need to hook up and lay it out."

Lawrence gave him the time and the spot. Chris said he'd meet him there and ended the call.

TWENTY-SEVEN

LAWRENCE NEWHOUSE stood in the heat of the bedroom he shared with Dorita's younger kids and slipped a lightweight burnt-orange North Face jacket over his white T. The gym bag, filled with money, and his daypack, containing the guns and Ben's carpet knife, sat on the bed.

He had been up, unable to sleep, for most of the night. He had stayed on his back, on the bed, his forearm draped over his eyes, thinking of what he was about to do. Pondering his strategy, and Chris.

Lawrence lifted the daypack and slipped one strap over his shoulder.

His smart little nephew, Terrence, came into the room. He grabbed his sneaks off the floor and looked up at his old uncle, overdressed for this summer day.

"Where you goin, Uncle L?"

"I got business."

"You a businessman?"

"You know I am."

"I'm gonna be a scientist," said Terrence, his face hopeful

and bright. "Look at the solar system through one of them telescopes and stuff."

"You can do it, Terrence. Just keep your head in those books."

Lawrence reached out and touched Terrence's warm scalp. The boy *could* do it. He had the brains. But he needed to get out of this place and away from his mother, who was too busy putting on weight and talking on her cell to get the boy in a position where he could succeed. Lawrence had heard of those charter schools the kids slept at, away from their homes. That was the type of hookup Terrence needed. But Lawrence didn't know how to make that kind of thing happen. It got him confused and angry to think on it, so he reached for the gym bag and gripped its stiff handles in his hand.

"I'll check you later, little man."

Lawrence walked from the room. He passed through the big area off the kitchen, where Dorita was sprawled out on the couch. Her little girl, Loquatia, was seated on the carpet in front of the TV, her hand in a bag of Cheetos.

"Where you headed?" said Dorita.

"Out," said Lawrence.

"Bring me back a soda."

"That's one thing you don't need."

"I ain't ask for your opinion."

"Okay, corn chip."

Lawrence kept moving out the door. He cared about his sister, he supposed, but damn, Dorita wasn't much more than two hundred fifty pounds of waste. He had considered giving her some of the money, but only for a minute. She'd blow it on stupid shit that would come to no good for the kids. Instead, Lawrence was gonna do something with it. One thing right.

Out on the street, he went to his Cavalier. Marquis Gilman,

his teenage nephew, called out to him. Marquis was standing around talking to some boys he shouldn't have been talking to. Lawrence walked to his car, popped the rear lid, and dropped the gym bag and the daypack into the trunk. Marquis was now beside him, looking at the trunk's contents. Lawrence closed the lid.

"You leavin out?" said Marquis, his gangly arms hanging loosely at his side.

"Nah, man. Goin for a ride."

"Looks like you takin off for real."

"I'm straight hood, son. Where would I go?" Lawrence put his hand on his nephew's shoulder. "Look, Marquis . . ."

"What?"

"I'm gonna go talk to Mr. Carter one more time. See if he can't hook you up with some worthwhile employment. But whatever happens, I want you to listen to that man and do what he says. He's lookin out for you. Ali is cool people." Lawrence made a sweeping motion with his hand. "You don't belong on this street. Time for you to make your move or you ain't never gonna get out."

"*You* stayed."

"Does it look like it was good to me?"

Marquis did not answer. Lawrence clasped one of Marquis's hands and put his free arm around Marquis and patted his back.

"See you up the road," said Lawrence. "Hear?"

Lawrence got into his car without looking back and sped away. A couple of blocks from the apartment, he stopped and threw his cell phone down a storm drain. He was done with it and didn't want to be called or traced. He was shedding his skin. He then drove over the Frederick Douglass Memorial Bridge and tossed something over its rail. On the other side of the Anacostia, he turned around, recrossed the river, and rolled back into his neighborhood.

He drove around for a while, till he spotted what he was looking for. Down around Firth Sterling Ave and Sumner Road he saw a boy, no older than ten or eleven, on a men's road bike that looked to be in perfect shape and was way too big for him. Lawrence pulled over and leaned out the open window.

"Young!" shouted Lawrence. "Yeah, you. Don't worry, you not in trouble. I just want to talk to you."

"What you want?" said the boy, who was pedaling the bike slowly in a tight circle.

"You about to make some money."

"What kinda money?"

"Kind you spend," said Lawrence. He killed the engine and stepped out of the car.

FLYNN AND Hector carried a roll of Berber out of the warehouse of Top Carpet and Floor Install in Beltsville and loaded it into Hector's van. Hector was not his usual upbeat self. He had been upset by the killing of Ben and his general air of optimism had been tested. But he was determined to work his way through it. He and the others in Isaac's crew, in the absence of Ben and Chris, had doubled their load and come through for the company.

Flynn's chest ached as he pushed the roll into the back of the van. He stood straight and waited for the pain to pass.

"You okay, boss?" said Hector.

"Fine," said Flynn. "This is going to that Tenleytown job."

"Tito gonna meet me there," said Hector, speaking of a new guy from the Dominican.

"Okay. Then you need to come back and pick up that roll for the lady in Tysons."

"We gonna take care of it. We make it nice."

"Thank you," said Flynn, looking Hector straight in the eye. "I appreciate it. I do."

As Hector drove off, Flynn entered the warehouse, passing the stage where a man spun a large piece of carpet levitated by air, and walked into the office area. Susie, the chubby girl with the fried-perm hairdo, and Katherine were seated behind their desks. Katherine had dark semicircles beneath her eyes. It was obvious she hadn't slept.

Flynn looked at Katherine and made a head motion toward the door.

"I'll just be a minute, Suze," said Katherine, and she got up out of her chair and followed Flynn outside.

They went by a parking area, crossed a narrow road, and stood in the shade of a lone oak.

"You hear from Chris?" said Flynn.

"No."

"We haven't, either. I'm in touch with Ali, and of course Amanda is sitting by the phone at home." Flynn touched Katherine's arm. "I don't want you to worry."

"It's like it was when Ben was missing," said Katherine. "It feels the same way."

"It's not gonna be like that," said Flynn. "Nothing's going to happen to my son and he's not going to kill anyone. Chris is tough and he's got character. This is going to be over with today and it's going to end right. Between all of us, we're going to find him. Okay?"

"I want to believe you," said Katherine.

"I promise you," said Flynn. Hoping that the sick feeling inside him, the helplessness, was not showing on his face.

*   *   *

CHRIS SAW the Cavalier, parked in the lot where Lawrence had said it would be. Chris put the van in a space alongside the Chevy. Chris had followed Lawrence's directions to a community park in Colman Manor, but he was in an unfamiliar place and felt lucky to have found the vehicle. Atop the Cavalier were a couple of loose ropes that went inside the barely open windows. Lawrence had lashed something to the roof of the car.

Chris only knew that he was in Prince George's County, somewhere near the District, having come through a tucked-in community that looked like a country town.

He locked the van, and, per Lawrence's instructions, found a nearby bike path sided by trees. He walked it for what seemed like a long while. Partway in, he realized he had left his cell back in the Ford, but he had come too far to turn back. Eventually he emerged from the woods and found himself on a wide road along a body of water. There were houses and streets on his left. He idly wondered why Lawrence had not told him to park on those residential blocks, which were much closer to the meeting spot. Across the water he could see a large dock and recreation area, and the famous tan-and-brown Peace Cross, a place his father had spoken of, once home to country, rock, and biker nightlife. Now Chris had a better idea of his location. He was somewhere near Bladensburg Road and the old Route 1.

The bike path continued, veering off the road and down a dip, going under a bridge. There he saw Lawrence in the shadows. A bicycle leaned up against a three-pole rail that separated the path and a drop-off to the water. An old white man, not much larger than a boy, was standing there, too. On the ground nearby were several blankets and a cooler.

Chris walked under the bridge and nodded at Lawrence. The little white man, unshaven, drunk, wearing a sleeveless T-shirt, raised his fists over his head and flexed his muscles.

"I'm fifty-five," said the little man, smiling, showing brown nubs that had once been teeth. "And I'll do fifty-five push-ups."

"Leave outta here, old-timer," said Lawrence, not unkindly.

"This is my house," said the little man.

Lawrence produced a roll of cash from his pocket and peeled off a twenty. "Go on, man. Get yourself some medicine. When you come back, we'll be gone."

The little man happily took the money and walked down the path in the direction of Bladensburg Road.

"Where are we?" said Chris.

"That's the Anacostia right there," said Lawrence, nodding at the river. "You know it flowed this far into Maryland?"

"I didn't."

"I'm tellin you, you can't know this city till you get on a bicycle."

"Where'd you get that one?"

"Bought it off some kid. It was stole, I reckon, so he made out all right."

Chris shifted his feet. "Why are we meeting here, Lawrence?"

"It's out the way."

"Tell me about it. I could have parked right in that neighborhood over there, instead of in that park."

"And now you gonna have to hike out a distance to get back to your car. Gives me time to put some space between us, what with me and my two wheels."

"Why would you want to do that?"

" 'Cause you ain't comin with me, man."

Chris squinted. "I thought you bought me a gun."

"I threw that cheap piece off the Douglass. It would have blown up in your face, anyhow. That is, if you had the steel to use it. I just don't think you do."

"You're right," said Chris. "I wouldn't have used it. I'm not about to kill anyone."

"So why are you here?"

"To try and stop you."

"Try, then."

Chris reached out to put a brotherly hand on Lawrence's shoulder. Lawrence slapped Chris's hand away and smiled.

"Don't be touchin on me," said Lawrence.

"There's got to be another way to solve this."

"Not for me."

"Tell me where you're meeting them. We'll have them arrested."

"You know I ain't gonna do that."

"We can talk about it, at least."

"You wanna talk now?" said Lawrence. "What about all that time in the Ridge when you refused to talk to me? When you showed me your back. Callin me Bughouse and shit, when I had a real last name. You think I don't know what y'all thought of me? All 'a y'all, except Ben. That boy had good in him, man. And I killed him." Lawrence poked a finger roughly into his own chest. "*I* did. This here got nothing to do with you. So go home, White Boy. Leave me to my thing."

"Listen," said Chris, taking a step forward.

Lawrence threw a right. It caught Chris square on the jaw, and he lost his balance. He went down on his side to the paved path. He rolled over and got up onto his knees. He had bitten his tongue and he spit out saliva and blood. He stood slowly and unsteadily. The landscape was tilted, and he tried to shake his head and make it straight but could not.

"That's right," said Lawrence. "Surprised you, didn't I?"

"Wait," said Chris.

"I'm about to clean you proper now."

Lawrence planted his back foot. Chris tucked his elbows in and tried to cover up, but he was too slow. Lawrence jabbed through the protection with his left and his fist found Chris's nose. The ring on his finger cut Chris, stung him, and blurred his vision. Chris dropped one arm and Lawrence grunted behind a right that had everything in it and Chris took the punch in the temple and was spun and knocked off his feet. He seemed to fall for a long time. His head hit the iron rail, and for a moment there was faint sensation and a downward float. He did not feel it when he hit the ground.

Lawrence stood over him. Blood flowed freely from Chris's nose. He wasn't moving. Lawrence crouched down and felt for a pulse. He did not find it and he began to panic and touched the artery standing out on Chris's neck. Chris was unconscious, but he was alive. Lawrence folded one of the little man's blankets into a small square and placed it behind Chris's head. He had seen this done on television shows. He hoped that this was right, but he couldn't stay.

Elated and horrified, he swung onto the saddle of the bike and pedaled furiously down the path in the direction of his car.

TWENTY-EIGHT

ALI CARTER stood inside the storefront window of his office on Alabama Avenue, watching William Richards mixing with the young men and women on the street. He had just met with William, and it had not gone well. He'd tried to convince him to return to his job with Party Land, which William had recently walked away from once again, refusing to wear the shirt with the balloon-and-clown logo. Ali was pretty certain that William was back to dirt and running with his boys. He had heard that William was beefing with someone and that this problem was about to boil over. William was too proud and stupid to walk away from it. His future, most likely, was grim. Anyway, Ali had tried.

Ali could not help everyone who came through his doors. Being completely honest with himself, he would admit that he could not help most of them or lead the majority of them to productive futures. If he were to think in terms of grandiose objectives, he would have to give up. It was impossible to pull large groups of young men through tiny keyholes. Ali had modest goals because that was how he got through his day.

Lawrence Newhouse's hooptie, the old Cavalier, pulled up in front of the office, a bike tied to its roof.

Ali watched as Lawrence, in a white T-shirt under a light-weight, rust-colored jacket, got out of the car. Lawrence opened the trunk and withdrew a gym bag. He walked toward the storefront, ignoring the snickers from the young ones on the sidewalk around him.

"Come on," said Ali, though no one else was in the room. "Come inside."

Lawrence entered the office. A chime sounded from a bell mounted over the door.

"Ding," said Lawrence, with a smile. He shook his braids away from his face. "Heard you been lookin for me."

"Come sit," said Ali.

They crossed the spartan room. Ali sat behind his desk, and Lawrence took a chair before it.

"I'm here," said Lawrence.

"Where's Chris at?"

"I had to drop him. That's right. Me."

"What do you mean, *drop him?*"

"I didn't shoot him or nothin like that. I put him down with my hands. He was tryin to stop me from doing this thing I got to do. Gettin all high-horse on my ass."

"Is he all right?"

"He's breathin. He fell down and hit his head. He ain't as rough and tough as he thinks he is. But he's gonna be okay."

"Where is he?" said Ali.

"On a bike trail, under a bridge. Near the Peace Cross, out by Colman Manor."

"Where exactly?"

Lawrence described the short way in and Ali wrote it down. Ali picked his cell up off the desk, and Lawrence listened as Ali spoke to Chris's father with urgency and gave the father directions to his son. As Ali talked, Lawrence took a black Sharpie from a leather cup filled with writing utensils and slipped one into the pocket of his North Face. Ali ended the call and placed the cell phone back atop the desk.

Ali's eyes went to the floor, where the gym bag sat. "What's in that sack?"

"My valuables. You don't think I'd leave them in my car, do you? In this neighborhood?"

"It's not so bad. Me and my mother live across the street."

"I know it. Gotta hand it to you, 'cause you got out."

"You could, too."

"It's too late for me."

"It's not," said Ali. "You don't have to do this."

"But I'm about to."

"I could call the police."

"And have me arrested for what? Thinkin on a murder?"

"I bet if they searched your car, they'd find a gun. That's an automatic fall for you."

"You wouldn't do that."

"Killing those men is not what Ben would've wanted."

"Don't start with me," said Lawrence. "You don't even want to put your hand near the flames I got inside me today. Chris did, and he stretched out."

The chair creaked beneath Ali's shifting weight. "Why'd you come here, Lawrence?"

"To appeal to your sense of right, I guess. To ask you one more time to get my nephew someplace good."

"I'm tryin to. But it takes baby steps to get where Marquis needs to be. Wasn't no leap from where I was to that house across the street, or this job I got right here. You can't just snap your fingers and make it happen."

"Take care of him the best you can. That's all I'm askin."

Ali nodded slowly. "I will."

Lawrence picked up the gym bag and stood from his chair. "Where the bathroom in this piece?"

"In the back."

Lawrence walked past the desk. Ali listened as the toilet flushed and the sink water ran. A couple of minutes later, Lawrence emerged from the bathroom without the bag and stood across from where Ali was seated.

"Place is dirty. You could use some new furniture, shit like that. Maybe a TV set that ain't broke, so the boys could chill in here."

"You forgot your bag."

"No, I didn't."

"What's going on, Lawrence?"

"Take care of your little niggas, hear?"

"I'm doin my best."

Lawrence held out his fist and reached across the desk. "Unit Five."

"Unit Five," said Ali softly. He dapped Lawrence up.

Lawrence grinned. "See you later . . . *Holly.*"

Ali smiled a little against a sinking feeling as he watched him step to the door. The small bell chimed as the door pushed out and Lawrence hit the sidewalk.

Ali got out of his chair and walked into the bathroom. There on the closed toilet lid sat the open gym bag, filled with cash. And on the mirror, written in black:

Your boy, Lawrence

Ali jogged out of the bathroom, went to the front window of the storefront, and looked out onto the street.

Lawrence Newhouse was gone.

*   *   *

SONNY WADE walked into a bedroom of the white rambler in Riverdale. Wayne Minors sat on the edge of the bed, shirtless and taut. He had been napping, and Sonny's heavy fist on the closed door, ten minutes earlier, had woken him up. Beside Wayne, the girl named Cheyenne slept nude atop the sheets. Raspberries of acne dotted her bony back.

"You been dozing?" said Sonny.

"I get tired after," said Wayne.

"I told you not to take no postcoital naps."

"Huh?"

"We got work and I want your head straight. Here." Sonny reached into his windbreaker and drew a Taurus .9 from where he had slipped it against his belly. "You're gonna need that."

"I got my knife."

"That's only good for close work. 'Less you plan to throw it."

"I could."

"This ain't no carnival. Take the gun."

Wayne took it and placed it beside him on the bed. He reached over to the nightstand and picked up the hardwood-handled knife with the spine-cut steel blade. He fitted it in its sheath, hiked up one leg of his Wrangler jeans, and strapped the sheath to his calf. He put on his black ring-strap Dingo boots, stood, and drew a black T-shirt over his head. He folded up the sleeves of the T-shirt one time to show off his arms and touched his wallet, chained to a belt loop, to make sure that it was secure.

"Say good-bye to your little slut," said Sonny.

"Don't call her that."

"Do it and let's get gone."

Wayne leaned over the bed and kissed Cheyenne's shoulder. His bushy mustache flattened out against her bone. He stood straight and holstered the Taurus in his waistband, under his T.

They walked into the living room. Ashley and Chuck were seated on the couch. There was a bong on the table before them, a ziplock bag of marijuana that was mostly seeds and stems, empty wine cooler bottles, crushed cans of beer. The television was on. They were watching *MTV Cribs*.

"You leavin?" said Ashley.

"It's time," said Sonny, his idea of a warm good-bye. He looked at Chuck, rolls of fat spilling about his waist, staring at the TV, too frightened to meet Sonny's eyes. "You never met us. Is that clear, fella?"

"Yes," said Chuck.

Sonny stood over Chuck and leaned forward. "You speak on either of us, my little buddy will come back here and carve you up."

Chuck's lip trembled.

" 'Preciate the hospitality," said Sonny.

Sonny and Wayne walked from the house. They got into the Mercury and drove over to the community center and park, where brown people were playing baseball on one of the diamonds. Sonny and Wayne got out of the black sedan and broke their cell phones on the hard road and threw the pieces into the woods. Sonny wanted no record of the incoming or outgoing calls they had made while they were in town, nor did he wish to worry on the tracking possibilities of GPS. They'd buy a couple of disposable cells at a convenience store when they left town.

They drove over to Kenilworth Avenue and headed into the city. Sonny had loaded the Mercury with all of their belongings. They had no firm plans or destination but were ticking with anticipation of the violence that was about to come.

Twenty minutes later, they were on New York Avenue. Sonny gripped the wheel of the fake-fur-covered steering wheel and spun it as Wayne lit a cigarette off a butane flame. He blew a smoke ring that shattered in the wind. Looking at it, his eyes crossed.

"What's postcoital mean?" said Wayne.

"Means after you stick her, stupid."

"My name is not Stupid."

"Hmph," said Sonny Wade.

They rolled through the open black gates of the National Arboretum and drove to the information center to get a map.

THE LITTLE man's name was Larry. He had returned to his home under the bridge, a brown bag holding a pint of store-brand vodka and a six of beer clutched under his arm. He had found Chris lying on the path with a blanket under his head. Chris was awake but motionless, looking up at the steel beams beneath the bridge floor. There was blood on his face. Larry wiped at it with a dirty rag, which only smudged the blood further. He covered Chris with another blanket.

"You're gonna be all right," said Larry. "But you need to lie there some."

"I gotta get back to my van," said Chris.

"You been hit on the noggin. You should take it slow."

Chris felt weak and a bit shocked. He peeled off the blanket and tried to get up on his feet. He was too dizzy. He sat back down, waited for the nausea to pass, and tried again. He stood carefully and gripped the rail.

"Who's that?" said Larry. He was nodding at the bike trail that broadened to a road.

Chris looked in that direction. A man with wild black hair was running down the road toward them. His feet were pounding the asphalt and dirt, and their heavy contact raised dust.

"Crazy sonofabitch," said Larry.

Chris issued a blood-caked smile.

THOMAS FLYNN walked Chris to Amanda's SUV and got him into the passenger bucket. He found a packet of wipes in the glove box and cleaned Chris's face, and once it was free of dirt and blood he inspected it.

"I should take you to an emergency room," said Flynn.

"I'm all right. I hit my head when I was falling, is all."

"All the more reason to get you to a doctor." Flynn shook his head, looking at the purple bruising that had come to Chris's face. "Why he'd do this to you?"

"Lawrence? I was tryin to stop him. But it was more than that. In his own way, Lawrence was looking to protect me. He wanted to keep me out of it."

"Do you know where he was going to meet them?"

"I had some time to think about it, lying under that bridge." Chris nodded. "I'm pretty sure I know where he went. It's a spot Lawrence took me to, over at the Arboretum."

"Then you need to call the police."

"Go ahead."

"*You* need to, Chris."

Chris looked at his watch. "It's close to four. He's already there."

Flynn scrolled through the contacts on his cell and found the one he was looking for.

"This is the number for Sergeant Bryant. Call her and tell her what's happening. She'll get some cars over there." Chris did not reach for the cell. "Do it, son. You've got to do what's right."

"I'm tryin, Dad."

"I know it. You've been trying all along. I'm sorry I doubted you."

"Forget all that," said Chris. "It's past."

They looked at each other across the seats.

Flynn held out his phone. Chris took it and made the call.

TWENTY-NINE

HE HAD parked the Cavalier in a small lot near the Capitol columns and untied the bicycle from the roof. It was now late in the afternoon and a drizzle had come that would soon turn to rain. Lawrence swung the daypack over his shoulders and got onto the bike.

He took the Crabtree loop and then Hickory Hill. He rode for miles. The rain cooled him and his pace was steady as he geared up and took the rise. The wind was pleasant on his face and it blew back his braids.

His prize possession as a boy had been his bicycle. When he would go out on long rides, to the Peace Cross, the Aquatic Gardens, and the Arboretum, he was far away from his roach-infested apartment, his smoked-up mother, her various men. He imagined that if he kept pedaling he would come to a place that was safe, find people to hold him instead of slap him, and be with adults who would talk to him with kindness and patience instead of sarcasm and cruelty. He never did find that place. But on his bike, for a short time at least, he could see it in his mind.

He pedaled up the road as the woods grew thick. He was

soaked with sweat beneath his jacket as he climbed the last hill. He passed a motorized maintenance cart, its driver giving him a small wave, as he arrived at the Asia Collection and its parking lot. There were no cars. It was the most out-of-the-way area in the park and also it was raining. There would be few visitors or grounds crew here today.

Lawrence got off the bike. He walked it off the road, past the brick house that held rest rooms, and carefully stepped down a lightly forested hill, holding and guiding the bike. Halfway down the hill he laid the bicycle on its side, partially concealed behind an oak, and covered it as best he could with brush and leaves. It was not hidden, but there was no place to keep it totally out of sight without putting it very far away. He would need access to it in the unlikely event that things went right.

Lawrence lifted the pack off his shoulders. From it he retrieved the Smith and Wesson combat magnum. He broke open its cylinder and thumbed six rounds into its chambers.

"Six is enough," he said, speaking out loud because he was nervous.

He snapped the cylinder shut and slipped the .357 into the shoulder holster he wore under his jacket. He drew the weapon cleanly and put it back in its holster. Then he took the Crain knife from the pack and slid it into the side pocket of his North Face.

He pinned the daypack under the bike and walked up the hill.

SONNY AND Wayne went into the Arboretum visitors' center. There were some old-folk visitors in the lobby and a couple of large female employees. One was complaining to the other about her man. The two white men with the outdated facial hair looked like they did not belong here or anywhere else but went virtually unnoticed because they did not linger. Wayne grabbed a folded information pamphlet that contained a map, and the two of them went back outside.

Crossing the lot, Wayne remarked on the numerous compact Jeep security vehicles and their drivers, rented cops.

Sonny said, "What are they gonna do? Only real police and criminals have guns in this town. Anyway, my Merc's got eight cylinders and they got four."

"What time is it?"

Sonny checked his watch. "Three thirty-five. Our friend said he'd be there at four."

"This *bro*-chure says the grounds close at five."

"We'll be done by then."

Sonny ignitioned the Marquis and took off. Wayne served as copilot as Sonny navigated the roads. Wayne was confused by the icons on the map, which he found overly clever and unhelpful, but signs on the shoulder had English words and clear arrows, and Sonny followed their directions up into the hills.

"How many exits you see on that map?" said Sonny.

"Looks like three. A service road makes four."

"Jesus, they're makin this easy."

Wayne lit a Marlboro, rolling the window down as Sonny arrived at the area, high atop a winding rise, marked "Asia Collection." There was a Cushman utility truck parked on the edge of the road, bales of hay stacked on its flat bed. Sonny put the Mercury into a lined space, head in, facing a small brick structure set down a stone path. He cut the engine.

It was raining harder. Wayne kept his window open, his arm leaning on the door ledge as he smoked, not noticing that he was getting wet.

"That can't be theirs," said Wayne, turning his head to indicate the truck.

"That's a vehicle for workers," said Sonny.

"So there's a third party here in these woods."

"Shame on them if they see us."

"Where's our friends?"

"They'll be here."

"You reckon there's two?"

"Well, there was that Afro American I spoke to. And Chris Carpet. Them and the smoke you butchered. They were all in this together. Criminals, like us. But not as hard as us."

Wayne took the Taurus from his waistband and pushed it under the seat. Its barrel had been cutting into his middle. He pitched his cigarette out the window and found a snow seal in the pocket of his Wranglers and carefully unfolded it. In it was a small amount of white crystal speckled with blue. He put his nose to it and snorted it up. He licked the paper hungrily, crumpled it, and dropped it on the floor.

"That did it," said Wayne, instantly lit. His eyes had begun to spiral.

"Now your nose is gonna bleed."

"Means it's good." Wayne nodded toward the small brick house. "Them's bathrooms?"

"No, it's a mo-tel."

"'Cause I feel like I could shit."

"Clench your sphincter," said Sonny.

Wayne folded his arms petulantly and unfolded them. "I need to walk. Look around. Could be they're lyin in wait."

"Dumbass. You think they parachuted in?"

"I'm sayin I can't sit still."

"Go ahead, then, but roll up that window before you do. That rain's gonna damage my velour."

Wayne closed the window. "You comin?"

"Nope. I think I'll stay dry."

"What if somethin happens?"

Sonny smiled. "I'll hear you scream."

"Or them," said Wayne, and he stepped out of the car.

Sonny watched him go down the stone path toward the rest room structure. It was hard to see him through the windshield, what with the rain. Wayne turned the corner and went around the back of the building and was gone.

LAWRENCE STOOD behind the brick house for a long while, but his nerves got to him when he heard the work truck come to a stop on the road. He looked around the corner and saw a young, heavyset female in an Arboretum shirt get out of the truck, a big cell or two-way holstered to her side. She was a white girl and she wore a rain slicker over the shirt and carried a bucket and hand shovel. If she saw him she'd see a hood rat from the side of town she never drove through, and she would get suspicious and maybe call security. Lawrence guessed she was one of those college girls who had majored in trees and plants. They had a name for that. Whore culture. Lawrence was too nervous to remember the word. But she was not the type to be cleaning out a bathroom. Wasn't no way she'd walk into the men's. Lawrence slipped around the corner and quietly pushed on the door to the men's room and stepped inside.

It was smaller than he thought it would be. Around a green metal divider, along one wall, were two urinals and a green metal stall holding a toilet. On the wall to his right was a white sink, a soap dispenser above it, and to the left one of those hot-air hand dryers that no one liked to use. Beside the sink, an office-sized trash can lined with a plastic bag. The floor was made up of small tiles in various shades of brown.

Rain tapped at the shingled roof. Lawrence heard the engine of a car, sounded like a big one, as it neared and then came to a stop.

He realized then that he had no plan.

In his mind, he had seen himself facing them, his gun hand hanging loosely at his side, his eyes steely, perhaps a small smile on his face, drawing quickly, beating their draw because they were white boys and slow, spinning the gun and holstering it before they even hit the ground. Ron O'Neal. The Master Gunfighter.

But here he was, low Lawrence Newhouse, cowering in a dirty bathroom. Trapped.

If one of them walked in, Lawrence would have to use Ben's blade. The sound of a gunshot would bring the other one, prepared, and that would mean that he, Lawrence, would be doomed.

Lawrence stood in front of the toilet stall. In his quivering hand was the carpet knife. The wood handle was damp with his sweat.

He shook his braids away from his face and tried to raise spit.

WAYNE MINORS had gone around the back of the building with the shingled roof and had found nothing but bright green ivy and a meter on its red brick wall. He had to go, but he preferred to urinate outside. Because he was still a child, he pissed his initials against the bricks. When he zipped up, he moved back from the wall and looked down a gently sloping hill.

He squinted through the mist and the rain. Down there behind a tree he thought he saw . . . yes, it was. A bicycle. Wayne stared at it, his mouth open, breathing through his nose. He got down to one knee and as his pants leg rode up, he drew his Rambo III knife from its sheath.

He gripped the hardwood handle and pressed the heavy-duty pommel and the steel blade against his leg. He went around the corner of the building and looked to the Mercury, parked in the space at the end of the stone path. He made a chucking motion with his chin but could not clearly see Sonny's reaction, or if he had one at all. The windshield was heavy with water.

One bicycle, one man. Ain't gonna be no problem. I'll walk out with a trophy and see the admiration in Sonny's eyes. Because I am his equal. I am not stupid.

Wayne turned and stepped quickly into the men's room.

LAWRENCE GOT a look at the man who had come to kill him as he emerged from behind the green metal divider. He was a little white man, tightly wound and strong, with a thick mustache and slightly crossed eyes. He held a hunting knife.

Lawrence opened his mouth to speak but could not. The little man giggled and came across the room. He was on Lawrence fast as fire, his knife hand raised.

This is the man who murdered Ben, thought Lawrence Newhouse, stepping back against the sink wall, frozen, unable to raise the Crain carpet knife, as he watched Wayne's weapon come down toward his chest.

The blade glanced off the holster and butt of Lawrence's gun. It surprised Wayne and woke Lawrence up.

This is the man who murdered Ben.

Wayne raised the knife again.

Lawrence grabbed Wayne's knife hand at the wrist and pushed him back. He danced Wayne across the tiles and into the green metal divider, rocking it. He had Wayne's T-shirt bunched in his right hand, still gripping the wood of the carpet knife. He spun him and held tight, pushing and lifting him, Wayne's feet grazing the tiles as they headed back to the sink wall, and Lawrence, with great force, slammed him up against the hand dryer. He let go of Wayne's shirt and moved the knife to the little man's neck and broke the flesh with the end, hooking it in beside the artery. Wayne's eyes pinballed in their sockets and he bared his teeth. He made an animal sound and freed his hand from Lawrence's grasp and stabbed at Lawrence furiously with the spine-cut knife. Lawrence gasped as the blade entered his chest again and again. Still, he held fast to Wayne.

Lawrence buried the hook deep and found purchase in the little man's flesh. He grunted with effort and ripped the Crain knife violently and almost completely through Wayne's neck, severing his artery and windpipe. Lawrence was showered in blood.

Wayne's head unhinged in a backward direction as he crumpled and fell. His boots kicked at the tiles. His head, loosely attached to his torso, floated in a widening pool of fluid. He had voided his bowels, and the stench was heavy in the room.

"God," whispered Lawrence.

He stumbled to the divider and leaned against it. He looked down at his T-shirt, drenched in crimson. He winced at the pain and dropped the Crain knife to the tile floor. He listened to the wheeze in his own breath.

Let me keep my feet.

Lawrence drew the heavy revolver from inside his shredded jacket and walked out of the men's room and into the rain.

The heavyset woman was now standing beside her truck. She saw Lawrence and her eyes grew wide. She turned and bucked. Lawrence saw her lift her radio off her hip as she ran into the woods.

He heard the opening of a car door. An old black sedan was parked at the end of the stone path. Its driver's-side door was opening and a big white man with a walrus mustache was getting out. He stood behind the open door and glass. Lawrence raised his gun and pointed it at the man's torso.

Lawrence saw the big man reach inside his windbreaker. His eyes lost their will, and his hand came out empty.

The man smiled. "Where's my friend?"

Lawrence did not reply.

Sonny Wade's hand slipped back inside his jacket.

"You ain't get to do that twice," said Lawrence, his weak voice lost in the rain.

"I can't hear you, fella," said Sonny, and he drew his .45.

Lawrence squeezed the trigger of the magnum. The .357 round shattered the window and blew a quarter-sized hole in Sonny's chest. The slug flattened, tumbled, and ruined everything in its path. When the lead exited, its hole was as big as a fist. Sonny grabbed the top of the open door, and Lawrence walked forward and shot him again. Sonny went down on his back.

It felt to Lawrence that he was floating as he moved crookedly to the car. He stood over the big man, whose shirt was moving in and out where he had taken the first bullet. The second round had entered Sonny's abdomen. His chest and belly were slick with red. Sonny was blinking his eyes slowly, struggling to breathe, the rain hitting his pale and frightened face as he pondered eternity. Lawrence pointed the gun at the big man's face and locked back the hammer. But he did not pull the trigger.

I'm not gonna give him that gift, thought Lawrence. *Let death laugh at him and walk toward him slow.*

Lawrence stumbled to the edge of the parking lot. He saw the path of wood chips and mud lined by beveled railroad ties. He made it there. He looked at his hand and saw that it no longer held the gun. He tripped and fell and slid down the hill. He managed to get back up. He saw the bench at the end of the trail, set before the ledge. He was there and he dropped onto it. He sat and looked across the treetops, down to the Anacostia. It was a wide ribbon of brown, and rain dotted its surface. He heard sirens and his vision began to fade.

This is where I want to be.

Lawrence stared at the river.

When they found him, he was staring at it still.

PART FOUR
THE WAY HOME

THIRTY

ON A Sunday late in April, the family attended early mass. They then visited Ben's grave at the cemetery and went to breakfast at the Open City Diner in Woodley Park. Afterward, Thomas and Amanda returned to their house on Livingston, changed their clothes, and put Django in the back of the SUV. They met Chris and Katherine on Albemarle Street in Forest Hills, where they all walked onto the entrance of the Soapstone Valley Trail in a tributary of Rock Creek Park.

They went along a flat stretch, followed the yellow trail markers painted on the trees, and navigated a steep slope into the valley. They stopped to look at a tall oak. On its trunk had been carved a heart enveloping Thomas's and Amanda's names, and the year 1980. A smaller heart was below it, bearing the name of Darby, Chris's childhood dog. A third heart contained the name of Chris and 1982, the year of his birth. Using her cell phone, Amanda took a photo of the tree. Chris and Flynn exchanged a look and they walked on.

Seeing no other hikers or pets, Flynn let Django off his leash. The Lab mix immediately galloped off trail and crashed into the woods in search of the creek, where he could splash in the water. They followed him there, Katherine and Amanda walking ahead of Chris and Flynn. Chris noticed the gray in his mother's hair as the sun, streaming down through the trees, highlighted it and brightened the water where Django played. There was a lightness in Amanda's step.

Flynn tripped on an exposed root, and Chris grabbed his arm before he fell. Steadying him, Chris smelled alcohol on his father and wondered when he had found the time to steal a drink. Chris made no mention of it. He felt that he was perhaps responsible for his father's deteriorated condition. Or maybe his father would have gotten to that place on his own, without the troubles they'd had. In any case, Chris wouldn't lecture him or question him in any way. For a long time it had seemed unlikely that they would all be back here, together and settled, as they were now.

"Thanks," said Flynn.

"That's what I'm here for."

"To prop up your old man."

"You're not so old."

"Feels like I am. I'll never lay carpet again, that's for sure. I can't get up off my knees."

"You've got Isaac and his guys for that."

"And you," said Flynn. "And your boy, what's his name . . ."

"Marquis."

"Yeah, him. How's he doing?"

Marquis was a work in progress. Chris said, "He'll be fine."

With some convincing from Chris and Ali, Flynn had put Marquis Gilman on. It was one of Ali's last acts as an assistant at Men Movin on Up. His boss, Coleman Wallace, had accepted a job in the D.C. government, and Ali had taken over the top spot. Ali was frequently on TV now as a spokesperson and advocate for at-risk boys, and sometimes as a voice of community conscience when boys got murdered. Chris smiled when he'd catch him on television, at press conferences and such. It was funny, realizing that all those cameras and eyes were upon him, knowing where Ali had come from. It was true that Chris was a little envious, seeing that Ali had done something meaningful with his life. But he was also very proud.

Flynn and Chris found a seat on some boulders in a patch of sunlight out on the creek. Amanda and Katherine were playing with Django on the bank, throwing a stick into the water, the dog's tail spinning like a prop as he watched the prize float on the current.

"You did good," said Flynn. "She's a solid woman."

"She is," said Chris. "You finally got your Kate."

"It's Katherine," said Flynn.

The stick went down the creek and neared a bend. Django waited until the last moment and jumped in to retrieve it.

"How's school?" said Flynn.

"It's all right. It's just one class. Most of the stuff, I'm familiar with. I mean, I already read all those history books you turned me on to."

"Stay with it."

"I'll see where it goes."

"And stay with our company. Isaac wants to expand, and we're gonna need your help. It's going to get better for you. Less grunt work and more management."

"There's money for all of us," said Chris, and Flynn blushed a little and smiled.

"Seriously," said Flynn, nodding his chin in the direction of Katherine, her strawberry blonde hair lifted by the breeze. "You're gonna be working for three soon. You'll need that paycheck."

"I know it," said Chris. "I'm gonna keep the day job. But I've also got my eye on something else."

"If you want to be a teacher, pursue it. I'll be there for you if you get jammed up. Me and your mom."

They sat there for a while, enjoying each other's company, saying little but not uncomfortable in the silence. Then Chris got up and joined his mother and Katherine, talking about the wedding and the baby that was on the way. Chris dutifully listened and acted as if he cared about caterers and floral arrangements, but they knew he did not and told him that it was okay to leave them to their conversation and fun. Chris smiled at his mother, kissed Katherine, and turned back to the rocks. Thomas Flynn was gone.

Chris walked through the woods. He got back on the trail and followed its markers south. A cloud passed overhead and the landscape darkened. And Chris thought, *Isn't it so.*

He was not unaware of his good fortune. He had been born in a well-to-do neighborhood, raised in a loving home. When he'd gotten out of Pine Ridge, his father had put him to work and his mother had continued to feed him and buy him clothes even as he passed from boy to adult. At twenty-six he'd come close to killing two men but was stopped by someone who sacrificed himself instead. Chris hadn't been charged or implicated in any way. His call to the police had helped, along with Bob Moskowitz, who was tight with the prosecutors downtown.

Chris knew that for everyone like him, who had good fortune, there was a Lawrence Newhouse, who had none. But it wasn't as if Chris would go untouched. His life would not always be a spring afternoon, sunlight streaming on his mom, a breeze caressing the hair of his beautiful lover, a strong dog joyfully playing in a creek. If he could have looked into his future, he'd have seen much happiness in the family he would raise, and fulfillment in his career, as well as wrenching disappointment, regret, and old age. He'd have seen his mother, alone and suddenly aged, praying the rosary in her room. He'd have seen his father lying on a morgue slab at the age of fifty-five, his face deeply cut from windshield glass, his blood alcohol level impossibly high.

If the storytellers told it true, all stories would end in death. *But that will come in time*, thought Chris. *Not today.*

The clouds broke as he went down a long slope and found his father, standing before the thick oak rooted in the valley floor. Flynn had his open buck knife in hand. He was carving Katherine's name beside Chris's, inside the heart on the family's tree.

"Dad," said Chris.

Thomas Flynn turned and stepped toward his son.

ACKNOWLEDGMENTS

Many thanks to Vincent Schiraldi, director of the Department of Youth Rehabilitation Services (DYRS) of the District of Columbia, for his good work and assistance. Also, thanks go out to the youth, staff, and guards at the Oak Hill juvenile detention facility for their candid opinions and conversations. My lifelong friend Steve Rados provided the carpet-and-floor-business expertise.

For more information on the promotion of a more effective criminal-justice system through reform of sentencing laws and practices, and alternatives to incarceration, go to www.sentencingproject.org.

Reading Group Guide

THE WAY HOME

A NOVEL BY

GEORGE PELECANOS

Questions and topics for discussion

1. Why is Thomas Flynn initially disappointed in his son, Chris? What are the expectations that the parents in the novel have for their children?

2. How are Chris's values different from his father's?

3. Discuss the manner in which Amanda and Thomas Flynn approach Chris while he is in Pine Ridge. How do their styles of parenting differ? Why is Chris more responsive to his mother than to his father?

4. Flynn often imagines what it would have been like if his two-month-old daughter, Kate, had survived. Why does this make it difficult for Flynn to accept Chris for who he is?

5. The other boys at Pine Ridge call Chris "White Boy" and tell him he doesn't belong there (page 59). Unlike the others, Chris grew up in a nice suburban home with two hardworking and attentive parents. Why do you think Chris ends up at Pine Ridge with these other boys?

6. A novelist named Mr. Sampson comes in to talk to Unit Five about his book *Payback Time*, which tells a story about a group of young men much like the ones at Pine Ridge. Lattimer, one of the security guards, argues that another one of Mr. Sampson's books, *Brothers in Blood*, promotes violence and disrespect, with only "ten pages of redemption in the

end," which he claims that young men like the ones in Unit Five won't even read (page 86). Is there a case to be made that such books promote violence, rather than a respect for authority and doing what is right? Would you agree with Lattimer that more books about "kids on the straight" are needed? Or are books like Mr. Sampson's more descriptive of the reality of at-risk young adults?

7. Education plays a key role in shaping the lives of the characters throughout *The Way Home*. Ben learns to read after leaving Pine Ridge. Ali graduates from college and then joins an organization that helps at-risk teenagers get back on track. How does further education open doors for these characters? What separates them from the lesser-educated graduates of Pine Ridge, such as Lawrence and Luther?

8. When Chris and Ben find the bag of money hidden under the floorboards, why does Chris insist on leaving it behind? When Chris says, "I'm sayin, there's no shortcut to where we're trying to get to. Just work, every day. Same as how it is for everyone else" (page 113), what has he learned from his time in Pine Ridge and from his father?

9. Lawrence makes a key decision regarding Chris and revenge at the book's climax. Discuss his motives. In what ways was Lawrence's childhood different from Chris's? What role does his childhood play in his choice to go on alone?

10. By the end of the novel, Chris is back at community college and taking a few classes. How have his life and attitude changed? What new responsibilities and obligations does he have?

George Pelecanos's favorite westerns

This piece, describing my seven favorite westerns, was originally published in *Uncut* magazine's "Magnificent Seven" column and was, by definition, meant to include seven entries. I cheated and made it eight. But even that was difficult, as there are so many westerns I like. So I have expanded the list. Enjoy.

The Magnificent Seven (1960)

A handful of professional gunmen led by black-clad Yul Brynner are hired to protect a south-of-the-border farming village from scores of bandits in John Sturges's western adaptation of Akira Kurosawa's *Seven Samurai*. Rousing entertainment and every boy's perfect action film, with a martial Elmer Bernstein score that will haunt you to your grave. Among the seven: Steve McQueen, Robert Vaughan, Charles Bronson, and, as the knife-wielding Texican, James Coburn.

One-Eyed Jacks (1961)

A superb psychological western, sensuous, brutal, and beautifully shot. Outlaw Marlon Brando goes after his former partner (Karl Malden), now a sheriff in a coastal California town. Kubrick began the shoot but Brando took over the directing reins halfway in. The performances are outstanding, with Slim Pickens, Ben Johnson, and a truly bughouse Timothy Carey of particular note. Great jailhouse brutalization scene between

Brando and Pickens, recreated by Peckinpah twelve years later in *Pat Garrett and Billy the Kid*.

The Man Who Shot Liberty Valence (1962)

The Searchers is the obvious choice, but this is my favorite John Ford western. It is, in many ways, his most complex and moving film. Rugged cowboy John Wayne saves city-slicker lawyer James Stewart from reprobate gunman Lee Marvin, sacrificing his own happiness and altering history in the process. Ford's tragic, noirish eulogy for a wilderness overrun by civilization was his own swan song as well; he'd never make a film this rich again. Wayne is outstanding.

Hombre (1967)

Martin Ritt's adaptation of an Elmore Leonard novel is a modern version of *Stagecoach* and an intelligent character study exploring the themes of race, heroism, cowardice, and greed. Paul Newman, blue-eyed and super cool, plays the title role, a white man raised by the Apaches who decides to save the ones he despises. Builds slowly and deliberately to a final showdown between Newman and a group of villains led by proto-badass Richard Boone. "Well now, Hombre," asks Boone, very casually, before the guns come out. "What do you suppose *hell* is gonna look like?"

Once Upon a Time in the West (1968)

Sergio Leone's operatic masterpiece is, on the surface, an epic tale of revenge, but underneath is the definitive take on the price of America's Manifest Destiny. Shot, in part, in John

Ford's beloved Monument Valley, Leone fires on all artistic cylinders, from the extraordinary opening title sequence to the last gunfight. Sound design, cinematography, and performances—by Bronson, Jason Robards, Claudia Cardinale, and especially Henry Fonda—are in harmonic balance, all brought to life by Ennio Morricone's Hendrix-meets-the-angels score. The main theme will be played at my funeral. A beautiful film.

The Wild Bunch (1969)

A band of aging outlaws who "came too late and stayed too long" make their last stand, taking on half the Mexican army in Sam Peckinpah's ode to friendship, honor, and bloody redemption. Peckinpah's stunner was a parable for Vietnam that turned peace-loving audiences on with its cathartic violence, in the process burning down the genre itself. Concludes with the Battle of Bloody Porch, perhaps the most visceral action sequence ever committed to film. Oddly enough, it's the quiet moments that stick with you. William Holden, Ernest Borgnine, Ben Johnson, and Warren Oates take the last walk, and blow it all to hell.

Pat Garrett and Billy the Kid (1973)

Peckinpah again, exploding the myth. This was a critical and commercial failure upon its release, but the years and a director's cut have given it a new life. Kris Kristofferson is the hippie-like Billy, James Coburn is the haunted Garrett, and a cast of supporting character actors drift in and out of the narrative like doomed players in a dusty dream. Rock hard, fatalistic Rudy Wurlitzer dialogue, and very hardboiled. R. G. Armstrong and Kristofferson do the jailhouse bit. Bob Dylan does the for-the-ages score. He also plays Alias, mumbles, and throws a knife. Slim Pickens dies to "Knockin' on Heaven's Door." Essential.

The Outlaw Josey Wales (1976)

The last great western. *Unforgiven* deservedly won the awards, but I believe that this is the one for which Clint Eastwood will be remembered. In the years following the Civil War, East-wood traverses the Midwest, searching for the Union rene-gades who murdered his family. Along the way he adopts a new family of friends, misfits, and lovers, but not before spilling some righteous blood. Eastwood directs masterfully, taking over for a fired Phil Kaufman, pacing the episodic script to perfection and giving it life. Name one red-blooded guy who can't quote stretches of dialogue from this film. "Dyin' ain't much of a livin', boy." 'Nuff said.

And:

Ride the High Country (1962)

This should have made my original list, as it is one of my fa-vorite films of any genre. Peckinpah's first great picture is an elegiac good-bye to the traditional western with an eye on what was to come. Randolph Scott and Joel McRae play aging gunmen who agree to transfer mine company gold into the high country of the California Sierras. With Mariette Hartley, James Drury, John Anderson, R. G. Armstrong, L. Q. Jones, and Warren Oates. Painterly cinematography by Lucian Ballard, memorable, offbeat characters, and a stunningly beautiful ending. In Europe the title was *Guns in the Afternoon*. "I just want to enter my house justified."

Seven Men from Now (1956)

The first of director Budd Boetticher's many collaborations with star Randolph Scott. All are worth watching but this is the best. Low budget and running at under eighty minutes, this packs a wallop due to its airtight Burt Kennedy screenplay, the director's use of landscape, and the dynamic interplay between the characters. Lee Marvin excels as the not-quite-villainous villain, exuding his big-cat grace and predatory sexuality to great effect. The final shootout predates Leone and was obviously a big influence on the Italian maestro, who would put his own stamp on the genre a few years later.

Hour of the Gun (1967)

John Sturges's sequel to his own *Gunfight at the O.K. Corral* is one of the finest revisionist westerns. James Garner plays Wyatt Earp as a cold-eyed killer; his draw is quick and his aim is true. Many actors have chewed into the role of Doc Holiday in its various screen incarnations, but Jason Robards locates the humanity of the character and makes it his own. Standouts in the supporting cast are Robert Ryan (as Ike Clanton), William Windom, Steve Inhat, Monte Markham, Albert Salmi, and a young Jon Voight as Curly Bill Brocius. John Sturges keeps the camera low, shooting up and mythologizing the players against the big sky and mountains. He also stages a hell of a gunfight. The cinematography is by Lucian Ballard. The Jerry Goldsmith score is one of the best ever composed for a western film.

Monte Walsh (1970)

Directed by noted cinematographer William A. Fraker, *Monte Walsh* is based on the novel by Jack Schaefer, who also wrote *Shane*. Noted for its depiction of the passing of the cowboy way of life, it is also a quiet ode to male friendship and honor. The scenes between the men on the Slash Y Ranch are incredibly rich. Lee Marvin (as Monte Walsh) and Jack Palance (as Chet) give the performances of their careers. A little-known film that I cannot recommend highly enough. With Jeanne Moreau, Mitch Ryan, Jim Davis, Michael Conrad, and Bo Hopkins. "I rode down the gray."

The Good, the Bad and the Ugly (1966)

When I land on this on television, no matter where it is in the narrative, I always stay with it and watch it to the end. I suppose there are "better" films, but there are few so consistently entertaining. Critics did not get Sergio Leone early in his career, but the moviegoers understood, even if they could not intellectualize it: they were watching populist art. There are too many extraordinary scenes to mention, but the wordless sequence where Blondie (Clint Eastwood) gives a dying soldier the last couple of drags off his cigar, Morricone's mournful cue ("Morti di un soldato") playing in the background, never fails to astonish. Here, in the swish-pan graveyard scene, and in the final shootout, the power of cinema has rarely been so bold. With Lee Van Cleef as Angel Eyes and a mind-blowing Eli Wallach as Tuco, "otherwise known as the Rat." Epic.

ABOUT THE AUTHOR

George Pelecanos is the author of several highly praised and bestselling novels, including, most recently, *The Night Gardener* and *The Turnaround*. He is also an independent-film producer, an essayist, and the recipient of numerous writing awards. He was a producer and Emmy-nominated writer for *The Wire* and currently writes for the acclaimed HBO series *Treme*.

Following is an excerpt from
the opening pages of

The Turnaround

TWO BROTHERS walked up a slightly graded rise toward a small market and general store called Nunzio's. They had just finished playing one-on-one at the outdoor court of a recreation center that adjoined an African Methodist Episcopal church. The older of the two, eighteen-year-old James Monroe, held a worn basketball under his arm.

Both James and his younger brother, Raymond, were long and thin, cut in the solar plexus and flat of chest, with good definition in the shoulders and arms. Both wore their hair in blowouts. James, a recent high school graduate, was good-looking and fully formed, and stood over six feet. At fifteen years old, Raymond was just as tall as James. As they walked, Raymond used a fist-topped pick to upcomb his hair.

"James," said Raymond, "you seen Rodney's new stereo yet?"

"Seen it? I was with him when he bought it."

"He got some big-ass Bozay speakers, man."

"Call it *Bose*. You sayin it like it's French or somethin."

"However you say it, those speakers is bad."

"They *are* some nice boxes."

"Man, he played me this record by this new group, EWF?"

"They ain't all that new. Uncle William got their first two records."

"They're new to me," said Raymond. "Rodney put on this one song, 'Power'? Starts off with a weird instrument—"

"That's a kalimba, Ray. An African instrument."

"After that, the music kicks in hard. Ain't no words in this song, either. When Rodney turned it up...I'm telling you, man, I was *trippin*."

"You shoulda heard those speakers at the stereo store we went to," said James. "Down on Connecticut? They got this sound room in the back, all closed up in glass. Call it the World of Audio. The salesman, long-haired white dude, puts Wilson Pickett on the platter. 'Engine Number Nine,' the long jam. Got to be the one record he spins when he trying to sell a stereo system to the black folk. Anyway, Rodney, you know he don't play that. So he says to the dude, 'Don't you have any rock records I can hear?'"

"Messin with the white dude's head."

"Right. So the salesman puts on a Led Zeppelin. That song with all the weird shit in the middle of it, music flyin back and forth between the speakers? One where the singer's talking about, 'Gonna give you every inch of my love.'"

"Yeah, Led Zeppelin...he's *bad*."

"It's a group, stupid. Not just one dude."

"Why you always tryin to teach me?"

"You shoulda heard it, Ray. Those speakers liked to blow us out the room. I mean, Rodney couldn't pull his wallet out fast enough. Fifteen minutes later, the stock boy is cramming a couple of Bozay Five-Oh-Ones into Rodney's trunk."

"Thought it was Bose."

James reached out and tapped his brother's head with affection. "I'm just playin with you, son."

"I'd like to have me a stereo like that one."

"Yeah," said James Monroe. "Rodney got the baddest stereo in Heathrow Heights."

Heathrow Heights was a small community of about seventy houses and apartments, bordered by railroad tracks to the south, woods to the west, parkland to the north, and a large boulevard and commercial strip to the east. It was an all-black neighborhood, founded by former slaves from southern Maryland on land deeded to them by the government.

By geography, some said by design, Heathrow Heights was both self-enclosed and cut off from the white middle- and upper-class neighborhoods around it. There were several traditionally black communities, most of them larger in area and population, like this one in Montgomery County. None seemed as secluded and segregated as Heathrow. The people who grew up here generally stayed here and passed on their properties, if they had managed to retain ownership of them, to their heirs. The residents were proud of their heritage and generally preferred to stay with their own.

The living conditions were far from utopian, though, and there certainly had been challenges and struggles. The early residents had owned their properties through deeds, but many houses had been sold to land speculators during the Depression. The properties were bought by a group of white businessmen who razed them, then built minimally sound, cheap houses on the lots and became absentee landlords. The majority of these homes had no hot water or indoor bathrooms. Heat was provided by wood-burning kitchen stoves.

Children had attended a one-room schoolhouse, later a two-room, on the grounds of an AME church. Elementary-age kids were educated there until the big change of 1954. Residents shopped at a local market, Nunzio's, founded by an Italian immigrant and eventually passed on to his son, Salvatore. Consequently, many grew up without much contact with whites.

Most of the roads in Heathrow had remained unpaved by the county until the 1950s. By the '60s, community activists had petitioned the government to force landlords to make improvements to their properties. Officials did so reluctantly. A women's association in one of the neighboring white communities had joined Heathrow's residents in forcing the government's hand, but by '72, the neighborhood was blighted still. Ramshackle houses, improperly constructed and "improved," were in disrepair. Rusting cars sat on cinder blocks in backyards among broken toys and other debris.

To liberals, it made for dinner conversation, the stuff of slow head shakes and momentary concern between the serving of the roast beef and the pour of the second glass of cabernet. To some of the middle- and working-class white teenagers of the surrounding area, who learned insecurity from their fathers, Heathrow Heights was the subject of ridicule, slurs, and pranks. They called it "Negro Heights." To James and Raymond Monroe, and to their mother, a part-time domestic, and their father, a D.C. Transit bus mechanic, Heathrow was home. Of them, only James had dreams of moving out and on.

James and Raymond came up on a couple of young men, Larry Wilson and Charles Baker, sitting on the curb in front of Nunzio's. Both were shirtless in the summer heat. Larry was smoking a Salem, drawing on it so hard and rapidly that its paper had creased. Both of them were drinking Carling Black Label beer from cans. A brown bag sat between them.

Baker had a wild head of hair that was matted in spots. He looked over Raymond with hazel eyes prematurely drained of life. Baker's face had been scarred by a young man with a box cutter who had casually questioned his manhood. Several people had gathered to witness the fight, the subject of rumors for days. Charles, bleeding profusely from the slice but visibly unfazed, had downed his opponent, kicked aside his weapon, and broken his arm by snapping it over his knee. The crowd had parted as a laughing, wounded Charles Baker had walked away, the boy on the ground convulsing in shock.

"Y'all been ballin?" said Larry.

"Down at the hoop," said James. It was the only one in the neighborhood, and he didn't have to elaborate.

"Who won?" said Larry.

"I did," said Raymond. "I took him to the hole like Clyde."

"You let him win?" said Larry, with a nod to James.

"He won square," said James.

Larry hotboxed his cigarette down to the filter and pitched it out into the street.

"What you all gonna do today?" said Raymond.

"Drink this brew before it gets too hot," said Charles. "Ain't nothin else *to* do."

Of them, only James had a job, a twenty-hour-a-week thing. He pumped gas at the Esso up on the boulevard and was hoping to move up from there. He planned to take a mechanics class. His father, who occasionally let him work on the family's Impala, changing the belts, replacing the water pump, and the like, said he had skills. James was hoping to hook Raymond up with an entry-level position at the station when he turned sixteen.

"You hear Rodney's new system?" said Raymond, looking

at Charles and not Larry. Raymond, being young, admired Charles for his violent rep and courted his favor.

"Heard *of* it," said Charles. "Hard not to hear of it, the way Rodney be braggin on it."

"He got a right to brag," said James. "Rod earned that money; he can spend it how he wants to."

"He ain't got to boast on it all the livelong day," said Larry.

"Actin superior," said Charles.

"Man's got a job," said James, defending his friend Rodney and making a point to his kid brother. "No reason to cut on him for that."

"You sayin I can't hold a job?" said Charles.

"I ain't never known you to hold one," said James.

"Fuck all a y'all," said Charles, looking past them and addressing the world. He drank from his can of beer.

"Yeah, okay," said James tiredly. "Let's go, Ray."

James tugged on Raymond's belt. They walked up the steps to Nunzio's market. On the wooden porch fronting the store, they stopped to say hello to a Heathrow elder who was retrieving her small terrier mix from where she had tied his leash to a crossbeam, used often as a hitching post.

"Hello, Miss Anna," said James.

"James," she said. "Raymond."

They entered the store and went to a refrigerated bin, where James found some Budding pressed luncheon meat that sold for sixty-nine cents. He grabbed two packages, beef and ham. Raymond got himself a bag of Wise potato chips and two bottles of Nehi, grape for him and orange for James. They stood on the porch and ate the meat straight out of the package. They shared the chips and drank their sweet sodas as they looked down at the street, where Larry and Charles now stood, having risen off the curb but still inert.

"What you gonna do now?" said Raymond.

"Go home and get ready for work. I got my shift at the station this afternoon."

"Rodney home, right?"

"Should be. He's off today."

"I'm 'a see if Charles and Larry wanna go over to Rodney's and check out his stereo. They ain't seen it yet. Maybe if Charles get to know Rodney, he won't be so, I don't know…"

"Charles gonna be what he is no matter who he gets to know," said James. "I don't want you runnin with him."

"Better than bein out here alone."

"I'm here."

"Not all the time."

Raymond had been stressing about recent incidents in the neighborhood, cars of white boys driving through, yelling "nigger" out their open windows, leaving rubber on the street and then speeding back up to the boulevard. It had happened more often in the past year. In one way or another, it had been going on for generations. Their mother had been the recipient of such a taunt a few weeks earlier, and the thought of someone calling their mother that name had cut James and Raymond to the heart. The only white people with reason to be in this neighborhood were meter men, mailmen, Bible and encyclopedia salesmen, police, bondsmen, or process servers. When it was drunken white boys coming through in their jacked-up vehicles, you knew what they were about. Always driving in quietly and turning around at the dead end, then speeding up around the market, where folks tended to hang in groups. Yelling that stuff and driving away fast. *Cowards*, thought James, 'cause they never did get out their cars.

James handed Raymond the bag of chips. "Do what you

want. Just remember: Charles and Larry, they ain't headed no place good. You and me, we weren't raised that way."

"I hear you, James."

"Go on, then. Mind the time, too."

James stayed on the porch of Nunzio's as Raymond went down to where Larry and Charles still stood, the bag of Carlings under Charles's arm. They talked for a little bit, Charles nodding as Larry lit another smoke. Then the three of them walked slowly down the block, turning right at the next intersection.

James kept his eyes on his brother. When he could see him no longer, he dropped the empty soda can in a bin and headed home.